Reviews of Rohan Quine's *The Imagination Thief*

See www.rohanquine.com/press-media/the-imagination-thief-reviews-media for all links to the following and other reviews.

"Rohan Quine is one of the most brilliant and original writers around. His *The Imagination Thief* blended written and spoken word and visuals to create one of the most haunting and complex explorations of the dark corners of the soul you will ever read. Never one to do something simple when something more complex can build up the layers more beautifully [...] suffice to say he is the consummate master of sentencecraft. His prose is a warming sea on which to float and luxuriate. But that is only half of the picture. He has a remarkable insight into the human psyche, and he demonstrates it by lacquering layer on layer of subtle observation and nuance. Allow yourself to slip from the slick surface of the water and you will soon find yourself tangled in a very deep and disturbing world, but the dangers that lurk beneath the surface are so enticing, so intoxicating it is impossible to resist their call."

"*The Imagination Thief* is one of those books that has originality stamped across it with a pair of size 12 DMs. An incredibly dark yet full and balanced with shafts of light picaresque through the recesses of the human psyche, it is an uncomfortable, troubling immersive experience that mixes text, audio and video taking us into places we would rather not go. It could be described as a cubist novel, taking each aspect of the torn mind and laying them out on separate planes through the different media."

"Rohan is one of the most original voices in the literary world today—and one of the most brilliant."
—**Dan Holloway**, author, poet and *Guardian* blogger

"Another difficult to classify book, but that's precisely why it works so well. Part literary fiction, part fantasy, it is a surreal experience which makes the most of its equally offbeat location. With a cast of unforgettable characters and a central premise both intriguing and epic [...].

[...] In Asbury Park, New Jersey, an abandoned holiday resort, preparations for the strangest and biggest show on earth continue.

They encounter an eclectic bunch of characters; lovers, enemies, slaves and masters, all of whom provide Jaymi with a wealth of material. But information is power, and more than one person wants access.

The swooping eloquence of this book had me hypnotised. Quine leaps into pools of imagery, delighting in what words can do. The fact that the reader is lured into joining this kaleidoscopic, elemental ballet marks this out as something fresh and unusual. In addition to the language, two other elements make their mark. The seaside ghost town with echoes of the past and the absorbing, varied and rich cast of characters.

It's a story with a concept, place and people you'll find hard to leave."

—**JJ Marsh**, author, in *Bookmuse*

"An intriguing book that addresses many big issues (love, sex, death, power, the nature and reliability of human memory, history, culture, human potential, the constraints of 21st century society, and more) [...].

[...] described with a larger-than-life intensity that put me strangely in mind of Coleridge's *Kubla Khan*—and occasionally its drug-induced origins too!

It's not an easy or comfortable read, particularly when closely examining mental and physical cruelty and violence between some of the characters. I read with a constant sense of foreboding. However even the most shocking passages are underpinned by the compassion, pity and tenderness of the narrator for all but the most brutal characters. There's also some very welcome, very British understated humour to offset some of the horror. The brevity of the 'mini-chapters' was well-judged—I felt I needed to come up for air after some of the short episodes, and to assimilate the latest action before moving on.

The immediacy of the story is more keenly felt because it is written in the present tense—always more demanding on the reader, I find, and even more so in this case because although most is in the first person, there are also many second-person narratives, where Jaymi is reading the minds of other characters and addressing them: 'You move closer...' That the author is able to keep the reader not only engaged but tantalised by this difficult mode of storytelling indicates the power of his prose.

Though it's very much a modern book, with the constraints of modern life as one of its themes, there are touches of the classic about it too, reminding this reader of Johnson's *Rasselas* […].

As I turned the pages, I found myself puzzling how on earth this intense tale would end. Without spoiling the plot, I can say I found the conclusion surprising, redemptive and satisfying.

[…] So, here we have not so much an imagination thief, but, to the reader, an imagination expander. Great stuff."
—**Debbie Young**, author and Amazon UK Top 1,000 Reviewer

"Novelist Rohan Quine not only has several books out. He also has a career in alternative modeling and film to look back on. Naturally, he has gone on to make a series of silent short films to go with an audio track of the author reading from his work. It's flooded with city lights, drugs and darkness. One foot in the New York Nineties, and one foot in today's London, it's both hypnotic and gut-churning."
—**Polly Trope**, author and literary editor of *indieberlin*

"To love some of these characters would be to doom yourself, you are simply asked to observe them; to see them as deeply, as thoroughly as you see yourself, such is the all-encompassing clarity of Quine's descriptive abilities.

[…] Rather than a violation, Jaymi's reading of this motley crew of players is performed with a tenderness and an unending respect for the spectacle of another's soul in its entirety laid bare to us. There is magic in the twisted minds as well as in the sublime.

[…] the decadently rich language of this novel makes it pure chocolate, wine and sex—you will need a cigarette as you turn the last page. This book reads like a musical. The words are liquid and melodic: always entrancing and encaptivating and rising to chorus-line lung-busting crescendos every time Jaymi unleashes his powers and the imaginations of his superbly diverse cast shine out of the page in an explosion of Sound and Vision. Given that he accomplishes this purveyance of the innermost soul with black words on a white page, what is indeed impressive is the sheer level of colour, smell, texture and heat that can be felt during these moments when we are invited to couple our minds with theirs.

As I have stated, this is a piece where the English language is flexed and stretched until it's sweating on the floor in its yoga pants, and yet there are plenty of examples throughout to demonstrate Quine's skill in summing up the state of a character in a few simple words.

[…] there are other characters too, such as Evelyn and Rik, who are able to find light and love in their lives in the same way that Shigem and Kim have, and the warmth and tenderness of these characters serves to further illustrate that in contrast Angel is unable to escape the darkness […].

[…] Despite Jaymi's authority as our narrator, the English language is the true star of this trans-corporeal, trans-reality, trans-possibility, trans-mindf*$k, all-transcending diva of a debut."
—**Jen McFaul**

"a dynamic that renders [narrator Jaymi] thrillingly amoral and makes this ambitious and unusual novel wholly unpredictable. […] he finds he can explore not only the real memories of his new friends but their fantasies as well. These sequences are incredibly powerful, richly poetic and unique. Rohan Quine is a very insightful writer, with an understanding and empathy that anchor these hyper-eroticised, often surreal flights in a comprehensible reality. There is, if anything, an embarrassment of riches here but that's a minor consideration. As a reader, you wonder what Jaymi would make of you, whether he would find you as interesting as the terrifying but beguiling gangster Lucan or his demented lover, Angel. Angel, out of his mind on drugs, female hormones and desire that seems to claw out of the page at you, is the exact opposite of the coolly aloof Jaymi […]. The freewheeling structure allows the author to dip in and out of different narratives and styles, worlds and fantasies. It also enables him to explore multiple genres, often within the same sequence. […] Despite the original structure, however, events do build to a tragic climax whose only predictability is that it is fittingly strange. I often like to mention other similar books as a 'way in' for review readers but there is nothing else like this novel and that is my best recommendation."
—**Andrew Wallace**, author

"It feels like something that will win major awards… I look forward to gritting my teeth and applauding loudly at next year's Booker."
—**Meg Davis**, literary agent, Ki Agency

"Rohan is a dazzling writer […] 21st century Beat Generation dreamweaver!"
—**Peter Godwin**, musician

"I finished *The Imagination Thief* late last night, and found it … many things, I suppose, but I know they add up to 'deeply overwhelming'. It took my own imagination prisoner for a long while, and I cannot think of a better accolade for a true novel. I can't recall the details of any earlier version (which is why I've been able to read this as from zero), nor can I find an earlier copy anywhere, but I don't remember that the older version ended the same as this—has it changed? Because now, I read the last few pages—the van trip back to NY—as completely new to me, and I thought you have wonderfully created a quite unforgettably convincingly-constructed exit for the reader from this (again, overwhelming) experience."
—**Dr Michael Halls**

"quite brilliantly written. I have now read it twice and think it is full of amazing descriptions—especially those detailing the backgrounds of the various characters as divined by Jaymi in his magic insights. I am not on the whole a fan of magic realism, if one is to call it that, but your prose is so lyrical and beautiful that I felt quite seduced by it. The same applies to your dialogue which is richly colloquial. I am sure that the writing alone will arouse the admiration of the discriminating reading public."
—**Jeremy Trafford**, author

"fiery work. How rollickingly it proceeds down to its last bloodily beautiful drop."
—**Willie Coakley**, poet

"This book packs many powerful items of weaponry behind the smooth flow of its surface, few of which are suitable for unsupervised children and many of which are downright dangerous even for adults. Whether exulting in the human imagination's most ecstatic heights, scraping its terrifying cellars, lightly conjuring its gentlest loneliness or rattling out its most raucous joys, *The Imagination Thief*'s language is fiercely vivid and polished, always fluid and precise, and very often explosively rich and rhythmic. Despite including lots of very natural and colloquial dialogue, the novel as a whole demands your focus; but it repays that focus ten-fold, with a ferocious and sensual dose of imaginative intensity and inventiveness that would be quite sufficient to fill at least two or three more normal/responsible/house-trained novels. Genuinely unlike anything else you'll have read, *The Imagination Thief* will take you places you have never been, it will slap you around with a dark and mirthful love that you're not expecting, and it will leave you richer."

—**Cradeaux Alexander**, actor, director and artist

If you'd like to be notified of future publications, you're most welcome to sign up for Rohan Quine's not-too-frequent newsletter at www.rohanquine.com/sign-up. Rest assured, such emails will be at supremely tasteful intervals and your details will be shared with no one else.

THE IMAGINATION THIEF

A NOVEL BY ROHAN QUINE

EC1 DIGITAL

The Imagination Thief by Rohan Quine
ISBN: 978-0-9927549-0-7

Published by EC1 Digital, London, UK

Copyright 2013 Rohan Quine

www.rohanquine.com/the-imagination-thief

Cover design by Andi Rivers
Funfair: photo by GTibbetts / www.shutterstock.com
Clouds: photo by stavklem / www.shutterstock.com
The Imagination Thief: photo by James Keates
Author: photo by Ruth Jenkinson

Epigraphs: Thomas Mann translated by David Luke;
Lautréamont translated by Alexis Lykiard.

This novel is also available as an ebook published by EC1 Digital and
the Firsty Group, and as an audiobook published by EC1 Digital.

I was too far to hear his words; but Alexander looked, and for the first time I saw his eyes. Them I remember like yesterday; my own mind less clearly; a kind of shock, a sense that one should have been more prepared.

—Mary Renault, *The Persian Boy*.

Once more he stopped to survey the scene. And suddenly, as if prompted by a memory, by an impulse, he turned at the waist, one hand on his hip, with an enchanting twist of the body, and looked back over his shoulder at the beach. There the watcher sat, as he had sat once before when those twilight-grey eyes, looking back at him then from that other threshold, had for the first time met his... But to him it was as if the pale and lovely soul-summoner out there were smiling to him, beckoning to him; as if he loosed his hand from his hip and pointed outwards, hovering ahead and onwards, into an immensity rich with unutterable expectation. And as so often, he set out to follow him.

—Thomas Mann, *Death in Venice*.

One should let one's fingernails grow for a fortnight.

—Lautréamont, *Maldoror*.

TABLE OF CONTENTS

PART III Monday: Alaia learns my subterfuge

PART IV Tuesday: Alaia acts too hastily

PART V Wednesday: I learn Alaia's subterfuge

PART VI Thursday: second spotlight with Alaia

PART VII Friday: Alaia receding

PART X Ghost town departure: revelation of Alaia

THE IMAGINATION THIEF'S LOCATION, ASBURY PARK:

Upscale Oceanfront Resort, Partial Ghost Town, National Treasure

This story's secondary location is New York City. But its primary one is the small town of Asbury Park, N.J., nearby on the Atlantic shore. For decades this was a popular and beloved resort. Among its many attractions, the wide-grinning face of Tillie, painted large on the wall of Palace Amusements long ago, was a prominent symbol of a place that tended to inspire the warmest of seaside memories in its visitors.

In the late twentieth century, however, it hit bad times. So much so that the eastern part of it, including the oceanfront with its long and once-bustling Boardwalk, became largely deserted—in some areas almost a ghost town. Although a few of the live music venues there continued their long and vibrant history throughout this time, nearly all the grand hotels now stood boarded up in grand ruin; some blocks of the street-grid lay desolate after their buildings had been razed; and one huge and very central newer structure ground to a halt in a state of abandoned half-completion that was destined to continue unchanged for more than another sixteen years until its eventual demolition on the morning of 29 April 2006.

The complex reasons for this decline may be read about in print and online—as well as accounts of the happier days that preceded it. The relevance of Asbury Park to *The Imagination Thief* is that the book was conceived and begun while I was staying there for two separate periods of one week each, in 2000 and 2001, visiting from New York. I took the first of those trips on a whim in order to start writing a story, because it was nearby and had inexpensive accommodation and was a lot quieter than the Lower East Side of Manhattan where I was living. Beforehand I had no reason to expect I would develop any particular feeling for the place once I was staying there, but this is what occurred—to the extent that I decided to use it as the book's setting. The handful of New York City scenes and characters that constitute the first twelve mini-chapters had been written a few years earlier, without then getting round to finding a home for themselves, but now I realised that these would make a good springboard for the book's main Asbury Park section that follows them; so the opening came ready-made, but from mini-chapter thirteen onwards a new tale was to be written.

What I started scribbling there, in a cavernous room numbered 629 on the north-west corner of Ocean and Sunset, happened to get put aside then for a few years after those two one-week visits, while I got distracted by various other shenanigans. Then it was resumed and put aside a couple more times, what with further delightful distractions, until it decided to get finished in its own sweet time now, like a drunken super-model staggering to the end of the catwalk with cocktail in hand. The street-plan, buildings, businesses and other locations described in *The Imagination Thief* therefore add up to an exact snapshot of the brief time when I chanced to be in town, because all these details were taken from precisely accurate geographical notes that I jotted down on an online map print-out while I wandered around. The only two invented locations in the book are the bar named Downstairs and the secret television recording-studio hidden inside the real-life ruins of the Metropolitan Hotel (now demolished). Since then, I've read that many structural elements have changed, but I've not had the pleasure of going back there, so I haven't seen them.

I was aware at the time, of course, that the town wasn't looking its best. Yet the spirit of the place transcended this and I found myself joining the ranks of those whose affections for it remained intact despite its ragged edges. Inevitably my affections partook of this very aspect of it, but they were neither ironic nor sentimental—they were just there. Since Asbury Park is an authentic cultural icon and therefore inspires many people to feel protective of it as a widely-shared symbol and plot of socio-historical ground, I was also aware that there was a certain cheekiness in my finding it so natural to use it as a setting, when I hadn't lived there and hadn't known its better days. From my descriptions of it, however, my affection for it is obvious, I believe; and in any case, something tells me the place will survive my cheek just fine, thank you.

I was aware too, gazing up at the resonantly silent Tillie on the Palace Amusements wall, late one night at the desolate far end of Cookman Avenue with the Atlantic Ocean booming on my left, that perhaps there was also an element of strangeness in pairing Asbury Park with the rest of *The Imagination Thief*. But life is full of strange juxtapositions and the strange beauty of all our internal imaginations—and that's where many of our richest possibilities are really on offer.

—Rohan Quine

PART I

GHOST TOWN ARRIVAL: SPOTLIGHT WITH ALAIA

1 A FUNNY TURN AT THE OFFICE

"Are you ready for this?" calls Raven to me from the corridor outside my office. "Don't forget we're pressing the button tomorrow!"

I sink back in my chair, my feet resting on my cluttered desktop. "Oh, I'll remember, thank you."

"OK, then. Goodnight." The main door hisses and clicks shut after her, muffling her steps across the stone floor of the outside lobby, where a lift-bell rings. To my left, the sun sinks over the Hudson River, turning its water into twinkly pink vertical strips between the towers of Battery Park City.

It's been a labour-intensive week, finishing a 300-page prospectus issuing nearly a billion dollars of notes for a blue-chip banking client. And now that it's all done, at noon tomorrow we press the button, as Raven said—meaning transmit it electronically to the cold light and scrutiny of the Securities and Exchange Commission. At which point, it had better be right. I think everything is right; but pressing this particular button is my responsibility, and if there is still some screw-up lurking somewhere in the document, then this particular promising little financial law career of mine could quickly head down the toilet. Sometimes I think that might be more interesting for me … but this isn't the moment to test that out.

It's eight-thirty. I'm the only one left on this floor of the building. Zoë will be here soon, to clean the rooms. It's funny, she so much reminds me of my ex-girlfriend, to look at. I've been tempted to tell her this, just for fun, but it's probably a good thing I haven't. I yawn. All right: I shall wake myself up with one more coffee, look through my SEC checklist for the last time, and then bust this joint.

As I wander down the corridor towards the kitchen, I am surprised to feel the gnawing of an entirely new disgust at these familiar surroundings, with all those trappings to be found in any big office: the endless heaps of paperwork, all so important yet always adding up to the same old shuffle of money among a small bunch of hidden, faceless, super-rich individuals; the weary photos of horrible babies on desks; the limp, cosy newspaper cartoons pinned to the beige partitions around the secretaries' desks; the cluelessly unpleasant items of clothing draped on chair-backs; the corporate photos of old white idiots with bad facial-hair choices, frightened eyes, stiff smiles and lazy imaginations. What bland beings they are!

—No, hold on, what am I saying here? Bland beings? That can't be right.

OK then, well why can't it be right? I'm sure the blandness I just perceived wasn't merely an illusion; so where and what exactly was it? I reach the kitchen, where several trays of ornate sandwiches, ordered to excess for some earlier meeting, lie around uneaten and ready to be binned by Zoë. Altering my drinks plan on a whim, I press the "CreamiChoc" button on the drinks machine. "Bland beings" isn't right, I see, because what's bland is not the beings themselves but the uses to which they are put, the dreary shapes and flavours into which so many of them have been squashed by career and survival. I taste my CreamiChoc, give it a nod of surprised approval and decide, on reflection, to add a little sweetener. Most people here seem as if there is nothing in their daily lives of any real enchantment, of any imaginative aliveness, of any of the bright inventive magic that some of them must have had something of once, long ago. They seem as if all that remains is what batters and constrains them into lazy habits. One or two may be doing a good job of concealing some kind of imaginative enchantment behind a veneer of drabness, but most of them are surely not such fine actors. I've talked about this deadening process a few times with my good friend Alaia, and she is less forgiving of its victims than I am: rather than blaming the situation they are caught in, she's more inclined to blame them for getting caught in it.

I empty an unfamiliar yellow packet of chemical sweetener into my drink and stir it gravely with a pink plastic swizzle-stick. Well, let's be honest, then: what a huge design flaw that is. What a flaw that the wild and beautiful voltages of so many millions of imaginations everywhere should atrophy from the greyness of external events and so be extinguished. That's a gigantic, fundamental, planet-wide fuck-up—no question.

What a stupid and disgusting waste!

Shaking my head in incomprehension, I mooch back up the corridor, sipping my CreamiChoc. I've never tried this drink option before, but it's very tasty, I have to say. I shall add it to my office kitchen repertoire, for sure: a close third, just behind EspressoChoc and Normal Coffee.

As I re-enter my office, I feel light-headed. Deciding some fresh air will do me good, I float across the floor and through the window-door to my balcony, where I lean on the rail and find myself dropped into the grand feast of a midsummer sunset spread across a panorama of towers and water. Poisoned sky, dripping orange through the twinkle of the river, presses down hot and thick upon the West Side Highway traffic surging far below.

Strange, but that stab of contempt I just felt in the corridor feels as if it's made my eyesight clearer, revealing the truth of this idyllic balcony scene we have here. This is me, Jaymi Peek, peeking out of two little eye-slit windows cut into the end of a thin trunk of flesh perched on this giddy ledge above a concrete highway. Each of these windows gives a little wet reflection of the sun across the river, till I feel myself swaying and shut them both—but the sun spikes the eyelid-blinds and tints them vermilion, like eye-shadow. I lay the back of a hand against my cheek, then a palm against my head above the ear. Behind me in the office, where the walls run with moisture, a sluggish ceiling-fan turns. Inside the building's outer wall a pipe gurgles, as if to break free and flex and coil around me hissing. Below me a siren wails up and down, continuous and smooth as a sine wave, curving where the straight-edged skyscrapers shine.

I rub my eyes. What on earth was in that CreamiChoc? Or that unfamiliar yellow packet of sweetener?

The last boiling drop of red sun sinks away, beside a far-off water-tower standing out sharp against the blood-glow along the horizon. Miles of air make the lights palpitate amid the grid of sad dock streets across the Hudson River. Up the sides of the city there's a whisper and a flicker—and do rats bare their yellow teeth on fire-escapes and sniff? So New York. A flick of lashes stirs inside the sticky dusk. I peer, to try to make out the eyes I thought I saw hanging there staring from behind the air...

Down across the Highway, among the towers' geometric shouts into space, children play on fenced-in patches of grass, their voices through the traffic like the tiny bleats of sheep. I picture bomb-blasts climbing inside the skyscrapers, ripping through their roofs and out among the clouds, air whisking in folds from the blades of helicopters with the flash of shattered glass. *A squint at great events,* through two soft windows slit across the end of a thin flesh-trunk upon a balcony.

As normal clarity curls tight and peels away, I see the perimeters of myself as a whole entity, with the understanding that a driver attains of a car he masters, a jockey attains of a horse that he rides as one with, or a person attains with a long-time partner—a mastery of the possibilities of this particular pairing. This arrival at a mapping of my self's edges gives me a clearer sense of how this vehicle interacts with what's around it, and how it could interact. I feel serene, clear, resilient, strong; my sight newly empowered, calm, compassionate, canny, observant, as if beginning again. I'm aware of the wide totality of the scene before me, aware of its larger reality, the elements of infinity and eternity within it. I feel a high like a substance-derived high, but clearer and deeper. I look about me and I smile. So there's all *this* around us and in us, in this beautiful empty cosmos, alone as we are in such a strange and fascinating predicament. I laugh aloud. What exhilaration! What riches of terror, beauty, horror and mirth.

As a use for all this, that extinguishment I was observing in the office behind me is like a mutilation of some kind. I was right to despise what perpetrates that ... and in effect, although inanimate, *it* despises me. I seek voltage and revenge, and I'm newly empowered (though I'm not yet sure quite how). OK, it's a battle. Time for action. Watch me now...

2 THE HUNT FOR WHAT MY EYES CAN DO

"Excuse me, d'you want your office cleaned, or shall I do it tomorrow?"

I give a start. Zoë is peering at me with concern from the balcony door, holding my waste-paper bin in a rubber-gloved hand. "Oh no! —Yes, I mean. Go ahead, thanks. I'm just leaving." I attempt a reassuring smile, walk past her into my office, grab my bag and sway out into the corridor.

"Are you OK?" she calls.

"Yes, fine, thanks." I reach the lobby, where an empty lift is waiting. Inside I press the button with the star beside it. That much I still know.

Still know? Why did I think that? In something of a trance I descend the steps outside, onto Liberty Street. Minicabs wait at the kerb, with scribbled four-digit numbers on sign-boards standing in their windows. I look at my building's façade of one-way-mirrored panels and walk towards one of these panels at pavement level.

As my reflection approaches me, in its black suit, white shirt and charcoal-grey tie, I look at my pale face and I am fascinated to sense something in my brown eyes that I've never sensed before. What the hell is it? It doesn't feel wrong, but it does feel new. I can sense it, even see it, right there in my eyes. Some brand-new power—some great new capacitance.

What the fuck has happened to me?

Pushing my gaze deeper into my own reflected eyes, I slip quickly into a vision just as vivid as the one that the rubber-gloved Zoë interrupted, but a hell of a lot quicker, lasting only a second or two. Within its flash, aeons feel nested in complex compression, as if I am seeing a collapsed version of the whole duration of human civilisation. Despite this, it manages to be essentially a still image, from near the Dunhuang watchtowers where the ancient road from China forks in two, so as to run either side of the desert's lethal thirst: one route along its north edge and one along its south where the dead tongues of Asia flow. Within this fork, expanses of salt rim a land-locked lake that appears and disappears every year according to whether the Tarim River flows or chokes; and I watch the lake swell and shrink in sequence, every year collapsed into a second, like the beating of a heart of salt. The lake is Lop Nor, and above it burns a hidden purple flame wider than a hill. I feel its quiet roar and crackle shoot around the earth's curve in every direction—sweet-smelling, silent, majestic and serene. I shall live and die and yet this flame will burn still, like a burning bell. Nations will fight from age to age and yet this flame will burn. Men will run through plains and will climb through city skies, but this flame will remain like a burning purple bell, floating huge above Lop Nor, dripping its elixir on the pale brown salt-pans, smooth and translucent as it carves out the desert bowl forever. When this speeded-up heart of salt arrives in the present age, I see that Lop Nor is now poisoned after decades of nuclear test bombs exploded around its rims ... but high above the poison burns the hidden purple flame, still.

I wrench my gaze away from my reflected eyes, and Liberty Street returns with a thump of reality. I walk away from the mirrored building and around the corner in a daze. And up through a crevice in the concrete horizon pokes the summit of the GE Building, central in the Rockefeller Center, way uptown. The GE Building—that reminds me of someone. "Marc Albright," I hear myself murmuring aloud. Marc Albright: the most powerful man I know about in detail, as it happens. The only person I know about in detail who's on my level right now...

Time to walk uptown. I shall think, once I reach him in his office.

3 SO NOW I'M ON A MISSION

As I thread through the people thronging Washington Square, the white Triumphal Arch looms. Approaching it, I drink with a rush the vista framed by its high stone: Fifth Avenue, running up the centre of the city, dead straight, like a spine. I steer around the Arch and up the vista, which fans to take me, reconverges after me and elongates ahead. Walls and windows tower either side—angles yawning downward to slide me up between them. If I glance left or right, a street unfolds to take my glance. Dangerously ascendant, I can hear the zeroes singing for me. Horns blare, engines pound and tyres grind sharp into black tar: visuals and music for my march towards a building whose approach I can feel.

A helicopter's clatter like a jagged scratch on velvet cuts the sky; I feel my clothes against my body and a drip of sweat trickle down the centre of my back.

The GE Building soars up ahead, and then around me as I push through its doors. Everyone inside is like a clockwork toy from a museum cabinet, gesticulating jerkily behind the dusty glass that seals them off from the obvious thunder's roar of what is coming, what has pulled me—what the destined meeting is whose thudding spreads already through the walls and through the city's groan, to grimy wire-fence city-limits and beyond.

How come all these people hear so little?

OK then. Stepping lightly on the sheen of stone, in rhythm with the thud, never hurrying, I pad through the lobby, under cameras, to a bank of lifts.

An open lift-door comes in frame. I enter, push the "close doors" button, hear a *ting* through the thud, and press the very highest button. The panelled wooden doors close. The lift moves and gathers speed, hissing up the shaft of the tower, like a piston. The heartbeat on the soundtrack grows in volume. Scarlet numbers flash: *ten … twenty … thirty … forty … fifty … sixty …* to a few unnumbered floors at the top. The lift glides smoothly to a halt. The doors open, I step out, the thudding ends.

I'm in a long, quiet, upper lobby, much more exclusive than the one downstairs. I am calm. I've come to try my abilities out, that's all. Well, why not? Wouldn't anybody else want to do so, in my shoes?

A receptionist sits at the far end of this lobby, with an alert half-smile. I pad softly over the stretch of thick crimson carpet, towards her.

Seeing the words "General Network" prominent on the wall, I remember whom I sensed downtown, whose name I murmured then, and whom I've come to see.

I reach the half-smile. "Hi!" I twinkle sweetly, "I've come to see Marc Albright."

Marc Albright. You don't just drop in on him out of the blue and expect his receptionist to buzz you in to him—assuming she wishes to keep her job, that is. What she won't have expected, however, and what she's just about to find out, is that on this occasion she'll have no choice…

Last week in a magazine I read a detailed profile of him that I shared with Alaia, including many photos from over the years, and I found myself fascinated to imagine what it feels like to run as ubiquitous a media empire as the General Network, and to exert such power over so many people, through what they see and hear. And knowing all this, I find that I can direct my senses to identify, locate and enter his presence here… Yes. I know which of these walls he's sitting behind—that one at the end of the corridor there, behind the yucca. Furthermore, it seems that my knowledge of who he is and what he looks like allows me to see the office he's gazing around. He's staying late at work, as usual. And I can tune in to his thoughts at this moment. In fact, before this receptionist makes her futile protest, I shall pick this up on the other side of the wall behind the yucca, right there—

4 SNEAK PEEK INTO A MOGUL'S MIND

Change of viewpoint. A black phone purrs in a south-east corner office, high inside the GE Building. An arm in a white shirt lifts the receiver, and a man's voice speaks with quiet authority: "Yes?… A visitor? We've scheduled no one… Jaymi who?… Jaymi Peek… You 'think I should see him'?… OK, OK, I'll play along! Make him wait a few, then send him in."

Yes, you're puzzled, Marc, but you've decided it must be a close family member who's persuaded your receptionist to act mysteriously. All right, you're happy to have a quick break. Your arm puts the phone back and joins its companion arm, folded on a lap facing out through the glassy night, four miles south through a crisp electric sky to the red lights winking on the towers downtown.

To most individuals, that silent red winking might look hesitant, softened and delayed by the distance, you reflect. To you, though, its nature is clear. It's the pulse of the power structure, hunched like a spider at the centre of its web, here in New York City—omnipotent, relentless, unassailable. And who knows that web and works that power structure as *you* do? Only a handful of other tycoons, hidden like you behind the noise of politicians and the flicker of the media, in office suites in New York, Washington, London, Tokyo, Hong

Kong… And the lights wink on, and off, and on, and off, above the restless night.

Brick by brick, shaft by shaft and pane by pane you built the tower of your empire: gradual, ineluctable and ruthlessly careful. And now, with its glinting keys a-twirl on your finger, you stand behind its highest pane and watch with a long-matured pleasure, as the masts on its roof fling away around the globe a world of signals that you authorise. How many d'you recall of the million bits of paper you have scanned like lightning in the course of your career, or the myriad phone-calls and meetings? Six days a week for three decades you have woken in Westchester at five beside your sleeping wife, exercised, showered, donned a faultless business suit and tie, eaten, processed paperwork inside your morning limo to Manhattan, worked demonically till night, been driven home, spent some time with your wife and gone to sleep, planning next day's schedule. (You brought, to your very first date with her, a résumé—remember?) You've lashed and slashed and slave-driven everyone at work, most of all yourself, for years and years without relent, to remain in the international corporate stratosphere. A hundred and twenty offices, in ten countries now. How addictive it has been! And how you've loved it, or could never have sustained such an effort.

No, you weren't too hard for me to pinpoint from the street downtown—a very big fish, on which to test my fishing line.

5 HOW TO SLAP A MOGUL AROUND

Your door clicks, you swivel in your chair, to greet … whom? Your son? Brother? Wife, down from Westchester, in town on a whim? But no: you start in your chair, to see a figure enter, dressed in a black suit, softly close the door and turn its gaze on you. It's thin, pretty, watchful, with big brown eyes that hold your gaze in silence as it pulses like a cat through the stretch of space between you. "Forgive me for intruding," the figure speaks and glides to a halt the other side of your desk. "My name is Jaymi. You're busy, I'm aware, but I shan't be long."

—And before Marc Albright can reflect, we are sitting face to face, either side of his desk. His corporate suit is topped by a head that is solid, wide; the face flattish, white, in its sixties, with clear grey eyes of bird-like brightness. I imagine that his perky half-smile would change little, whether it heralded a business handshake, a brutal put-down or an anecdote at a dinner table after his plate had been cleared by unnoticed hands. He shakes his head. "Who are you?" he barks.

I haven't planned this, but as I hoped, I know exactly what to say: "Marc, look harder. You'll remember."

He looks harder indeed, and just like music, I make us both focus on a scene from his internal landscape. The scene is startling and vivid, and for him clearly "primal" in some deep way. I watch him while he thinks of it; and while he stares at me, the eyes of *that* figure stare him down—the eyes from the ballroom party, just as they stared him down across that crowded ball without a warning, cutting straight through the heads of a hundred other guests when he turned to fill his champagne glass—eyes he'd not expected but had known before, from somewhere. Singled out and pinned where he stood, glass in hand, he knew that he was powerless against this figure, though no one else seemed to be aware of it at all. Never since that evening in the ballroom has its blazing golden gaze left his memory. The figure seemed above the crowd, its eyes strangely one: Marc felt as if he stared at a great gold Cyclops three metres high, sprouting horns like a Baphomet's, its claws hanging down resting easy on the grey heads carpeting the ballroom, its heavy eye transfixing him—

"*Stop!*" he cries.

"Yes, Marc," I murmur. "I can fuck with your head—so listen hard. But I'm not here just for that. I'm here for enchantment, and for business. Your ballroom remains yours and mine alone to know about. But everyone has primal scenes and private screams and radioactive mines, like yours. Their own magic ballrooms, wonderful and terrible, which everyday life tends to cancel and destroy." His eyes make me think of a hunted baby eagle, as I turn up the pressure. "When I turn on the gaze I aimed at you just now, those who look at me will not look away until I let them, as I'm lighting up their scenes in burning bloodlight like they've never seen before." I pause, to let this statement sink in—into me as well as into him, since I'm learning with amazement while I speak. I lean in towards him and raise the voltage still higher, until he's pinned onto his seat. "And the hundreds of millions who don't dare look at their own scenes will be forced to look—d'you hear me, Marc? Self-knowledge breeds thinking and compassion, every time, across the world. That's evolution, that's enlightenment of mankind, facing into cold dark space as we are. You and I are pushing out and upward at the forefront of a species we must teach, for time is short. And listen closely now"— and his fingers grip his desk, as I walk with the angels here—"*you* can make them look at me and learn what they need to learn from inside themselves. *You're* among the few who can ensure that they look at me, for *you* run the biggest broadcast network in the world, don't you, Marc? Let's work together, therefore, and drag our species upward just a little. Let's realise that aim, because together you and I possess the means for it. You know this is your duty. I can see that you do." I lower my voice again, to a level tone of business. "So listen to me now, Marc: following publicity in every market globally, you'll present a prime-time broadcast of that gaze of mine—just a close-up—with worldwide exposure. Everyone will view it very differently, I promise you, but everyone will view it ... and you'll reap unheard-of profits, as you're also recognising right now. Yes, you're correct, the nuts and bolts will be a challenge, but the big picture is that you know very well we do have the power to achieve this, don't we? *Do you understand?*" My gaze grips him mercilessly, one more second, then I let him go.

Knowing to give him a quick break, I glance down at the varnished wooden angles at a corner of his desk. In so doing, I register that there is a distinction between how I looked into him from the corridor and how I looked into him just now: from the corridor my looking was unseen by him, whereas just now of course he was all too aware of being forcefully hypnotised and dragged around on a journey I controlled... Hmm. I wonder whether I could have done just the first type of tune-in, the unseen passive kind, if I'd been sitting here interacting with him? Or would our interaction have meant that he became aware of my doing so? Hmm. I must test that out on Alaia. When I next meet her, I'll look into her and see whether she becomes aware my doing so. That's a great term for the unseen kind of looking, by the way, a "tune-in"—that's exactly what it felt like in the corridor. Why did I not stop to work all this out, before I set off from Liberty Street? I'm lucky to have been able to work it out on the hoof... Now Marc interrupts my train of thought, however, shaking his head and frowning: "But how exactly would this work?"

"Let me clarify the mechanics, Marc. I have two kinds of special sight, which feel different, both to me and to you. I have an active hypnotic one, which I just used on you, so you know the effect of that. It takes control and drags you on a trip around the depths of yourself, scaring up any of that old radioactive magic you have inside you. Right? And then I have a passive secret sight, which people don't know I'm using, although it shows me what's inside them just as clearly as the other sight does. I also used this passive sight on you, from the corridor, because I already knew enough about you to do so—and I saw you looking at those red winking lights and thinking how there's only a handful of men in the world who really know how to work those power structures, such as your humble self etc. etc. and blah blah blah. *Right?*"

He flinches.

"Right," I say. "OK, let's say a live TV camera is set up and pointing at me, and I'm looking right back at it, staring into its lens instead of into someone's eyes. *I* shan't see anything because a camera has nothing to see inside it, none of that old radioactive magic for me to scare up... But the TV-viewers will see exactly what they'd have seen if I'd been standing right in front of them. And they'll be affected just the same." He makes to speak but I forestall interruption, starting again now to accelerate the force and speed of my speech, so that by the time I am finished, he is once more pinned to his chair. "Now, a live broadcast of me using my secret passive gaze would be kind of boring, wouldn't it: the only thing our audience would see would be just my face in close-up. But if I'm aiming the active hypnotic gaze at the camera, live ... well, then we're talking 'must-see TV'. You see where I'm heading, Marc? When I level *that* gaze at the camera, the one I gave you a sample of, then I'll hypnotise the viewers into unlocking so much imaginative magic in themselves that they'll be addicted to watching the General Network forever! Are we having fun yet?"

He considers this question.

"During the broadcast," I continue, "I shan't know what I'm unlocking in them. The only way I could know would be afterwards to take a passive look at someone's memory of the broadcast and see what I'd scared up in that particular person. Information only travels one way through the camera and the TV screen. But that just leads me to the clincher, Marc: alongside the basic hypnotic effect, I'll be projecting my own red-hot imaginative stuff. It'll mix with every viewer's own imagination in a unique way, but they'll all receive the same original stuff of mine, and they'll all recognise that stuff by itself as a big part of the unique live experience they had. And you'll have captured my stuff by itself, from when we broadcast it, so you can then sell it to all those viewers in various formats and re-issues with all kinds of bonus features and fun add-ons, and they'll all buy it! D'YOU UNDERSTAND ME, MARC?"

I see his bird-eyes have understood very well. "Yes," he nods, wiping his forehead. His attention tears itself away and into the distance, where I leave it for a moment to machinate undisturbed, like a percolating coffee pot.

I'm happy to have a moment's respite. I'm flying blind here, and what I'm doing is not easy: I challenge anyone else to slap a mogul around like this. Then, without warning, I observe another inspiration assemble itself in my mind and climb to its feet like a self-erecting tripod. Forget walking with the angels now, we've moved on from that. This has the feeling of a shark swimming right through me; those tripod legs have streamlined into fins... Downtown tonight, I saw how right Alaia is, never to deviate from despising what she despises. I vowed voltage and revenge—and here I am finding them in Midtown. I think my memory of her contempt helped nudge me here. Well then, let's cut her into the action! Why not? I break sharply into Marc's silent cogitations: "And for even greater profit-ability, I've even got a red-hot original soundtrack to offer, which I'll tell you all about in a moment, if you're good. No lyrics, I can assure you."

He nods with interest, and something about his distance of manner suggests that the avenues of possibility I've sent his imagi-nation scurrying down are wide enough to accommodate Alaia too. Excellent. We'll be coming back to her, then—oh, we'll be coming back to her.

"Yes…" he says. "I suppose this proposal of yours is within the realms of possibility." He gives a thin smile, feeling his way forward, not meeting my eye. "In fact, I find that I wish it, because your demonstration spoke for itself and your proposal makes sense. I only wish I'd been in more control of my discovery. You've been unfair, but you've succeeded." He breathes hard and looks around, wrapped up in his thoughts. "This is extraordinary, and new, and quite unexpected … but sometimes such a thing happens, and this is evidently one of those times." He swivels his chair back towards the downtown towers. Those red aircraft warning lights wink on, unending.

The analytical lucidity of his last speech, under the circumstances, is impressive. "It's a pleasure to deal with you," I state.

He swivels his chair round towards me with apprehension, but I have shielded the active hypnotic gaze and am instead wearing an expression as if to say *Yes, I've shielded it, and from now on I undertake that you'll remain on the same side of it as me, rather than be its target, so that we can both direct it at other people instead.* I see his acute perception pick this message up. His apprehension subsides and that perky half-smile begins to return: "So this is just business," he thinks.

To jolt him once more (he must not get cocky), I reply to this aloud: "Yes, it's business. Big business, I believe." His smile fades. Now he needs "clubbable", I think. I rise from my seat, spread my hands easily, wander round the desk and pat him on the shoulder. "From now on I'll give you some privacy. How about we wander over to those rather comfortable-looking armchairs and sketch out a few general terms? Do I see a bottle of whisky over there? I must say I'd love a drink, if you're offering."

He jumps to his feet and strides across the office. "Me too," he booms and rubs his hands together.

Two hours later, having agreed some basic practicalities, both signed a very general letter of intent and set up further meetings, Marc and I leave his office, step out onto the pavement on Rockefeller Plaza and part with a handshake.

So now I've pressed the button.

6 MY ABSENT DEFAULT PERSONALITY

I turn the corner and wander down the block to the Sixth Avenue subway, processing what exactly has happened tonight. It seems, in short, that something extraordinary occurred at my workplace, which gave me a new and wondrous power of sight into the imagination of another person, either in the form of a clairvoyant tune-in or a hypnotic scouring, and that I was then cheeky enough to come here straightaway and use this ability to compel the commissioning of a television programme. Did I really just do that? Yes, I did. It's hardly just any old television programme, either: it's an enormous television event, focusing on me. Children, don't try this at home. And not only that; it seems I involved my friend Alaia in the project, following no consultation with her whatsoever. Perhaps I'd better phone her now.

"Hey," she says, and at the sound of her sleek familiar voice I feel a touch of sanity.

"I've got some serious news," I say. "Can I come round and tell you?"

"OK, sure. Where are you?"

"Midtown. I'll be half an hour."

So it's fixed. Descending the subway stairs, I apprehend that I'm frightened—really scared—of what else may happen, any moment, of a comparably great and unexpected nature. The instant of sanity in Alaia's voice just now was too brief. I dare not think about madness, though the topic lurks somewhere in the wings of my mind; how could it not? I grip metal handrails and analyse the geometric qualities of ceramic tiles and light-fittings; I drink in the symbols on subway maps, focus on the typefaces and orthographies of printed words, and dwell on the satisfying numerical construction of Manhattan's street grid. Anything abstract or mineral, anything plain and hard and non-human, I fixate on, as a clean, clear, unambiguous anchor for my sanity.

By and by, this incipient panic starts to dissipate. I begin to risk less hard, more ambiguous objects. I flick my gaze from one fellow passenger to another. So far, so good; people don't seem to find me any stranger than they usually do. So my powers aren't visible. Thank goodness. It would truly alienate me if they were. I suppose I could have concluded this from my walking earlier to the GE Building, but I was catching no eyes then and in any case that walk now seems like a long-past dream. I catch a couple of people's eyes now, as if not intending it, for just long enough to tell they are not registering anything too odd. And I note that I am not seeing into people. I can feel that I *could* see into them, if I directed myself to—but I've had enough of that for one day. Except for Alaia: maybe I'll just have a quick look into her, when I reach her place.

However, something is wrong. It feels as if something subtle has gone missing in me. What is that? I step off the F train at Second Avenue station, find a subway official and ask if he knows of any imminent train delays, just to hear myself interacting ... and it sounds like somebody else is asking. Or rather, I feel as if I don't know in what personality to ask. I mean, in what default personality; for there doesn't seem to be one of those in me any more. I could ask him in dozens of ways. But what would be my own way? How did I use to interact when I could just be my own spontaneous self, a few hours ago? How did I choose to respond to things and perceive things, when I did so "naturally"?

It wouldn't have occurred to me that one could lose such a thing as the memory of one's personality. I shouldn't have known what such a thing might feel like. But now I know. And I think I need to fix this, before I lose track forever of something that was preciously mine.

7 TELLING ALAIA WHAT'S HARD TO BELIEVE

These concerns seem to recede, as I settle into a chair on the flat roof of Alaia's apartment on the south-east corner of Houston Street and Norfolk Street, holding up a Southern Comfort Manhattan with a cherry. She emerges from the stairway door and comes up the shallow gradient towards me on her high heels, tapping a finger-nail against one of the free-standing drainpipes that rise in a line down the length of the asphalt roof, each pipe terminating above head-height. I clink my glass against her Black Russian (her cocktails are well-known) and decide to try out the little test I planned in Marc's office—just an instant's tune-in, to see if she becomes aware of it. So while we small-talk, as she settles down, I shoot a sudden clean glance into her. The thoughts I happen to catch—concerning whether the chair is steady, whether we're too close to the parapet, whether her hair is right, at what angle the present lighting will fall upon her face for my benefit, and whether she should have chosen a twist of lemon rather than the cherry for my Southern Comfort Manhattan—are an authentic mess of Alaia-flavoured practicality in motion. And perceiving she has no knowledge that I'm in there with her, I cut short the tune-in. So that question's settled.

Alaia Danielle is a singer, or a vocal performer, with a growing underground following. I first met her a couple of years ago at a party in Chinatown: not in an apartment or a club, but in a raw warehouse-type space, convened over the course of a day or two by semi-spontaneous phone-calls and texts. It was evident that this had once been a whorehouse, from the eight or ten mattress-sized cubicles with numbered doors, in which beer and various drugs were being consumed. She had just arrived alone, climbed six flights up a narrow stairwell from the rainy sweaty street, passed through the approving band of Italian guys working as security at the door and bought a beer, and was now standing in the crowded corridor between doors 1 and 2, smoking and sizing up the crowd. Her long straightened hair was pulled back, as it still is, from a smooth black face that I've always thought of as "aerodynamic", and was held in a small band at the back, from which it fell to her shoulders; and as it still is, her expression was sleek and sharp, with something in the poise of the eyes that promised not to suffer jerks gladly. The two of us started talking, got on well, laughed quite a bit, talked about her boyfriend (now ex-boyfriend) who wasn't with her that night because they were going through some hassles, and got very pleasantly drunk. Since then we've stayed in touch, and by degrees over the last few months she's become one of my best friends.

"OK, here's the story," I say. "Do you remember that list in the magazine, of the ten top media moguls?"

"Yes." She lights a Virginia Superslim. "I called them perpetrators."

"Yes. D'you remember the great Marc Albright, CEO of the General Network?"

She nods.

"I just met him."

"How?"

"I'll tell you. But not only did I meet him. We spoke at length too."

"You're joking."

"No I'm not. And not only did he and I speak at length." I lean towards her. "I persuaded him to give you and me a two-and-a-half-hour prime-time slot on a mainstream GN channel, in a month or two, for an international broadcast of us in concert."

She serves a full beat of silence, exhales a puff of smoke, and says with probing humour in her eyes, "You lie."

I reach into my shoulder-bag, extract a page and hold it out. She grabs and inspects it, and I watch her take in the discreet letterhead, our names, the words "Letter of intent", and doubtless other subtler indicators of legitimacy that I haven't yet thought to locate. Then she starts to read.

"'Concert'?" she asks at last. "But you don't sing or play an instrument. Or have you taken up your childhood violin again?" She glares at me, then back at the paper.

I take her drink out of her hand, place it down on the roof and put my own beside it, rim touching rim. "Alaia—look at me."

She looks, and I slide my outer gaze aside, baring the sensors and projectors of the inner one. Her dark eyes flash with defiance for an instant, of course; then they grow serene and widen, as I take control.

8 THE STATUE OF BLACK SUGAR

Inside her I see thoughts, memories and feelings, as with Marc. But because she is already a dear friend and he was not, looking into her is both odder and more natural than looking into him. How beautiful she is! What a cool, analytical nature I'm seeing, yet with such passion behind the cool. And what warmth I feel towards that black star-shaped point of insecurity at the centre of her.

But I'm in here to demonstrate my abilities to her, not just to nose around. I'm here to lead her and me on a compulsory Alaia-based equivalent of Marc's random ballroom scene. Let's say two memories and a fantasy ... so first I select a shard of memory from your teens, Alaia, there in the bar where you prance on the podium, your hair electric blue. My viewpoint hangs in the air above your audience, invisible to you. You move like a lithe brown spider or a fierce slinky alien, flipping left to right, a cool dragon-child—and I'm sad I didn't know you then.

Secondly, there you are just two weeks ago. A much quieter picture; but what a fly young woman with your cool eyes and long sleek hair, wearing headphones, coiled up downstairs in front of those gauzy white curtains, which are here swaying in a slight breeze. As you scribble in your journal, I hear your voice sounding in your head: "The woman at the window ... that's me. Out there, four storeys down and one block over, people pass down the wet black of Essex Street, in cars, on journeys of their own, every one hidden in the dark between a white light and a red light. The thought that I'll never know who they are, or what it's like for them when they're alone, would once have sounded a clap of wonder, sorrow and excitement in me. Now, I have a calmer sense that our separate existences, tucked in between white and red car-lights, are simply how things are. Maybe I'm just discovering new beauties in isolation. If only life were easier." You lay down your journal and stare into the distance, thus setting off your sleek profile against the gauzy white curtains *just so*, without quite knowing this...

Then thirdly comes a fantasy of yours, evoking how you will be at a time very far in the future, when you'll have become a statue in an empty forest clearing somewhere—a statue fashioned out of smooth sugar coloured pure black, and wearing mirrored sunglasses. Your slender carved hands hold a scarlet rose, with a grip that looks limp but is unbreakable. Violence at demonic voltage, hard as a light-bulb, is coiled in this statue. From underneath the black flames of hair at your neck hangs an icicle of blood. But now I'm startled to recognise my very own disembodied viewpoint come hovering into the clearing, within this established fantasy of yours, and home in upon your statue in order to check on my own reflection in your mirrored glasses! I wasn't expecting to bump into myself here. Your statue fantasy-self smiles and emanates, as if on heat, a smell of musk. You can't coil around the hovering Jaymi viewpoint, because it is just a viewpoint and you are just sugar; yet it seems that you want to. Suddenly your lips move, whispering the strangest fire-and-brimstone language, and it's almost as if this fantasy self-image of yours is making a kind of love with me as it speaks: "A black comet streaks along the dust lanes of the Milky Way," your statue-self says. "Sunquakes boom through space, like the songs of whales through oceans. The great Basilisk cuts planets on its plate, where the blue of flaming methane licks. When life awoke in dark matter, neither the galactic hiss nor the endless background flux of waves stopped to mark its waking; nor did the liquid electric effluxion and resonance of airwaves three stars above us split the night in any great surprise. Giant discs have risen near the ocean horizon; towns have fallen into dust and been enfolded into mountains; and Violence, Religion, Injustice and Death, like the tides of the seas, have inundated the shadowfields: yet still we are not noticed by the Bloodstar, that sphere of pulsing scarlet fluid hanging at the centre-point of all black space… Well, so be it." You fall quiet and still again. In mixed joy and sadness, the Jaymi viewpoint slithers from the clearing's light and slips away in forest, as your statue gaze follows it, ambiguous and hungry.

9 ALAIA GETS EXCITED

I hide my inner gaze again and touch back down with her, here upon this rooftop on the Lower East Side. I retrieve Marc's letter from her grip, where it's been clenched throughout our journey, lay it down and take her hands in mine. She lets me do this, but stares at me as if I have two heads.

"The situation is simple," I say, not quite convinced of the truth of this. "I shan't intrude into you again like that. I'll respect your privacy from now on. But I had to do that once, so you understand what I'm talking about and believe me when I say this broadcast of ours will be for real. I don't know how, but I seem to have learned this kind of hypnotic gaze that takes whomever I'm looking at on a forcible journey through themselves, as I just did with you. I did the same to Marc Albright too, earlier tonight. I chose him because of his power, but I'm pretty sure it would have worked on anyone." She stares at the contract, unfocused. "Or else I can do a 'tune-in', as I call it: if I'm with someone, or if I'm not with them but I know them, then I can see into them without their knowing. I can't see everything, but I can see quite a bit of their mind and imagination and fantasies."

She sits there, staring at the same clump of downtown skyscrapers Marc stared at earlier—though from closer here, from a different direction and with yellow-grey mist now wrapped about them. "Jaymi, how the fuck did this happen?"

"This will be hard to believe, I know, but it's true, as I've just demonstrated. It all began with a CreamiChoc at work, though I don't know if that's what caused it."

"It began with a *what*?"

"A CreamiChoc. It's a kind of vending-machine drink. Sort of like a mixture of..." and I proceed to tell the tale of all the steps that have led me to this point tonight. She lets me finish. Then she grills me about those steps, from every single angle. I can hardly blame her; I should probably have done the same to her. Then from disbelief she passes slowly to belief, from seriousness to laughter, and finally from wide-eyed wonder to greedy-eyed scheming. Just as I might have expected!

Then she grills me about what exactly we'll be doing during the broadcast. I explain that I shan't be tuning in passively to anyone, but hypnotically projecting an active gaze that'll work differently in every watcher, depending on their particular mind. I say the broadcast will consist of just a close-up of my face in real time, speaking no words but staring at the lens, to a soundtrack of her live and unaccompanied voice (I hope) running free with the kind of beautiful swoops and wails with which I've heard her mesmerise small audiences in various downtown venues—a startling and unearthly sound that has started to gain her a well-deserved cult following. "Marc's intention is to simulate a stadium performance—you onstage, and then above you a big screen with me projected on it live. But since not even he could sell out a real stadium for an unidentified act, he's going to record us on a sound-stage and then insert cut-aways of a digitally created stadium audience."

"Right... Jaymi, how long do we have?"

"All I know so far is that in a few weeks' time, on a Sunday afternoon, we'll be driven down to the sound-stage in Asbury Park, and on the same night it'll be broadcast live."

She stares at the towers, where the red lights wink through the yellow mist. "I'm dreaming!" she cries out, shaking her head. But she believes it, at last, I can see; she believes it. She jumps up, I follow her, and then we're dancing around the flat rooftop, laughing and jubilant, threading our way in and out of the line of vertical drainpipes, swinging ourselves around one or other of these. Even in her jubilance, however, her mind is working, as I see when she swings herself around one pipe with the lights of the night reflecting sharp off her silver stud-earring. The pipe is next to me, so her face is suddenly right in mine and our gazes latch onto each other from very close up in a split-second's freeze-frame that hits us both, with her eyes asking *Where are you taking me, Jaymi?*

10 ANGLES OF GLAMOUR

At nine next morning, referring to the letter of intent that Marc and I signed, I make a round of calls from my home phone to several high-powered intellectual property lawyers, to ascertain which one I'll be instructing with regard to the protection of my and Alaia's rights in this broadcast. Once that ball is rolling, I head to my workplace in the mid-morning, to take charge of the pressing of the button to the SEC at noon on behalf of the prospectus team, which goes as smoothly as I could have hoped. The customary post-button-pressing celebrations pass with great and forgettable pleas-antness, whereafter I take immediate advantage of my hard-earned brownie-points by arranging to take a couple of weeks off, citing vague holiday plans. In the early afternoon I visit the lawyer I've selected to represent Alaia and me, one Bedford Pickering III, in his offices on Broad Street, sign some paperwork with him and make an advance payment against some very fat fees.

Then in the late afternoon Alaia and I have an appointment at the General Network, to meet a trusted deputy of Marc's who will oversee our broadcast—one Jason Carax. When she and I arrive, Marc is not in evidence but a receptionist shows us to a conference room and tells us Mr Carax will join us soon. As soon as we are left alone, we find ourselves gripped by such a sense of anticipa-tion at the whole direction of events, that with very little warning our usual professional demeanour devolves into a fit of whispering, nudging and uncontrollable girlish giggling. Angry at myself, I whisper furiously to her that this is hardly our best self-presentation to the General Network and we should cool it, because it's quite possible we're being seen and heard right now through cameras and microphones hidden around this conference room. Alas, this just sets us both off even more, till we are heaving and drooping off our chairs for minutes on end, with tears of adolescent mirth streaming down our faces.

At last we get it together.

Really, what was that about? Ridiculous silliness. Mustn't happen again. Especially not during the broadcast...

But now there are voices down the corridor and the sound of one person approaching. Curious to see who will enter the room, I see a tall, middle-aged man in a pale grey designer suit coast in through the door with a laid-back tread. His longish, gently stream-lined black face is friendly and mild, but his eyes acute. He inclines his head a moment, in a suave and understated bow: "Jaymi, Alaia. Congratulations, you are both now icons!" he purrs. Though there's interest and mirth in his eyes, his emotions are hidden. He takes a seat across the conference table. "I'm Jason Carax, VP Live Events. I'll be executive-producing, and I'm delighted we could help to put this broadcast event together. Unfortunately this meeting will have to be a brief one, but we'll no doubt catch up again presently. I'm afraid the Asbury Park sound-stage won't be available until the day of the broadcast, but we have world-class facilities here in the city, which my assistant will show you. Meanwhile, if I can be of any help, please don't hesitate to give me a call," and he hands us his card.

Tickled by this smooth opacity, I'm curious to take a quick look inside him—strictly a passive one, of course ... and the first thing I find, Jason Carax, is a memory of twenty years ago. You're boarding a bus, on which you slip away west across the marshes on the highway from New York to the airport, sealed in your headphones, through airport lounges, over moving tunnel-floors, through the gates to a plane, and the music seals you off while you shoot down the runway and climb through the air and curve around and streak across the ocean, sunset-crystal through the moving glass, and down again, through gates and further tunnels, to a city where you bus, train and quick-change and out through the streets under European skies... You walk, meet and talk, part and meet, look and ride and run and drink, then you head for another town and start the show again and fix those Internet connections and make a rendezvous and shine again with the people, then slip away, blurred in an audio-electrical cultural haze of many countries, chic hotels and continental glamour, plane-wheels and plastic, foreign coins and fluid motion, from nation to nation: "London—Paris—Rome—Berlin—Athens—Barcelona," say your eyes, "cities never-ending—a playground, almost like a video. So come with me now, we'll escape, don't you think?"

Jason, you manipulator, player, analyser! This is fun. Fast-track to yesterday, and there you are planning, scheming, framing, mixing on your laptop and phone and even diagrams on paper—slip and slide, and take us on a streak through the airwaves and out across the Web in fashion spreads. Turn poison into mercury and measure our temperatures; gauge the looks and market them to next year's beat. Is that fire in your eyes or the glow of machines? I take another peek in you, to settle this dilemma, and I smile then with pleasure, as a clear silent stream of words glances through the air at me and onward far beyond me, like quarks in a particle accelerator... *"Allure is a beautiful lie... Some people have a crackle... My people's people will talk to your people's people... Your entourage will have an entourage... Image as a second language... Plastic daydream... Dying young is such a good career move... I like to pit one demographic against another... I was skinny in Paris... French philosophy has the rigour of a good perfume... Media-genic... My fire is a glazed fire... There are those who make you and those who buy you... The secret of success is to be the ultimate extreme edition of yourself... It's so sterile, you could write an essay about it!... I'm too famous for a business card... It's without irony, and defeats any you bring to it... The public wants an Icon to be first euphoric, then tragic... It's always reassuring to see other people's frenzy... Making tragedy's too obvious—I like to make myth... Abstraction: the perfume... I want to make a drama out of my inability to resolve an identity... If I ran a club, then even if you were refused entry it would still feel like sex... Perfect, sanitised angst... I'm your wispy myth... I can't breathe in this mask!..."*

What a hoot he is, I do confess. I feel like responding to his quarks with a fillip of hypnosis, saying "OK Jason, picture me a face like the sound of the slinkiest and coolest pulse of electronic music, with space between the cheekbones of its high flicks of treble and a wet bass weight within those lips I want to kiss upon a poster on my bedroom wall! It's Jaymi's face—mine, the face you need to see on me, for now it's up to you to frame it to perfection, for the world. Angles of glamour on a face so bewitching, it is painful to the viewer—*that's the brief, so get going—off we go now, chop chop!*"

That would probably backfire in some way, however, so I strap it down. "Well, thank you, Mr Carax," I say aloud instead, proffering Bedford Pickering III's card. "This is our attorney's card, so I'm sure we'll all be in touch with one another." I give a little bow, like the one he gave to us; and he's gone.

As Alaia and I cross the downstairs lobby together, she mutters, "We'd better deliver."

"We shall."

"By the way, you're not having any secret tune-ins to me, are you?"

"No, of course not; I promised you." We walk on. "Good choice of pin-number for the ATM, though. Nobody would guess it."

She hits me on the arm, grinning, but through her grin I can see she's nervous about the broadcast.

So am I. Still, now that I'm getting used to having these new abilities in general, it's become absolutely clear that I was made to possess the power that they give me. This feels like no more than a simple truth. To perceive and appreciate the richest and subtlest elements of a person, instead of just guessing at these elements through an opacity of flesh that lacks the inclination to confirm one's guesses and the verbal ability to convey the same rich information in words: this is merely what I should always have been able to do. Why on *earth* did I have to wait years for this ability to arrive?... What a waste of time. Oh well—better late than never!

11 LUNCH WITH A SHARK

The next four weeks are like a rapid-edit montage: Alaia and I planning and rehearsing; Marc's awesome publicity machine confecting a global buzz around what has now been named *Sound & Vision*, "an exclusive live broadcast of an international act at a secret location"; universal expectation swelling up at such a high-profile TV event; and obedient debate swirling over who or what the act will be. Rehearsals occur at a small GN sound-stage under the GE Building. These involve interminable hours with me under her close scrutiny, while she is invisible to me. The reason for this is that she is shut away in a sound-recording booth, in front of a microphone, watching a monitor that displays what is seen by the camera right in front of me—my face, projecting through my eyes. The rest of me is off-camera, perched on a tall seat. She vocalises, with her inimitable combination of wildness and minute control, to accompany the imaginative material I'm projecting; I then interact with her; and we thereby shape and hone what we shall present live. We are expertly helped, whenever we need it, by an otherwise silent studio engineer named Anne, of whom we see little because she tends to be either in a control booth or in the shadows behind the lights that are trained on me from around the camera lens.

After the two-week holiday I booked off from work is over, I return to work whenever I can, telling Raven and my other colleagues nothing of my life's recent changes, until I have expended the great majority of my annual holiday allowance. Nobody remarks much on my timetable; luckily, we are in the company's summer lull. I am hazily aware that after this broadcast I may not have to work again—but I have decided not to think about this possibility until *Sound & Vision* proves itself to have been a reality.

One morning when I'm at work, Jason phones and requests that we meet for lunch, specifying that he and I are to meet alone. He gives the name and location of a Midtown restaurant I am not familiar with. Expecting the venue to be chic or at least tasteful, I am surprised, when I get there, to find it is one of those tired and anonymous tourist-oriented restaurants that come and go in the Times Square area, such as no real New Yorker would ever choose. A suspicion flickers up in me: does he not want to be seen, today, by any of his colleagues?

As I skirt around a horrible bawling child in the doorway, whose tourist parents are making a weary scene and whose face I must remember not to kick as I pass, I see Jason through the window, sitting jammed into a small booth in a corner. Languid in his pale grey suit, he looks somewhat out of place, being surrounded in this aisle by noisy and vilely occupied perambulators. A tall fruity drink stands on the table in front of him, topped by a garish paper mini-parasol. He watches me approach him. "I hope you like my taste in restaurants," he says, extending his hand. "The perfect atmosphere!"

"This is quite the place of the moment, I've heard," I reply, raising my voice to be heard above the din.

He inclines his head away from the corner of a duvet-sized map of Manhattan that is being wrestled with by a pudgy redneck seated in the adjoining booth beside a vacant-eyed, gum-chewing wife.

It's a buffet-style restaurant, so we get up in turn and fill our plates. "Thanks for meeting at short notice."

"Oh, sure. Alaia and I don't start rehearsing till two-thirty today."

"So, you're waltzing, you two?"

"Waltzing?"

"Moving forward with the project?"

"Oh, yes. We're working out some fabulous things for *Sound & Vision*. There's a ship—the biggest and most beautiful ship you've ever seen—and the turning of the world in a sidelight, and—oh, just gorgeous things. It's hard to describe them, like trying to describe music in words. You'll see it all."

"Great. I'm sure you'll want to maximise the impact of this gift of yours, this special sight?"

"You could say so," I reply, trying to work out why we are here. I can't help noticing how, while seeming just to be toying with his food, he seems to have consumed almost a third of a plateful already, with a sharky, deadly efficiency, while I have barely started mine. How did he manage that?

"Yay! So what would you say are your prime missions in using these abilities? I understand they're pretty new?"

I decide we must be here for some sort of pep-talk, so I relax. "I'm glad you ask, Jason." I spear a small gherkin with my fork. "And since you do ask, well—it sounds idealistic, but I want to use these abilities and this broadcast to help encourage people to transcend the everyday, just through really delving down into their own internal landscapes of imagination and perception, and exulting and delighting in all those riches. Which is a pastime that too many people seem to have had drummed out of them, you know? In most people's daily grind, look what they're up against: not enough attention or power or respect; not enough time left, after just getting by; always somewhere the threat of pain, injury and decline; always somewhere the threat of losing everything they have; plus the simple financial inaccessibility of most of the interesting things and adventures in life... In the context of all that shit, for many people it'll be a revelation to be compelled into intimate reacquaintance with the beauty of their own internal landscapes, which they'll have forgotten to look at for too long." I notice that I've been waving the small gherkin around on the end of my fork, rather dangerously, and I stop this. "That's my light-up-the-world mission! The second mission is more of a challenge: I want to deliver a big fuck-you to the average, the bland, the stale, the stupid, the dead, the waste of life. Like *corporate* culture, for instance ... er, well, not *your* corporate culture, of course, that's very different, I mean you're part of the solution here! You know what I mean... Anyway. And then finally, I want to re-learn my own 'natural' personality, because I feel I've recently lost track of some of that." I pop the well-travelled gherkin into my mouth at last, and masticate. "Does that make sense?"

"Absolutely." He nods in thought. He has finished his entire plateful, while I am still only a quarter of the way through mine. "Those aims are rich and varied. I'm impressed. And since you're so alive to possibilities, I have a proposition. Your contract with the General Network for this broadcast event is great. It's a cool gig! But you can expand from that. I've been thinking about how you could maximally exploit your content-gathering and your content-transmission at the same time. 'Cos you do both those functions, have you thought about that?" I shake my head. "Your passive gaze, as you call it, will do the gathering, and then your active gaze will do the transmission. After the *Sound & Vision* broadcast you'll have a week of down-time in Asbury Park, while Marc decides whether he can milk you for a second event."

"A second event? Really?"

"Oh, sorry, didn't we tell you that? Yeah. So anyway, while you're down there, why vegetate? Here's what I'm seeing—check this out. While you're there, you pick four individuals that you've got to know in Asbury Park, then you tune in on them in serious detail, with that passive gaze. Then after gathering as much as you can remember from their heads, you'll go to the studio, turn on that active hypnotic thing, just like you're doing for the broadcast, and you'll project all those people's material out again into a camera where it'll be captured in all its raw glory. You'll do that several times, till we've gathered enough. Then a post-production team will splice all that raw stuff together and use cutting-edge software to compose it into a free-standing, wholly man-made 'human imagination'."

"Fascinating. Is this for scientific research?"

"In a way, yes. What I'm proposing is a licensing agreement, between us two and another corporation I'm dealing with—a household name, which is pioneering a brand-new marketing science. You see, our man-made human imagination will be used as the framework for a state-of-the-art interactive cartoon spokesman for this corporation. They're planning a global brand overhaul." He taps me on the hand. "This will be way more than a regular spokesman. A regular spokesman isn't much more than a logo with a script. *This* spokesman will be the first use of a fully interactive suite of software they're developing, which we hope will one day be installed on every new computer and mobile device as a basic browser plug-in. But as the first public use for that software, this spokesman will allow the company to speak powerfully to the children's toy market, because children will love him—and the whole religious market, because Christians in particular will respond to him—plus the adult sex market, of course—and even the toilet-paper market, because of his softness."

"His *softness?*"

"Jaymi, you need to understand that this cartoon corporate spokesfigure is, in fact, a sheep."

I stare at him, dumbstruck. I should have guessed it would be something tacky like this. So much for those noble aims of scientific research. "…A sheep."

"A lamb or a sheep, yes. Probably a sheep. Let's not be snobbish here. I've commissioned detailed market research and financial projections. This could be very big business for you and me." He looks me hard in the eyes. "And this has nothing to do with *Sound & Vision*. Marc knows nothing of this, and he will continue to know nothing. Is that clear? Nothing in your contract with the General Network precludes this spokesfigure work, because the end product of this work won't contain any picture or sound that's recognisably you. I have a copy of your contract here with me, as well as a copy of the research and projections, in case you'd like to see them now."

"But Jason," I groan, "you want me to use this great new gift of mine, which is a real and rare opportunity for the betterment of mankind's imaginative wealth and self-knowledge, just to make a 'spokes-sheep' for some kind of toilet-roll manufacturer?" I fix him with a piteous look, calculated to appeal to whatever vestige remains in him of aesthetic seriousness, decency and right-living—aesthetic morality, perhaps. But the piteous look will be a non-starter, I observe; so I change tack and slide into a conspiratorial brightness. "Tell me, what do the mass media and social media mean? Let's use my gifts to explore that. You're in a very interesting position within that matrix…" But this is going nowhere either, any more than the piteous look was, and we both know it, so I peter out.

He waits for me to do so, then nods earnestly and lays a printed graph on the table. "Here are the financial projections," he begins, and then says something so fluent about profit margins that my eyes glaze over straightaway. He continues with an eloquent monologue about the graph, for perhaps two solid minutes. I sort of keep up with what he is saying, while he is saying it, but find that I cannot remember any of it afterwards. I think it boils down to *Sound & Vision*'s being a one-off, whereas this deal will give me an income for life. And anyway, what do I have to lose? Nothing, of course, since I'll never be recognisable in the final product. And what do I have to gain? Well, at the very least, one hell of a lot!

He becomes deadly serious. "Only two other people will know about this, aside from us two, and that's how it will stay." He stares at me sharply, with a quick flash of murder in there somewhere. "Both of them are necessary to us for this. Nobody else is. Person number one is the broadcasting engineer at the Metropolitan sound-stage. That's the facility in Asbury Park. He'll record the material you deliver from your four target imaginations. He's very up and coming, the third or fourth most eminent on the east coast, I'd say, and set to be the pre-eminent one after the broadcast. His name is Rik Chambers." I nod warily. "Person number two is your door-opener in town. We can't have you getting material from anyone who works in the facility itself, because they might make trouble if they ever recognised elements of their own imaginations after that material has reached its final manifestation."

"They might recognise themselves in the sheep?"

He nods. "Then things could get messy and litigious. Too risky. We need you to take raw material from people in town, outside the Metropolitan. The common herd. People who would have no clue how to start making any legal trouble even if they do recognise their own imaginations in the spokesfigure one day. People who have no money for a lawyer's consultation and maybe even just a hazy idea of how to get to New York from Asbury Park. Your door-opener, therefore, will be Evelyn Carmello. She works as a GN driver, moving talent between the City and the Metropolitan, but she's also a round-the-way girl who grew up in Asbury and knows the folks there like a native, which is essential. You should know that she's also Rik's girlfriend."

"OK, well, we'll see. I'll check with Alaia—"

"No you won't. You most certainly won't do anything of the kind, because this has nothing at all to do with Alaia. This is strictly between you, me and the two individuals I've just mentioned. And that is *it*. We have a confidentiality agreement with the corporation in question, and that is written in stone, Jaymi. Alaia will know nothing about this. Nothing whatsoever. *Ever.* It's not a singing sheep."

"Look, Jason, I don't actually have to—"

"*I* can step on your broadcast any time I want to." He glares at me, with that trace of murder once again. "And if I did, then *my* career would carry on, up and up and up, thank you very much. *You* get only one shot, however. *This* is that shot." He sinks back in his seat and grins. "And you really don't know what you're doing, right here and now—do you? That's painfully obvious, I can assure you. Oh, what are you going to do, Jaymi? Start hypnotising me into backing down on this? I don't think so, do you? Because even if you succeeded in doing that, during just this meeting—then guess what. Would it be surprising if you were to hear this evening from my assistant that your broadcast had hit 'unexpected difficulties' and had had to be mysteriously cancelled? I think it would be surprising if you *didn't* hear that, because I can see in great detail a thousand unexpected difficulties that might arise for such a complex project as *Sound & Vision*; I don't think I need to bother giving you any examples of them. Look at my position and look at yours. You hit a bull's-eye when you went to Marc's office that night, sure. But the end result was he OK'd you as a project and then handed you over to me, so he could get on with running a conglomerate. He's moved on from this already, believe me. That's how he works. What I say about you *goes*, as far as he's concerned. I hold all the cards here, don't

I? You're bright enough to see that. It's amazing, frankly, that you've got this far—so don't fuck it up, please, just play the game."

His eyes stare into mine, a quarter-smile buried somewhere in their mercilessness. *You shark!* I think, my mind and emotions racing. So this was my pep-talk: being blackmailed, in effect, into being a commercial imagination-cloning machine. I'll be stealing the imaginations of four human beings. An imagination thief—that's what he wants me as. Yes, I'm hired, as a glorified photocopier. And aside from depriving our selected targets of privacy and compensation, he is also driving an uncomfortable wedge between Alaia and me, for I shall now have to keep her ignorant of secret recordings and such like, which she'll probably sense and resent. She can't stand being kept out of the loop. I assume he must have blackmailed or bribed Evelyn and Rik somehow too. Jason is living dangerously, for sure, by going behind Marc's back. I can't be a hundred per cent certain he'd back up his threats by sabotaging my broadcast, but I'm sure he would succeed if he chose to, so I have no wish to test him out on this. (The task of locating and hypnotising a comparable entertainment mogul into arranging a similar broadcast is a little too fraught to contemplate.) I hate having my new abilities hijacked for the making of a tacky interactive cartoon sheep, instead of using them for works of artistic, scientific or social value ... but having got so close to making *Sound & Vision* a reality, how can I jeopardise it? I have to admit he's got me massively shafted, and the only honourable course of action will be just to roll over like a pussy.

"Yes, I'm thoroughly in agreement," I breeze, turning back to him with a bland smile. "By all means let's move ahead. I think it's a fine opportunity."

"Excellent choice." He clinks his fruity drink against my coffee cup. "So here's a basic letter of agreement between you and me, just so I've got a signature from you." He pulls a business envelope from his suit pocket, opens it and lays a short letter in front of me ready to be signed. Yes, of course he would. "Very straightforward, for now, as you can see. We can iron out the details later. As it says here, you're guaranteed a handsome minimum."

There he speaks the truth, I must admit. I nod, then sign. "And a copy for myself?" I try.

"On reflection, I don't think that will be necessary, no."

We pay and rise to leave the restaurant. My mind is churning. "What happens next?"

"Next, you just go down there and give one hell of a fantastic broadcast, Jaymi," he beams, shaking my hand. "And enjoy it, dammit. You will be changing the world, down there. How did you put it? 'Adding to mankind's imaginative wealth and self-knowledge'. Have at it! Why not? Then afterwards, Evelyn will brief you on the other stuff." And once again his smile disappears, without a trace: "But don't you *dare* fuck up…"

He turns and melts away into the Times Square crowds.

12 RELENTLESS WAKEFULNESS IN THE BELFRY

After the Times Square ordeal, I decide I shall put Jason's "other stuff" out of my mind and just focus on the imminent *Sound & Vision*. Through rehearsals, Alaia's and my mutual responsiveness has evolved into a fertile give-and-take between our eponymous sound and vision, evoking cathedrals of beauty and power, leading us to a tentative confidence that this will be a uniquely beautiful audio-visual spectacle, the like of which we have never quite seen or heard before.

The night before the broadcast, when we have no more rehearsing left to do, Marc phones me. "Great news! Public expectation for *Sound & Vision* has reached such a height that I've been able to set up a second broadcast event for you both, to be aired this coming Thursday evening."

"*What?* Marc, that's four days' time! No, we need far longer than that. This first one's taken weeks."

"Nonsense. This is show business, Jaymi, you have to crank it out!" He cackles raucously. "No, seriously. Jason's assistant tells him you've been moaning that you have too much material now for just one broadcast. Am I right?"

He is sort of right, in fact. "Well, I suppose that is true, as far as it goes. But—"

"There you go, then. Beware of answered prayers, eh? Hollywood calls only once, you know, and you'd better say yes when it does!" He cackles again; he's having much too much fun here. "Look, you and

Alaia will be experts at this, after tomorrow night. You'll put the second one together in time for Thursday, don't you worry. So, do I have your agreement?"

"Well, OK," I sigh, "but—"

"Excellent choice." Those words echo strangely in my head, as he continues, "Console yourself that I've resisted setting up a third broadcast event, until we can gauge public demand and optimise its timing."

"*Please* continue to resist that, Marc. Have you told Alaia about the second broadcast?"

"I'm just about to call her."

"Shall we see you down in Asbury Park?"

"Alas not, dear boy, I have too many commitments. Our two Pacific Rim divisions are de-merging just before midnight tomorrow. Good for the balance books, don't you know. I shall have to be on hand here. But I assure you I shall be with you in spirit, and I shall certainly take a break earlier in the evening, to watch a little television in the office here. Which is a fitting honour for you, by the way, as I haven't even plugged the damned thing in for months, so I hope I can remember how to do so!"

Since my first big encounter with him in his office, I have felt an odd aversion to the idea of tuning in to Marc again. That first meeting was such a legendary bull's-eye that the prospect of revisiting the same ground in any way has always felt more than just unnecessary: it has felt like a perilous proposition, even sacrilegious, as if it might in some unforeseeable way endanger my position on this precarious pinnacle where I find myself. Also, with the two grand broadcasts now facing me, my poking around in Marc's head would feel as off-putting for me as it would be for an actor on stage to think not about his character but about the financial structure of the theatre itself. As he speaks on the phone, however, I do permit my sight to reach in and grab one tiny salient picture from him. It comes from not much deeper inside him than my daily image of him from outside, residing just within the shallows of his surface, as it were … and in a high square tower in your mind's epidermis, Marc, are bright white walls, and in the centre of this belfry is a never-sleeping, desperately alert white head, rooted there in the floor, whose job it is to keep an eagle-eye upon the distant mountain valleys to be seen through the unglazed embrasures in the belfry walls. The head is wide and solid, in its sixties, Marc, its features somewhat flattish. It is powerful, reporting to no one, a head to be respected—yet I also feel, somewhere, a tiny fleeting something of pity at the spectacle of such relentless wakefulness.

"So onward, then!" he booms. "Good luck tomorrow. Get some sleep."

Just for an instant I hear this last word as "sheep", but then realise it's not. "Thank you, Marc."

"Oh, you're welcome. You're only making us all money!"

13 THE SILVER VAN TO THE GHOST TOWN

I awake to the big day. Tonight we perform, and I can hear the zeroes singing for me.

I get up at leisure, text Alaia "Did Marc call you about Thursday?" and receive the reply "Yes—EEK!" I get dressed, eat, get various things done around my apartment here in the Riverbank West, which I've been neglecting during this rehearsal period, and pack for a week. The journey there will be short, and I know that once we've arrived we shan't have too long before the broadcast, so I ready myself for the camera here. The picture will be a close-up from about shoulder-height upwards, with essentially no alteration of framing throughout; so I wear the simplest black long-sleeved T-shirt with no other attire visible to camera, to offer no distraction from what I'll be projecting.

At the appointed hour I get a text from an unfamiliar number, saying "Outside." I step onto my balcony, here near the top of the tower-block, peer down and see a small silver van parked on the street. I gather my things, lock up, descend in the lift and emerge at Forty-Third Street by Eleventh Avenue. The afternoon air is warm on my face. There's that sleek little van, and in the driver's window the face of a Latina in her twenties smiles out at me, smooth, sunny, round, with a faint sass within its clear warmth. This must be the mysterious Evelyn Carmello. "Hi Jaymi," she calls. I like her straightaway. I lean against a lamp-post and fold my arms. She stares at me. "Well, come on!"

"I don't know," I say. "Should we cancel?"

She raises her eyes and points behind her to the van door.

I step across the pavement. "I feel like a little boy on his first morning of school."

"Well aren't you cute—we should put that in a press release." She clicks the van door open for me.

Up three steps is a small living space in black and silver, with a tiny table and a few very basic facilities including a TV and a mini-fridge, then further back a dozen fixed black seats with windows on either side. I slide the door shut behind me, put my bag down and sit in one of the two front-most seats.

She eases the van from the kerb and sets off across the Avenue. "This is like a concert tour van," I say. "And I guess this is a kind of concert tour, though a brief and unnatural one. So let's do this right: for the next couple of hours of our life, on this tour van, our every passing feeling will potentially be product or merchandise."

She picks this up without dropping a beat: "Oh, you know it. This tour will be a legend. One day they'll make a road movie out of it. See that little fridge there? Look inside."

I get up and open it. "Oh my god. A comprehensive array of intoxicating beverages!"

"I'm driving, so I'll just have a whisky."

I turn, and glimpse her twinkly eyes and freckled nose in the driving mirror. "What kind of whisky?"

"Bourbon. What are you having?"

"Chocolate-flavoured soy milk."

"*Soy milk?*"

"That's the modern-day rock'n'roll lifestyle. The hard stuff is so two-decades-ago." I pour out a tall brown glassful for myself and hand her a tumbler of bourbon on the rocks, as we turn onto the far side of the West Side Highway. The scurrying of cars reminds me of a jazz trumpet's sound, the sunlight pours through the van's open windows and I feel a burst of exhilaration at what's coming tonight. "You know," I announce, "I think this trip is going to be a giggle."

She bangs her hands on the wheel and whoops back at me, "It's gonna be a blast!"

There's no doubt about it: although it's evident that I retain the ability to make plausible good-natured conversation with someone I have never met before (admitting that the bubbly Evelyn is hardly a test of such abilities), I have nonetheless not ceased, since the onset of my new abilities, to feel as if my conversational contributions are turns in a role-playing game uttered by some skilled participant other than myself. She doesn't seem to be hearing anything odd, but from inside it feels as if my best guess is to aim a straight line from what I'm thinking to my interlocutor's likely understanding of this thinking, and to hope that this line, in passing through the interface between us, will crackle up a little constellation of exchanges that'll be appropriate. Perhaps this is what I and others did in conversations before my new abilities arrived; but I can't quite be certain of this, for in those days I didn't have this feeling. I didn't feel that I lacked the basic clothing of a default personality. This reminds me: "Oh. I suppose, before we pick up Alaia, I should ask you about, you know, Jason and—"

"Let's get the broadcast over with first. We'll get onto the other stuff afterwards."

So "the other stuff" is still on. Well, at least we're all calling it the same thing.

We exit the Highway onto Houston Street; then before long she pulls up at the corner of Houston and Norfolk, and there's Alaia.

"Hi Alaia. Hop on in," says Evelyn through the window and clicks open the door for her.

Alaia's faint smile seems to burn through the air at us. "Evelyn? Hi." She climbs into the van and slides the door shut behind her. "Good afternoon," she says to me and sits, with that demureness which I know to be deceptive, on the seat across the aisle from me.

I notice Evelyn is sending a quick text. "OK then, let's roll," she says. "This is how we roll." She turns and hands to each of us a print-out of our call-sheet for the evening, headed "General Network— Metropolitan Sound-stage", featuring a simple but precise timetable for our arrival and studio call-times, culminating with the broadcast at eight o'clock and signed off by Rik Chambers.

When I look up from the sheet, we are coasting fast down the elevated FDR Drive, passing the end of Wall Street. I catch Alaia's eye. "Ready?" I ask quietly.

She holds my gaze. "Yes, I'm ready. And you?"

Evelyn presses a button and the windows all glide shut.

"Yep."

We turn our heads to opposite sides, as daylight fades away, an underpass slants up in streaks on left and right, and the van swoops down to the Brooklyn-Battery Tunnel.

14 THE SMASHED VIOLIN

Just as she mirrored my exuberance at the start of our drive, Evelyn now echoes our reflective mood as she hurtles us through the tunnel, unspeaking. Once back up in the afternoon sun, we bomb down the Brooklyn Queens Expressway, over the Verrazano Narrows Bridge, across Staten Island and onto unfamiliar southward highways.

As she stares out at the industrial spaces flashing by, Alaia's fingers still clutch her call-sheet. Pretending to doze, I tune in to her thoughts (I'm aware I promised not to, but just one more time) … and I find you're churning with excitement, Alaia, and a touch of self-admonishment: "I'm tense again—*don't* be tense. Calm down. Put the call-sheet down. There—it's on the seat now. But of course I'm going to be tense. I'm allowed to be: this broadcast's the biggest break I've ever had. Look at Evelyn, so comfortable up there. She drives the van as if she were wearing it. And look at Jaymi, curled up pale there, asleep. I've never seen him with his eyes closed for any length of time—not even on the sound booth monitor, I think. I like it; it reminds me he's human, like before his sight. I should have known he'd be looking glamorous already, early in the day—it's exhausting. Flawless natural make-up for the camera, of course. Well, I'm quite happy to be un-glamorous for the journey, thank you… Is this broadcast of ours lunacy? I know what my voice can do, and I've seen what that gaze of his does, up on screen: but what will we actually be *doing*? Just wailing and staring. That's all it is. Now that is just lunacy! Then again…" Your eyes narrow. "Then again—*just you wait, you motherfuckers!*"

That's more like it! Your head rests back, your eyes close gently, and I see that you're starting to drift away and lose focus.

I slip my vision out of her and open my eyes. That was dangerously addictive, but I'm not going to spy on her again, because I promised her I wouldn't. That was the last time.

Up in the driver's seat with her back to us, Evelyn barely moves. How sunny and curved she is, in her bright orange T-shirt. Her shape makes me think of a big viola, or the violin I used to own. I haven't thought about that in a while. I used to play it under a favourite tree in the woods near where I lived in Nebraska. I'd go to that tree many evenings, alone, to play my violin at dusk; a secret place. One evening when I was sixteen I started to play, then a band of other kids appeared around the corner, who had seen me and followed me. Expecting violence and abuse, I carried on playing, thinking that I may as well do so, since it would make no difference to what would happen. To my amazement, however, it did make a difference, because they just came up and listened, not even interrupting me with very much talk. I should never have expected it, but eventually some were even dancing in the clearing, to my music! After that, there was no more violence or abuse from them, but every few days they would follow me again, and hear, and dance in the clearing at dusk ... until one day a band of parents followed them and found us at our ritual. To my shock and grief, a couple of the parents grabbed my violin and bow, smashed them against my tree, told me I was perverting the other children to make them like me, and if I didn't leave town they would hurt me badly. They grabbed their children and left. I was shattered. Only one woman turned back towards me with a hint of compassion, to say she had heard there were many violins in New York City, so maybe I should try living there instead. Then she hurried after the others. I decided that at last I was leaving there forever. I ran to the home I lived in, put all absolute essentials into a bag, ran away to the highway and stood there with a sign saying "New York". Soon a truck stopped, bound for Boston, and I climbed aboard. *Escape at last! Never should I go back. No more need to hide!* My mood soared above the truck. The driver was taciturn, which suited me perfectly. Physically immobile but inside aflame, I let the hours and the miles and the land slide by, through the afternoon and onward, as the truck thundered east across the heartland of America, the sun swung low through the giant sky behind us and the shadow of the truck ran away upon the road ahead...

And now this tour van streaks along, some years later in a very different chapter, its engine pounding smoothly as its shadow runs beside us. I seem to feel the turning of the earth and the planets, and enormous hidden powers all converging on the coast here—ghost trucks thundering up the highways of America from every state, intent on some explosive goal I cannot now escape.

Alaia's still asleep. I check the time: in another twenty minutes we'll be there. I rest my head back. Evelyn must have turned on the radio, but hasn't tuned it well. Unadjusted, it sputters through a spree of signals, snatching fragments up or ripping through a no-man's-land between stations: heated talk, bland voices, earnest weather, urgent traffic; surges of classical or twangy country music, cut with advertising jingles; and wastes of crackle, wheezing, cryptic blips or dirty foundry roars. Voice, noise or music, all is random and detached, but makes its own sense somehow. "*All the way down the east coast!*" shouts a distant, raucous voice. "*All the way down the east coast... Come back fat as a rat!... Why be a loser when you can be a winner?...*" Another shimmers in, chilled-out, from many miles away: "For the next thirty minutes, I'm going to give you a special phone number, where you can call me, so I can send you a special gift, this week. Get your paper and pen ready, because I have a special phone number..." Montage: truck-stops and isolated diners on the highway, a cellophane wrapper blown across a lonely intersection, stabs of preaching through the babble, unreal city... What exhilarating multitudes of detail in the world, and how prodigious their minuteness of unfolding. A low electric growl like a worm out of mud comes, rises to a hum, to a whine and a squeak, before vanishing to dogs' or even bats' realms of hearing.

A sign—"Asbury Park 5 miles"—streaks by.

Then through the crackle comes a strain of faint piano, transporting me to something so long-lost and forgotten, from my childhood or another's, that it fills me with wordless vivid sadness and magic: hiding in the shade of a square monastic cloister, where a sunlit fountain softly plays and chuckles at the centre, I flit down one long side of the square, on my tiptoes silent past twenty cracked columns, till I near the open door of a chamber in a corner. I creep to the door and peep within. An old man plays on an ancient yellow piano, never looking at the keyboard but up towards the ceiling, with the sweet tender smile of past hopes, past loves and faded glories long vanished, now revisited a thousandth time but never quite recaptured—

a swelling, yearning, faded music once acclaimed but now forgotten, played with a lyric grace and fond regret that slows the blood and saps the will. He's the composer, I realise. Around him, collapsing stacks of books and papers, scores and jottings, broken metronomes, bric-a-brac and knick-knacks rise from the floor and up the walls on every side, as if they hold up the ceiling. The old man has lived here a lifetime, clearly. Here he plays, all day and every day; and here he'll die, in one year or twenty, unchanged. Here, in this place of tranquillity, I start to feel my energy and hope draining out, sucked away by a heavy past that isn't even mine: if I don't watch out, I'll enter, settle in an armchair and take root, and then surely petrify and very soon be cobwebbed...

Stirring, I shake my head, bump it on the window and come to life.

15 EVELYN'S TOUR OF THE GHOST TOWN

"Wake up, you two," Evelyn calls. I wake and see Alaia stirring too. "We're entering Asbury Park now, my home town. Some call it a bombsite, but I hold it in great affection, so be careful what you say!"

All I've heard about Asbury Park is that it's a run-down seaside resort about half an hour away from New York City. On the left, yellow tape is stretched across the steps leading from a boardwalk to a wide and deserted sandy beach where a notice reads "No Bathing". A road sign tells me this is Ocean Avenue, and there indeed is an ocean. Coincidence? I think not. In stark contrast to when we set out, the afternoon has become grimly overcast and it is starting to drizzle. "And it's perfect beach weather!" hoots Evelyn. "All right, I'm going to give you both a quick tour, since you insist. There on the right is the Berkeley Carteret Hotel," and she points at a high brick building, "the only hotel remaining that isn't ruined or a flea-pit. It's always mostly empty." Beyond it are two wide empty squares of grass, with a gaggle of grey geese on them. We pass some low concrete structures interspersed by a few elegant but run-down seaside buildings with ornate decorations—most of these buildings locked, shuttered up or wrecked, with old paint peeling off walls and wooden facings. "There's the venerable Madame Marie's psychic cabin on the left," continues Evelyn as we cross Fourth Avenue, "closed due to unforeseen circumstances."

I seem to hear a bird's shriek, rich as a peach, and I picture it poking out its orange bill from shadow: I lean to the right, peer up and see a corner of the sky lying drowned behind the long-abandoned shell of a half-constructed multi-storey building. Years of aborted half-completion have encrusted its protruding metal concrete-reinforcing rods with rust where they poke up from the columns like frayed wires from a broken appliance. I see no great bird, I must have been hearing things. "That lovely eyesore," says Evelyn, "is Joe Carob's carcass-building. Also known as C-8, from its old tax ID number. It makes some people so cheesed off, they have a hard time even acknowledging its existence—though it's kind of hard to miss, being smack in the middle of town and the biggest thing around. It's the great unmentionable, so I'll mention it: ladies and gentlemen, the aborted Ocean Mile Condo. Unfortunately uncle Joe ran out of cash in '89, after eleven storeys of bare steel and concrete. And to think, it was going to be sixteen floors of bare steel and concrete!... I seem to be the only one who feels it has a certain charm, just because it was part of my childhood, which was a beautiful time for me. So I say, 'Thanks Joe!' I could never tell that to anyone who comes from around here, though—I think I'd get lynched if I did."

On the right comes the boarded-up ruin of the Albion Hotel, then on the left a weeded-over miniature golf course. I've picked up some of her goofy enthusiasm, I must say: already I do find myself feeling a real affection for this place. She swings us right on Second Avenue. "There's the Stone Pony on the left, still jumping; there's been a lot of live music in this town. Back there was the Atlantis with the rainbow sign. I think they'll be pulling down the Albion later this year." Looking right on Kingsley Street, I see beside the Albion a building in a two-storey L-shape, enclosing an empty space where pebbles push through asphalt. Up the outside stairways, the dead-looking upper doors are numbered still in sequence, squatted in or empty, with the windows shuttered. "And this is where I worked the street a few years back, when it was busier," she says, turning left on Kingsley Street. "You'd never guess, to look at me, of course."

The drizzle comes harder. A sense of exhaustion presses down from the sky through the weed-edged fragments of flagstone and grass, where I'm pleased to see no children play. Looking down Second Avenue as we turn again, I see several large houses with grand porches and balconies, some boarded up, which gives the street a spooky air. A train siren blares on and off, across the town, headed somewhere from somewhere but not stopping here. Lone figures scurry round corners in the middle distance. Yet, there are sporadic signs of life, amid the wreckage: on the right another gay bar, Zippers, then an older-looking girly-bar next door called Seductions, then some run-down shack-like bungalows. The grimy Flamingo Motel proclaims vacancies on First Avenue. On our left across a wide space the Empress Hotel is shut down, but Evelyn points to it: "In there is Paradise, where my friend Shigem works. It's a club, I'll take you there." Turning right on Asbury Avenue, I see on my left a shuttered green building labelled Palace Amusements, bearing two primitive painted renditions of a grinning fun-lover's face. Next to him is a gay pornographic cinema, then the Talking Bird Café, both functional but closed. "That was Tillie," says Evelyn, "another little part of my childhood. He's watched us like that for twice my lifetime, but I hear he's going to be demolished, so enjoy him while you can... And here we are." The van glides to a halt. "The town has great parking, don't you think? OK, end of tour, we can go back to New York now … oh no, sorry, there's a concert first."

I look around for a building that might be expected to house a high-end sound-stage, but all I can see, aside from houses, is the wide, shuttered façade of yet another boarded-up hotel on our right clad in peeling white paint. Its decrepit façade bears no name, but on its roof, facing the sea, stands a line of big letters adding up to half a name—"METROPOL". "It's in *here*?" enquires Alaia.

Evelyn nods, chuckling. "Let's be fast going in, please. We try to be unobtrusive. Plus, in view of the broadcast it would be good if nobody in the houses across the street sees you, Jaymi, so try and keep your face down."

She spirits us through an inconspicuous, unmarked door. I feel a sense of unreality, as if I am an actor on the silent screen or a chess-piece in a game (black knight, I think). I glance at Alaia. "Isn't all this strange?" I mutter to her as we hurry after Evelyn.

"Yes," she murmurs. "I feel like a chess-piece."

"*Really?* You as well? Wow... By the way, which piece?"

She glances at me darkly: "D'you need to ask?"

I do need to, in fact, despite her seeming to think I shouldn't.

Before I can decide how to press the question in a tactful way, however, we have entered an empty white hallway of faded grandeur, featuring a curved white marble staircase lined with balusters like fat white pawns.

Did she mean the black queen? I should guess so, intellectually, but I could be wrong. It would seem somewhat excessive to tune in to her, just in order to find this out (and of course I shouldn't do so now anyway), but I must admit I'm curious.

16 READY FOR OUR CLOSE-UP

From nowhere there appears a young white man of about thirty whose angularity of face and body has a forceful irreducibility, a toughness of will and a perceptive directness that cause me to feel two reactions at once: envy of what can only be called his all-around coolness; and a faint pang of inexplicable sorrow. But now he smiles and in a laid-back Scots accent says, "Hey, how's it going?" and shakes my hand. In these words I recognise Rik Chambers, the broadcasting engineer whose praises Jason rang and one of our two accomplices in "the other stuff". I've spoken with him on the phone a few times. From hearing that easy, level lilt, I wasn't expecting someone as wired as I'm seeing. His leisurely warmth and sharp, humorous eyes establish an atmosphere of calm and focus, however. A great combination to put ourselves into the hands of, for *Sound & Vision*. "Welcome! As you can see from the call-sheet, I've not given us too much down-time before we go to the studio, because I wanted us to get straight down to business without hours of flapping about and losing focus. Evelyn'll show you up to your rooms, where you can freshen up and have a bite to eat if you want. Then she'll come back up to fetch you at seven, and we'll get you wired up. Could I ask that we leave all mobile phones upstairs, rather than bringing them into the studio."

As she leads us up the stairs, Evelyn points down at a door across the hallway, saying "Breakfast room". In the upstairs corridor she indicates a couple of adjacent doors, each with a piece of paper fixed to it bearing one of our names. She then returns downstairs, while Alaia and I exchange a look of conspiratorial trepidation and diverge through our appointed doors.

My room has a window just beneath the eaves, overlooking a pleasant square of trees and grass on the inland side of the Metropolitan. As I freshen up, I wonder who else has been allotted this room over the years. Who else has paced up and down here, or sprawled on the bed, before being shepherded down to perform in one of the studios? I check my clothes, freshen up my make-up in the mirror, set my phone to silent and leave it on the table. Ten to seven. I pour myself a coffee from the pot on the table, sit in the armchair by the window and consume a chocolate bar from a handy plate of snacks.

Calm and focus ... calm and focus.

A knock at my door, then another at Alaia's. We emerge from our doors at the same moment and join Evelyn in the corridor. Alaia has changed into a smooth and elegant black silk dress, at which I smile approvingly. "OK, so they won't see it," she says, "but they'll hear it."

"Sure is one hell of a noisy dress," chirps Evelyn as we bustle along the corridor.

"I didn't mean it in that sense," returns Alaia crisply.

We are led back down to the main hallway, then down a long, dim corridor, till we reach a door beneath a green light. Inside it is a low-lit and low-ceilinged room full of impressive-looking audio-visual equipment. "Hey," says Rik. The door clicks shut behind us, and another light above it on this side changes from green to red. "So here we are. Everything's set up, ready to mesh with your inputs: lights, cameras, sound, stadium audience, big screen."

"Where's the rest of the broadcast crew?" I ask.

"New York."

"Oops," says Alaia.

"No worries! It's just us four here, but I'm looking at the rest of the team in New York, through the monitor here." He does a thumbs-up sign at a monitor whose back is facing us, then grins. "He just gave me the finger. The cheek of it, you can't get the staff these days. Anyway, we're all set, they might as well be in the same room with us. Do we have any mobile phones here?" We shake our heads. "Are we absolutely sure?" We nod. "Good. Alaia, if you could take a seat in the sound booth," and he points through the door of what looks like a built-in wardrobe, where a tiny but comfortable cupboard space contains the same set-up we've rehearsed with: a microphone at which she can stand or sit, facing a monitor that displays where I shall be. "Bit of a noisy dress," comments Rik, as Alaia shuts herself inside and Evelyn clears her throat. "You won't be thrashing around too much in there, I hope? Because I tell you, these mics—"

"I stand statuesque," announces a voice from the sound booth.

"OK then. Jaymi, let's have you right there in front of the three cameras, on the mark. Would you prefer to sit or stand?"

"Sit, but high."

"Try this tall seat here, then." I hop up onto it. "Is that good?" I nod.

"D'you want any make-up?" asks Evelyn.

"No, I'm fine, just give me a minute before we roll, and I'll give it last looks," I reply, holding up a translucent powder compact before returning it to my pocket. "Are we shooting 4K, like you said?" I ask Rik.

"We are indeed—I've been looking forward to it for years."

I stick my tongue out at the invisible Alaia, through the cameras, and she blows back a raspberry at me.

"Alaia," says Rik. "At whatever vocal pitch you can get the loudest, could you give me a smooth gradient, over about ten seconds, from silence up to your loudest, please…" And so it carries on, for at least half an hour: assisted by Evelyn, Rik leads us in a quiet, expert fashion through more and more minutely calibrated tests of her sound and my vision, several times in each case, making tiny adjustments of every kind. Phone calls to the broadcast crew in New York are few: he and they evidently add up to a well-oiled machine.

At last his tests come to a finish. "That's it, then," he pronounces quietly. "Jaymi, if you'd like to give it those last looks." As I blot and lightly powder, I notice he is speaking in a slower, softer voice than before, with a simple, serious calm. He would have the right stuff as an astronaut, I think. I could also imagine him walking over with authoritative calm to take the gun out of a gunman's hand. "We have ten minutes left," he says. "Any burning questions from either of you, please ask. If not, may I suggest you both just remain still in your own spaces and don't move. Rest … and focus. When the time comes, I shall say a countdown from ten to one, indicating seconds remaining till we're live on air. 'One' will be the last thing you hear from me. Then a second later you'll hear and feel the space of the stadium. Then off you go—it's all yours." He pauses. "Are you both set?"

"Yes."

"Yes."

"Good."

And no further word is said.

Within a few seconds after this cessation of all verbiage, I become aware of every tiny sound and movement around me in the studio. Evelyn moves, somewhere not far behind me. I let my eyelids gently sink, and start to still my mind.

Hundreds of millions of eyes, around the earth, are about to focus only on my face and Alaia's sound—none of them, except for a handful who work in the General Network, knowing quite what to expect of us.

The biggest thing I've ever done.

Probably the biggest thing I'll ever do.

And soon I grow as focused, as calm and as alone as I have ever been.

17 SOUND & VISION

It seems that a lot less than ten minutes has passed, when the return of Rik's level, quiet voice cuts into the extreme stillness that reigns. Before even the split-second of the "T" in his word "Ten" is finished, however, I know that this must be the inevitable countdown, right here upon us, at last.

In the middle of me now is a circle of uncanny calm, an empty round spotlight on a smooth black floor. Somewhere beyond the edges of this circle, a tiny intellectual voice in my head reminds me that he won't say "zero". I can't engage with anything intellectual now, but I absorb this little reminder lightly, around the edges of the spotlight, as being not without its helpfulness. Meanwhile the clear, calm, relentless countdown continues: "... nine ... eight ... seven ... six ... five ... four ... three ... two ... one..."

A huge distant murmur arises, and swells loud.

The audience! Digitally created, to stand in for the millions at their television sets around the world. "Well, that's showbiz," I reflect.

Here it is, then, *Sound & Vision...*

Space unfurls, ballooning forward, up and out in front of me. Ten giant floodlights rear up skyward, from the highest outer rim above the stadium's upper circles. The dizzy fall of bluish-white light across a landscape of several hundred thousand tiny heads below is fierce—and yet it's also feeble, spilling to the ground beneath the cold gigantic darkness of infinity beyond it.

And now the floods start to dim, very slowly.

The crowd's random babble dims along with the floods, while a unified cheer fades in from round the stadium. I close my eyes, seated here in my hidden perch above the big screen, and listen. I let my eyelids open and raise my glance. The cheer swells louder and the floods keep on dimming, till for two or three seconds just a scratch of blue filament in each of the ten banks of huge glass bulbs is left against the blackness. Then this dies too and faint stars appear instead, dotting the entire sky. The cheer simmers down again, to quiet and expectancy.

My outer gaze descends from the minuscule stars, to alight upon the central of the three camera lenses ahead of me. The focus of the audience approaches its peak. I slide my outer gaze aside, laying bare my sensors but not projecting anything. Immediately, I feel the hushed attention of every person present as a soft silk string, fired out across the stadium and sticking to me—soft and intelligent, the optical fibre of a secret human spider.

Behind me where I'm perched, a dim glow fades up, to silhouette me, as arranged. The big screen beneath me shows its first image— just my head, full-on but silhouetted black against the glow. In the instant, as the audience observes this and murmurs, I feel an outward pulling of attention on my face, from every seat around the stadium, non-physical but potent and growing all the time: a pull, from eyelash-close to the spanning of a dam across the width of a valley...

The moment of optimum audience focus arrives. The surface of the deep blue night is a-shiver, like a shiny poster rippling in a breeze. Lamps around the cameras burn bright and light me up, so I burst alive and huge upon the giant screen below. A tiny curling spotlight like a hair hits Alaia far beneath me where she stands on the stage underneath the big screen. I open my projectors, and my eyes on the screen flood the lower echelons of the stadium with ocean, and the music of this ocean fills the watching bodies, buoys them up and carries them, as if the most bewitching tide of melody and harmony were sweeping them in circles. Fluorescent waves lap the shore, the scent of brine suffuses the enormity of space ahead, then over the horizon it appears ... *the greatest ship you've ever seen!* Gliding through the silence behind the ocean's music, it's the size of a range of hills, the shape of an oil-tanker, deepest black, its many decks twinkling with strange lights—bewitching on the night sea. Who knew this ship would come? My projectors insinuate the shadow of a question: do you want this? *Yes!* my sensors catch your answer, huge and immediate. I love your answer and I love you too, although I know that love is pretty easy at this distance. Yes, of course you want this ship, though I know you didn't ask for it. You're mesmerised, there where you sway among the waves before its majesty and magic ... so take this ship, it's yours!

Its prow rides higher in the sky than the floods, and the stadium revolves. Alaia's voice rises through the splashing of the waves, to a chorus of voices that pour from the ship's decks as honey into black sea or willow sap weeping into plum-dark depths. Figures can be glimpsed on every level of the vessel, silhouetted on the ballroom glow inside it. Most of these are standing at the railings of the decks, staring out across the water at us huddled in the stadium, while others float behind them down the length of the ship. Some figures must be three metres tall, one or two with antlers of some kind. Sea-hounds leap where the lush foam dances underneath the prow, their yaps like squeaks across the gulf of air and spray. The vessel towers closer, but our viewpoint rises, sweeping up till we're above it, floating in among its aerials and minarets and turrets. Steam wreathes around us, belching up from the funnels. On a tower near below, a mighty searchlight revolves every fifteen seconds, like a lighthouse, flinging out a path of white a mile across the waves. Ahead, where the sun has set, a band of sky is clear scarlet.

As Alaia's song wells through my eyes and fills the space of air, bells boom vast somewhere further round the earth's curve, silent cracks of lightning flicker white through the scarlet, and I feel your adoration through your million spiders' silks.

Her sound grows in volume, and the audience is silent. Never has a sound like this been heard on earth before: a voice that is thunder and lullaby, channelled from above, beyond and inside the world, of a beauty that is terrifying, wordless and sublime. No words could evoke it, for her song's the song that made us and our words; the wail of all destruction and creation, made as sound. Monolithic slabs of grey longing, big as mountains, push across the sky—a skeleton of girders equipped with the strength to march around the world and push the world's horizon round the world's curve, but also with a human skin's naked sensitivity.

So now you are attending, I say to every one of you: inspect these golden eyes on screen, and know that you have seen them before, in your own mind. Hear what you heard then, but hear it loud and clear, for this screen is even bigger and the pupils of these golden eyes are even deeper black. To everyone, your own primal scenes flicker up on screen within my eyes, and music plays that's *you* alone, sky-high in the airwaves—a grand, eternal music that will always play inside you. You hear it through this golden gaze, surging ever onward, drowning out the crackle of the flames of the oilrigs at night on Arab desert sands, miles underneath you.

Far above Alaia and myself, giant powers feel a fold of time and matter soften round us, aching out a passage like they haven't felt before: they push and fill this passage out, with cosmic enormity, then spin us in an arc that is greater than a galaxy but smaller than an atom, with an ecstasy beyond physicality, beyond mind or thought or the bars of time and matter. Here beyond consciousness, we let these powers resonate, through my eyes and through her voice, and down through the stadium.

The screen has grown to fill the sky. Each of the golden-grained cymbals of my irises is bossed with a perfect central black sun, in exquisite radiance of heavenly geometry. My lashes curl as long as constellations; my eyebrows sweep across the sky's northern hemisphere, in thin black sleekly-tapered arcs. Eyes and lips of a flame-girl, dissipating into air! And telescoped within the blinding grandeur of this face and voice, the turning of the earth's nights and days shines divine through the vastness of space, while the years and aeons unpeel—billions of tons of rock and atmosphere and water, on an orbit that is breakneck, but luminously slow...

The glance of the sun across the surface of the planet, through the whirl of its dawn around the volume of its sphere, lights the points of its peaks and the spumes of its waves in the tiniest of detail, in a sidelight that defies any labelling of colour.

From the screen in the stadium a flood of purple flame spreads. A fountain of unearthly colours, tastes, sounds, scents and ecstatic touch pours out from screens around the world; and the oceans rise a fraction.

My face fades to black on screen, Alaia's voice fades out, and *Sound & Vision* glides to the smoothest of halts.

PART II

SUNDAY LATE:
AFTERGLOW WITH ALAIA

18 THE WARM DOME OF SMILE

"Cut," says a quiet voice.

Dark, quiet. Where is this? A fluorescent light flickers on. Ahead are three cameras; over there, a bank of faders. The studio. After what I've just been through, it looks tiny. *A squint at great events, from the windows of a narrow room...*

There's a whoop, in Evelyn's voice. The lights that have been trained on me from around the lenses, cocooning me in my own space and obscuring what is behind them, are turned off and Rik is revealed behind the central camera, grinning in a small corner of the studio.

Evelyn appears beside me out of nowhere and gives me a hug. "Hi!" I say. "Where did you pop up from?"

"You didn't know? I was crouching behind your chair the whole time, in case you started swaying, but you never did."

"Well, thanks! I had no idea. Could you see anything?"

"Are you kidding? Aside from watching the back of you, I was just looking at Rik in case he needed me to do something urgent. I don't know what the front of you looked like. Did it go well?"

"Oh yes," says Rik, stepping out from behind the cameras. The clock on the wall tells us the show was an hour long, as we rehearsed it. I must struggle, however, to make any connection between this unit of time and my own live experience just now, which feels both shorter and longer. Rik flicks a switch, steps forward and gives my hand a leisurely shake. "Good work!"

"You too. Did we get it all?"

"Yeah. You were shifting just a wee bit to left and right, now and then, but I kept you centre-frame." He looks at his phone. "Playout's just texted me: the GN's estimate of viewership during the last few minutes of the broadcast was thirty million in the US alone."

The sound booth door opens and out steps Alaia. For a second I merely recognise her, in the same way I just recognised Evelyn and Rik. Then the memory hits me, like a thunderclap, of what an extraordinary otherworldly experience she and I have just undergone together, in a place that felt quite elsewhere, ending only about a minute ago. I feel euphoria at our having come through something so ambitious, which could have gone so wrong but never did. I glance back upward at what a flight of ecstasy she and I just created, and am filled with a glow of warmth for this brilliant and beautiful woman whose gaze meets mine. Inexorably we smile, time slows, and for a moment we are nothing but the sole cohabitors of a warm dome of smile.

A telephone starts flashing. "Gotta get this," says Rik. "Studio. Hallo Marc... Thank you... Every last thing went smoothly, yes... Of course we shall... Yep, I'll be doing that over the next few days, and I'll get Evelyn to deliver it to Jason... OK, I'll hand you over to him."

"Jaymi!" booms Marc. "It was all I was hoping for, and more besides. A fantastic opening salvo. How d'you feel?"

From close up, I watch one of my fingernails tapping the metal of a microphone stand. "I'm a bit delirious right now... Thank you for this, Marc."

"You're most welcome. All set for the second one on Thursday?"

I laugh weakly. "Oh dear, no peace."

"Certainly not."

"Yeah, we'll do something ... I mean, *yes, we'll do an amazing show!*"

"That's the spirit! Rik'll steer you right. He's on top of it."

"Yes, yes he is. Would you like a word with Alaia?"

"Please!"

"OK, here she comes." I hold out the handset to her.

While she talks to him, I wander around the studio, still returning to earth. Then soon enough, the four of us are stepping out into the long, dim corridor. Rik locks the studio door behind us. "OK, kiddies, I'm going home," he yawns. "I got about two hours' sleep last night, setting up, so I can feel an appointment with my bed coming on." He puts his arm around Evelyn's shoulders. "Why don't I see you two performers back here at twelve tomorrow, and we'll start work on Thursday's instalment."

"Eek!" says Alaia. "See you at noon, then."

Evelyn points up the corridor for us, towards the main hallway. "Go that way, you'll know where you are," she says. "We're going upstairs. We just got a new apartment, up at the back of the building. You should both come round one of these evenings."

"OK, that's a date," says Alaia.

19 FLAMES, LUCAN, KEV

"I think I'd like to get outside for a while," I say, caressing the white marble balusters of the staircase as she and I climb upstairs. "Touch the ground, see the sky, for a dose of reality." There's a problem with this idea, however: anticipating media speculation about us and our hide-out, Jason instructed us both, in GN head office, to stay hidden here inside the Metropolitan throughout our stay in Asbury Park. "I mean, I see the sense in Jason's curfew, but I know I'll be able to hypnotise anyone we meet outside into not spreading the news of our presence here. After all, I made Marc set the whole broadcast up, so I don't think this would be too much of a challenge in comparison."

Alaia frowns. "Let's not jeopardise anything." We stand in the unlit corridor outside our rooms. "It feels late, but it must only be about ten o'clock. Seems everyone here has finished for the night. Evelyn didn't look as if she wanted to sleep yet, though ... didn't you think?"

"She was just going back with Rik. I must say, I'm still wide awake."

"You know what we should do. Get on with preparing for Thursday's broadcast—right now, preferably. You know how little time we have."

I raise my hands, shrugging. "What can we do right now? You know that's not going to happen tonight. It's just not the kind of thing that happens, is it? So let's not sweat it."

We stare fixedly at each other, through the shadows, for several seconds.

"Ah, fuck it, let's go out," she says.

"All right, you've persuaded me."

Five minutes later we leave our rooms, go back down the staircase, tiptoe through the deserted hallway and slip out into the open air of Asbury Avenue. A naughty children's sense of escape from school overcomes us, and we skip to the right across the empty road, stifling giggles in the dead quiet. A nearly full moon pours light through the warm air. This strange little town is our oyster—where shall we go?

We turn left at random, down Heck Street. Towards the end of this short block a voice calls "Hey!" and a tall, slim, African American guy lopes over to us from the stoop of a run-down residential hotel on the left. He's in his late twenties, with alert, restless eyes. He stops dead, staring at me. Following the cliché, his mouth falls open. "Shit!" he cries, steps back, then leans forward again to peer at me. "Damn! Was that *you* on TV tonight? That *Sound & Vision* thing? Was that you? I was just watching you!"

Well, this is a great start to our secret stroll. I nod warily.

"Goddamn! You just bust my head. Who *are* you?…"

I recall Marc insisted that the broadcast explain nothing about either Alaia or me, but merely showcase her voice and my face, without explanation. His best idea, I thought. "Jaymi," I say, holding a hand out.

He looks down at it and shakes it gingerly, as if it might come off. "Flames…" He turns and directs a low whistle behind him. A car engine purrs into life, just beyond the hotel, and a black Cadillac with its roof down rolls unhurriedly around the corner. "This is Lucan," mutters Flames.

As the car creeps towards us, the presence of the man in the passenger's seat is so strong that the driver is eclipsed: lit with shocking clarity beneath the yellow street-lamp, his overpowering eyes, set in a strong, handsome black face, flick from Alaia to me, from Alaia to me, from Alaia to me. He's in his mid-twenties, wearing a black vest, very powerfully and smoothly muscular, with his hair shaved almost down to nothing. This is the face that Flames and the driver and anybody else who may appear will obviously obey: there is so little question about this, that I very nearly laugh. The Cadillac glides to a standstill beside Flames. Still looking from me to Alaia, the man in the passenger's seat smiles, slowly, and his smile spells trouble, violence, sex and danger. He opens the car-door and steps up onto the narrow grass verge between the pavement and the road. A full two metres tall, wearing black jeans and black combat boots, he raises one hand easily, rests it on the nape of Flames's neck and squeezes hard without effort; Flames's shoulders rise, he grins, laughs and half-crumples down. Not looking back at him, Lucan saunters over to Alaia and me, plants himself right in front of us, legs apart and arms crossed, and looks us up and down without speaking. A big, flat, golden crucifix hangs from his chest, whose bulk quite dominates my field of vision, so close to me has he parked himself. "What the fuck are *you* doing in Asbury?" he growls in a deep voice, grinning down insolently at me.

So he saw the broadcast too. I was wondering.

"Hi Lucan," I murmur, and without moving I unfurl at him a look that's hypnotically controlling to the absolute maximum. His grin disappears, he stares daggers for an instant ... and then you grow stiller, Lucan, don't you, as I pull out all the stops and aim the fiercest blast of power I can muster through my eyes, as much as I have ever emitted. I do this not for amusement, but because it's clear you're someone for whom it will be advisable that I do so: both because of your own willpower, which will try to dominate me if I don't dominate you first, and because the others here will take their lead from you. Through the excessive voltage I'm directing at you, I'm hoping this process will be very short, because I don't want it to disrupt our exchange and make you lose face in front of the others. I therefore have no time, right now, to drag you and me around any of your head, as I did with Marc and Alaia. I simply convey two simple messages to you, with enormous force and clarity: you will ensure that our stay here remains safe and low-key, and there will be no bombardment of us with questions.

I cut this intrusive gaze off dead, and see him snap back into the present, swaying slightly. "What the fuck are we doing here?" I echo him, filling up the pause in which he now regains his bearings. "Good question!" I put my hand on Alaia's shoulder. "Well, I guess we're just passing through." Lucan nods, summons up his grin again and turns back to face his companions. I am pleased that despite the pause, our flow wasn't too broken; and despite his continued aura of defiance, I can see our pecking order has been established and my requirements have been impressed upon him clearly.

Our attentions are distracted by the driver, who emerges from the Cadillac and ambles towards us with a kind of heavy waddle: when his right leg steps forward, his bulky mass leans slightly to the right, then back to the left as his left leg takes a step. In his thirties, black, his heavy thick-set face is sluggishly chewing gum. He stops, looks me up and down, spits his gum out onto the grass verge and glances at Lucan. Then he inspects Alaia. "Look at that pussy!" he says in a coarse, mocking voice, "I'd like to dick her." Alaia folds her arms, with her iciest *you wish* expression on her face. "I'd like to pork her, but you know me, I could fuck a stab-wound."

"Kev, hush," says Lucan.

"Yeah, Kev, you're being a little slow here," says Flames. "If you take your finger out of your ass, you may recognise someone from the TV tonight?" and he points at me.

"And Alaia was the voice you heard," I say, pointing at her.

"You could say we weren't expecting you," Flames answers me, and glances up at Lucan.

Kev frowns and shifts himself nearer to peer at us, especially me. Presumably seeing the truth of Flames's reference to the television, Kev goes quiet. "Man," he mutters, seeming not to know what else to say, then mumbles on inaudibly, shifting from one leg to the other.

I have scant wish to see anything inside him or to hypnotise his ugly presence, if I can possibly avoid it, and I'm glad to see it's unlikely to be necessary. For both Flames and Kev clearly take their cues from Lucan, whose next utterance causes Kev to stare at him in surprise, perhaps in reaction to its unexpected level of welcome and respect: "You heard of Downstairs?"

"Downstairs? No," I say.

"It's a bar," growls Lucan. "Let's go. Flames, get in the back with Sound and Vision."

20 PARANOIA BY THE WIRE-NETTING FENCE

So Alaia and I precede Flames into the wide rear seat of the Cadillac, and Lucan and Kev get into the front seats as before. "Next we pick up Damian," Flames informs us. "Then there's no one else to pick up, and that's a good thing—'cos Sound can sit on Vision's lap, but Damian is sure as hell not sitting on mine."

Soon we pull up outside a spooky, verandah'd structure on Second Avenue and Bond Street, surrounded by larger, dilapidated houses. "Damian was gonna be watching TV too," says Lucan, leaning around in his seat to address me, "so you knock on the door. We'll give him a surprise."

"Yeah!" holler the other two, Flames slapping his thighs with glee at the prospect.

"Alright," I sigh. This is just silly, but Damian will be recognising me soon enough anyway, so we may as well get it over with on his doorstep. In any case, I have to admit that the prospect does tickle me a little. "Alaia, come with me, we'll surprise him together," I say, and she follows me out of the back seat.

"Bell number one," Kev calls after us, guffawing through his chewing-gum.

She and I set off up the front path. "Jaymi, you're encouraging them," she says. "You're all the same, you boys. So much for keeping a low profile in town."

"We are *not* all the same," I say with a hint of sharpness. "Lucan's going to behave—you saw me make sure of that, didn't you? And all the others follow his lead."

We reach the porch, where a small card printed with a U.S. flag is taped up beside an Edwardian bell-push moulded like a petal, bearing the name "Damian West" in narrow, handwritten capitals. "Wail at him, sugar!" Kev wails out to Alaia from the Cadillac, and I can hear Flames cracking up in the back seat.

"This is ridiculous," fumes Alaia. "What am I, a performing seal?"

"Alaia, this is just the price of stardom and fierceness," I say, raising my finger to the bell-push and having to hold back a sudden wave of laughter.

She turns and gives me *the look*, which has been known to shrivel cacti at thirty paces.

The look is not destined to last its usual duration, however, for as soon as I have pressed the bell-push and the bell rings inside, we jump back in shock, as a savage barking erupts from beside us in an alleyway where three large guard dogs leap up behind a chain-link fence, snapping viciously.

The front door opens and the gaunt, unshaven white face of a man in his fifties peers down at us, with a paranoid, shifty, evaluative expression. His gives a low whistle; the dogs fall silent, but continue to pace and pant behind the fence. The man's temporal bones stand out prominently from his face, leading back to his ears, and his cheeks are sunken with leanness. The impression is not one of frailty, however, but of brutality and wiriness. I see that in the shadows, by his right leg, he is holding a small hand-gun, and I step back off the porch, pulling Alaia with me. I'm hoping this quick retreat will reassure him that we are not about to lunge forward and throttle him, which is what his expression might suggest he expects.

Now comes his recognition of me from the television earlier: I can see his half-concealed surprise and befuddlement, as I'm sure Alaia can. His eyes flick to her, in search of some similar recognition, perhaps … but no, he draws a blank there. He puts the gun away in the pocket of the well-worn black leather jacket he's wearing. There is a moment of odd silence among the three of us: it is, after all, something of an odd meeting.

At last the other three's laughter can be repressed no more and billows out behind us. Damian's eyes dart to the road and clock the Cadillac. He speaks at low volume, fast, as if there's no time to waste: "Is this some kind of joke?" he asks me. "What the hell d'you think *you're* doing here?"

Flames jumps out of the car and springs up the path like a long-legged spider, giggling, then flails in surprise as the dogs explode at him from behind the fence. Damian whistles them quiet again. Flames recovers himself and reaches the porch: "Jesus, Damian, will you get rid of those stupid dogs? Anyway, just shut the fuck up and come to Downstairs, we don't have all evening for you to shift your ass. Come on, jump in the car, we're out of here," and he runs back down the front path again.

So we all pile into the Cadillac. With Kev and Lucan in the front, there are now four of us squeezed into the back seat, as we head west across Main Street: me on the right with Alaia on my lap, then Flames bouncing around in the middle, then Damian scrunched up at the far left.

21 ANGEL'S WINGS IN THE DIVE-BAR

Downstairs turns out to be a busy, no-frills dive bar on Summerfield Avenue, west of the tracks. Following my tacit agreement with Lucan that he will make sure Alaia and I maintain a low profile, I've not heard him relaying this instruction to Flames, Kev and Damian. Yet it's as if he has conveyed it to them somehow without words; because upon entering Downstairs, this trio undertake no publicising whatsoever of her and me, but instead just shepherd us inside in a low-key manner, to a table in a low-lit area near the back. Lucan steers me into a chair positioned so that I face across the table into the corner of the room, and says I'm not to go to the bar. Several people are curious when they see us slipping past, but our haste and the low lighting and the smoke all conspire to ensure that anyone who did see *Sound & Vision*, of which there must be some, do not in fact recognise me. In addition I see that Kev has been given, or has assumed, the task of discouraging others' interest in our party; for he manages always to loom large and unwelcoming between us and anyone who shows signs of wanting to approach us, until they lose interest. Downstairs is clearly home territory for Lucan and his crowd.

It turns out Flames has come here to work a shift behind the bar, where he will soon be taking over from someone else. "Drinks time," he says. "Vision? Sound?"

We all place our orders and he darts off. "I'm timing this," says Kev, glancing at his phone. Then in just another minute or so, after I have had chance to do little more than take my jacket off, Flames sweeps back to the table with an entire round of seven drinks on a tray. "Fifty-five seconds," Kev announces.

"For Jaymi and Alaia, red wine," says Flames as he places them in front of us. "For Lucan, straight whisky. "For Kev and me, beer. And for Damian, grapefruit juice."

"Alcohol's a rank poison," Damian mutters.

"That's good," says Lucan, slapping him on the back, "we need you sober back there," and he jerks his thumb towards the corridor at the back.

Making this fifty-five-second total genuinely noteworthy, there is also the seventh drink. One cherry garnishes a brown-brimming cocktail glass, handed out by Flames to one who cuts in from some-where, passing Kev without obstruction—a dark-eyed Latino boy of maybe twenty-one, whose spiteful sleek depraved face radiates decadence and damage from its sharp beauty. "And for Angel, one Manhattan," Flames announces, takes a bow and returns to the bar.

With the arrival of drinks, talk around the table starts to drift and split. This newest face, I observe, is active here, though incongruous. He is shadowy, effete, both unhealthy and luminous: I picture him a pirate-queen scuttling up the masts of a slave-ship, to keep watch. Aside from a silver earring in his right ear, a shiny black vinyl bras-siere is all that he wears above the waist, above black leggings and pointed black boots. Through his smooth brown skin I can sense the charge of nerves around his ribs beneath the faint swell of his breasts. His smooth little torso is built like a whip, thin and supple. Beauti-fully tattooed down the length of his back is a stark, emblematic pair of angel's wings, cross-cut with faint lash-marks. Half the time his mouth, with its lips painted cinnabar, is sulky; and half the time his teeth are bared, jaws tense and snapping like a starved baby she-wolf. His voice is intersexual, with a degenerate breathiness underlying a fluid steel edge and a slight lisp on every *s*. A clean but musky sexual scent coils about him, even through the smoke. When his eyes fix mine for the first time, I have to make an effort not to flick my gaze away, so potent is the damage and so luscious is the blackness of fever within them. Hard excitement and the pulsing of attraction to the beauty of the dark spills out of him, as if his sweetest wish is for a violent revenge against life and all who live it.

One hidden thing do I let myself tune in to as yet, for a split-second only: tattooed on his forehead, in an ink that's invisible, a single word flickers up and shouts out—SLAVE.

He leaves the group and heads towards the rear of the bar. Passing by, Flames peers down at Angel's glass on the table, saying, "Angel's lost his cherry—but I thought that was years ago?"

Hearing, Angel turns: "Don't make me slap you, Flames—I only need to look at you, to know you need slapping." And he turns away and slinks to the corridor's mouth, like a little black dragon with a scorpion's sting.

Another thing I was expecting was that Damian, Flames and Kev would need to be stopped by Lucan from firing a bunch of questions at us about *Sound & Vision*, how we achieved it, what we're all about and so on. However, except for a quiet aside to Angel, who then glances towards me and Alaia, Lucan never has any confidential words with any of the others—and yet none of them questions us at all. For fifteen minutes I wait for them to do so, but then when it still hasn't happened, I see that it's not going to. I feel a tiny amused sting of pique give way to simple curiosity about this. I suppose Lucan must, again, have conveyed this requirement to the other three without words. Such communication must have been honed through many dealings. Or as I begin to perceive, for all their apparent free-wheelingness, Lucan's crew is in fact very careful never to take any initiatives in his presence. By themselves, they would probably have been inclined to ask questions; after all, they were unaware of my tacit agreement with Lucan, and Flames did say I'd bust his head earlier tonight. But it seems that none of them wants to be the first to ask us anything substantive. What respect for him this would seem to indicate—a respect that I begin to sense is more like fear. And remembering Lucan's big hand at Flames's neck on the street, squeezing without effort until Flames's knees buckled, I suspect this fear even borders on terror.

As a result, all we get is a lazy swirl of high-spirited chatter among the seven of us, random and good-natured. It occurs to me that maybe the engine driving Lucan's strict enforcement of my request that Alaia and I not be grilled, although everyone in our group seems to have watched *Sound & Vision* and so must be curious about us, is that he fears I may look at him hypnotically again and so make him lose face here in his power base. He could have taken revenge by overpowering me physically, and he has the aura of one who will have considered this as an option, but he hasn't done this. My active hypnotic look at him on the street was discreet enough, to all but him and me, to have done no real damage to his image; but he may reckon that the gaze I turned on him is too quickly deployable for him to make any hasty moves. So, amid the noisy high spirits prevailing at Downstairs, we end up just having a loud good time, saying not much of substance: within half an hour I am tipsy and within an hour verging on drunk.

When I slip down the corridor at the back, I see Damian must have left us without my noticing, for here he is beside the doors to the toilets, selling drugs to a couple of punters. He has raised the collar of his battered leather jacket, making himself look even shiftier than usual. His customers eye my approach with suspicion, but he grunts a curt reassurance and they return their attention to him. Someone has thrown up pungently, I surmise when I enter the gents. As I stand at the urinal, Damian finishes his sale. "Someone bring a mop and bucket here," he bellows down the corridor towards the bar. He spits savagely on the glistening floor, then tries to wipe the sweat from his tired face with his hand, but only succeeds in smearing it around.

The only illumination in here is from the bright yellow bulb of a street-lamp shining through the broken window from outside, where furtive figures go in and out of shadows in an alleyway. Finishing at the urinal, I peer with curiosity through the thick sultry heat, to locate the source of a constant jagged buzz, and discover that it emanates from an orange neon fuse nailed to the grimy bricks outside the broken window. Seeing this, Damian cracks the first grin I've yet seen on him and mutters at me, as if unearthing a conspiracy, "That's the 's' of 'Downstairs'," and grimly nods.

22 NO ENCHANTMENT WITHOUT ORDEAL

Before coming to Asbury Park I tuned in to hardly anyone, wishing to safeguard the success of *Sound & Vision* by honing only my projecting abilities, rather than risk developing any tendencies to fall into the relatively lazy processes of a tune-in. This remains my mindset, in light of the coming second broadcast; but with the first one so triumphantly concluded, I decide I can afford to cut myself some slack in the tune-in department.

I look around. Hot, sticky, summer night at Downstairs. Music pumps, whisky flows, and lights full of smoke bathe bodies full of blood. Under the deep red light, I see Angel's make-up sliding down … and it's time to tune in to you now, my little demon vermin Angel! Let's see. For you, as in the tales, there has been no enchantment without ordeal. I assumed you were Latino when you first appeared, but now I perceive that your family was Armenian. Your self-image from antiquity, however, is a Persian one—the Persian Boy, of course. You see jewels, incense, flowing verse on scrolls of parchment, flaming candelabra in the harem around you, and purple eye-shadow when you glance in the hand-mirror. A barred window gives upon a courtyard of spiky flowers, palms and the cool splash of fountains. A flute trills, behind silk that hangs across a door; smiling women swirl, you whisper, and your whisper is an influence and seeps across an empire, now long vanished.

From birth onward, here in Asbury Park, you were scorned, and your spite took shape and grew. You were victimised and beaten, and your cruelty shot roots down and drank and pulled, tight as wires, through the earth. The beauty that bewitched you and the beauty that was in you were rejected and dismissed by those around you, and your viciousness unfurled like an icy metal flower. These elements inside you gathered force and locked together in infernal harmonies, until a great black symphony of Angel towered raging like a hellish dark mill against the sky inside your head.

Your brows were too arched for the oil-spattered trailer-park you lived in on the west edge of town, where abuse between the motor-homes spoke to you in simple terms: *I'll slit your pout wide, freak, I'll carve pleasure from your mouth and throat—how about a sweet smile cut with this knife, and not your rat-faced sneer? Don't fuck with me, bitch.* And yet with longing hot and tight you yearned to spend yourself upon these other boys, the only boys you knew, and yearned to stay their target forever, as a home.

And meanwhile, slanting from the billboard on the highway, the film-star flickered down upon you like a whip, and you were certain they would find you sprawled dead and hard beside the grey electric fence behind your trailer-home, his image burned tiny on your retina.

There's a place of enchantment, you knew, where the Full Moon in Scorpio irradiates the brightest, with wisdom and secrets, ancient powers and some smoke and mirrors too. So you ran through the night streets and flat deserted waterfront, through lanes of yellow lamps, always looking for this place—felt its whisper round the corner, heard its giggle from the next block, retreating—caught its black velvet breath around the angle of the bricks before it whisked away. Running, running, running, always gaining on it, slowly... And still the little boy-girl inside you runs the streets at night, seeking that retreating thing, and gaining on it, slowly. (But I found it first, in Manhattan, and that's why I'm seeing into you—and why you saw the broadcast and watched me with avidity enough to twist the knife of your own rich pain.)

Back at school, when the teachers bade you drink your poison up like a good girl, you'd slip through the alley-way where hypodermic syringes and empty lipstick cylinders would crunch beneath your boots. There you built heaps of trash you named as your enemies and then, one by one, set them toxically ablaze with a yelp of splashed gasoline and matches. Sudden blotchy hands gripped the window-bars beside you, from inside that shack of cinder-blocks, and you screamed and fled, and later you were jittery with excess coffee in the smudgy cracked window of the Coffee Cup Café, the ashtray heaped up with spent cigarettes you'd sucked to death.

I see you then at seventeen, scything the long grass, for pennies. Of course you are left-handed, and of course the scythe was made for a right-handed person and was thin and broken anyway, but there you were, slashing at the rank growth pressing in upon you.

The wildest crew came to let you join them, like a mascot, subjecting you to verbal abuse that was constant but grudgingly affectionate. You played it very cool, but you never stopped picturing their masculine bodies all around you, black and naked underneath the baggy clothes they wore, and then began the permanent erection that has never left you ever since—the constant hard excitement in the one tiny part of you you've always yearned to hack right off.

Few were the channels that were free for you to flow down, and darkest out of those felt the channel that you took. For then you took a room in Damian West's house awhile. He ran Lucan's distributions here in Asbury Park, day to day, then as now; and he took you in, desiring your respect and companionship, and feeling some affinity and germs of compassion. He lived on Bangs Avenue and Langford Street then, surrounded by guard dogs, hand-guns and flick-knives.

He was gruff in manner, bleak in outlook and oozed paranoia. Sometimes, sitting in the Spartan kitchen eating simple food, he'd tell you of his drug deals, prison times and acid-flashed service in Vietnam. He wasn't much fun, but he was your protector, for which you were grateful. Never did he hit you or insult you, but treated you instead with a trace of old gallantry and only took a token rent from what you earned turning tricks, provided that you helped around the house. Even his dogs seemed to treat you with gentleness.

Then you and Evelyn would haunt the strip on Kingsley Street, throughout that summer when this town seemed bigger than it now does, both wearing little in the hot sticky nights. She was sweet and tough; she talked you away from anorexia, and made you laugh and even lent you money once or twice. She and you had good times, in among the bad, on that grimy strip where motorcycle horns cut the fetid yellow lamp-lit air.

And what a fierce street whore you were: where your heels scraped the pavement a red gash would surface, while you swung your arms, sauntering, and sucked a Capri cigarette. One night you decided, you would move to New York City and would knock 'em dead. But straightaway a picture of yourself in the New York winter flickered up: a figure floating through, swathed tight in a long coat topped by a sleek-boned she-male face, unfocused, in among the cars across the oil-slicked pavement, desperate and gorgeous, up and down the tangle of expressway ramps by the Macombs Dam Bridge upon the southernmost concrete rind of the Bronx... You shook your head and landed back at Kingsley Street and Asbury Avenue, where Tillie grimaced down at you and seemed to shake his head. Something in that picture of yourself made you sense it: New York would kill you, somehow. No, you'd stay here for now.

Then Lucan saw you one night, summoned you and scooped you up, plucked you out of Damian's, installed you in his own house, and no one ever messed with you again. Then you rode high: you travelled round town in Lucan's car, had respect and more money than you'd ever had. Throughout that first month with him were warm thunderstorms and muggy heat, and every clap of thunder announced your arrival here as someone whom the others had to know and take account of, whose power, crime and glamour stood plain, written high across the sky. They were avid to explore you and the trouble in your eyes. The beauty you'd exploited as a whore was now legitimised by Lucan, growing legendary beside him, as the girls watched in envy. God you looked fantastic! The downtrodden past was gone, and wide countryside opened up, lit in flashes on the summer sky across which you fluttered like a little black metallic butterfly.

How your life then accelerated. Lucan and Angel—untouchable power and untouchable glamour. What a legend! Oh, that Dark Summer, soaked in Ecstasy and petrol fumes, semen and sweat, while the music pumped relentless through the warmth of the air around the corners of the buildings and the flashbulbs popped—till the alcoholic glamour of the white and yellow lights streaking by you through the night swerved down into red-shift and gorgeous splintered-metal smells of sex-drenched death...

For all around the pair of you, throughout that Dark Summer, there were gang wars and car crashes, accidents and murders, for month after month, while the parties lasted days and the drugs took you higher, ever higher, every week. You and Lucan lived at the centre of the parties, the centre of the drug trade, the centre of the worst of the bloodshed too, and yet you both were unscathed; and Lucan's opposition was destroyed once again and his power strengthened further, and the bloodshed stopped.

One day you heard with glad surprise that Evelyn had gone straight and was staying straight—drove a van now for some high-end company or something. A real job. You don't see her much, but when you meet you both say "Hey bitch" and hug and think of Kingsley Street, then slide away again along your own separate rails. Sometimes she comes to Downstairs with friends, gets drunk and is hilarious at the bar. Lucan isn't close with her but knows of her and trusts her, so you're free then to join her and you have a lot of fun; but you're always in groups of people, so you never get to talk to her in private any more.

You're tough as nails of tungsten and the bravest of them all. You've always jumped the ship's plank first, while the crew goggled safely down at water that you alone would brave—green, sticky, glowing water, pregnant with tentacles and eyeless-headed long necks of algae-smeared flesh, with curling mist and bubbles gulping up from the deep. Every day you're down there, and every night you climb back alone to the pirate ship, unsung … but I shall make you one of my chosen four, I promise, Angel, so *I* at last shall sing you, to the camera!

23 A DECLARATION OF WAR AGAINST LUCAN

As with all of the few tune-ins I've ever permitted myself in the company of others, I have remained socially functional throughout my tune-in to Angel, if a little quieter than usual; and although this was a deeper tune-in than I've ever done, my transition back into full social involvement is only a small jolt. I'm exhilarated to recognise how much my ability to cope with and wield my sight has developed, since my initial nervous testing of its parameters on the subway after first meeting Marc.

A pleasant surprise appears beside me, in the shape of Evelyn, who is talking with Alaia on the fringes of Lucan's gang. Alaia was right, then, to say that Evelyn hadn't looked like someone who was ready to sleep when we all left the recording studio: for here she is, with a glow fresh and used, out on the town and up for more fun. "Jaymi!" she says. "What a small world. We're going down to Paradise right now, the three of us. I'm driving us."

At this moment, I notice Flames becoming aware of a bulky object sitting on his busy bar-top draped in a black cloth, inconspicuous but mysterious. Curious, he removes the cloth, then jumps back in horror to see Lucan's head with two daggers stuck deep into its forehead. "*Oh, SHIT!*" he shouts, staggering back. Talk in the bar dies down, as everybody turns and stares at Flames, then at Lucan's severed head. A horrified intake of breath makes way for a brief stunned silence, then a slowly rising babble. Flames's composure is not restored when out from the crowd steps Lucan, head intact, and stands before the object, glaring fiercely at it. "Lucan! Oh it's *you*, thank god. I mean I knew it was you, but—well, I don't mean *that* thing was you," babbles Flames, and tails off.

The likeness is striking, capturing both Lucan's beauty and the violence in his eyes, although the original is superior in both details.

Lucan looks up and stares around. Silence falls. "That's a declaration of war," he states with a menacing calm. "Who made it?"

There are sidelong glances, mumbles and shiftings of feet.

"Angel was next to it at the time," blurts Kev; and without a sound being uttered by either him or Angel, the air between the two becomes a poisonous furrow of hissing bile and snake excrement.

"And Evelyn was pretty close," jokes Flames, but as soon as he has spoken he winces.

"Trade rivals in Red Bank," grunts Damian. "They could have had someone sneak in, park this here, then sneak out—easy."

As general talk wells up again, there's a tug at my sleeve. It's Evelyn, pulling Alaia and me quietly towards the door. "Let's go," she mouths in silence.

24 ON THE SKY, THAT FACE

"We don't wanna be in there right now," she says outside, chivvying us to the van. "This could start a war again. But I'm not gonna think about all that shit tonight, because we're going to Paradise. There's only about an hour before it closes, but we should go say hallo to Shigem. I'm on his list. Though if the door-whore saw the broadcast, I doubt we'll have any trouble getting in for free anyway—Shep wouldn't exactly complain about that kind of publicity for his club."

"Talking about publicity," says Alaia, looking troubled as we climb into the van, "I'm sorry we're not being as discreet around town as we're meant to be."

Evelyn flaps her hand through the air. "Ah, lighten up. Rules are there to be broken, so let's just have fun. We may be dead tomorrow."

Soon she parks the van back outside the Metropolitan and we get out and walk three blocks to the club's entrance, where many cars are now parked. The girl at the door doesn't bother looking for Evelyn's name on Shigem's list, perhaps thinking it too late for lists, and doesn't seem to recognise me either, but just waves us inside. Evelyn heads to the bar to get us drinks, while I take in a smallish but happening venue with banging sound and light systems, almost filled with a reasonably cosmopolitan crowd that must have come from a catchment area quite a lot wider than just Asbury Park itself.

Electronic dance music pumps across a busy floor. "There's Shigem," says Evelyn, pointing towards someone I recognise from somewhere, and we set off through the crowd. After a moment I remember that I first noticed him earlier from the Cadillac, while the car was sitting at a traffic-light on Main Street, right beside where he was on the pavement talking to a girl. The first thing I registered then was a golden bracelet with the name "Shigem" engraved on it in slick squirly black letters, because it reminded me that Evelyn had told us this name during her guided tour when she first drove us into town. I almost tuned in to him then and there, but Angel ended up beating him to this honour because we were all too much in transit in the car, so I should not have been able to give Shigem a proper tune-in. The only thing I got as far as picking up from him was that he was Malaysian. He had long black hair with platinum-blond highlights in, warm bright eyes, and beautiful high-fashion facial features that were nevertheless prominently acne-cratered all over, especially on a pair of perfect high cheekbones. Here in the club he's dressed with stylish flamboyance and a certain flash and trash, like a whore on Jalan Raja on a hot Kuala Lumpur night in Fashion Week. A thin silver earring hangs from each ear, and the word "Virginity" is tattooed on the honey-coloured skin of his left shoulder in the same script as the name on the bracelet. Inhabiting the femininity of his slim and delicate body with a simple, quiet and sensual pleasure, he reminds me of sunlight and moves with divinity.

Here he's in his element, much more than on the street. Hosting a club night, it's clear he is a natural. Just within the time we take to cross the room and approach him, he has mixed in all directions. Tied to no one, he succeeds in connecting with everyone: faster than quicksilver, light as air and never once intrusive or demanding, he yet reaches somehow into every person's presence, one to one, and draws them out and upward like a chime through the strobe-lights. Riding the crowd, he electrifies the dance-floor with effortless charisma, in tune with the dirty hard electro playing, as he lights up the faces and the spaces in between them with the bright sexy flicker of his presence. He curls his fingers round in the air as he speaks, and I see that malice cannot touch him here: no matter what may happen in the outside world, here in club-land he's unbeatable. If all the land were set up as a chic nightclub, he'd be absolute monarch. I lean over to Evelyn. "Why is he not in Manhattan?" I ask.

She laughs: "I dunno—because he's here, I guess. And he's ours, and he's *way* too good for Manhattan!"

We have nearly reached him, but now he becomes embroiled in conversation with a group, without yet having noticed her, so the three of us hover nearby. As we dance, I contemplate him where he stands half turned-away, his left shoulder facing me with that word "Virginity" … and while we wait, Shigem, I think I'll take a look inside you, before we've even met. And although I've been half-expecting that your mind would be a nightclub mind with "disco" VIP Room emotions to match, this is not the case. You see what you're doing here as showmanship, neither more nor less. You do it, as you should, because you love it and it pays you and you know you're the best—and you wish that the days were as dark and bright as this room, and that people spoke in dance music, permanently liquored-up and high like these. And yet you function in the real world too, I see, with only subtle changes and little disappointment.

But here's a rich crevasse, for me: I see how you were several hours back, at home, when you settled down to watch *Sound & Vision*. As Alaia's voice welled up, you sank to the floor and sat immobile, gazing at the TV screen. Silent tears sprang forth and ran down your cheeks. For hers was a song that had echoed in your head since early childhood, a song with untranscribable notes, without a name, which you'd treasured in yourself as yours alone … but here it was *without* you, for all the world to hear, paired up with that beautifully alien face on the screen. Somehow Alaia had discovered it—but how? It had always emanated from forbidden lands of cruel sun and sweet sensual nights; and it poisoned with bewitchment of yearning and delirium and glimpses of sublime bliss, ensuring that the real world would always, ever after, fall short. The first time you'd heard this song, coiling like the vapour of a scarlet wine throughout your head, you knew it was forbidden but ignored this of course. Often since then you'd heard it carried on the wind, in the fevers of the deep small hours, blown across a hundred years to land in you. It always sang of sweet dark and sorrow and enormous love, unearthing ancient things within yourself while it played.

And always joining this song, from your childhood onward through the years, every time it welled from your depths or echoed off the folded hills of the night, there would float up, several seconds after its opening, *that face*, Shigem... Oh, *that* face: yes, you know the one, I think. It's this face, my own, upon the screen you watched tonight, in its soft unearthly lighting and the smooth coloured make-up that you saw on it—the first time you witnessed it projected without you, in the outside world, for all to see. So large had it always loomed, for you, that it seemed to float upon the sky, its gaze ever fixed on a point above your head that you couldn't quite reach. But its gaze from the screen today looked *at* you, and you shivered to be looked at thus, for nothing of yourself could you hide from it. Somehow I'd embodied it. How? But there it stayed, on the screen, in all its melting permutations, with your endless private song wrapped divine around its lineaments—a shatteringly magical conjunction that floored you. Every last thing in you it saw, accepted, knew, without expression. "You've got *everything*," you mouthed at me onscreen, in silent passion. This face, you saw, was all you really needed to know now, and all the rest would follow. It's the only game in town, so to speak, despite the anguish of your knowing you will never be inside it. Along with Alaia's song, this face has lived in you since boyhood, Shigem, and will remain in you till death. It's majestic and familiar—rich and inevitable—powerful and beautiful—addictive and eternal!

25 THE FIGURE IN THE CROWD IN THE MIRROR

Evelyn shakes my arm, and I snap back from inside Shigem to Paradise. "He's still chatting," she says. "Let's get another drink, we'll catch up with him in a minute," and she pulls me in the direction of the bar. "The bar's better lit, so you'd better hang back a bit, behind us two."

Standing in the shadow of Alaia, I watch the crowd reflected in the mirrored wall behind the bar. There in the distance is Shigem; then much nearer to the mirror there is Evelyn, laughing; and standing near her, with eyes open wide and an opaque smile, is a slim, dark-haired figure—oh but that's me of course. And there's Alaia right beside me, lighting a Virginia Superslim, or trying to, with a match that isn't working. I take a book of matches from my pocket, turn my gaze from the mirror to the real-life Alaia, strike a match and hold a yellow flame in front of her. She waits for it to finish flaring, sucks it through the end of her cigarette, nods me thanks and turns her attention elsewhere. I drift my gaze back to my unexpected figure in the mirror, which is the only figure, out of all those in the tableau, who shows any consciousness of someone else looking in upon them, of someone outside them in a different dimension: the only individual in the composition to look outward at the viewer, like that figure in the Bosch picture who fixes the observer with perceptive eyes from in between the heads of unperceptive companions, who is often thought to be Bosch himself. The frozen transience of the figure in the bar-mirror mural reminds me of the figure of a boy I once saw who'd been preserved since Roman times by ash, whose delicate build and size were mine, with the faint ashy shape, on a round little head, of a sort of Roman buzz-cut, just as my own hair was cut then, and vague eye-hollows where I stared back at length through the centuries...

The bartender blocks my sightline, cutting off this outsider view of myself. He's a young white man in his twenties whose blond cropped hair, handsome face and shirtless body make up a generically attractive ensemble. As I watch him, however, this generic allure starts to assume its place as packaging for a content richer and subtler than expected. There's a quietness, seriousness and simplicity to his movements and expressions, as he serves customers, which suggest a considerable emotional vulnerability under the watchful care of a rather greater strength, coupled with a touch of sadness somewhere. Evelyn bubbles up and puts her arm around me. "Hi Kim," she says to him.

"Hi Evelyn. What can I get you?"

"I'll have a Bud. Have you met my friends Jaymi and Alaia here? They were just doing a broadcast earlier. I was helping out." I sense Alaia deciding not to question again the wisdom of such further indiscretion, in view of Jason's bid for secrecy. I have to confess we're doing a disastrous job of keeping a low profile tonight. But Evelyn turns to pre-empt her: "It's OK—Kim doesn't even live in Asbury, he's just bartending on a trip here from London." She turns back to Kim: "Is Shigem packed up yet?"

"No, he still has a lot to do. We have a few more days left. You've met Shigem?" he asks me.

"We tried to, just now," I say.

"I first met him about three months ago in London where I live," Kim explains with a smile. "He was visiting there on his first trip from here. We fell in love pretty fast." He has a light English accent that I know isn't from London but cannot place any further.

"Cool," says Alaia. "He's kind of in demand here, but we'll have another go at meeting him in a minute."

"How will you stay together?" I ask him.

"He's going to have to move to Britain with me, because the U.S. doesn't let me move here for him, which is pretty dumb. We'll be moving out of here for good in a few days."

"I hope you're happy there," I say.

"Thanks! Gotta go," and he turns to a customer. I'm not going to tune in to him now, because I want to finish with Shigem first, but I realise that in all of Kim's clear-eyed candour he hasn't yet shown any signs of recognising me from the broadcast. This is interesting, in view of the fact that his boyfriend Shigem watched it in spades, as I just explored. Did Kim not watch, or has he not recognised me here despite Evelyn's introduction of us, or is his recognition concealed for some reason?

26 SHIGEM AND I ON THE DANCE-FLOOR

I tell Evelyn and Alaia I'm going to have a wander round, then I find a perch behind a railing by the dance-floor … and there you are, Shigem, you beautiful creature. So what happened next, once you'd heard that voice and seen that face on TV, for all the world to hear and see? Well, first you sat there, gob-smacked; then your intellect chipped in, to tell you that your overwhelming feelings were triggered by a highly-crafted television spectacle that meshed with spells you had inside you anyway. You shook your head. Was beauty such delusion, then? you wondered, then remembered that you'd asked yourself this very same question once before, in little-boy language, when you were a little boy, with your toes in the sand beneath the serpents and the dolphins on the wall of the Convention Hall.

Just before you'd asked this in your little-boy words, you had run down the sand with tiny steps toward the sea, beneath a sky you carried in you—a sky filled with heavy planets, dark brown caverns and the glint of pink stars on gigantic deepest blue—a magic sky amid ten thousand less enchanted skies. The sea had been mercury, not sinking through the sand but sliding waveless across it. From the ocean, standing there, you had conjured copper snails, silver dolphins, uranium express-fish, chromium sea-snakes and worms of plutonium, and watched them dance in front of you, bursting and sprouting in the quicksilver bay while you paddled and you capered in the shallows. Dry shiny drops had splashed up from your hand when you'd stooped to flick the liquid up. Then the slope of the scene had curved up, until above you there had been a shaft with shiny spinning galleries rising to a sweet space of honeylight in giant circles telescoped within one another, out beyond, to where *this* face smiled down at you from here and now. Your ground had risen upward, with a great turn of gears ... but then you'd looked again and seen that all of that had not been real: there were no heavy planets, caverns, pink stars or deepest blue, no snails, dolphins, mercury, express-fish, worms or sea-snakes, and no shining shaft or galleries or honeylight or face.

Instead, you just looked east, across a flat dull sea, beneath an empty grey sky.

So then came the moment when you asked it, all those years ago: was beauty such delusion? You shouted out your version of it, out across the sea and up ... a question you'd forgotten till tonight and *Sound & Vision*. You were the sweetest little boy I've ever seen—and see today still, beneath your skin, behind your warm brown eyes. (Concealed in my futurity and great elevation, I *was* still here above you, of course, but how well you'd done to see me even once, from that beach. I bounce back an echo to you then, from here and now—but no, you turned away.)

The last of your innocence I see was aged six, when on golden days you'd picture a ride upon an ostrich through the sands of Arabia. Sun-birds would shriek and coo, electric flies would buzz, and sylphs and gnomes would speak in dimpled voices from the undergrowth (for this was your very own version of Arabia). Once you saw a chanterelle beneath a mauve rose: you dismounted from your bird and ate your *tulipe à l'orange*. Through the woods you spied a lake and scampered over to its shallows, where shubunkin and raspberry-tangerine-coloured ribbon-fish with helicopter ears buzzed and scuttled in the weeds, leaving spiral wakes. Glow-fish wiggled and a silver scallop winked from the sandy lake-bed. You looked up and dusk had fallen: tiny black horses and a mincing giraffe ringed a carousel built upon a cloud near the moon. Puffballs of shadow swelled huge among the hills, and rose and burst in the night in coloured fire.

Cut to age thirteen, and the sky-eggs are gone: I see you wander past the strip-bar Seductions, through its pool of seedy neon light, your face breaking out all over, just at the start of your eleven years of acne, while above you on the glass was the scarlet neon outline of a nude recumbent woman. In reply to her, across the street in Cindi's Beauty Parlor, now closed for the night, a neon sign "PRETTY NAILS" flickered, weak and pink behind the dusty glass. "Pretty nails," you murmured, gazing vacantly across at it, your legs and arms quivering inside as you spoke.

Later in your teens, there you are with your friends, in Ronelle's, out of town, all dancing round your handbags on the floor, waving drinks and laughing by the thump of the speakers. The beat never ended, on those trips: too much vodka, cheap drugs, uncontrollable erections and flawless coats of deep crimson polish on your nails. Beneath your skilful make-up, your cheeks erupting fiercely always, painful in the slow queue below those white fluorescent lights; but never a lack of teenage kisses, heart-to-heart talks walking home, drunken sex and tissues scattered all around the room. Up just in time for a late, late lunch, still drunk, and prone to fainting, as you always were, but starting nonetheless to plan tonight's fun and frolic … and how you'd not have missed all that, for the world.

Coming up to date, I see you not long before your recent London trip, sitting lonely on the platform in Asbury Park station, across wet tracks from a northbound train that was pulling out, pulling away the beautiful boy who held your gaze unblinking as he disappeared forever, down the tracks and into a point. And you never even spoke to him or knew him. *Follow the tracks to nowhere, your tiptoes on the rails, Shigem.* Amber, red, green in the mist—flee this town, through the asphalt metal night beyond the railroad crossing.

Throughout these years, when you woke in the morning, a metal will awoke with you. Expecting to be battered by the day, this will pushed you onward undefeated, so you never had depression or despair for more than seconds: knocked down constantly, you always raised yourself from the ground and pressed ahead through the rain, with an eye on the horizon and the other in the mirror, dodging bullets, leaving most of those who knocked you down far behind. Every day this metal will lifted up its toughened self and climbed inside a truck's cab. A hundred years of discipline would turn the key, set the gear, and pull away at measured speed, cracking off the rust of the night and warming up for the long, long haul yet again, with no one's help. This will of yours had fuel for a thousand miles a day. Below the froth and shimmer of your surface, this will was sober, plain as pewter, serious and functional. Unlike yourself, it sought to see and not be seen; it didn't care about acceptance or fun, for there was driving to be done. When you called a halt to the day, it stopped, parked and fuelled the truck, reclined and fell asleep. And there it is inside you still, anchoring the flutter and the spume of your presence, in perfect health and good for another million miles.

I check the time on my mobile. In ten minutes the club will close, the music cease, the house-lights blaze and then inevitably Evelyn will introduce us, knowing neither whether you have noticed me nor what I've seen in you concerning me. Because of this, would it not be classier and kinder if I introduced us now, within the music on the dance-floor, with neither talk nor ceremony? Yes.

I step from my perch here, down to the dance-floor, and move across towards you. You see me, and before your astonishment becomes a thing emotional to comment on or act upon, I've grabbed it with my eyes and pulled our gazes up inside you—up, where you leap high and streak through ice and sand, where the telegraph wires sing with frost, bodies scurry, wind soughs through the branches like a million years ago, magic circles curl away, and the planets sweep and turn and the stars spin and fly.

The last two long hard dance tracks are slamming, with the dirtiest and deepest thumping bass I've ever heard and stabbing hooks of merciless, ecstatic, driving power. For these two tracks, you and I dance together, never touching, never smiling, but staring at each other's eyes with clarity and ease. As the crazy-deep climax of the last track comes, we are easy in the knowledge that we don't need to speak about the broadcast at all, and we smile for the first time.

Here, several hours after *Sound & Vision* ended, you conclude a high-speed journey: you accept that although I can't be Kim for you, I yet return to you the love you poured in my direction when it bounced off the glass of your TV screen at home.

—But of course, I can make you into another of my chosen four here in town, as I vowed tonight I'd do for Angel too! OK: your lovely image, my Shigem, will spread its fire and fluid far beyond your life, I shall ensure it. Fifty light-years in all directions, the broadcasts of fifty years ago hurtle outward in a huge swelling bubble. From the tops of the spires of the old stone cathedrals is rising a vast new cathedral of airwaves, multiplying, reconvening, splitting, being mirrored. Through Rik's camera, this bubble will be fed with your image, so the rhythms and the visions of your dreams will run forever there, memes in proliferation, standing out Shigem-shaped, hard against the blackness, twisting outward further, mating light with other memes and surging out of sight beyond the curvature of space…

For I love you, Shigem, across the world or here in Paradise, forever; and I'll never leave your side or let you down, throughout eternity.

27 A DEVOTED FAN OF ALAIA AND ME

That deepest, darkest wonderland of bass and hook fades down in volume as it thunders, till it's sucked in tiny through the meshes of the bass-bins. Whoops greet the DJ, the house lights fade on and Evelyn bubbles up beside the pair of us. "I'm glad you two met," she says, putting one arm around his neck and one around mine. "Did you catch *Sound & Vision* on TV tonight?" she asks Shigem, and points at me and at Alaia who approaches now and puts her arms around Shigem's and my necks, opposite from Evelyn and making up a circle.

"I did, and it was amazing. He was telling me about it," Shigem replies, and he and I share a glance.

"It was so cool," says Evelyn. "And no screw-ups in the studio."

"They announced there's another one on Thursday?" says Shigem.

"Yes," says Alaia, "it should be even better. Must-see TV!" She makes a brief secret face of panic at me, as if to say *Who am I kidding?*

We don't know WHAT we're doing on Thursday yet! to which I reply by bouncing my elbow lightly on her shoulder.

As the dance-floor empties, we cross to where Kim is breaking down the bar. In an absent way he sings along to the lyrics of the track playing quietly on the club's sound system; and I am struck by his voice, which is clean, vanilla, supple, pure and filled with earnest beauty. It's a voice of great wholesomeness, picturesquely sad and honest, redolent of goodness—and a little white lie, I think.

"Hey Kim, did you see *Sound & Vision* on the TV tonight?" asks Evelyn.

"No, I had to set up here. I think I heard something about it ahead of time, but I can't remember what. Was it good?"

He's not sounding as if Shigem has told him anything about his own experience of it.

"Jaymi and Alaia here were in it. It was really neat," says Evelyn. "You won't find a good-quality copy online for a while, but I can lend you a DVD." She lowers her voice. "Just don't tell anyone else I lent it, and don't lose it or I'm in trouble."

"I shan't. Thanks, I'd love to see it."

"Hey, do you two want to come see a friend of mine?" Evelyn asks Alaia and me. "I have to go sell her some grass tonight."

"Competing with Lucan?" I ask.

"No, he doesn't sell that. I won't stay long, but you should meet her. She's quiet, she never goes out and doesn't hang out with anyone, but I like her."

I glance at Alaia. "I'm on," I say. "What's her name?"

"Pippa." She turns to Shigem and Kim: "I'm going with Jaymi and Alaia to see a friend of mine. Do you two want to come?"

"Do I know them?" Shigem asks.

"Pippa Vail. You know her?"

"Sure, I've seen her round, for years," he says. "I don't know her well." He looks at Kim, who nods OK. "You know everyone, Evelyn!"

"You and me both, babe! We can walk there from here."

So the five of us leave the club and head up the width and quiet of Asbury Avenue. At Heck Street we hang a left, just as I did earlier tonight with Alaia. And just like then, Lucan's posse is in front of Flames's place at the end of the block, with Kev's Cadillac purring at the kerb. Back here from Downstairs, they now include Damian and Angel. "Hey, Shigem!" Kev calls, his piggy eyes close-set, his mouth hanging open. "Why you always walk like you got a penis up your butt?" and Flames and Damian snort.

"And why d'you always talk like you got one in your mouth?" Shigem fires back.

The whole gang hoots with lazy laughter, Flames nudging Kev and asking earnestly, "Yeah, Kev—why is that?"

Kev looks annoyed, torn between targeting Flames or Shigem. "Fuck you," he finally manages, his words landing somewhere in the space between the two targets.

Lucan spits. "What you doing with the white boy?" he calls, nodding his head to indicate Kim. "You need flavour." Angel flicks a look of curiosity at Lucan.

A beat. "And how d'you know what I need?" Shigem replies with careful lightness.

Without warning, Lucan then targets us with a silent but shocking gesture, in imitation of his own decapitation—a vicious slice through the air just in front of his neck, his hand flashing in the yellow lamplight, his large eyes blazing and burrowing into each of our faces. Alaia, Evelyn, Kim and I exchange glances. I realise that Lucan must be hoping this gesture will trigger some response from us that reveals something about who may have left the severed wax head of himself on the bar. Then I notice that fear is flashing through Shigem's face. My mind flicks back to Downstairs a couple of hours ago when the discovery was made: Shigem wasn't there, I'm sure of it. No, of course he wasn't, he was in Paradise and I hadn't yet met him. In fact, he and Kim are the only ones in our group here who weren't present there in Downstairs—the only ones, therefore, who won't have known what Lucan's gesture referred to just now. And Shigem is alone here in knowing Lucan but not knowing what the gesture meant, so of course he'll be frightened. He probably thinks the gesture referred to a genuine decapitation in the near future, rather than a fake waxen one in the near past; and I'm guessing he fears this promised treat may be his own specifically, since Lucan happened to have been talking to him in particular just before the gesture. That was just unfortunate timing, I believe—and very much so, because despite the distance across the street I'm pretty sure Lucan is now staring fixedly at Shigem alone. Though Shigem has now concealed his fear, Lucan can hardly have failed to notice it when it was flashing out like a beacon. And judging by Lucan's stance, I have a nasty feeling he is increasingly inclined to construe that flash of fear as guilt.

"OK, guys, sweet dreams now," calls Evelyn, blowing a generalised kiss across the street and turning away.

"Will you dream of me, honey?" calls Flames.

"No," she chirps.

"Sure you will."

Two or three different conversations hang unfinished in the air but contrive somehow to cancel one another out, as patterns of attention start to fracture. Although the two groups are facing each other, neither is very coherent physically. It happens that in Lucan's group it is Angel who is standing nearest to ours, with points of yellow street-light shining off his black vinyl brassiere, and in my group it is I who am standing nearest to Lucan's: Angel and I are thus no more than a couple of metres from each other and both somewhat apart from the rest. Evelyn is gearing up to move my group on, but first I fix Angel's eyes with my own. Back at Downstairs I looked around among his memories, but now I aim a hypnotic suggestion at him, forcing him to feel that he's known about "Jaymi and Alaia" for half his life ... so you picture that cabaret bar, don't you, Angel, where you sat years ago when you first heard Alaia singing through these eyes and started feeling sucked in: that saxophone of creamy chocolate velvet wine, spilling out its jagged notes of dark muscled flesh that coiled around you as you leaned your body forward, your elbows on the sticky bar, loath to believe you were there among the first to hear a sound you knew immediately would ripple out through history! Remember how your feet tapped the footrest on your bar-seat; remember how you reached for a white book of matches without looking down for it, to light another Capri up and draw it down deeply, your eyes growing wide until they blinked in the smoke? You shook the match out when you felt the flame approaching your golden-painted nails, tossed it somewhere down, surrendered to the pulsing of the beat beneath the saxophone and felt the tears start behind your eyes, alone within the crowd. Every girl you'd ever yearned to be, and every boy you'd ever wanted, were summed and projected in the pairing of Alaia's voice and these eyes—remember? Then afterwards you wandered in a daze through the streets, saw the moon looking down at you, inscrutable and ancient, and you knew that my Vision and her Sound were in your blood for life... And though beneath this street-light my gaze looks as frail as an eggshell gaze glimpsed passing in a limousine, it's raped you nonetheless, through the airwaves and light waves, consensually, for life!

28 WET GREEN EYES OF PIPPA IN THE TAKE-AWAY

I let him go. The face-off has now broken up and the rest of our two groups are wandering off. Mine gravitates to Evelyn, who leads us to the end of the block and right onto Sewall Avenue. Once we have turned the corner out of sight of the other group, a few seconds elapse before Shigem asks, "Was he looking at *me* just now? I think he was."

Evelyn puts her arm around his shoulder. "I know what you mean, honey, but I don't think he meant you specially, because that gesture, that was from something earlier," and she gives a quick account of the waxwork head at Downstairs, which is tasty news to him and Kim.

"Still ... it did kind of look as if he thought Shigem was responsible," says Kim.

Evelyn glances at him, nods slowly and comes to a halt at Emory Street. "We'll come back to this. OK, this is Pippa's building," she says, indicating a grimy residential high-rise on the left which looms up a dozen storeys. "But before we go up, let's grab some food over there." So we carry on a couple more blocks, to where the Hop Shing Chinese take-away is still open on Main Street. "Go ahead," she tells us on the pavement outside it. "I'm going to call Pippa, to see if she wants us to bring any food up."

After we've all placed our orders at the counter inside, a quiet voice on my right crackles, "Egg foo yong, please." I turn and see a vacant-eyed, light-skinned black woman in her thirties, wearing a clean dark-blue sweatshirt with matching dark-blue sweatpants and a pair of black silk gloves. Her prominent green eyes look wet and hurt, as if she's been crying hard, though there are no tear-stains. "That's all," she mumbles, distracted. Her gaze meets mine, and is then through me and beyond me, far away. I scent some emotional damage or absence in her, some churn of loss or deadened anger. Questions arise in connection with her order, simple though it was, and while she deals with these I notice there are tiny hesitations and freezes throughout her actions, as if all her movements have a slight stammer. There's a sense of catatonic indecision and volcanic red embarrassment inside her. I realise that whenever she becomes aware of anyone watching her, she blushes; and those eyes really do look as if they must be regular water-pipes. At last her food arrives, along with ours. She pays, picks up her bag, turns away and floats out from this fluorescent box and into the summer night.

"Pippa," calls Evelyn as I follow her out. "I'm meant to be coming to your place now. I thought you'd flaked out, girl! I just left a message on your phone."

"Sorry," Pippa blinks. "It's always later than I thought…" She trails off, then starts again, as if confiding to Evelyn, "I once answered a pay-phone on the street. A man said he was behind a window, looking down at me. He said he didn't know how to come down and meet people, and he wanted me to visit him because calling the pay-phone was the only way he dared to ask for company. I said sorry, no, but it probably wouldn't make a difference anyway…" She notices the four of us standing around her with bags of food, and trails off again. "Oh…" she says and blushes.

"Pippa, this is Alaia, Kim and Jaymi … and I think you know Shigem?"

"Oh, hi … hi … hi… Hi Shigem, yeah, I've seen you round…"

"Did you catch that *Sound & Vision* thing I told you about on the General Network tonight?"

"I don't know," she says vaguely. "The TV's always on but I keep the sound off."

"If you don't recognise his face," says Evelyn, pointing at me, "then you didn't see it… No, you didn't see it. Anyway, they're friends of mine from New York. Can they join us at yours for a while?"

"Oh … sure…" and she looks at us shyly.

29 FLIGHT FROM ARVERNE

So the six of us head back to the high-rise, follow Pippa into the lift and ride to the eleventh floor. Her apartment is a reasonable size but dim and cluttered. Ornaments of angels seem to be everywhere, in various sizes and colours. The whole effect is rather spooky and disconcerting.

"Good view," I say at the window, where a poky balcony overlooks most of Asbury Park.

"The ass of the nation," she murmurs, depressively and yet somehow with a hint of affection for what she is describing. I notice that although everything here suggests she lives alone, the small dining table in the corner appears to have been laid for two. Presumably for a guest, although she doesn't come across as one who would have visitors, except for Evelyn, whom she now pays for a bag of grass.

Pippa makes mugs of tea and we all start to eat, half-watching subtitled cartoons on the TV. Meanwhile, chatting now and then on auto-pilot, I take a look inside her ... and I see you, Pippa Vail, in New York, in a brown and grey project in Arverne, south-east Queens, a distant-eyed child in a slum by the sea. You were still a small girl when your parents got themselves out of there at the end of the 'sixties, dreaming of a new life here in Asbury Park when it was lively, a life without the pressure and the danger of the city. They quit their rotten jobs in a burst of liberation, loaded up a van, returned the landlord's key and drove away, down to here, both on air. They had scraped together enough to rent a small bungalow, almost a shack, two blocks from the sea on First Avenue and Kingsley Street. A cabin by the sea... But then began the downturn: no jobs in Asbury Park or Ocean Grove, no money, alcohol and tension in the bungalow, and then in 1970 your father was killed in the race riots here. Life and joy were happening elsewhere, had passed you by, it seemed. Your mother died soon, of nothing memorable, and now you feel the best thing to do would be to walk down the beach at night and just continue walking further out into the ocean. You can go there any time, down the sand, to the phosphorescent sea. It's always there at night, you know, a few blocks away from here, its whisper an enticement.

I see you aged twelve, sweet and sullen—but that sweet and sullen girl found a tunnel, clambered inside, and thus climbed into you, Pippa, and buried herself alive.

There was a man in your life, for a while, after you moved here to the high-rise. He even quit his shit-job in the factory on the Bayonne waterfront, to come down and live with you, here beside the sea. It didn't work, however. I suspect he thought you saw, around the two of you, oppressive scenes of horror, retribution and smoke; but did he never notice your sweet little snub-nose profiled against any scene you might be in? Could any such scene be so bad, with such a nose? He never tried to fathom you, he only left you pregnant, not long before you miscarried. Before he left, you planned to escape him. "I could walk out any time," you thought, "and hit the ground running—maybe never touch the ground! I'll start a brand-new life, and then…" but you always trailed away here. That was years ago. Perhaps he'll realise yet what he lost, though more likely he will not. Then perhaps you'd want him back, though more probably you wouldn't.

Since then you've had friends, sometimes; but one thing you have never found, never coming close, is a lover who will stay with you for any length of time, who will be there and give to you. I doubt you ever will, though I shan't tell you that. So ingrained is your alone-ness, it is sensed at thirty paces. There are other things in life besides cohabiting with someone; but you, it seems, are set up so you need someone first, before the rest could occur, and so the rest never will. There's one consolation, though: you may come back to earth for your next life, Pippa, if there is such a thing, and then perhaps you'll find your lover then—you never know, you may! Then maybe he will want to fly away with you, to somewhere, then maybe you will fly away together to a happy land, forever, or at least another town…

By chance you had in fact turned the TV sound on, just before our broadcast, so you did hear Alaia's voice from down in your bedroom. The song you heard ran sky-high, slow and all-embracing through the airwaves of your head: you'd known the song before, you felt, with that one man of yours, in the sweetest early times with him, in moments in his presence when you stepped for the very first time into new internal continents inside yourself. (Hard to know those steps would turn out the only ones you ever took there.) Memories of your two shadows falling on a building wall, doubled up with laughter in a summer long ago, were unlocked by this song: shadows photographed on plaster and filed in the album of your memory. A dying love affair in Asbury Park.

Sometimes you think you feel another man calling out, across this town, across the world, around both the past and the present, to address you. He calls through that song inside your head ... and no, you won't meet.

Such promise in you, Pippa—what went wrong? It seems your personality did not grow a backbone: no one, ahead of time, thought to say you'd need one. Living's such an effort. (Who arranged that? and what a great mistake it was.) The weight of your body leads to stasis, by nature; any other action is unnatural, for you. The play of your attention leads to silence, by nature; any other noise is unnatural, for you. The spanning of your vision leads to darkness, by nature; any other lighting is unnatural, for you. Paralysis—an illness.

A wave of sadness breaks, as you see how "too early" overlapped with "too late". Or maybe there was just a blip of time between those two periods; but alas, you didn't recognise this blip when it arrived in witty camouflage, and so you didn't know to act while it was still happening, and now the blip's gone, taking its camouflage with it. Here's a cool idea, though: perhaps that fleeting blip was all the more resonant, for never being utilised!... Is that of any use to you? No? No, I guess not.

I bring my tune-in to a close. So there she is. I suspect she'd have it otherwise. So should I, big time. Funny how things turn out.

Kim walks in through the door at the far end of this long sitting room, returning from a trip alone down Pippa's dim hallway. I register that he is looking extremely troubled. I flick my eyes away before he can catch me observing this, then slide my gaze back onto him to find he has quite concealed that other expression as he strides up the room smiling and joins us in the light here.

30 THE SMALL BLACK TOOTHBRUSH

"I'm tired," proclaims Evelyn, finishing her food. "Pippa, honey. Nice to see you on my monthly grass visit. If you ever want to get out of

this apartment and come play in the real world, give me a call, OK?"
She looks at the rest of us: "Nobody else needs to leave."

"No, we should get home too," says Shigem.

"And I need to sleep," says Alaia, "I'll walk to the Metropolitan
with you, Evelyn."

Is Alaia going to ask me, I wonder?

"You too?" she asks me.

"I don't think I am, quite yet. But I'll be following you soon." I
look at Pippa, who gazes emptily through me.

Goodbyes are said to the other three, then once she has sat back
down, tears run from her eyes. At first she tries to hide this, but then
stops bothering. Her weeping feeds on itself, swelling quickly but
quietly in intensity. I sip my tea. At last she stops, exhausted, blows
her nose, blushes, tries to speak, mumbles "Sorry, I cry all the time
but I hate it that I do."

"Why d'you cry?"

"I don't really know. Maybe because everything's wrong. Once it
starts, it's hard to stop. It's getting harder too: one day I'll probably
start and never stop. I have to drink a lot of water, to keep me topped
up!"

"Is it of help?"

"No, I feel like a bomb that can never blow, it's too wet." She
stifles a sudden savage sneeze, and in her head it sounds like celery
fibres snapping. She raises her head from it, damp-eyed and sniffling.
"When I was pregnant I drew the child's outline in ink on my belly,
but it didn't last. Pain dripped through me. It made me so angry, I
became this green seething gnome, which I hated, which made me
even angrier... Quite fun, really!"

"Let's have a sunny picnic," I suggest, standing up.

She laughs through her sniffles and gets up too. "OK, sure. What,
right now?"

I put my arms around her. "No, Pippa, not at four in the morning.
I'll call you and we'll fix it. Let me take your number." She scribbles
it on a scrap of paper and hands it to me, then I follow her down the
sitting room and into the darkness of the hallway from which I saw
Kim returning earlier. She flicks a dim light on, half-illuminating a
narrow, cluttered passageway, surprisingly long.

Halfway between the sitting room and the front door of the apartment, a bathroom door approaches me on the right, standing open, with a yellowish light on inside. I glance in, while we pass it. Nothing special there ... but then I frown, drawing near Pippa at the front door, thinking back to my snapshot of that yellow-lit bathroom.

Nothing special about that room at all. Yet my snapshot does contain one detail that I cannot help but zero in upon now. I zoom in to it, in my memory. Yes! Mounted there on the wall, just beside the basin, was a toothbrush-holder. Hanging in this holder was a big blue toothbrush. And half-hidden behind that—a small black toothbrush.

Standing at the front door, she turns her head to face me as I near her. I take my leave with a kiss ... and while I'm close, I look behind your eyes and see beneath the sadness a happy place, somewhere, remaining from before, that lets its sun through your eyes now and then, spilling onto other people if they're lucky to be with you when it spills. In that place, the place you should have been, fountains fling up jets of spray on mossy stone cherubs; strips of lawn snake away between high beds of flowers, where you sprawl in the grass, and the parties last days and nights and afternoons and further nights. You run through the moonlight across the portico, along the terraces and down cool woodland paths to obelisks and urns in the dappled light of stars. You've never taken a trip to such a place from Asbury Park, but you've always known that once you lived there, strange to say—once upon a time you lived that life, Pippa Vail, for a lifetime, somewhere—an endless Indian Summer in a palace!

"Looking forward to that picnic," I say.

She sends her empty smile across the lift lobby at me: "Me too."

I head for the Metropolitan on dead quiet streets, towards the glimmer of the dawn across the ocean ahead.

PART III

MONDAY: ALAIA LEARNS MY SUBTERFUGE

31 WE'LL ALL ADORE YOU

I wake at half-past ten, to my alarm and the scratching of the gulls in the eaves through the window. I walk across the room and peer down at the green space outside, which my journeys last night informed me is Liberty Square. I see my phone on the coffee table. I had forgotten its existence throughout last night. Glancing at its tally of new texts and voicemail messages that have been accumulating silently since the broadcast, mostly from New York, I make a snap decision: these are all products of such a different world and such a different headspace from those I'm currently inhabiting here in Asbury Park, that I'm not going to deal with a single one of them for the few days I'm here. I shall be officially uncontactable. Otherwise I'm going to get too distracted with stuff that can wait. I'm meant to be in hiding, after all. So I'm going to leave it on silent and carry it, but answer only if it's Alaia or Evelyn or Rik or Marc or Jason or Pippa or anyone else I may meet in this strange little bubble of exile.

I get ready at high speed, knock on Alaia's door, hear no answer and head downstairs. In the room that Evelyn called the breakfast room there is a buffet of which I make good use, attended by a polite but wholly uncommunicative Mexican girl who flits on cat's feet between this room and some hidden kitchen, as if serving at a delicate funeral.

As soon as I've returned to my room, Alaia emerges from hers and knocks on my door. I bid her enter and she bursts in, emanating a glow of exhilaration. "Good news?" I ask.

"Nothing in particular. Unless you count the fact that I was just looking online and found that millions of people are talking about us two, all around the entire world, after last night. And I don't mean bad stuff. It's amazing, fabulous stuff! D'you want to come see some of it? Jaymi, our lives have completely changed now."

I laugh and reflect on this for a moment. "You know what? I don't. Not yet. Not before the second broadcast. It'll distract me while I'm on camera, I know it will. I'm going to wait till we're back in Manhattan, then just go through all of it. It'll be a very Manhattan thing to look at! If our lives have changed as much as you say, which I can believe, then we'll have quite long enough to inhabit all that. We'll have no choice. But this town is on a different planet from that, and I want to keep things peaceful and isolated and strange, just for the week that we're down here. This is an unrepeatable and unique little Sargasso Sea of time and space, that we'll never get again—our very last week of privacy, before the dam bursts forever. We shouldn't squander it with texting."

"Privacy, such as Lucan hustling you into Downstairs, facing you into a corner at the back and putting a paper-bag over your head?"

"Um, I don't remember the paper-bag, but yes, that was the kind of restful privacy I'm talking about, compared to what's coming next week. But here, I'm not going to answer any calls or texts from outside this little bubble we're in. This thing's staying on silent."

"I'm with you there. I haven't been answering either."

Soon we're both back in the studio, for our noon appointment. "OK," says Rik, "so you know Marc's fixed the second broadcast for this Thursday evening. That's three and a half days away, which pushes us *unmercifully* for time, but we can't do anything about it, so we'll just have to make it work." Alaia grimaces. "Jason's no help there, he's also been pushing for Thursday because apparently that's the day of 'maximised cross-fertilisation of viewer memory and word-of-mouth', whatever that means. Anyway, two things here. First off, Jason's given that broadcast a name: he's calling it *Big Bang*."

Alaia frowns. "OK. Sounds a bit like a circus act."

"That's fine," I say. "We are a circus act."

So *Big Bang* it becomes.

"Second thing," says Rik. "An idea that may help us, so let me know if you're both on for it. I hope you are. Jason's OK'd it already on the phone, 'cos he knows it'll turn out at least as good as last night's. To take it to the next level, how about we don't air live, as such? I suggest we air an amalgam of three short sessions we record over the next three evenings—the first tonight, the second one tomorrow Tuesday, and the third one Wednesday. Along the way, I'll be putting the three together, through some new software that processes the picture and the sound in fantastic ways." A faint cloud must have flicked across our faces, because he hastens to add, "Don't worry, I'm not going to tweeze you around so much that you'll be unrecognisable."

"Well, that's all right, then," says Alaia. "I just don't want to sound like some scratch mix of myself."

"Alaia, we'll all adore you."

"Well, I wasn't really thinking of that—"

"Sure you were—I mean, no of course you weren't," he says, slapping his cheek.

"OK," she laughs.

"Fine," I say to Rik. "It sounds like your non-live idea may have saved the day there. So, less pressure than yesterday?"

"Not really. Our schedule's tight as a gnat's fanny, if I'm to get the post-production done in time. So let's treat these three as fully live, and let's shoot the first one tonight at seven. By the way, d'you two have the content sorted out?"

"Oh, just that little matter of the content!" laughs Alaia.

"*Content?*" I say. "No, we thought we'd skip that bit... Oh all right, if you insist, we can rustle up a little something."

"Cool beans. OK, let's just get a few tests done. If you could each sit where you sat last time." We take our places, as he starts flicking switches and checking monitors. "Alaia: at whatever vocal pitch you're loudest, could you give me a smooth gradient, over ten seconds, from silent up to loudest, please."

I hover my index fingers over my ears.

"Why are you putting your fingers over your ears?" demands Alaia from inside the sound booth.

32 EVELYN PICKS IMAGINATIONS TO THIEVE

After several hours of intensive and inspired rehearsal work, the three of us are contemplating this evening's recording with a lot more confidence than we expected. In the late afternoon Alaia and I return upstairs, where she says she's in the mood for taking it easy awhile, so we split off through our adjacent doors.

Once alone, I remind myself that now *Sound & Vision* is over, I need to find out about the secret imagination-cloning business, away from Alaia's ears. I close my window quietly and dial a number on my phone. "Evelyn, it's Jaymi," I say in a low voice. "Should you and I be talking about something?"

"Yeah, I think so," she says. "Why not come round here: go down the corridor, past the studio and up the stairs to the top. I'll let you in."

At the end of the corridor, therefore, I climb two storeys up the narrow back stairs, probably the staff staircase when this was a hotel, and knock on the door. Evelyn opens it and ushers me into her and Rik's apartment, an attractive and well-windowed space that's recently been renovated and painted in solid blocks of bright colour. "Where's Alaia?"

"Lying on her bed."

"Good." She makes us coffee and I settle back into a deep-purple-leather-covered sofa in the sitting room. She curls up opposite me in an identically covered armchair, which makes a spectacular contrast with the bright yellow T-shirt and magenta skirt she's wearing.

"Jason said I should get some instructions from you," I begin.

"You bet." And she proceeds to confirm everything Jason told me about his secret imagination-thieving deal; I even recognise some of his phrases. She clearly paid close attention to his plans and is intending to execute them to the letter. There's something she's not telling me, though. What's missing, I realise, is her own opinion of all this. I don't know whether she's a party to this scheme under duress from Jason, or gladly. I decide to refrain from asking her this, however, thinking it best to feel my way forward; so I restrict my questions to the logistical. Basically, on behalf of Jason's anonymous household-name corporation, she and I must select a "balanced, cheerful, family-rated quartet of target imaginations"; then I must use my passive gaze to tune in to and gather up swathes of intimate detail from their internal lives; and then I must blast all that stuff out again into Rik's camera using my active hypnotic gaze, exactly as I used that gaze during the broadcast except that now I shall be blasting out those other people's imaginative stuff instead of my own. A few such recording sessions should suffice, Rik has estimated, to give Jason's client enough raw material from which to assemble a full, man-made "human imagination" for the company's pesky interactive cartoon spokes-sheep.

She then starts relaying something else from Jason, which he didn't say to me, about how the sheep's logical facilities won't need to be stolen from real people in the same way but can just be plugged in from existing logic-based computer programs. My mind starts to wander, rather as it did with Jason's financial graph, so while I half-listen I can't help myself tuning in to her for a moment ... and I zoom in on a pair of childhood memories, Evelyn: the chime of the ice cream van with garish cones and faces painted gaily on its sides in faded letters, as you giggled with a girl who was a friend, but whose face is a lacuna in this scene. And linking chime and giggle, an old rock song heard in Frank's, up on Main Street, where you went with a boy who came to town for a brief while but then moved away again and so fell out of touch—a boy called Romel, whom you thought of, when he went, as Romel-we-hardly-knew-you. What's this ghost of your former self saying to Romel in Frank's, with such enthusiasm? Neither you nor I can lip-read your younger self's words, but the urgency of your chatter is at least preserved in the faint tug and ache of this small memory, and maybe also somewhere in the memory of the vanished Romel.

"Who'll be the targets?" she asks.

"Er ... well, how about you? You'd make a great contribution to a sheep's imagination."

"No, thank you, Jaymi. Anyway, our targets have to be *outside* the Metropolitan."

"Hmm." Thinking back to last night, I remember that I've already earmarked Angel and Shigem, for starters, but I'm curious to see whom she suggests.

"All right, I'll choose," she says. "How about Pippa, Kim, Shigem and Angel?"

"What good taste you have! OK, fine. You know them better than I do. I'll leave you to take responsibility for the choice."

"Oh, sure," she says. She looks into the distance, with a hint of glee in her eyes. Then she reaches for a pencil and a scrap of paper, writes out their names and slides the scrap across the sofa towards me, with a flicker of irony, like a cool teacher assigning a perverse bit of homework. I pick it up and inspect it.

Pippa Vail.

Kim Somerville.

Shigem Adele.

Angel Deon.

As I contemplate these names, randomly applied by general agreement to four people I have known for less than one full day, it strikes me that by steering me towards them, Evelyn might be thought of as having somewhat subverted Jason's "balanced, cheerful, family-rated quartet of target imaginations". They're an OK balance of races, I guess, and Kim and Shigem are good-natured enough, but something makes me wonder whether Jason would see any of these as quite what he had in mind for the spokesfigure of a corporate client. I suspect Evelyn picked them out as a result of little more than her own arrant nosiness concerning imaginations she's curious about. I wonder how conscious this motivation was. I'm just about to ask, when I stop. Such derailing of Jason's plans is suddenly appealing to me, I have to say. It would constitute a mischievous kind of sabotage on my part, which would serve him right for threatening to sabotage *Sound & Vision*. He won't know our selections aren't quite what he asked for, until it's too late. Anyway, such judgements are so subjective; we might have picked these in all innocence... Well, maybe not. Jason's pretty sharp. Still, what leverage will he have over me, after *Big Bang*, if that goes as planned and the millions roll into the GN? How much would Marc then care, if he saw my duplicitous signature next to Jason's on that secret letter agreement? If he saw that, he would also see that Jason had blackmailed me into it. No; the more unsuitable the targets, the more fun it will be for me. "Should we consider Lucan?" I ask Evelyn.

She peers at me, tilting her head to one side: "Don't go there! That's a bit too blatant."

From this I deduce that she's on the same page as me, where Jason is concerned, though she doesn't want to say so aloud. She didn't like being railroaded into this by him, any more than I did.

"By the way," she says, "just between us, I delivered a copy of *Sound & Vision* to Kim this morning, since he missed it on TV last night. That still leaves Pippa who didn't see it, but at least three out of our four targets saw it."

"Hold on. You gave it to him because you knew I'd approve your ready-made list of targets, including him?"

"Yep," she chuckles. "Jaymi, you don't seem to have noticed, but in secret I actually run the country. OK then—let's go record your first secret imagination-cloning session." She reaches for her phone.

"What, right now?"

"Why not? I could tell you were taking a lot in last night."

"Was it that obvious?"

"Not to any of them, but I could tell. Don't forget, I'm up to my neck in this with you. I think you tuned in to all four of our targets."

"Actually just three of them. I didn't have time to plunge into Kim."

"Fine, we'll get cracking with the other three, then. Jason wants results here."

"Do we have time, before the *Big Bang* recording?"

She checks the time. "Easily. It won't take you more than, what, half an hour to project what you remember, will it?"

"I guess not. Damn! I was hoping to take it easy."

"You'll get enough of that when you're dead. Hey babe," she says into her phone. "You in the studio? OK, we're both on our way. Those four are confirmed now." She rings off. "Rik's ready now."

"You just told him 'those' four are confirmed…"

"Yes, he and I chose them for you last night. Let's hit it, Jaymi! Put that coffee down. Go go go! Bam bam bam! Chop chop chop!" She takes my hand, hauls me to my feet, ignoring my laughing protests, and steers me towards the door.

Why do I get the feeling I'm not in control here?

33 THEFT ONE, AND HOW TO BE IGNORED

So here I am in the studio, with Evelyn and Rik only, psyching myself up to project my first three tune-ins, and here they come…

First up is Angel's violent childhood, as I plunged down into it in Downstairs; his lusciousness and poison, his shacking up with Lucan and his sheer survivor qualities.

Then comes Shigem's boyhood sky full of planets, as I saw it there in Paradise; his will, like a truck, within his own vulnerability, keeping his enchantment intact through the years.

And finally comes Pippa with her hard and lonely upbringing, one real relationship that didn't work out, and her bits of joy, like shadows…

Once I start projecting, I'm pleased to discover that a small corner of my mind remains free to analyse what I'm doing, while I'm doing it, which certainly wasn't the case during the broadcast. This is one respect in which this particular process is subtly different from anything I've done before. (I suspect it would have taken me a while to think of trying this particular pursuit, incidentally, so I'm almost grateful to Jason for forcing me into the discovery of a third kind of inhabitation of my abilities.) Basically this feels like a milder version of the hypnotic projecting that I used for the broadcast and for showing Lucan who was boss and for imprinting into Angel his phony sense of having worshipped Alaia and me for years. This is still *active* like those hypnotic projectings were—in contrast with just a passive tune-in during conversation—and this is also still visible to the camera and would be visible to anyone if I were looking into their eyes. However, compared with the hypnotic kind of active projection, this here is a lot less demanding on me and requires me to be a lot less hyped-up, because I'm not having to scare up any of my own material and voltage but am merely relaying other people's, accessing my memory of their imaginations and minds as if I'm replaying video and audio.

On the emotional side, at the start of my projection of each imagination I have a feeling of "confessing" things that I'm not guilty of myself, but in each case this soon turns into an exhilarated awe at that internal landscape … then an understanding of how it ticks … then through that understanding, a growing love. In fact I soon find it's the strength of this love that I most have to cope with, in order not to derail the faithfulness and efficacy of my projecting—as if it is now I who must take care not to let myself be hypnotised by my targets. I didn't expect the strength of these reactions in me, which are noticeably more powerful and concentrated versions of what I felt while I was doing my original tunings-in to gather the material itself.

In no time it's all over and I am filled with emotion at having inhabited so intimately these squirts of flesh-bound passion and pain, ambition and anguish, laughter and weakness—the three of them here for such a short while and soon enough to die, leaving no lasting record of their own complexities except what I'm laying down here in Rik's camera.

"You OK, Jaymi?" asks Evelyn, her hand on my shoulder. "What did that feel like?"

I slide into unexpected chuckling, as an emotional release and also at how very obliquely these emotions lie in relation to the business of assembling the one-line statement that'll best answer this most natural of questions. "It's quite a trip to have been privy to all that, and empowered to preserve it," I say.

"I bet. I wanted to watch you on the monitor, but I could only snatch glimpses of it because Rik had me monitoring the brightness gauge the whole time, which I'm guessing was probably a less interesting sight."

"You were doing noble work," Rik tells her. "We had to keep it within those parameters and we don't have the playout guys in New York to do it for us. In fact, I think we've found your niche—custodian of the brightness gauge."

She snores aloud, then checks her phone. "OK, I don't think we have time to watch it now, before you and Alaia are back in here—"

"Oh yes, I'd forgotten about *Big Bang*," I say. "So much for taking it easy today."

"So we'll watch this some time later. But I'm gonna text Jason and tell him we've started. He may call me right back and ask for details. If he does, do you two want me to say you're here with me? Anyone want a word with him?"

Rik and I each gaze at a different part of the ceiling, in separate assessments, then shake our heads in unison.

While she texts I contemplate her with mixed feelings. There's no escaping the fact that in steering me towards these four imaginations in particular, rather than others she didn't know, she was betraying her old friends Angel, Shigem and Pippa and her new friend Kim. There's also, of course, no escaping the fact that I myself am betraying the four of them too, by doing the actual spying. But what could I have done to avoid this? And how on earth can I abandon it, now I know the beauties in at least three of them? "You selected well," is what I find to say to her, but refrain. "Were you watching just now, Rik?" I say instead.

"It may sound strange, but no, not really. I know you weren't doing the full hypnotic thing you were doing in *Sound & Vision*, so I could have watched you today, from that point of view. But like in the broadcast, you were shifting slightly throughout the whole time, so I had to keep you centre-frame, or it'll look like I was crap behind the camera. There's no enjoying the show for me, I'm afraid—no television-watching for the Camera Operator, especially when he's D.P. too."

"Hold on, you just said I wasn't doing the full hypnotic thing here, so from that point of view you could have watched me tonight. D'you mean you didn't watch me in *Sound & Vision?*"

"Damn straight I didn't! Even if I hadn't been busy keeping you centre-frame, I wouldn't have watched you while you were in that mode—a fat lot of use I'd have been, hypnotised! I'd have wound up pointing the camera at the coat-rack and broadcasting that. Then I'd have been at the Job Centre next week, while the GN share value plummeted and Marc stuck pins into a wax model of me and urinated slowly down his trouser-leg... I did look at your eyes now and then, but I always looked away again."

Strange that this had never occurred to me. "And Evelyn wasn't watching either, because she was crouching behind my chair or watching her brightness gauge."

"Yep," she says. "In this room you were supremely ignored, Jaymi."

"So I see, and I'm considering the adoption of a wounded expression."

"Don't worry, we did watch a copy of *Sound & Vision* later, that I took home on disc," says Rik, with the ghost of a smile.

I look from him to her, then back to him. "Well?" I chivvy them. "*And...?* Anyone have a good trip?"

They both grin. "Not a trip, exactly," he says, "but I guess it did contribute to a fucking good shag."

Well, there's something else I wasn't expecting. "I'm honoured!" I declare.

Before long, we creep out of the studio and off in our respective directions down the long dim corridor, hoping not to bump into Alaia, since she would of course be fatally curious as to what we had all been up to.

No sooner have I lain on my bed and closed my eyes, than my peace is interrupted by the chimes of six o'clock from the grand-mother clock in the corridor, which is the signal for Alaia and me to start getting ready for our first official, above-board recording for Thursday's *Big Bang*. I hear her door open and a knock at mine. "Come in."

She enters, looking coolly radiant in that smooth black silk dress of hers, refreshed and psyched-up for the recording and unaware of all the hard labour I've just been putting in downstairs.

To help her refrain from asking where I've been for the last hour or two, in case she knows or cares that I was gone, I throw her a distracting titbit. "You know, I think I'm going to use this visit for something else, aside from the broadcasts."

"What's that?"

"Well, when I gained the sight, I think maybe I lost something too."

She nods.

"Alaia, why are you nodding? That wasn't in the script."

"You did change slightly. You became a teeny bit ... blander. More blank."

"I was going to ask if that was evident, but now perhaps I shan't. Yes, I'm in the market for a personality. I seem to have mislaid some of my own."

"It'll come back, don't worry. Meanwhile, you're a lovely clear lens."

"Gee, thanks. Anyway, we're bumping into a bunch of people we've never met before and probably shan't meet again. How often are we going to find ourselves in Asbury Park again? So I'm going to take a trip or two while I'm here—trips into people. I'm going to tune in to a few of them without their knowing."

An element of challenge enters her demeanour.

"I'm not going to hurt them or give away their secrets," I say. "It's just a bit of research into what I may have lost, so I can find it again. I need to know what it was, in case it becomes too late to re-learn it. I have become too much of a blank slate, it's true. I felt it as soon as I first left Marc's office. With people, it feels like I'm just mind and power now; I need to find instinct again. So I'm just going to delve a bit into … the forms a personality can take, I guess. And the limits of those forms—the different ways of being a perfect version of a self. And if I investigate the shapes people can take, maybe I'll even find out something of why they're alive. Does that make sense? I'll only be doing this for me, I assure you."

"Yes. I never realised spying was so noble."

"But I'm not going to spy into you, you have my promise."

"You'd better not!" she says, her finger pointing at my face, with only the modicum of a sly smile to mitigate the warning.

I take hold of her warning finger and hand, then let these go. We stand in awkward silence. "Maybe I also want to see if any of them need waking up."

She softens at this and turns away to go to her room: "Oh, they will," she says and lets my door close behind her.

For the camera I reproduce *Sound & Vision*'s natural make-up (which Shigem saw as so lush and smoothly coloured) and change into the same outline of simple black. In doing so, I catch a strange, dissociated glimpse of myself in the wardrobe mirror, seeing my slim form and watchful eyes as if they belonged to someone else, just as I did in Paradise.

A few minutes to seven. I stand at my window and listen to the distant sea, centring myself into maximum calm and focus. Then a bell somewhere across town tolls the hour … and it's time for the studio, for she and I are *on!*

34 *BIG BANG*: SONG OF DEATH

This time the three lenses are angled in relation to one another—one straight ahead of me and one on each side at forty-five degrees to that, like the mirrored panels of a vanity mirror on a dressing-table.

Aside from ratcheting up the intensity a notch above last time, we've decided that tonight Alaia will be dominant, with me taking my lead from her vocal input; then for the remaining two sessions she'll return to taking her lead from the face on the monitor in her sound booth.

There are the last-minute technical checks and double-checks, like the first time; there is the same quiet, inexorable progress towards a state of utter calm and focus, like an empty round spotlight on a black floor inside me; and at last Rik's countdown. He has made the opening wrap-around material similar to last time, as a kind of branding technique, and here it comes: the distant murmur of the audience, the ten giant floodlights above the stadium, the dizzy fall of bluish-white light across the landscape of heads, the dimming floods, the rising cheer, the scratch of blue filaments against a starry sky, the growing quiet, the faint light behind me, silhouetting me on the big screen. I feel the outward pull; I slide my outer gaze aside, baring the sensors that can feel the spiders' silks; the night shivers, then I burst onto screen with the lights around my face, while a spotlight like a hair picks Alaia out, tiny on the stage far below...

Strange that I never thought to wonder, until now, how Rik included that tiny image of her down there, when there's no camera pointing at her. Since it's only from this great height that she's ever seen by the television viewers (or by the digitally-created stadium audience, indeed), her image is probably small enough for Rik to have got away with just importing and animating a still image of her.

I fling this distracting intellectual analysis away, since her voice is now taking the lead as planned, with my gaze as responder and back-up, in a subtle overture ... and to every one of you who can hear her and see me, it seems you are walking over fields with a mystery friend to whom you cannot turn but who feels like a part of you, and from this companion a full, swelling voice wails and keens. This friend is yours alone—exotic, from an ancient place, with eyes that see what you see and silence swelling loud beneath the wailing of its passage through the fields with you. It constitutes a procession in itself, dark, bejewelled and smiling at you, though you still can't turn to face it.

Warmed up now, she accelerates. Her voice pushes outward, and hollows out sound, out of silence—volume out of nothing, as the Big Bang pushed out brand-new space at the speed of the light that was born of it. She carves out a bowl of sky and mountains with her song: you who listen find yourselves standing on a mountain pass, looking down at Lop Nor, the deserts all around it and the mountain bowl around those, wider in enormity with every passing second. Clouds boil and bubble on a level with your feet upon the pass. While you watch, cities sprout, proliferate and die, miles below you. Her upturned black face flings its inexhaustible magic out across galactic space-time, where (at her will) powers of ten collapse and stretch, collapse and stretch, collapse and stretch, into icy-golden ladders out of sight into infinity…

This being her journey, we take a darker turn than anything I'd have served you by myself. It's as if, having just sketched the birth of space, she now bewails with tangy glee your wretched place within space—her song nearly cheerful in its rhythm but evoking the sound of your soft human lips on your hard stone planet, where you cling like red-nerved molluscs on a rock. Obviously those soft lips shouldn't have been housed in this cold glinting song of death and planets, glass and rock and falling steel: what vicious force inflicted *that* upon you fleshy squirts?

Her sphinx voice curls around your dreary snarls and mocks them, with goddess-like serenity and power. Through the litter and the dirt, round the jagged little corners of your fibreglass and concrete and your gaudy plastic shop-fronts, behind the stench of fates and minds, their limits, spite and hate—can you hear the haunting wail of her unfair perfection, huge and dark and female in the lower sky? Always seeing where you're at, but not inclined to save you; apt to raise you up but leave you hanging; heavy and oppressive, but alluring as a drug. She's Alaia—but she's gone, just an instant before you see the form of her. She draws you on in anguish that you'll always fall short of her, and yes, you always will … but then again she might just be lying when she says that, or lying now in saying this. Reach for her (she'll make this very difficult), and some of you she'll break in two and some she will caress, while seeming to imply there's a reason for these differences—and yet she may be lying by implying so. Reach for her, she'll kiss you, lick your ear or make you kill yourself. Reach for her, she'll undulate a tentacle of shivers through your flesh or lick your eyeballs. She'll light you up with wine, or burn your mouth away with acid, making certain that these outcomes are not in your control. When the sun blasts fire on the globe's other side, you may hear her. Catch her late tonight, behind the siren of the train in the distance, when you half-wake: the train roars along the blasted viaduct, screaming, and drowns out a screech from an arch underneath it as the siren blares on for a whole long minute, stops a moment, then returns for another blaring minute ... and you'll arch through her colonnades and spin your hula-hoops along her yellow-twilit viaducts among your sweaty sheets, every one of you. But when at last you see her, then she's gone! Did you ever feel led-on? D'you think she lies? Listen hard.

Her notes grow in violence—huge hammers smashing down on every beat, as if to kill it, and slamming in to crush your heads and bodies. Whatever words you try to say, she melts them to a primal scream. You bounce up cliffs on the surge of her sound, while the hammers swing relentless through the blood-spattered stadium; and up above the carnage, the angles and the curves of my face float serene...

At last you can face your mystery friend upon the fields, and you find, too late for rescue, that this friend is her too. Beyond the horizon, gun-beats billow, dry as thunder and as heavy as the Pyramids—a grand weight of cosmic sound that gives the planets gooseflesh. Then she leaves you dead and steps away through the fields, across the plain, staining the horizon with a spired plume of emerald smoke and icy flowers of mist. She slopes away a sudden hundred miles to a cavern where a different moon sets, pale and vast above a tiny crash of waves, and majestically she vanishes; and there we end.

35 CHEAP CHAMPAGNE AT EVELYN'S

"Cut," says a quiet voice.

Dark, quiet. Where is this? A fluorescent light flickers on. Ahead are three cameras; over there, a bank of faders. The studio. *Again a squint at great events, seen from a narrow room...*

Rik pops up from behind the three cameras. Evelyn gives a joyful whoop, standing up from behind my chair. Alaia comes out from the sound booth and the two of us high-five.

I find myself in rather a dreamlike state as the four of us leave the studio. "OK, you guys, we got a fridge-ful of cheap champagne upstairs," says Evelyn, "so let's go drink it."

Well, if she puts it like that, how can we refuse? So down the long corridor we bubble, past a screening room, up the servants' staircase and into her and Rik's apartment.

My dreamlike state transmutes very easily into the effects of the promised cheap champagne, and then further into great mirth when Evelyn, peering at me from close up, gives me neither warning nor reason before sticking the very end of her tongue unmistakably into one of her nostrils.

"That shouldn't be allowed!" I say, recovering the power of speech from the clutches of my laughter.

"A useful skill, that one, I can assure you," laughs Rik.

Then I realise something else that's funny, as well as thought-provoking: "Hey Evelyn," I say through my subsiding giggles, "when you watch that footage of Angel we recorded, you'll see yourself standing on the strip with him, wearing that *exact* same magenta skirt you're wearing now! Isn't that interesting, that it lost nothing in translation through his memory? I bet that skirt paid for itself—" and I grind to a halt, remembering that Alaia is perched on the back of an armchair nearby, listening most curiously. *Oh shit!* my face broadcasts without speaking, and I see her take this in too, before a frown of fascination and bewilderment spreads across her features.

An instant of guilt flickers between Evelyn and me.

Well, Alaia won't be letting that one go. No, she'll sink her teeth into it and chew away at it until it's dead.

Oops.

"OK, Alaia—come with me, honey," says Evelyn, taking charge. "I need to talk to you alone. Alaia and I are going down the corridor to the little girls' room," she tells me.

I glance towards the door of the kitchen, where Rik is making drinks. "If Rik comes back in and asks for you, what shall I say?" I whisper.

She cracks up with laughter. "Jaymi you doofus, Rik's *in* this with us! He was our cameraman this afternoon, remember? So please tell him Alaia and I have gone to sniff coke... No, seriously now, the reason I'm taking Alaia out isn't because of him—it's because we're just about to have other guests who can't hear any of this, OK?" She exits the room, pulling along an increasingly mystified Alaia who turns upon me a flash of dark interrogation.

Oh dear. There goes the confidentiality of our agreement with Jason, already. That didn't take me long. I'm going to get a grilling from Alaia, once we've left this gathering. Still, at least now Evelyn and Rik and I shan't have to walk on eggshells around her to preserve her ignorance.

I hear Rik's phone ring in the kitchen. After a moment he emerges into this room, saying "Guests," and leaves the apartment. For a minute I sit alone, then I brighten as I hear that the voice of Rik is accompanied by those of Shigem and Kim. Kim follows Rik into the kitchen to deposit the bottle they've brought, while Shigem and I hug in a quick greeting without words, giving me an extreme close-up of the topmost squirls of his "Virginity" tattoo, the rest being covered by his mauve T-shirt.

Soon Kim emerges from the kitchen with Rik, comes up and shakes my hand. "Evelyn lent me a copy of *Sound & Vision* this morning," he says. "It was incredible. It swept me away, it was wonderful. It was like a drug—you two were like a beautiful drug. The effect reminded me of when I used to put the headphones on every night before I went to sleep, and lit a joint and listened to music that I absolutely adored, really loud, and just went somewhere else, somewhere beautiful—but you two achieved that without any joint."

"Thank you, Kim," I say. "Thank you very much." Watching him speak so straightforwardly, I realise that what he just said was something I've wanted to hear all my life. It's obvious, I suppose, at least with hindsight, but I'd never identified the desire as such. And now it's been identified, I observe that it survives in me for only a few seconds more before I register its fulfilment and consequent demise. So that's what it feels like to have a lifelong wish granted! Most such wishes, once identified, survive rather longer than the may-fly life-span granted that one.

"What exactly were you both *doing* in the studio?" asks Kim. "I couldn't quite work out how it must have been set up."

"I'll tell you," I say. And I do.

36 KIM'S DEAD SUBURBIA

Nearly an hour later, long after Evelyn has brought Alaia back into the room, I hear a tipsy Shigem say to Kim, "Let's get drunk on cheap champagne—it's wisdom, you know," and he starts opening another bottle. "Shit, I've broken a nail." He examines the damage, finishes the bottle-opening, pulls a thin silver bangle off his wrist and aims it successfully onto the neck of the bottle from quite a distance. "Gotcha," he tells it, "now you're dressed for the occasion. Anyway," he continues, refilling their drinks and presumably continuing a conversation they were having a minute ago, "yes, I'd say there is a certain sadness in your eyes."

Kim nods. "I can see it in the mirror."

"I wondered if you could."

"I'm happy with it, though. It seems like an intelligent reaction to the world, wouldn't you say?"

"Do bears shit in the woods?"

"Plus it's mine. Riches should be got from it."

"As they are," says Shigem.

"I'll drink to that." Watching them clink glasses, I tune in to Kim's own memories of his childhood … and I see you aged seven, by the sea, which was your friend in its impersonal enormity. Although so many eyes had looked upon it, yet to no pair of eyes had it cared to explain itself: you liked that.

I see you aged ten, growing up amid a stretch of tame suburbs on the edge of Southport. (So the English accent I first heard in Paradise is identified.) You walked in the night past quiet suburban houses, where the window options numbered five in total: a few uncurtained windows blazed openly with gaudy life; other ones afforded only glimpses of this, through twee net curtains or between solid curtains; a third kind showed solid curtains pulled across, lit around the sides; a fourth, solid curtains too, but unlit round the edges; and the fifth kind, darkened rooms with curtains wide open. Such were the permutations, and onto any one of these, bluish television flickers might be added. Occasionally, from blocks away, a shout would come, or the slamming of a door, then an engine and a dog's bark, then nothing but the humming of the white street-lights. Every window stood removed, beyond an empty garden; but nowhere was a window that enticed you anyway. No one on your street was the same age as you, at all; but even if they had been, you'd probably not have clicked with them. Those of your age whom you knew from school, who lived elsewhere: you didn't truly want to be with those either. You didn't quite connect with them in any solid way—well sort of, one or two. But no one whom you knew had a life that *attracted* you. Throughout those years you wanted many things, but only some of these could you have named, if you'd tried. Much time would be needed, so it seemed, and much boredom, till you found individuals who excited you. For years until you found them, though, suburbia would yawn at you, with solitude and waiting games and emptiness and comfort, while at night your feet stepped through a thousand white pools of light, the dogs barked a block away and bluish flickers played around the curtains in the windows.

I see you aged twelve, first realising the word gay applied to you, and feeling simple pleasure that the attraction you'd felt since age six, though seemingly natural, in fact belonged to something as alternative and interesting as this.

Next, there you sat upon the carpet, aged sixteen, smoking hash with the others. All were under threat from one another; yet fun was had, with music and videos, here in the living room of someone's absent parents. You were cooler, in many ways, than anybody else here, and yet in other ways you lagged behind in this respect. Often you were unsure which score applied. For you there were stabs of tension, sudden mirth, and even bits of friendship—but always at the headache-making price of fitting in and guessing how not to veer beyond "unusual" into "wrong". How little of yourself could you have shared with the others here. How different you felt—and how glad you were that you had not been any one of them. Your sexuality was merely one part of this, for there was so much more, too, that would have been alien to most of them, if you had just been your natural self and spoken your intelligent mind. So of course you tended not to speak. How exhausting and how limiting they were, with their mediocre cluelessness that pushed you into such quietness, then. What a waste of time. (No, not all of them—just most.) Drunk or stoned, you and they went through the kitchen to the back garden terrace, each of you making jaggedly politicised tracks among the others, trapped tiringly together; while you, saying nothing, just drank in the clean, cool, clear, black, non-human sky like a draught of freshest water.

I glimpse you not long after, on that dim bus at night with the others through the countryside in France, your reflection in the window and the same music playing at the front again and again, and the furtive talk of smuggling fire-crackers through the border...

I see you in that nightclub in the suburbs, on that nameless faceless shuttered shopping street, just one time, where "Suburbia" was playing. A fight between emotionally retarded yobs began, at which you smiled to see them both really damaging each other, drawing blood and breaking bones and both deserving every stab of pain and much more besides. Then you left the club, caught a bus and gazed out through the window at the terraced houses' sad sitting rooms and sad bedrooms, glimpsed behind squalid curtains.

Somewhere the *electric* stuff was waiting for you—wanted by you—hunted by you, Kim! But it wasn't quite *here* yet. Never quite *here* yet. Not ready *yet*, Kim. Please wait and want and hunt for very much longer, Kim. Please wait for boring years of stupid, putrid school, Kim...

But while you wait, what fun it was, back there in the club, to see those macho morons hurt and stab and slash each other's hateful backward faces, and if only they had died of it!

37 FLASH OF WEASEL EYES THROUGH THE KEYHOLE

I surface from Kim, impressed at finding such resonant depths where I had wrongly expected something a little more bovine. I must have been extrapolating from his placid surface. I see Shigem is now wandering away to join Rik, Evelyn and Alaia across the room, where Rik is working spontaneous electronic magic: from different angles, two small camcorders point at a tipsy Evelyn sitting cross-legged in front of a TV screen that is being fed in split-screen mode by the camcorders themselves, resulting in two infinite regresses of her half-profile, now being further tweaked by various exotic pre-set effects from the camcorders.

"Evelyn, are you satirising my studio set-up?" I call.

"No, Jaymi, you're still being supremely ignored. Hey, Shigem honey," she says as he approaches her, "you coming to join me on TV?" Shigem shakes his head with a passion. "OK, well what about Alaia? Give us a wail now, girl!"

"We don't have sound-proofing in here," Rik reminds her.

"Well she can just sing quietly, then," says Evelyn.

"What shall I sing?"

"I don't know, something cool like you'd sing for Jaymi on screen—only it's *me* instead!"

"In that case, how about 'Rudolf the Red-nosed Reindeer'?" suggests Rik, and Evelyn throws a pillow at him.

"Oh, Jaymi," says Kim beside me on the sofa. "I've been meaning to tell you, I saw something weird at Pippa's."

"Really? What?"

He pauses. "I was going down that hallway ... and there was this little door in the wall. Not short, but narrow. There was a faint light coming through the hinge, though you couldn't see through. There was a big keyhole in the door, and I felt a really strong urge to look through. So I bent down and peered in, and I nearly screamed, because inside was some kind of toilet cubicle, and it was just dimly lit, but there was a person sitting there, naked in a wheelchair, right close in front of me, staring at me with these weaselly eyes, level with the keyhole... You remember when Lucan's gang was across the street from us?" I nod. "You know which one Angel is?" I nod again. "Well, this figure looked just like an identical twin of Angel. I didn't know what to do. I thought, he must be able to see me out here, he's so close to me—but his eyes weren't showing any signs of seeing me. Then I remembered it was really dark out here in the hallway, and light in the cubicle, so of course he wouldn't be able to see me. I also wondered if this person was unconscious, or in a trance, or maybe some kind of vegetable who wouldn't be able to see me even if the light were on my face. Or maybe he'd be able to see me, but he wouldn't be able to look like he was seeing me, because he was paralysed or something. I remembered where the hallway light-switch was, from seeing Pippa turn it off earlier, so I crept along the wall looking for it. And as I went along, I noticed there were no squeaky floorboards and I know I always move quietly, so I thought that with no light and no sound, maybe that figure still doesn't know I'm here? Then I found the light-switch and flicked it on and crept back to the door and started bending down again—but I stopped dead when I was halfway down to the keyhole, because right there in front of my face, on the door handle, was this small smear of stickiness… It looked like it was congealed blood, or something like that, I couldn't tell. I jumped back, feeling freaked-out, then I just flicked the light-switch back off and ran up the hallway and back into the sitting room and joined all you guys again."

"Wow… Who the fuck *was* it?"

He shakes his head and gives a shudder.

"How well d'you know Angel?" I ask. "Could he have a twin?"

"I've never spoken to him. I've only been here a month. Shigem says he hangs out at Downstairs, but we never go there. Last night on the street was the closest I've ever come to him. I told Shigem about it on the way home from Pippa's, and I should have waited till this morning instead, because it totally creeped him out and gave him nightmares that kept waking us up—he was thrashing around the bed. He scares so easily. But no, he's never said Angel has a twin. Not that that means much, because they've seen each other around town and met a few times, but they've never associated and they don't know each other much. Shigem knows a lot more about Lucan, though he wishes he didn't, because Lucan's always teased him and scared the shit out of him."

"Action," calls Rik, and I turn to see that as the camcorders start to roll, Evelyn slowly crosses her eyes and does her trademark insertion of tongue-tip into nostril, as I saw her do earlier, while Alaia begins a rendition of "Rudolf the Red-nosed Reindeer".

I *knew* they were satirising me!

38 KIM'S AMBER DAYS

The alcohol is having a fine effect on the gathering, and soon Shigem launches into an anecdote that I can tell will be a long one. I do lend half an ear to it, as it certainly fits the mood; but the greater part of me is inconspicuously finishing off my tune-in to Kim, now that his childhood has piqued my curiosity ... and I see you, Kim, there in your first college room, which you loved for being yours alone, at half-past-eleven in the morning, at your window with a coffee. Underneath a still, damp, stone-washed sky was a lane, little-ridden, lightly mossed, leading to the stark brown bulk of the Library. Along the lane's far edge, a blond boy wandered past—quite pretty, dressed in a black coat and black-tie, returning home from some night out. Blue smoke rose as he took a languid draw from his cigarette, his hair hanging forward in a pale curved spray. And you sipped from your coffee mug, and idly watched him down the lane and vanish round the corner.

The hazy amber days you lived there were a gorgeous alcoholic social haze of serious fun. You wasted not an instant of those years, and nothing can alter that. They're sealed—yours—and perfect.

Reclining on the warm grass beside the river late one night, you heard sweet thin notes approaching through the clear air. A girl alone in a small canoe floated from the shadows of the trees to your right, drifted past and down the river to your left, around a stone corner, underneath the Bridge of Sighs, and disappeared. For minutes more, her piping trailed behind her, faded, and vanished.

From the window of your last room, you looked across the front court: through fountain spray and through the arch, to tiny figures ambling in the haze along the distant road; then coming back, nearer figures by the river, framed in the arch; then back nearer still, upon the lawn just beyond the arch; then here in this front court and down beneath your window. That soundtrack was playing, and now it reached the infinitely creepy-sweet "Mysteries of Love". And through your leaded window, all those distant background figures, standing still or gesturing in talk or crawling antlike across the frame, were sealed in a different world, photographed and laminated here in your memory.

Then London, in a strange room, with telephone numbers. I see you pushing on, through a spitting London rain, past the black-painted rust-spotted wet metal railings enclosing the grass in a lonely residential square. Pushing along in the rain to a boy you loved or thought you did, who loved you back or thought he did, you were edgy with uncertainty, the promise of togetherness, and imminent aloneness. *'Cos you know as well as I do I can never think of anyone but you*, went the song. Alone in buses and trains, reflecting, questing, staring at the distance, always seeking something, someone, somewhere else perhaps... You heard the silence beat behind the bustle and the rain: beating on and on, while you rushed through the rain to some suburban street you'd never seen before (and yet would see a few more times, a few), and the system of the city worked around you, oblivious. Sure, you'll be all right, you thought—but where was the outside lightning, to answer yours that always seemed to flash alone without direct reply? And your symphony revolved within you, underneath the plane trees and past the wet railings, as the rain pattered on. Then, by and by, Kim: your face in the rain ... last chance on the stairway ... alone in the social whirl ... I'll never see your eyes again ... *dance away...*

Once you saw, waiting on the platform of a station, a tall platinum-blond spiky-haired boy in sunlight—striking, thin and sexy in a long-sleeved black-and-white-striped T-shirt, and he settled right then into your lifelong memory, just before your train pulled away from him forever.

A last small residential square in the afternoon. Soft weather, damp air. You accessed the square itself, found a hidden wooden bench, and sat. The odd bus passed, beyond the railings. A breeze blew the wet black branches of the trees, and their few remaining brown leaves spiralled down around you onto dripping shrubs. A grey squirrel hopped among the leaves on the lawn, as it nibbled at an acorn. It saw you, stopped nibbling for a second, then nibbled on. You held each other's gaze.

39 YOUR PAINTED FACE ALIVE AND SMILING

I join in a small round of appreciative applause for Shigem, who has just finished his extended anecdote. A part of me did continue to attend to him throughout my tune-in to Kim, and did enjoy what he was saying: it's just that this part of me seems not to have included much of my memorising faculties, as I can now recall little of what he said, whereas I do recall most of what I just saw in Kim.

"You know, I still can't get over how strange it is," says Alaia, "to see this apartment, plus that whole high-end studio, tucked away in this old building. From outside it looks like such a ruin."

"Isn't it fun?" says Evelyn. "It was Jason's idea. He wanted somewhere we could do low-profile recordings, where people wouldn't think to hang round outside waiting to catch a sight of some big-name talent going in or out. And it worked—a lot of people still don't know we're here."

"That was all, while he was planning it," says Rik. "But when we started renovating, it became a wacky mission for him to build the least likely-looking high-end facility on the market. When we got to kitting it out, he told me every delivery truck had to have 'demolition' painted on the side of it, in a plausible way, so everyone would think we were just clearing out old shit, not bringing new shit in. The trucks had to back right up against the building, so all the kit could be slid inside without anyone outside seeing it."

"Did this really fool everyone?" asks Alaia. "There must have been a lot of activity that couldn't be hidden. Like connecting this place to the cable networks, or whatever it's connected to. Plus renovation noise."

"All those things were carefully planned to be super-quick," says Rik. "Some people registered that something was moving in here, but they probably thought it was just some obscure little office looking for a dirt-cheap rent. To this day, nobody in town here knows it's as high-end as anything in New York."

"Quite a few people in town know by now that it's some kind of recording studio," says Evelyn, "but they're pretty hazy about it, 'cos there's no sign saying 'GN'—just those few old letters standing on the roof, from when this was a grand hotel."

"Yeah," I chip in. "With just those left up there, if I hadn't already known we were coming to somewhere called the Metropolitan, I'd have assumed this clapped-out old hulk was just the Metropol."

"There used to be a modern little car-port tacked onto the front of the big old entrance porch with the columns," says Rik. "And it had plastic lettering around the top of it, which did still say 'Metropolitan Hotel' for years after the place became a ruin. But it was so tacked-on and tacky, that although Jason wanted the whole place to remain a general ruin on the outside, he did have the car-port taken off."

Seeing Evelyn get up and head across the room, I rise and wander after her. Once we're alone in the kitchen, I murmur "I'm sorry I gave the game away to Alaia earlier, I am such a dipstick—"

"Yeah, nice work," she replies, giving me a hug. "You'd make a great undercover agent." She takes a pack of beer cans from the fridge. "Will Alaia be discreet? My job's on the line here."

"Oh yes," I reply, tuning in while I speak … and they've known you here for years, Evelyn, circulating through the streets, adding to the summer with your laugh. What fun it was, to lose control on a Friday night or a Saturday night, or both! What a rush to trip on acid, lying on the grass among the ducks on the island by the bridge on Sunset Lake with friends, after you saw that band play at the Saint over on Main Street. What better use of dollars than to drink them in a bar or on the beach beneath the summer stars, as someone played drums in the distance? All those words and laughs and fights and flashes of metal and cash and alcohol have flown away, and that whole scene is mostly gone; but how enriched you were by it, and how you returned the favour. They all saw you climbing into cruising cars at midnight, and sniffing coke in alleyways and nightclub toilets, your painted face alive and smiling, high from the scent of the gasoline and fuel oil spilled on the pavement where your high heels strutted. Outside the deli by the hole in the wall you would stand with your arms folded, leaning on the pay-phone, thinking of the coins and the bills in the pocket of your tight blue jeans, as you cocked an ear to some wild tale that the glamorous proto-anorexic Angel was telling you, before he found Lucan: in your eyes, as you heard him, were fun, compassion, sparkle and humanity. At Kingsley and Second was the corner where you sold yourselves, surrounded by the bars and clubs and empty lots and run-down homes and crumbling hotels. What a shit job, but you both made the best of it.

You'd never known another place to live than Asbury Park; you were used to it and loved it with a rough love, as home. Back then, it was only the marginal who moved here; most people bypassed this bombsite-by-the-sea full of people who would stay and die. Slowly since then, however, different kinds of people have been moving in, unexpected people. Jason came, for instance; and though he went away again, he left behind the sound-stage and hired you to drive for it.

And so you left the street and stayed off it, but you're independent always. You move in your space with the beauty of a swagger, like an everyday assassin. To the drum-beat inside you, you shake your hips, flick your long black hair through the air, and run with no gang. It seems you hang with everyone, and yet you are a lone wolf, a sunny band of one. Good god, you're beautiful.

"Beer?" she offers me.

"No thanks. You know, I never could be doing with beer."

"Really? What else is there to drink? Aside from bourbon."

"What else? There's a whole range of effete and picturesque cocktails for every occasion."

She creases up at this. "You're cuckoo!"

"Evelyn, I distinctly saw you drinking champagne earlier tonight."

"I was just slumming it, for you. I'm having a Bud, thanks." And she grabs a can, rips the top off and takes a long swig.

"But there's just so *much* of it," I reason, "compared with the other options. Where d'you put it all?"

She swallows, looking sunnily up at me, and I can see the beer fizz popping behind her eyes. "You piss it out, what d'you think?" she blinks.

"I mean where d'you put it before you piss it out?"

She lifts up her bright yellow T-shirt, slaps her curvaceous tan stomach and cackles raucously at me, "Right here, honey!"

40 ALAIA GIVES ME A GRILLING

The grilling I was expecting to receive later and elsewhere from Alaia occurs here and now instead, when she and I are dragged into a spare bedroom by Evelyn, who evidently reckons this will be the place to provide us with adequate time undisturbed. I suspect Evelyn is right in this, because when she led the two of us out of the sitting room, Rik and Shigem were just embarking on a new and complex set-up of camcorders, clip-lights and television, this time with Kim in the hot-seat, in search of newly exotic flavours of infinite video feedback. Not that there's anything for us three to keep secret from Rik—but we can't, of course, have Kim or Shigem overhearing any discussion about my spying into people.

In addition to this being a spare bedroom, one end of the room has been taken over by Evelyn as a working area of her own. A Friesian-cow design covers a desk-chair in front of a messy desk, amongst whose fertile clutter I spot a pink MP3-player hooked up to a pair of good speakers flanking a framed photo of that Adewale guy as Adebisi in *Oz*, with the mark of a lipsticked kiss on its glass. (How *just* adorable.) Alaia stands in the middle of the space, I sit on the cow chair facing the middle of the room and Evelyn reclines on the bed.

Now that Alaia knows about my imagination-cloning deal, from Evelyn's private explanation to her earlier, she disapproves of it on aesthetic grounds and she lets me know it. "Jaymi: the point of *Sound & Vision* was to enrich the world and remind people of what's fine and most valuable in themselves, and here you are making a tacky corporate cartoon."

"Well," I squirm, "not everything that we put out, as a species, is going to be high art, you know."

"No, but you know damn well that this corporate cartoon thing's going to be designed to appeal to the lowest common denominator, like some toxic daily newspaper or some horrible piece of shit on TV. Whatever the details of it, its flavour's going to be exactly like a tabloid, obviously—in other words, idiocy and ugliness. It'll appeal to the most mediocre impulses in every one of the tens of millions who see it; and by engaging with those impulses, it'll strengthen and perpetuate them, without question. You know it will. That's *real damage*, right there—real damage that Jason's client company is doing, and I know you can see that. Whenever a powerful company pulls that same old weary poisonous shit, it's unforgivable, *every single time it happens*. Are you disgusted? I am! It lets every last one of us down, as a species." She folds her arms and glares at me.

None of that surprised me at all, but I can tell Evelyn wasn't expecting it. "Alaia ... this sheep thing'll be pretty dumb, sure," she says. "But where's the harm in it?"

Alaia smiles at her, with affection but a hint of sadness somewhere, deciding what to reply. At last she says: "Look, I just find the debased things in our cultural output hideously ugly. I believe they've cheapened and saddened and slowed down the achievement and potential of the human race as a whole. And there's a small but significant part of me that's remained in a state of permanent, low-level shock, throughout my life, that at least a large minority of people don't see and feel the same."

Now it's Evelyn's turn to decide what to reply. "I understand," she says. "But it's just a stupid cartoon. And if it wasn't going to be this stupid cartoon, then it would be some other stupid cartoon instead. That's just how things are, so what's the big deal?"

"You're right, that's how things are—and that's the problem. For me that's a very big deal, because I'd like us to evolve from that ... and Evelyn, *we could evolve*."

Evelyn gives her a look both admiring and sceptical. "Then we'd better hope for some good luck, 'cos I know what people are like."

"Yes, but people can improve. And I'll do what I can in that direction. Talking of which," she turns to me, "this secret deal with Jason basically adds up to snooping on people. And stealing intellectual property from them. You know that, don't you, Jaymi?"

"You're right," I say, "but I was out-manoeuvred. I think that if I hadn't agreed to do this, Jason really would have sabotaged *Sound & Vision*. Would you have been prepared to sacrifice that, just to avoid a bit of sullying and snooping and stealing?... Anyway," and here I feel a first flicker of mirth, "what's a bit of sullying and snooping and stealing, between friends?" and I reach forward to slap Evelyn on the thigh, at which she smirks. "—Alaia, don't answer that. No but seriously, are you telling me you'd have sacrificed the chance to perform in the broadcast?"

Alaia raises her eyebrows and draws her breath in, ready for a considered moral verdict.

"Mind your nose on the ceiling, honey!" chirps Evelyn.

Alaia emits a fierce equine flash of a look at her. "I shall have to think about it," she concludes.

Evelyn croaks out a laugh as dirty as a drain. "You won't think long, let me tell you! Come on, girl, you gonna get all high-maintenance on us? Jesus, cut us some slack here! This is how life works—and life's too short to try and change life. At least mine is."

Alaia responds with dignity: "Look, I just don't feel comfortable parading four other people's private imaginations, memories and fantasies in front of millions of people, without those four individuals' permission."

"You're right again, of course," I say. "But I don't believe anyone will recognise those elements or trace them to their owners, because the company, whoever it is, is going to mix our four together, then out of that mixture they'll just grab what they want and cook up a single imagination. Then they'll bury that with all kinds of other ingredients that'll probably also help conceal our targets: it'll be integrated with some basic logic, for example, plus no doubt some goofy appearance and a really annoying, bleating, baa-ing voice…"

"Perhaps they'll call it Baaasil!" whoops Evelyn and cracks up, rolling around on the bed and thumping it with her fists.

Alaia laughs, despite herself, then turns to me: "Well, you're sounding quite the corporate sheep yourself there. Perhaps they should just program you as this character?"

I look at her dryly. "You know, it's not too late for me to put you into the sheep. What d'you think, Evelyn, shall we change our list of targets?"

Alaia dives her hand down and pokes me in the stomach.

"Plus," I add, "we didn't exactly pick the kind of targets Jason said we should pick, did we? I mean, Kim and Shigem are sane, but Jason wanted stuff that wouldn't frighten Middle America—the place that's frightened of everything and would certainly be frightened of those two. Plus we've got a terminal depressive and a gangster's masochistic moll mixed in there too. So they may not even be able to use what we give them. I guess we just slipped up with our choices," and I glance at Evelyn.

Alaia stands in thought a moment, then addresses Evelyn. "So ... hold on. Remember when I apologised to you in the van, after we left Downstairs, because Jaymi and I weren't doing a very good job of staying low-profile? You told me to lighten up, and said what were rules for, except to be broken."

Evelyn shrugs. "That's my philosophy, yeah."

"Sure, but what I'm getting at is: if you knew about Jason's cloak-and-dagger spying operation, then you knew Jason couldn't really want us to stay buried in the Metropolitan. You must have known that those instructions you gave us never to show our faces outside were just bullshit, because Jaymi needed to find targets. That's why you dragged us to Paradise and Pippa's."

She's sharp.

Evelyn concedes. "OK, yeah yeah yeah. But Alaia, what could I do? You didn't know this then and I wasn't allowed to tell you."

"And *you*," Alaia turns to me. "When you and I went out into town after the broadcast, with all that scampering and giggling about our making an escape...? It wasn't spontaneous at all for you, was it? You were levering us both outside all along, just to look for poor innocent creatures to spy into—"

"Ain't nobody innocent around here!" snorts Evelyn.

"That is *not* true," I say.

"It sure is," says Evelyn.

"No, I mean it's not true about the scampering and giggling being fake," I say, stung by this. "I wasn't thinking about target-hunting at all, I was just elated after our broadcast. I promise you, Alaia: *my scampering and giggling were NOT FAKE...*"

They stare at me, taking in my passion. Then Evelyn bursts out laughing. After a few seconds Alaia follows suit, then after another few seconds so do I. I sink back onto the chair and Alaia sits down on the edge of the bed, where Evelyn is now lying back, bubbling with mirth.

"Well, I'm glad this all came out," grins Alaia. She looks at Evelyn. "And all because you wore that whorish magenta skirt."

"When you see that skirt in Angel's footage," I remark, "I think you'll agree his memory had stored it up as being even shorter than it is, by the way. Or have you had it lengthened since then?"

When we have recovered our composure, Evelyn sits up on the bed. "Look, the bottom line is, it's a done deal. We're in too deep, there's no getting out of it."

"We're in too deep, no doubt about it," I reply.

"So hey—let's just go back to the others." She gets up off the bed, crosses the room, opens the bedroom door and heads back up the hallway.

I get up from my Friesian chair. "We're steeped in sin," I murmur to Alaia as I pass her in the bedroom doorway.

She narrows her eyes and compresses her lips without speaking, and gives me *the look*.

"By the way," I tell her, "last night when all of us were across the street from Lucan's crew, you and Evelyn were busy with idle chit-chat but I was doing something useful: I was hypnotising Angel, in silence, into believing he's known and loved you and me for half his life." *The look* dissolves, in mid-smoulder. "Oh yes. No messing around, I took him right back to that cabaret bar where he first heard you singing through my eyes, as it were—you remember it—where he first became sucked into our magic, knowing it would go down in history. We have a real devoted fan there now."

"Jaymi, that's outrageous. You can't go round doing that to people, it's not fair!" she says, then joins me in cracking up with laughter again.

"But don't you just think he'll make such an *adorable* fan?" I ask. "Hmm. Anyone else you'd like to see as a fan?"

"Don't!" she says. "Just don't."

The hot-seat on the sitting room floor in front of the TV is no longer occupied by Kim but now by Rik, with Shigem pointing the camcorders at him. "Where have you lot been?" asks Rik, probably guessing what we'll have been talking about but feigning ignorance.

"Shooting up," says Evelyn. "I know you guys don't do it, so we didn't invite you."

After a drunkenly entertaining half-hour viewing trippy high-lights from various inventive experiments with infinitely regressing video images of Kim and himself, Rik goes off to bed, having to get up with efficiency tomorrow in order to process tonight's *Big Bang* recording and get ready for tomorrow evening's. I too take my leave, and Alaia, Shigem and Kim get up to follow suit.

41 IT'S ONLY A SHELL

I return to the quiet of my room and sprawl flat. My head still echoes with our conversation in the bedroom. It's funny, I came down here thinking I would be in charge of things, that this would be an adventure we'd control. After all, we'd rehearsed enough. Outside the specifics we've presented on camera, however, it's felt as if we've just been swept along. Well, we'd better hold on tight, then.

My alarm clock tells me it's a quarter to two, but I'm not sleepy yet. It occurs to me that the only kind of tune-in Jason mentioned in Times Square was the kind I should do in the company of whomever I'd be tuning in to; and so far this is the only kind I have done here. I recall, however, that if I already know who somebody is, then their live presence isn't necessary for me to be able to tune in to them. I first discovered this on Liberty Street when I located what I can only describe as Marc's "frequency" up in the GE Building, and then again when I tuned in to him through his office wall behind the yucca. Surely, then, I should be able to locate our targets' frequencies from right here? After all, in relation to these four I've now done much better than just reading a detailed profile on them, which was my sole source of knowledge about Marc before Liberty Street: I've not only met these four but even tuned in to all of them in person already. Let's try it, then, solely for the sake of Jason's thieving deal.

I close my eyes and hold aloft in my mind as vivid a picture as possible of Kim and Shigem, assembling this both from their physical presence here in the Metropolitan and from my tuning in to Shigem last night in Paradise and Kim tonight. I throw this picture out into the world and send my attention bounding after it like a dog in pursuit of a rubber ball. Straightaway I find my attention is hauled sideways towards the window and somewhat downwards too, to home in on where the pair of them are crossing Liberty Square, having left Rik's and Evelyn's not long after I did … just as Kim is saying, "Oh, I told Jaymi about the figure at Pippa's."

"I hope I don't have more nightmares about that tonight," says Shigem. "Those nightmares just went on and on. There was another part of them I forgot to tell you about. I kept wanting to look through those door hinges you mentioned—maybe because you said you couldn't see through them in real life—but someone kept telling me I was too trashy to look through them. Am I trashy? I don't think I'm as trashy as people probably think I am, but maybe I'm trashier than I think I am. You're not as trashy as me, I know that. How did you manage that? Maybe it's just part of me. When you grow up around brainless chatterboxes like my family, you have to fend off the trashiness—I could just feel waves of it coming at me throughout my childhood. My sister used to decorate her room to match her rabbit."

Leaving the square, they disengage hands, as a figure appears a block or two ahead. "You're as strong as anyone," says Kim, laughing. "I used to think you were a fragile fern, you know."

"Oh, some of me is pretty quailing and fern-like—you won't be entirely disappointed." The figure up ahead disappears into a house. "But the rest of me is about as subtle as a truck, it's true. I'm glad you're perceptive and not just a male bimbo."

"Have you been with many bimbi?"

Shigem nods. "Usually not the brightest bulbs in the box." He feels his right ear: "Oh, I've lost my ear-ring. It's a disaster. I wonder if it's at Evelyn's or on the street?"

"Shall we walk back and look for it on the ground?"

"No, it was just a cheap one." They walk on a bit in silence. "… But I don't think it was trashy. It was just a simple silver hoop. Well, silver-plated."

Turning around while they walk, Kim stares back towards the ocean, at the carcass-building, which stands open to the night between its bare concrete columns. "I wonder how long that building's going to stay there as only a shell," he says.

Shigem pretends to break down in tears. "*It's only a shell!*" he wails.

42 THE LAST MUSIC KIM HEARD
BEFORE SHIGEM

As Kim stares at him in amusement at this effusion, I hurl myself into a freeze-frame of Kim's mirth-squinting eyes ... and I see that for the last two years, Kim, just before you slept, you'd recline most nights with a drink and a joint, to hear that music at top volume through your headphones. Mixed with tobacco, the hash might burn unevenly, one side a bit faster than the other, whereupon a dab of spit on the runaway red side would help even things out. Ahead of you would be the whole album, whichever one it was, with some tracks to be repeated along the way—a prospect of pure pleasure. Then often when this pleasure came, it turned into ecstasy (it's not too strong a word) and you'd be off, deep within the Wild of it, mating with it effortlessly. You could have lived in this music, if that were possible. It did everything you required at just the right moment, though always fresh. It constituted a fantasy play land of joy and sadness, constructed like a great delirious climbing frame from which it was impossible to fall and hurt yourself, or an enchanted factory or city of tunnels and halls, lights and colour, movement and exhilaration, all harmoniously interlocking, from its big-booming architectural shell to the highest-pitched aerial or finial, rich and self-generating... In some sense you wanted to be the music. How much easier and simpler life would then be—in comparison with the messy-sludgy-OK thing it was in reality. What exquisite sound and vision you would then be: what a permanent delirium! And although these nightly ecstasies of hash-enhanced music have had to stop since you met Shigem (for they do demand solitude, and anyway you both quit smoking when you flew here), nonetheless the rich watermarks of their magic will always remain in you.

Late in the course of one of the last such musical sessions, however, you spotted a new thing. High upon the façade of the multi-storeyed edifice of sound that you were inhabiting at that moment was a small traditional balcony with balusters, rather tight and sombre for this building's style—and suddenly you knew that this balcony signified a parting with this music. Not goodbye forever, because you would still be able to hear this music and would certainly do so sometimes, but a subtle and deep intimation of goodbye nonetheless, such as is elicited by the sight of a railway terminus from which you're about to leave a city or a continent you've called home, or by the ringing of a telephone heralding what you know will be the last conversation with somebody you've known well. You must move on, the balcony told you. This would be the last time you heard this music in this old way. No figure would emerge behind the balusters and wave goodbye to you, or even just stand there, for it wasn't a balcony made to be used: it was as functional as those tiny stone balconies under certain windows on high old city buildings where, out of forty-eight offices on a façade, only a couple have such windows and yet the occupiers of these two are probably not aware of their privilege, since their balcony is either just an ornamental detail almost flush with the external wall or at most a thin vertiginous dirty concrete space hardly wide enough for a chair, accessible only via a window-door the key to whose painted-over lock was used once ten years ago and now is lost... "Curtain. 30. Finis," said the balcony to you, and then said nothing more, while the music it was mounted on went ahead and played on and wound down at last and reached its natural and appointed end. Adieu, you replied; rest in peace.

And so the music ended. You took your headphones off and lay still. The clock upon your bedroom wall ticked, and you thought of how you tended just to watch and not say much—after all, you were shy, and there was usually less to say than people thought there was. You felt time passing, dripping, slipping, ticking—gone, and gone, and gone. You saw the days fade away and started wishing x and y and z had come, but knew you shouldn't think of things that might have been, and much time remained to you, ahead of you, as yet.

Indeed it did. For that night, by chance, was the night before you finally met the dose of spice and joy whom you'd sought so very long throughout those tame Southport suburbs and beside those London railings...

43 MALAYSIAN CHILLI PEPPERS

I propel myself up and out of the freeze-frame of Kim's eyes, which reanimate; he finishes his laugh of surprise and steps on down First Avenue.

The pair of them reach Shigem's block. "I can't imagine why I'm thinking of this, but there's a punishment in the Malaysian penal code," says Shigem, "which is to have a peeled chilli pepper inserted up your bottom. It's true. It's an old Malaysian custom. I can't remember what it's a punishment for, but I just know it would happen to me immediately if I ever went there. I'd just find myself committing that particular crime and getting caught. I'm glad my parents moved out of there and came here instead—it was a narrow escape."

"No chilli peppers, growing up here?" Kim asks, as they turn up Shigem's front path.

"It's not a part of state law here—probably just in the Deep South. I was different, growing up here, always. I was stared at everywhere and cauldrons of abuse were poured on me over the years, but I smashed my way through it all. There were fights in the street, too—and I fight like a girl in the rain, so don't get on my wrong side."

"I think I'll deliberately get on your wrong side now; I'm curious." They close the front door behind them and head up the dim creaky staircase, suspending the conversation until they are inside Shigem's room. "What kind of friends did you have?"

Shigem pours drinks. "Being seen around with me always took a bit of courage to do, but some people did it anyway, so I loved them just for that. I felt like an acrobat on the high wire sometimes. I felt like a freak, with general tragedy looming over my head. I assumed that sooner or later someone would want to kill me because I was me, or a house would collapse on me, or a flower-pot would fall off a roof and *pop!* I'd be gone—curtains, funeral, weeping into hankies at the grave, widow's weeds and all that. I felt 'tragic' for a while, I did. But it's funny, I wasn't really miserable enough—at least not as much as a tragic person should be. 'Cos I guess a tragic person should be really miserable. And I was only slightly miserable."

"Or maybe it was just a small tragedy. At least you enjoyed it."

"Oh, I had a front-row seat for it, and it was always picturesque. My hopes for love, of course, were just a-wisp on the breeze. People always said I was a complete slut, and for two or three years I guess I kind of was, despite being such a pizza-face, but that's over now, it's in the past. I'm not even attracted to that many guys, but people still whistle and say lewd things, like you saw last night and those other times. I could always talk, though, I'd put someone down whenever they really deserved it—though I couldn't do that with everyone here. But I only did it when they deserved it: I hate it when people are bitchy for no reason, it's so lame. I mean, how boring to be bitchy for no reason except your own insecurities. I'm mostly insecurities, as you'll have noticed, but I never inflict them on other people. I think you should start out by respecting someone, don't you?"

"They often don't turn out to deserve it, but yes."

"I always start by giving someone the benefit of the doubt. Because I love people, generally. I don't know why, but I do. It's just individuals I can't stand."

"Funny, it's the other way round for me, I love certain individuals but I don't like the mass of people."

"Oh my god—another great subject to disagree about. You wouldn't think we'd known each other for a whole three months already. Aren't we meant to be drying up with the topics by now?"

"We could always pretend to. Shall we sit here morosely for a while?" Kim yawns. "Sorry, but I need to sleep."

"You're too pretty to be sorry."

"So are you," says Kim, kissing him.

"So you say. Well, at least I'll confess to having a pair of sensual, pouty and very kissable lips." He giggles: "Evelyn was impersonating my lips on camera tonight. She was so funny."

Thinking back, Kim surmises that at the time of these hi-jinks he must have been busy telling me about the mysterious figure at Pippa's.

"She is such good vibes," continues Shigem. "I was once at a kind of cocktail-party that was really stiff, everyone standing around in fifth position, but then she arrived and the whole thing just took off. I'm not so into cocktail-parties—give me a nightclub and I'm happiest."

Kim laughs. "That reminds me: a friend of mine had a dance teacher who used to make every student come to every class with a 50p coin. To start the class he'd always stand, quite naturally, in something like fifth position. Then he'd clap his hands, saying 'Girls—places!' and they would each have to clench their 50p coin between their butt-cheeks and keep clenching it while they did bar exercises, so they had a financial interest in maintaining their buttock-clench, as well as an artistic interest. If anyone's 50p fell out, as it often did, this teacher would pick it up and keep it, saying 'Thank you!' Up and down the whole class he'd go, pocketing 50p coins: 'Thank you!... Thank you!... Thank you!...'"

They climb into bed and turn the light out. "I don't believe that!" laughs Shigem, squirming his back into a comfortable position against Kim's chest.

"No, it's true, I swear…"

44 THE FIVE TIMES I HYPNOTISED SOMEONE

I slip away and find myself back in the Metropolitan, sprawled on my bed. My first reaction to this tune-in is a feeling of enormous affection for the two of them. In addition I decide that in future I shall just tune in to one person at a time, as I was doing there when I was delving into Kim's memory of his music-listening: this single kind of tune-in feels almost as if I'm talking with the person, and is evidently a lot richer and subtler than the kind of shared tune-in I was doing for Kim's and Shigem's mutual experience of home and of the rest of their walk either side of Kim's music memory. What's seen in a shared tune-in is no less clearly seen, as far as it goes, but it would appear that only now and then does it penetrate into either one of its subjects, tending to hover instead more superficially between them. For instance, the only time my shared tune-in entered Kim's own thoughts was when he realised he'd missed Evelyn's horsing-around on camera because he'd been talking to me; and it didn't enter much inside Shigem at all.

I'm startled to see from my bedside alarm clock how short my time with the pair of them has been, in real time: it's still only a quarter past two. My phone vibrates—Evelyn.

"Looks like you're not sleeping," she says.

"Hi! No, I'm not tired. Where are you?"

"In the van outside the Metropolitan, parked in the square. I can see your lights on. Wanna come to Downstairs, for the hell of it?"

"How many of us?"

"Alaia's in the van with me."

Minutes later I'm climbing into the van, where I settle into one of the seats at the back. Alaia is sitting in the passenger's seat ahead of me.

"We were just at Downstairs already, before we drove back here to see if your light was on, and I overheard Kev say Lucan wants revenge on you," says Evelyn, with her hand hovering near the ignition key.

"Which could be bullshit," says Alaia.

"But we thought we should come get you and go back there, if you were awake, because if Kev's telling the truth, then you just being there with us might help Lucan get over it instead of building you up into some great absent enemy. You don't want to become Lucan's enemy. Or Damian's, by the way."

"Revenge for what?" I ask.

"Kev told Flames that Lucan's mad because you caused him to lose some face in front of Flames and Kev on the street," says Evelyn. Her hand abandons its hover near the ignition key and she turns round in the driver's seat to face me. "What exactly happened there?"

"Well, when Alaia and I first bumped into Flames on the street, and then Lucan appeared, I could tell immediately that this was a guy I needed to persuade to be discreet about our presence here in Asbury Park. Because if he were discreet, I could see that all the others would be too, and if any of them wanted to reveal our presence then Lucan would step on that idea. This was back in those innocent days of not wanting to leave the Metropolitan, you understand. So the only choice I had was to give him a quick hypnotic gaze, to impress that on him and show him who was boss."

Evelyn tortures herself with glee over this. "Jaymi, *nobody* shows him who's boss! People have ended up with parts of their anatomy missing, for trying to do that. Or else lying face down, heading out to sea."

I grimace. "So, loss of face was the problem, was it? Hmm, I guess he might see it that way."

"Er, yes, I'd say so."

"You know, you should really be careful about using that hypnotic gaze in everyday situations, just at the drop of a hat," pronounces Alaia, turning all the way round in the passenger's seat and shaking her head sanctimoniously at me.

"Yeah, you should be really careful, it's just too dangerous, Alaia's right," says Evelyn, turning all the way round in the driver's seat and shaking her head too; and they both sit there shaking their lovely heads at me, as if synchronised.

For some reason, this really gets my goat: they are like some accusatory double-act. "Look, give me a break. I've used the hypnotic gaze, as opposed to the secret gaze, only *three* times…" I glare at them both, and they at least stop shaking their heads. "No, hold on, *four* times." I look away, thinking back. "No, *five* times. Plus of course I used it in *Sound & Vision*, and then today in *Big Bang*—not much of a show otherwise. Plus of course I'll need to use it several more times when we record imagination samples with Rik. *However*, to a person, as opposed to a camera, I have used it only five times, and every one of those five was unavoidable. Indeed, may I remind those present that without some of those occasions, we wouldn't be standing here."

"We're sitting," murmurs Alaia.

"The *five times* I've looked into somebody in that active hypnotic way," I persist, restricting myself to a quiet, level, tight tone, "rather than just the passive secret way I normally use, are as follows." Now Alaia does a Hitler-style salute, back down the van at me, which I ignore pointedly as I start to enumerate the five on my fingers. "There was Marc in his office, to make him see how he'd benefit from setting up all this. There was you on your roof, Alaia, to bring you into the project. There was Lucan on the street, to show him who would be boss in this three-horse town. There was Shigem at Paradise"—I refrain from saying this was to lift him smartly up out of what looked as if it might otherwise become an unhelpful infatuation with me—"for my own reasons. OK? And finally I did it to Angel across the street, to make him believe he'd always been a devoted fan of Alaia and me, which I seem to recall your enjoying very much, Alaia, when I told you about it." This tickles Evelyn greatly, reminding me that I have not, until now, got round to telling her of this little present I made to Angel. "That last one with Angel was unnecessary, I do admit, but it was the only one that was. It was just a piece of mischief I couldn't resist, which I'm not going to get into the habit of."

"All right, I think we all need to take a deep breath and calm down," pronounces Alaia, while Evelyn rolls around with satirical goofiness in the driver's seat. "Especially Jaymi. It's been a very long day for him already and I think he's tired and fractious."

"I am *so* calm," I say. "I am *so* chilled, I'm almost on the floor. That's how chilled I am. Look at me—don't I look chilled? To quote Angel, don't make me slap you…"

At last Evelyn's fingers turn the ignition key and we set off along the quiet streets.

45 A DECLARATION OF WAR AGAINST KEV

Downstairs is only half as busy as last night, but again I keep my head down as we enter, until I am seated facing across a table into a corner, away from the rest of the bar. This time it is not a table at the back but one tucked away at the very front of the establishment, beside a small grimy window onto the pavement. "Did you miss me?" Flames asks Evelyn, from behind the bar nearby.

"No," she chirps.

"Damn! There go the free drinks."

"There's no such thing as a free drink," she says. "Could we have a beer and two glasses of red wine, please. Is Lucan gonna be here tonight?"

"Probably soon." He peers towards her. "Hey, *I* remember that necklace! Let's see, who was it bought you that?"

"Yes, it brings back happy memories, Flames—what store did you mop it from, I forget?"

"They were leaner days," he shrugs. "Still, it's very telling that you wear it here for me. Very telling…"

She blows a kiss, turning away from him, and Alaia gets up from the table to pick up the drinks. Evelyn lowers her voice to me: "This place is quieter than usual because certain people don't want to risk being around any more trouble, after last night. If Lucan arrives, just nod and say hi, then I'll butter him up and we'll all just hang out here a while and then leave together, OK? Oh, and I need to tell Lucan it couldn't have been Shigem who planted that wax head. Kev told Flames that Lucan's toying with the idea of punishing Shigem for it, which is ridiculous."

"Yes, ridiculous," I say, and I could almost persuade myself I feel my pupils widening a fraction when I think of his face. "But Shigem was in Paradise when the head appeared. He was hosting in the club before we arrived there. There'll be dozens of witnesses to that."

"Yeah, but Lucan could still claim that Shigem was behind the head and got one of his friends to plant it here. Lucan just needs to find a culprit, because it's starting to look like he doesn't have a clue who left it, which he doesn't."

Returning with the drinks and hearing some of this, Alaia sits and quietly adds, "Kev also told Flames that he hears some of Shigem's friends from Paradise may have been in here last night."

"That's bullshit," says Evelyn. "Kev's just stirring up trouble and trying to keep the heat off himself. That is so mean. He is such a smear."

"Could Kev have planted the head?" asks Alaia.

"Let's keep our voices down," says Evelyn. "I don't know, it's not impossible, though the sculpting's got to be beyond his powers."

"Has Lucan approached Shigem about this yet?" I ask her.

"I don't think so, but Shigem will be freaked-out if he hears he's under suspicion from Lucan. Lucan's teased him and scared the shit out of him for his whole life. He's so sweet, I'd just hate to see him get hurt."

"Me too," I murmur, remembering my tune-in in to him and Kim, just before we came here—which reminds me, I haven't yet told Evelyn and Alaia about that mysterious figure at Pippa's apartment, as reported by Kim. He didn't say anything about its being secret and I don't see why it should be.

I therefore relay what he told me, with every detail I can recall, eliciting predictably horrified fascination from both of them—especially from Pippa's friend Evelyn. "I guess I'll tune in to Pippa tonight and see what I can see," I conclude.

"It's too late to visit her now," says Evelyn, "especially since we went round there late last night—and that only happened because I was making a delivery."

"...Oh! No, I forgot to tell you that I don't have to be with someone, in order to tune in to them—so long as I know them, or know a lot about them. I was half-aware of this already, but I only just confirmed it upstairs: I tuned in to Kim while he was going home with Shigem after your place tonight."

"Jason never briefed me on that," says Evelyn. "Alaia, did you know that was possible?"

"Yes, because Jaymi told me."

"Incidentally," I add, "I don't think Jason knew this about tune-ins, because he learned about my abilities from Marc, not from me. And Marc's entire interest was in the hypnotic gaze instead: on camera, passive tune-ins look rather like paint drying, so they wouldn't have done the GN ratings much good."

"If Jason thought that tune-in targets need to be present in person for a tune-in to happen," says Alaia, "then I guess he never thought to wonder how you homed in on Marc from Liberty Street and then ran him to ground."

She's onto something there; I hadn't thought of that. "Unless Jason *did* wonder that, but never mentioned it—"

"OK, OK, OK, you guys," interrupts Evelyn, whose interest in this particular nicety seems strangely limited. "Jaymi, when we drive home past Pippa's tonight, you are *so* tuning in to her, and you are *so* having a serious snoop around, through someone else's life ... isn't he, Alaia?"

Alaia gives a poised sniff. "I'll concede this one," she says.

Through the little window beside me I spot Angel on the pavement outside. He is dancing alone, lewd and rude, as if he owns the space, obscenely gyrating his bottom independent of the rest of him, with one hand in the air and the other on his hip. Upon his tight black T-shirt, just above the gentle undulation of his breasts, hangs a little silver crucifix. I tune in, as he moves ... and I catch you imagining, Angel, that you're just a skeleton with flesh around it, and then recalling with unease that you are just this—and always in your head, like a drug, that sultry thrumming beat. Beneath the smooth seductive curve and flicker of your subtly made-up eyes and face, the starved baby she-wolf inside you licks her wounds and cocks her ears, hunting for the next scrap of trotting meat to spring upon and fight and bite to death without getting killed or hurt—knowing she will always have to do this until she is sprung upon and bitten to an agonising death herself, by something bigger, stronger, faster. That's just nature, after all. (Great design, don't you think?) So on you dance, alone in the light, lewd and rude, your bottom still gyrating independent of the rest of you, awaiting just that bigger, stronger, faster thing to bound up beside you, bite you through with its canines and chew you up with snapping bone and ecstasy of pain.

Right on cue, the Cadillac purrs around the corner and stops beside you, in a pool of yellow lamp-light. You stop your dance and wait there, your torso trembling invisibly. Lucan climbs out from the passenger's seat at leisure. He grins and half-snarls, pantherine, and gestures with his head towards the door beside this grimy little window where I stare out—and you, of course, follow. You follow him through the front door nearby us, over there, with a smugly chewing Kev not far behind.

Hardly have you been inside for a moment than there is a shout behind you. You and Lucan wheel round, and there beside the door is Kev, holding a black cloth that he has just pulled off an ugly, stupid-looking, life-size wax model of his own head with a dagger stuck gruesomely into each cheek up to the hilt, positioned on the cigarette machine. Though startled myself, I continue to tune in to you behind your little wolf-lips where a smile plays, as Kev spits his gum onto the floor, lunges forward, pulls the daggers out and puts them down, leaving the head looking even worse than it did, and stands there at a loss to know what to do next. "Oh, Kev, it's very flattering!" sniggers Flames, and Lucan shushes him. You squirm forward, still smiling to see Kev drape the cloth back over the head, pick up the draped head, approach a trash-bin, think better of this, then finally hustle the bundle onto a shelf under the bar.

The entire clientele has gathered near the bar, some looking quite nervous. As conversation bubbles up again among them, you stand near the cigarette machine, between the crowd and the wall, still half-dancing, with your little bottom waggling and gyrating as it did outside. But it stops waggling when you notice that Kev has drawn an angry-looking Lucan into a corner and is muttering into his ear, casting looks in your direction: planting poison about you, obviously, as confirmed now by Lucan's doubtful glances at you. Oh, Angel—you know you should really go join them, remonstrate, take control, as you usually try to, but you're so spacy from the drugs and that sultry beat in your head and all those hormones in your blood, and no food, and no sleep but tossing and writhing and churning in bed throughout the few hours last night when Lucan was asleep and so left you alone.

You see Lucan move away from Kev and head back to the front door, beckoning you to follow, which you do; just as I follow you, inside myself, from my table here. When you reach the pavement, Lucan has already walked to the Cadillac and is standing by its open rear door, awaiting you. You walk to him and straight past him, and climb into the car in silence. Kev gets into the driver's seat. Lucan closes the door behind you, staying on the pavement, and leans down towards you. From opposite sides of the window, just before the car moves, you and Lucan each rest a hand, palm-down upon the glass for a second, in the same place, staring at each other. This romantic gesture, unexpected in itself, especially in public, is rendered all the more assaultive by the evil promised in Lucan's smile and by the need in your eyes to be its victim. Positioning himself so the others cannot read his lips, Lucan mouths in silence, "You're my dog." The Cadillac pulls away and you settle into a poisonous silence with Kev.

Yes, you really are spacy, you realise, from the skunk you smoked before you came to Downstairs and from that never-ending sultry beat in your head, but nevertheless you attempt a piece of clear thinking, here in the cavernous back seat of the Cadillac: those hormones are ramping up your system to a fever-pitch, you decide, and now the time has come for you to insist that Lucan stop forcing them into you. You try to remember how long it has been. Two years, you believe. For about two years Lucan has taken steroids and male hormones, in a cocktail that has enhanced his magnificent natural musculature and made him by slow degrees even more obsessively horny than he was already. More to the point, however, for the same period he has force-fed you with a similarly powerful brew of female hormones which, as well as creating your beautiful little breasts, has also made your passive receptive horniness even deeper and more constant than it was to begin with, so that it has now become an almost relentless pressure and hunger. By the time the Cadillac pulls up at Lucan's house, further along Summerfield Avenue, your eyes are half-closed with exhaustion. Yes, it's time to insist...

46 ANOTHER FURTIVE ESCAPE

I feel a tug on my arm. Evelyn is catching the attentions of Alaia and me and pulling us into a careful, low-key exit, like yesterday. "This is getting to be a habit," she says, back in the van. "We don't want to be in there right now. But I'm just going to wait here a few minutes, because if there's violence in there, I wanna hear it."

"So much for hanging out with Lucan," I say.

"Don't worry, this new head of Kev will have grabbed his attention away from you," says Alaia.

"Unless he decides it's me who left the heads," I say.

"Well, was it?" asks Alaia. "You were pretty close to this one when the cloth fell off it. I don't know—what do you think, Evelyn?"

"Alaia, I'm trying to cover up for him here, can you work with me?"

"Lucan looked furious," says Alaia, "just like when his own head was discovered. Can't he see the funny side? They're probably just some practical joke."

Evelyn laughs. "You're not from round here, are you. Lucan's actually got a good sense of humour—but not when his pride is attacked, or his business. Nobody here with a brain would play a practical joke on him. Think about it: he controls the hard drugs market here in Asbury and surrounds. It's a very dangerous job. That's why he only smokes skunk and never takes the stuff he sells. He can't afford to take any chances or let his vigilance slip. It's also why he's a vicious thug, in case you didn't know. That's not just for fun, it comes with the job. Permanent telephones are carved, from time to time. Sometimes people disappear."

"Permanent telephones?" asks Alaia.

"You ever seen someone with a scar from their mouth to their ear? Maybe you haven't seen any yet. I can think of two in Asbury Park itself and at least one other nearby. That's their reminder: they can stay here and they won't be hurt again, just so long as they don't step out of line again."

"Charming," says Alaia. "Who does the carving?"

"Welcome to the real world. Lucan and Damian. Kev's mostly hot air. Look, I can flirt and horse around with Lucan in Downstairs, partly because I know he won't come on to me, but also because I know exactly the line not to cross. That's his public home, it's a place where he's used to constant respect. So picture it: a model of his own head is placed in the middle of that home, with two daggers in his forehead, and it's uncovered in front of everyone. Is he going to think that's funny? The first thing he said was, 'That's a declaration of war.' He labelled it quietly and he was right. Sure it was a declaration of war. Just the fact that someone dared to do it—that was the declaration, more than the head itself."

"And the attractiveness of the model suggested a certain seriousness in the declaration," I add.

"Uh-huh. And then a model of Lucan's driver appears with a dagger in each cheek. That was also a challenge to Lucan, not to Kev. Kev's a real dim-bulb, you may have noticed. Angel and Damian can't stand him—Lucan likes it like that."

"Divide and rule," says Alaia.

"Yep. So the Kev head just confirmed the declaration of war and took it to a whole new level. The temperature is hot in this town right now. If another turf war starts, you two should start obeying Marc for real and just stay in the Metropolitan. You could become a lightning rod, otherwise. And I fear for the life of the person who left those heads, when they're uncovered."

"Who could it be?" asks Alaia.

"I have no idea. Oh, Jaymi, you know what we need to do tonight, don't you?"

This sounds ominous. "No, what?"

"We need to do a second secret spokes-sheep recording with Rik."

"Do we have to?"

"But you loved doing it this afternoon."

"Yeah, but two secret spokes-sheep recordings in one day! And on the same day we did the first official session for *Big Bang*. What am I, a performing monkey?"

"Yep," they say in unison.

"I bet you took in stacks of material tonight," presses Evelyn, "at my place and Downstairs. You don't want to forget all that, do you?"

"Yeah, all right," I sigh.

"Good, I'll wake Rik when we get home. A shame to drag him out of bed, but tough shit—Jason's paying us to be on call at any time of day, for whenever you have enough to deliver."

Aha! So Jason is paying Rik and Evelyn, just as he's paying me. I wonder whether their renovated new apartment in the Metropolitan is some part of that payment (with their rental contract's future renewal as an incentive, perhaps, to co-operate with Jason's spying shenanigans)? "Did you speak to Jason about the first spokes-sheep recording?"

Evelyn nods. "He said, '*Yay! He's waltzing.*'"

"Yes, he would."

"I'm so curious to watch this," says Alaia.

"It's not a real hypnotic gaze," I warn her. "Not like in the broadcasts. It's still active projecting rather than passive tuning-in, but … it's more like a screening of third-party material. For the first session Evelyn found it more interesting to watch the brightness gauge instead, but—well, Evelyn, you tell me, when you glanced up from the gauge now and then during the recording, what did you see?"

"You staring into the camera like a rabbit in the headlights."

"No, I mean whenever you glanced at the monitor itself, to see what I was projecting." —But actually her description of me just then was interesting, and not what I'd have expected. "By the way, what made you think of a rabbit in the headlights, specifically?"

She considers a moment. "I think it was the long, furry ears, Jaymi."

47 PIPPA GOES TO GREET
A GENTLEMAN CALLER

At last Evelyn starts the van. "OK, it was just emotional violence in there tonight," she says.

"My favourite kind," I say. While we wait to cross Main Street, I see Pippa's high-rise ahead of us, and tune in … and I see you spent the day sitting, staring at the walls, until the evening, Pippa! You could have gone out, talked and laughed and eaten, danced and drunk, thrown up and had a blast running round, but of course that's not your style. Or gone to the Casino on the beach—that's much more you, since its roof is caved in and trees reach to the ceiling of the hall where shows were once staged. You could have crossed the sand, beneath the shells and the ships in relief on the Casino walls, and sat by its further side and watched the dark sea slosh and boom right in front of you.

But no, you did none of that, for here instead you perch on your balcony and stare across the night-time town, in a clean brown sweatshirt with matching brown sweatpants. On the small folding table beside you is another one of those details which, like the dining table laid for two or that companionship of toothbrushes, is more suggestive of some cohabitor here than of the solitude with which your presence seems so instinct—a pair of mugs with dregs of tea in them.

Several blocks ahead and to the right, the concrete carcass-building rises—gorgeously disastrous, unmentionable, eleven storeys high, picked out by the scattering of streetlights below it. It's more perhaps a monstrous abortion than a carcass, never having even achieved walls. You feel as small as the gnats, flies and moths that crawl these walls and flick and swing around the dim electric bulb hanging down from the concrete of the balcony above. "The balcony scene," you muse, "there's always a balcony scene." How visible you feel beneath your light-bulb in this outdoor cell, for all to see and to know by seeing, high upon the front of this lone grimy high-rise, thrust against the face of the night just ahead. The dusty glass wind-chimes hanging near the bulb give a tinkle in the faint breeze. A pane of frosted glass cuts you off from the balcony beside you belonging to your neighbours, who never use it and have never spoken to you. Feeling as if you had been killed, you register that the scene before you is assuming the grain of this same feeling, until the sky is like the inside of a skull and the things around you reside in the fibres of your own once-enchanted mind, aborted hopes and carcass dreams. You're vaguely aware that this expansion into the night is something of a fallacy, but it affords a modicum of escape, so you stick with it.

As the days keep on relentless, the things around you cycle every twenty-four hours and they seep into your being with addictive repetition, till you're made of them: the sad front rooms around the space across the street, the coming-on and going-off of street-lights, the quiet, then the swishing of the wind in the trees, the night-time shouts, passing talk and then quiet again, and best of all, the sighing of the sea when the wind is in the east.

You peer over the balcony rail and see a car pull up across the street, with a shadowed figure in it. Male, you believe. You know you shouldn't think this, but there genuinely is a chance, albeit a very small one, that this will be a man who knocks on your door, enters, recognises you, takes you in his arms and completes your life. You will thereby have got what you think you need, without even leaving home. Your mind, you're aware, is getting mushy after so long in here, but the light is dim, so maybe he won't notice your confusion. But oh, suppose he knocks and is the one for you, and yet you fail to notice? You must be careful, when he knocks, to remain attentive to his face. You tiptoe to your door, swing the cover from your spy-hole and peep through its wide-angle lens at the stained concrete lift lobby.

After ten minutes at the spy-hole, you return to your balcony. You watch the trees, unmoving. Looking from your high-rise grave, you know the truth and it's appalling: as part of being alive, you should have had the ability to run through the fields of the sky, chase the clouds and shout your joy to the world like a child running wild on the beach on an afternoon that never ends, with someone whose presence and attention give you meaning. And although you lack this scenario, it remains desired nonetheless, like a magic song playing behind a wall you cannot break through. Whatever forces were responsible for it, this arrangement was clearly, both at first glance and upon reflection, a colossal and painful mistake, like a huge steel and concrete carcass-abortion at the heart of a very small town. Tears stream hot down your cheeks and round your nose, from a silent howl.

The planes have departed; you have no voltage left. You see too clearly, Pippa Vail, and I wish that I could help you, but I don't see how I can.

48 DOES LUCAN HATE SHIGEM?

Evelyn's eyes swim into focus, peering at me through the rear-view mirror. "Earth to Jaymi. You back with us? Did you see anything?"

"I certainly did. It was … difficult to summarise, but ever so Pippa."

"I mean," says Evelyn, patiently, "did you see that narrow door in her hallway?"

"Oh. Sorry. Forgot."

Alaia turns in the passenger's seat and scrutinises me around the head-rest: "Jaymi? Covering up for Pippa, are we?"

"Just tired. Plus, it was a bit of a rushed tune-in, may I say? I felt a bit chivvied there."

"Hmm," says Alaia. "I don't know. I shall have to think about that."

"Oh well, next time," says Evelyn, parking outside the Metropolitan. "You know, the more I think about it, the happier I am that this second head appeared tonight. It'll mean the heat comes off Shigem, because it's appeared only a day after the Lucan head."

"But couldn't Shigem have been responsible for both?" I ask.

"No, because the second head takes things to such a new level, it's cranking up the disrespect so high, that I don't think Lucan can pretend to think Shigem did this. If Lucan suggests that Shigem would dare to plant the Kev head, knowing the atmosphere that existed already after the Lucan head, then Lucan might start to look stupid or desperate."

"So what you're implying," I say brightly, "is that if Lucan decides Shigem couldn't have made the second head, then Lucan will be less likely to think he made the first head either—because his not making the second head means that, *as* a possible perpetrator of just the first head, Shigem *didn't* already have any more wax heads in his criminal record than any other possible perpetrator had, including the head that was still in the future."

Evelyn peers at me in the overhead mirror, then bursts out laughing. "You're seriously cuckoo, Jaymi—that's way too logical!"

"But couldn't different people in fact have been responsible?" I continue. "Why not? If so, then Lucan *could* still say Shigem left the first head, even if we've established he couldn't get away with saying Shigem left the second one…"

"Cuckoo!" calls Evelyn. "Cuckoo!"

"Guilty as charged," I say. "But aside from my guilt there, what I'm saying is also true!"

"Granted," says Alaia, "but if there were two perps, then it certainly looks as if they both went to the same sculpting class."

"Maybe they did," I say. "Maybe we're onto something here. Evelyn, who teaches handicrafts in Asbury Park?"

By now, hilarity has erupted. "*Anyway*," says Evelyn through her laughter, "whatever ridiculously cuckoo way Jaymi wants to analyse it, the important thing is that I think Lucan may now have to find someone else to point the finger at."

"I hope so," I say.

"I vote for Kev," says Alaia with venom.

"By the way, does Lucan hate Shigem?" I ask. "How much does he even know him?"

"They've never hung out together and Shigem doesn't go to Downstairs, but this is a small town," says Evelyn. "Shigem's hard to miss, he's been here all his life and he hosts Paradise, so Lucan knows who he is. Lucan calls him batty-man, chi-chi-man, femian, shemian, even though Lucan himself is with Angel. But I think Lucan's now just acting out of some gut reaction that Shigem is selling out by being with Kim." Alaia nods. "Especially since Shigem's leaving town for Kim—even leaving the country for him."

"Why would Lucan think being with Kim was selling out?"

"Kim's a white boy, Jaymi—like you, you Nebraska boy. Can't just ignore that. I don't think Lucan can, anyway."

"Damian could be from Nebraska," I say, "though not as wholesome and corn-fed as me, of course."

"Damian's better at the permanent telephones than you are," says Evelyn. "I don't know, Lucan's been here all his life and he knows Shigem's been here all his life too. So although they're very different and Lucan calls him a pussy-boy, Lucan probably has a grudging respect for him somewhere, just as a home-town boy."

"And even a subtle feeling of betrayal, just at his leaving?" I ask.

"Could be," says Evelyn.

"Especially with Kim," adds Alaia.

49 THEFT TWO, AND NATTERING ABOUT BIKINIS

We get out of the van, slip through the unmarked door into the Metropolitan, through the hallway, down the long dim corridor and up the back stairs to Evelyn's door. She goes in, then after a few minutes emerges with a sleepy-looking Rik and the four of us go back down to the studio.

"Fresh as a daisy, I see," Evelyn tells him.

"Fresh as a badger's armpit," he says.

"We're not doing proper camera make-up for these recordings for Jason, are we?" asks Evelyn.

I shake my head. "I shan't even end up recognisable, from these."

As I settle myself comfortably onto my tall seat, I realise I'll be projecting from no fewer than seven segments of tune-in, all done today since the first secret spokes-sheep recording we did this afternoon. It's now nearly 4 a.m. by the studio clock, and I'm going to award myself a late lie-in tomorrow morning. —Oh no I'm not, because there's my late-morning picnic date with Pippa. *Damn*, why did I suggest the morning to her? "Action," says Rik. Oh well, here goes…

So first, from the party, comes Kim's childhood in archetypal suburbia: comfortable, alone and always behind-a-pane-of-glass from what he wanted.

Here come his golden days at college, not studying; then fun in London and the quest alone for love.

And here, from my tune-in to him and Shigem together, comes their both setting off home earlier this evening from Evelyn's and Rik's apartment upstairs, looking back towards the building that was only a shell.

Here is Kim's freeze-frame on the street outside, and his memories of music alone through the headphones in London with his first sense of passing time.

Here are the pair of them together again, finishing their journey home tonight: talk of Shigem's growing up, a love for masses versus individual people, and so to bed.

Here is Angel's lewd dance, the she-wolf inside him that will eat or else be eaten; his sinking, his spaciness, his need to be a victim; and his drive home with Kev in horrid silence in the Cadillac.

And here at last is Pippa: her not going out tonight to trip the light fantastic; her relentless days, her visitor, her feeling she's been killed.

I cut through my active gaze. The image-stream's tail-feathers streak away and dissipate around the camera lens, like a ragged end of celluloid spinning to a halt around a spool on a projector. The tiny red light beneath the lens dims to black.

Rik flicks the studio house-lights back on. I take a deep breath. For me, that required just as much stamina as our first imagination theft did this afternoon. "You were right," I tell Evelyn. "My memory couldn't have held much more than those, so I'm glad we captured them before they started seeping away. It makes you realise what a huge volume of stuff just gets wasted, through leaking out of our memories."

Evelyn snorts: "Good riddance, to most of it!"

"Were you projecting anything from Angel?" asks Alaia.

"Well, you saw the dance on the street and the she-wolf and—oh, you mean you couldn't see the monitor? I knew Evelyn would be glued to her brightness gauge, but I thought you'd be able to watch." We all look at Rik.

"Yeah," he says, "if I'd been more than half-awake I'd have remembered to say: from now on we can watch these after they're done, but while they're being recorded the monitor's going to be over here, just so that I can keep an eye on the framing. Sorry, but I need Jaymi to be doing his thing without being aware of anyone just 'watching television' in real time while he's doing it."

"I don't mind if Alaia's just watching—or Evelyn," I say.

"Yeah, but I do," he says, "because for me it would then start to feel like a live taping of a TV show, which is an entirely different vibe from what I need here."

"That's fine, I don't mind when I see it," says Alaia. "I was only asking if Jaymi projected Angel, because I'm sure Lucan abuses him. I can sense it."

"Yeah, he thrives on that," says Evelyn. "That was his specialty when he and I were hooking. He constantly had bruises and black eyes."

"How can he thrive on that?"

"He does," I say. "I saw a foreshadow of it today and it was included here. You'll see when we watch it."

"I can't wait to see me wearing this skirt on Kingsley Street, from the recording this afternoon," laughs Evelyn. She looks at the clock. "It's too late to watch these two sessions now, we'll see them tomorrow. What top did I have on with this skirt?"

I cogitate on this. "A kind of bikini, I think. I remember your golden rings, though."

"OK, are we going to be nattering about skirts and bikinis all night?" asks Rik. "Because I have a date with a pillow right now and we should lock up here."

"Maybe Angel does thrive on it," Alaia says. "But he still wants revenge on Lucan. Real revenge; I can sense that too."

"Well, maybe he'll get his revenge one day," I say.

She shrugs. "People usually don't."

"I bet I was wearing that pastel yellow bikini top with this skirt. Was that it?" Evelyn asks me.

"I don't think so," I say. "Anyway, would you really have put that with bright magenta? A bright yellow like this one works fine, but a pastel yellow?"

"*Hallo*," says Rik. "I hate to interrupt the fashion commentary, but I'm locking up the studio now, and you can sleep on the nice hard floor here, if you'd prefer it to a soft bed."

"It would be a bold contrast in tone as well as colour, yes" pronounces Alaia, "but that's not the same thing as a clash—"

"*Look!*" says Rik. "I'm going to get quite cross in a minute. I know I'm just the trog behind the camera who's taking care of the trifling matter of the second global broadcast event, and of course I'd never dream of processing Alaia's voice until it's unrecognisable there—"

"We're gone!" says Alaia, shooting him a flirtatious look, and we all step out of the studio.

50 UNNERVING THINGS IN PIPPA'S BEDROOM

Back in my room, I am quickly in bed, with the alarm set for my late-morning picnic with Pippa. It's now half past four in the morning and I should sleep, but of course that last hypnotic effort in the studio has left me more awake than I was before it.

Pippa herself should slow down my mind, I decide. I'll use her as if I'm counting sheep: how appropriate! Perhaps I can also rectify my omission this evening when I tuned in and I forgot to look out for that narrow door. So I shoot my attention upward … and I find you, Pippa, naked in your big double bed in your depressing, cluttered bedroom, with your eyes wide and glassy. Just your presence in this bedroom gobbles half the room's space, for even when you're out, your emotional machinery remains here—parked across the end wall, complex and heavy as an outsized organ, with struts and pipes and pedals and a rack of tubes and valves, half atrophied. It's too bulky to move and would probably not survive disassembly and reassembly elsewhere, so here it stays, playing soft and sad to itself, never stopping, like a haunted organ playing in an empty red theatre that's been locked for years.

The only illumination in the room is the dim bedside light, but I notice there's a book lying open on each of the two bedside tables. Your bedroom door is closed, so from your current vantage point I cannot see your hallway or that other, narrow door; but I cast around inside what I can see of the boarded-up warehouse of your mind, in search of anything relating to this … in vain, for now. A thousand faces flick across your bedroom's television screen, muted, from that other world outside you. Some of these faces stare right at you here in bed, craning their heads in to peer through the glass screen as if through a window in the corner of your bedroom, mouthing things you cannot understand.

Your ears push five slim pale-brown fingers out, one by one, into the dim room: you feel each finger squeeze out its girth with a pop, wriggle off across the pillow, then halt at the pillow's end and sniff the air, scratching and stroking at the cotton with its long crimson nail. The fingers melt to snails' horns, twirling at the pillow corners, each one freezing as it sees the people pouring through your bedroom from the TV screen: a cavalcade of bones and air and dust beneath the glamour of their chatter and their flesh; celebrities twitching in the back seats of limousines, pretty little skeletons, brittle dry voices… Their teeth gibber words out, which hang upon the silence pressing in from behind.

A sound-stream you've heard across the years rushes past you: an actor bites an apple in a spotlight while a pre-recorded crunch booms out from hidden speakers; the empty bus at night hums and wheezes through the empty square; a buzz of hornets cuts the air, and artificial bird-song warbles and trills above the manufactured sound of a fresh, moist meadow. A grand noise of yearning beauty swells, then inside it in the distance is the sound of children playing in that wasteland between the Arverne projects where you grew up. You think you hear your own childish speech among these voices, and the five-year-old buried in you stirs. Again behind the stillness you can hear the greater silence, and the even greater darkness behind what's visible. Mercifully at last, a cone of black descends, and sleep.

...But while you sleep, the hits just keep on coming, Pippa Vail! You raise your heavy skull up off the pillow and you peer out from inside, from just behind the eyes—watchful for meaty furry spiders on the walls behind your angel statuettes, where they often crouch, flexing their hairy thighs and picking at their teeth. Before they can beckon you to lick them, as you usually must, you're startled to notice that your television's on. Did you leave it on, at lights-out? Surely you wouldn't have. It shows, furthermore, a thing it's never shown before, in all these years: a simple, plastic, old-fashioned wall-clock, in black and white, mounted prosaically upon an institution wall, its second-hand sweeping round behind the window-bars... The picture cuts to you, where you clutch at your fire-escape railings, in the sky. Around you are long, bendy, lighted candles swaying in a faint breeze. A dry nose pushes from your left, and inside you the fossils of your lust stir a second, but it's obvious from the space in your eyes that for you the sky's gone out: your face has grown blind as the face of the moon. You see no further out than the colours on the inside surface of your skull—brown, black and purple. You hurry up the steps of your fire-escape, swilling and pushing along within your coat of flesh; the handrail is worn thin and limp by the touch of many dead hands. You see your goal ahead: a brittle husk, frail and translucent, hung aloft against the blackness of the cavern of your head. And the stairs up inside you end in death, with a stabbing scent of cheeseflesh and blood-lemon streaming away from your ears like the memory of a dream at dawn.

Soon it will be dawn and the end of this night. And within you as you sleep, the thing that never had the strength to birth itself, thus remaining trapped there and leaving you intact, stirs now, pressing slowly and carefully at the inside of your abdomen. Thin skin seals its eyes; webbing coats its teeth and joins its fingers. You stir with the thing inside, and underneath the curve of your sweet little snub-nose, your mouth grins wetly in the dark.

PART IV

TUESDAY: ALAIA ACTS TOO HASTILY

51 EVELYN'S FLING WITH FLAMES

Next morning I leave a note on Alaia's door saying "At picnic", sneak out of the Metropolitan and set off for Pippa's high-rise. The morning is sunny and hot, yet when Pippa opens the door she is dressed in what I'm coming to recognise as her trademark outfit, having seen her in two differently-coloured versions of the same thing—a clean dark-green sweatshirt and matching dark-green sweatpants, with the same short black silk gloves. Her long hours of fitful sleep and fevered non-sleep, of which I saw a brief slice last night, have left her looking exhausted. Her presence feels, for want of a better word, scraped. She seems eager at the prospect of our picnic, however, and we set off towards the beach, carrying plastic bags and finding it entirely comfortable to say almost nothing to each other.

Coming down Second Avenue, we see Evelyn on the left. Before she notices us, a voice calls her name. She turns to see Flames outside the deli on Kingsley Street on the sunny pavement, making eyes at her, and I sense a bit of history flickering between them. From her body language, her unspoken thought would seem to be: *You wish, don't you, Flames.* "Hi Flames!" she breezes … and I can see your memory of your very first meeting, when you knew that he saw you as wild, free and self-sufficient, walking with a sway through the beauty of the night, like a part of the night itself—a sweet, sexy woman whom he passed at a corner. The second time he saw you, you were parked in your van with the door open, staring through the windscreen in thought. On your pale brown skin a simple golden band necklace hung and flashed in the sunlight, and when you saw him watching you, from some way away, you knew what he was thinking: *Oh girl*, he was thinking, *how beautiful you are.* You smiled through the windscreen and touched your golden band. He saw you as embodying how lovingness and warmth could exist in a natural and instinctive form, whatever kind of place it found itself; and when he looked in your eyes, then he felt plugged in to a warm electric fountain of rich brown light.

Your awareness of him grew, then, slow and sure, until a gorgeous realisation came to you: you wanted to look at only one of those around you, who wanted to look at you alone—Flames Alleyne. You loved the way he moved. When your gazes met, you loved the kiss in his eyes that were the colour of an earthenware coffee-pot. He sounded golden, when he spoke. You knew that this was way premature, but in your mind you tried the magic word *boyfriend* and felt its warmth. His dark sensuality and sharp edge of wildness bewitched you.

So, before too long, the morning sun streamed, hot and seeping, through the open bedroom window as you both woke, sleep-warm. Breathe in the sky! In a horizontal talk you informed him, later: "It's amazing, but from age twelve until now, aged twenty-five, every single period of mine has started one or two days past the full moon. It's strange, I guess." And so it went, and then for a while you made music, as you're happy to recall, looking back upon the two of you in various scenarios: as good friends, laughing; as lovers, under neon or in bed (milky meat of coconut, with pomegranate glaze); or as sensuously deep appreciators of the simple deliciousness of those hot croissants and butter, that morning after that drunken night.

And by and by it ended, too, having run its course. "You know," you told your sister on the phone, "whenever I suggested an idea of my own, I could see Flames wondering if I wasn't turning lesbian: he says they're the only women who are allowed to have ideas of their own."

Nonetheless, it was a precious and important chapter in both your lives, if brief. You won't be spending time alone together any more;

but you know that he remembers, he knows that you remember, and you'll each take the memory of the other to your deathbed.

52 MORNING PICNIC WITH VODKA AND BURNING TYRES

Trudging on down Second Avenue beside Pippa, I realise I shall see Flames in a new light now, as rather richer and more lyrical than I've been seeing him. So, when Lucan squeezed the nape of his neck and Flames's shoulders rose and he laughed and half-crumpled down, Lucan was squeezing just beneath the cubby-hole where all that history with Evelyn lives! What a strange arrangement.

While Evelyn chats with him, she sees us and gives us a wave. As we pass close by them, she catches my eye, subtly indicates Pippa and half-winks while Pippa is looking away: *Jaymi, don't forget to find out what you can, about what Kim glimpsed in her hallway* is clearly the message. Indeed I shan't.

Pippa and I continue one further block, to the miniature golf course. Its narrow lanes, bridges and archways, stretching perhaps ten metres, haven't seen a golf-ball in years, but are now weeded-over, here and there crumbling and returning to a state of mud and scratchy grass. We step across the low fence and find a tiny roundabout to lay our picnic gear on, with a hillock on either side of it where we each sit comfortably. No one is around us on the wide, dusty streets, though I suppose some people can see us from the handful of residential windows we can see. Litter is strewn picturesquely about. Some time earlier this morning a car was smashed and torched across Ocean Avenue, outside the hulk of the old Albion Hotel, and although its interior is no longer hot, its four burst misshapen tyres are all still smouldering on their blackened hubcaps. Smoke coils out from the cracks around the door of the boot, suggesting that a spare tyre inside it is smouldering too. The reassuring scents of gasoline and burning rubber fill the air.

I've brought a fine smooth Chopin vodka and some good picnic apples, plus a carton of Lucky Strikes for Pippa, and she has brought white Wonderbread, plastic cups, paper napkins, a couple of knives and a packet of fat mini-wheels of Laughing Cow cheese. "A discerning choice of cheese," I remark. "I'd say the money-cheese, in fact." She nods gravely, then beams wide. I pour a couple of generous shots of vodka into the plastic cups and hand one to her, and we bump our cups together, before downing them and gazing out to sea. We meet each other's eyes and there is genuine fondness there, in both directions. I suspect she feels secure in the knowledge that I shall never judge her or demand anything but just accept her as she is. As for me, I have to say I find her depression as relaxing as it is profound. For without being callous, I feel no pressure to achieve anything in relation to her, at least as yet: I've seen what it's like inside her, but can do nothing to help, except just to be kind to her and enjoy her company for the duration of our friendship, however short or nebulous this may prove to be.

I smile as I watch her silk gloves tear open the plastic packet and dive inside it. "You know what," I say, "I'm going to come by your place with a copy of *Sound & Vision* and show you something from it. You should find it fun, I think." One of the mini-wheels on her plate has a tiny smear of something red and sticky on it, I notice; she must have nicked her hand with one of the knives. "And if I ask you nicely, maybe you'll even turn the volume up a bit on the TV—Alaia was in fine voice, I can assure you." I pour us each a second generous shot of Chopin, then shine up the apples with a clean paper napkin. When we've downed our shots, she pulls the short red plastic tab protruding from the oblate spheroid of wax enclosing the first cheese wheel she's grabbed, opens it, and takes a bite of cheese and a bite of bread and we laugh at the funny name of the cheese and the sweet little picture of the laughing red cow on its label. "Moo!" we say to each other several times, and laugh. A gentle warm swimminess spreads within me. I like her, I really do.

I pour us a third vodka, she opens more Laughing Cows and we settle back more comfortably among the paraphernalia of the golf-course. I peer at the various miniature castles and mounds, roundabouts and gateways around us: "Gateway 3" one of the structures is marked, I can't imagine why. "What a cosy niche we have ourselves here!" I enthuse. "And how comforting that wrecked car is: it distracts us from ourselves, suggests there's something really happening in our world here this morning, some activity beside ourselves … d'you know what I mean?"

She just nods and smiles, but I can see she's not *just* nodding and smiling: she really does know. I look again for that sticky red smear on the cheese, but it's gone.

I pour us another generous pair of shots, which we knock together again before downing them. "Would you prefer a walk?" I ask her.

"No, no—let's stay here, please," she murmurs. After a pause she grins, becoming drunk, and asks, "D'you have a special person in your life?"

"Not at the moment," I say. "Do you?"

"Oh, yes!" she nods and giggles, then falls silent.

"I'm glad to hear it," I say, and announce within myself that the most graceful and fitting course of action now will be to accord her the simple dignity—here I hiccup loudly—of telling me as much or as little as she wishes, and not a jot more than this, nor indeed a tittle less.

And so we chat inconsequentially, with the greatest of mutual pleasure, and then lapse, by and by, into the warmest and most coppery of brown studies—two figures reclining nobly in a bucolic afternoon landscape. To stretch my legs I stand up, sway a moment, and squint towards the sea: upon the sand is a flourish of surf, and windswept is the shore...

53 THE MEANING OF A SPOTLIGHT

In the early afternoon I take an affectionate leave of Pippa outside the Metropolitan, return to my room and dance around it for pleasure, during which Alaia knocks and enters. "You look happy," she observes. "Was it a liquid picnic?"

"You guessed it! So, at seven we're doing our next recording session for *Big Bang*, yes? And I get to lead you this time, because you led me yesterday." She nods. "I can't *wait* for it! Alaia, isn't this whole thing just a blast?"

"Yes it is. And we have time beforehand to watch your spokes-sheep material, with Rik and Evelyn. Fancy doing that? We could call and see if they want to watch it now—no, hold on. What am I saying? You and I finally have the chance to watch *Sound & Vision* now... We're the only two who still haven't seen it yet, remember?"

"Oh yeah!" We stare at each other with amusement.

She looks at the television in the corner, which I have never thought of turning on. "Wait," she says, disappears to her room and then returns with an unmarked black DVD case. "Rik gave me this, which is what went out on TV. And there's a DVD recorder under the TV. What are we waiting for?"

"I have no idea. OK, let's call Rik and Evelyn and fix a time to watch the spokes-sheep stuff later this afternoon. How long was the broadcast?"

"Well, we were one hour—remember?!—plus Rik said there's about ten minutes of stuff wrapped around that."

So Evelyn and Rik are called, an appointment is made for four-thirty, a "do not disturb" note is taped to my door, our phones are switched off, the curtains drawn, the DVD recorder turned on, the disc inserted, the TV set to drink from the recorder, the menu navigated and the "enter" button hovered over by Alaia's right index finger.

"Ready?" she asks. I nod. And we watch...

I realise straightaway that this broadcast will make a strange juxtaposition, for me, with the drunken whimsy of the picnic I've just had. As soon as it begins I sober up fast, for it is no kind of mirthful viewing: not that it's entirely without flashes of implicit wit, but these are subtle rather than funny and in any case they must be engaged with on the broadcast's terms, not on the viewer's. The viewer is not in control of *Sound & Vision* at all—not even these two viewers, although we aren't ourselves actually hypnotised by it, knowing far too well how we achieved the effects we did. In this, my first "outsider's" viewing, I see more clearly that what my eyes achieved in the broadcast, aside from the scaring up of each viewer's own internal magic for them, was a selective but rich celebration of one viewpoint on this bizarre state we call being alive—my own viewpoint, as it happens, but representative of a multitude of viewpoints.

What can I say except that it is powerful and beautiful, we are blessed that it happened, I am grateful for it and shall die much the happier for knowing it was put out so widely. It is itself, in sum, and funnily enough there is not a hell of a lot for her and me to say about it to each other: most of what is to be said has been said already, either by us in what we presented, or just by the fact of its broadcast and reception. Quite what it means that such a specific set of idiosyncratic material from inside these particular two individuals was transmitted and consumed so globally, I'm not sure. I suspect it may mean nothing more than that with good fortune we managed to effect such global transmission and consumption for ourselves, in place of some other duo's effecting it for themselves. In other words its cultural meaning is a retrospective, simply historical one, rather than one deriving from any culturally prescriptive wisdom on our parts: it was these two who pulled that off by the method they did, and there it is.

We're both rather zonked by it, but we get it together to trundle unspeaking down the marble stairs at four-thirty ... and then with rather a jolt we are in the studio again, crashing back into the good-natured quotidian chit-chat of Evelyn and Rik. We didn't tell them earlier that we were going to watch *Sound & Vision*, and the prospect of mentioning it now seems superfluous, so we don't.

"I had about two hours of sleep last night, I'll have you know," says Rik. "After our little four-in-the-morning stunt, I was up first thing today, bright and breezy, working on something a bit more above-board—the first *Big Bang* session we recorded yesterday. That's some heavy shit there, you two, and it looks fabulous."

Of course—I'd almost forgotten about the song of death Alaia led me on!

"How does it sound?" she asks.

"Well, when I said it looks fabulous, I meant it sounds fabulous," he assures her. "Great audio always makes the lighting look better. Anyway, just for now, here's those two spokes-sheep sessions we recorded yesterday. I haven't seen any of these myself yet, I haven't had time."

In contrast with the *Sound & Vision* broadcast that Alaia and I have just seen upstairs, these two secret recordings are not an over-whelming experience for me, because I've already been through the material twice—once to take it in and then again, more emotionally, to project it. Nevertheless, it is of course fascinating for me to watch my own eyes spilling out parts of other imaginations and memories, instead of my own. I suppose that in contrast with the broadcasts, the relationship in these spokes-sheep recordings between me and the four internal lives I'm conveying is more like that between an actor and four different characters being played by him.

The others, however, are amazed. Evelyn in particular, since she knows three of our four targets well, is leaning towards the TV screen with her mouth hanging open. "That is *so* fucking weird!" she squeals. "There are Jaymi's eyes as usual, but then there's a great *whoosh* of Shigem spraying out of them, or a *whoosh* of Angel or—that is just a mind-fuck, Jaymi!"

"That's the only word for it," agrees Rik, shaking his head in wonder.

"I sort of felt as if we shouldn't be allowed to see into people like that, but I wasn't about to look away," says Alaia. "Also, I may be wrong, but wasn't there something funny about the second recording, the one you did last night while I was here?... There was Kim as a boy in the suburbs, and then him at college and looking for love in London, and they were pretty rich and 3D, like the whole first recording session was. But then when he and Shigem were walking home at night through Asbury Park it suddenly went 2D, like a cartoon." I nod vigorously. "And then we went back to the rich 3D from that freeze-frame of him into all that stuff about the music he used to hear. But then it went 2D again for the rest of their walk and while they were at home—"

I can contain myself no longer. I feel like a gardener whose juxtaposition of vermilion globes of physalis with spiky purple Peruvian lilies has been understood and commented upon by a casually passing citizen: "Alaia, you are so sharp, I wish I'd packed my thimble. Allow me to introduce you to the delights of the *shared tune-in*, to more than one person at a time: a new and exciting model of tune-in, which is responsible for the 2D, cartoony, more superficial bits you noticed." I turn to Rik: "Those can be used for the spokes-sheep's memory of being a small, uninteresting lamb." I return to Alaia: "And perhaps you also noticed..."

"Oh, Jaymi," says Evelyn after these analyses have run their course, "did you find anything out from Pippa this morning about you-know-what—the figure in her apartment?"

"The what? Oh no, sorry, I completely forgot about that. We were having too good a time together, getting drunk."

"Well, a fat lot of use that was!" says Evelyn, raising her eyes to the ceiling.

I feel a trifle piqued at this. "It wasn't meant to be useful, it was meant to be *beautiful* … and it succeeded, I can tell you."

We split up into two pairs, for now, agreeing that we shall return here to the studio just before seven, to lay down the second of the three *Big Bang* sessions. As Alaia and I approach our rooms, she turns to me in the darkness of the corridor: "I saw that foreshadow of abuse you mentioned. I mean after Angel dancing on the street and after him as a wolf … that constant feeling of fear that he's going to be eaten by something, or someone, with no let-up for him, ever. That constant sinking flavour, the constant churning and pumping and pressure and that spaced-out drive home, as if he was headed into horror or disaster… Something there smells terribly wrong to me. I don't like it. It made me shiver, like a really bad dream or a horrible truth that grins through the wall." I think back vividly on all she is referring to. "I'm worried for him, Jaymi. Where he's headed…" She shakes her head. "See what else you can pick up on that, please."

"OK," I nod.

We split off through our separate doors.

54 *BIG BANG*: RETURN OF THE GIANT SHIP

Seven o'clock in the studio, and Rik installs us in our places, in our accustomed black: she hidden in her tiny cupboard of a sound booth, and I on my tall seat. With Evelyn's assistance he runs through his customary last-minute technical tests, some of which involve technicalities I don't understand but whose occurrence I look forward to and actively savour, for the incomparable rush of imminent performance that they herald. Since we have already laid down *Big Bang*'s opening instalment yesterday in the form of our song of death, today's short second instalment requires no tension-building lead-up from a dark stadium with just a silhouette of me, but will instead plunge us straight back into the midst of our trip. This time, therefore, the lights around the three angled cameras are already shining straight at my face. As when on stage between spotlights and footlights, I can thus see little of what is in front of me, beyond the light that fills the air itself and picks up tiny dust motes. On a level with my eyes I can just about make out those three all-important black circles which, it is to be hoped, can see me about a thousand times more clearly than I can see them: I decide to take it on trust that Rik has remembered to take off the lens-caps... "What are you grinning about?" Alaia's voice breaks in gently from the sound booth, and I recall that she has a high-definition monitor right in front of her displaying every flicker in my face: she must have seen something related to my reflection just now about Rik's taking the lens-caps off. "Yes, don't forget I have a monitor in here," she says... So she saw that as well! I wonder whether I am really that transparent?... "Yes, you're that transparent," she replies.

I laugh aloud. "OK, you in the airing cupboard there, so let's keep up that level of attentiveness to me. We need to keep on dancing toe to toe, here. D'you think you can keep up?"

There's a snort from the sound booth: "Honey-buns," she says, "the question is, can *you* keep up with *me*? My milkshake brings all the boys to the yard, but d'you have the stamina, babe? You got the wing-span to fly with the eagles? We'll see, sugar."

"Bring it on, baby," I reply, "bring it on."

"I do love your *work*, Jaymi, my petal—*love your work*."

"Love your work too, pumpkin." (This kind of trash-talking is something we used to slip into in the rehearsal studios in New York, in what now feels like a former life. I'd forgotten it, but it's lovely to be picked up unexpectedly by it and just carried along.) "So, to confirm we're in sync, my sweet: when we wrapped up here last time, I believe we'd just got to where you sloped away a sudden hundred miles to a cavern where a different moon sets, pale and vast above a tiny crash of waves, and majestically you vanished—right?"

"Yes we did, my love," she says, and an electric surge of warmth suffuses me. No doubt seeing this surge through one of the cameras or on his own monitor, the unseen Rik, somewhere beyond the lenses ahead of me, begins his countdown from ten. This is not what was promised; there was meant to be a tad more dialogue and a few minutes of focusing before the countdown, as there was yesterday. But he's spot-on in his decision to throw us into the deep end: my exchange with Alaia had just the energy that I require to summon up the return of the giant ship, and that she requires in order to follow me. Oh, he's good, he is—like Jason said he was.

OK, now it's easy, bring it on. The countdown ends. From my eyes I feel the pull of photons streaming, turning digital in camera and shooting out to north, south, east and west through the air across the sky around the world. Every single viewer then is off alone, town to town, continent to continent: through the slums of Rio or beneath the Arctic Ocean, to their own bright heaven or their own torture chamber. What I myself believe in, while they're drowning in this gaze, they cannot know. The make-up round my gaze is bright and sharp and rich as amber, while the gaze, cold-blooded as an angelfish, flutters cool and alien. The combination deifies and makes of me an icon on the screen—a creature born of exquisite light, inaccessible, a fever dream beamed from the most elite suites of the airwaves.

Meanwhile Alaia's voice is like electric music spilling out through my eyes in all directions, rich and unstoppable. Gleaming machinery unfurls from this gaze, to fill the stadium. Note by indefatigable note, I unfurl it, adding to this city of machinery—silver insulator-cones, glass wires, pylons of platinum and red pipes pumping in an everlasting symphony of movement. I swirl around amongst it, come upon a porthole, stand in it with hands and feet splayed within its circle, and peer down. Underneath me are the outside walls of the great ship I conjured up in *Sound & Vision*. West across the ocean, the sun presses down in a wet sprawl of sunset and sinks through a giant hole of liquefied red; while thousands of miles underneath this, the Burma Lagoon bubbles silently and twinkles at the pale scintillation of dawn on its surface.

I climb to the ship's highest bridge, raise my arms and dance, slow and stately, by myself. I'm nearly home now, alone—away from the noise and exhaustion of people. There's space above my head going upward forever, and beneath the ship's keel, ocean depths. In blissful liberation of aloneness I shout, across the scarlet-flashing surface of the grand Pacific plains stretching radiant for thousands of miles in all directions. I shout aloud to no one in the night, from my tanker's bridge, and yes—I'm almost home, away from Earth, away from life, and bound for better, higher, cleaner planes of empty nothingness forever! Oh, *bliss* of death and sweet dissolution, at last...

Before I say goodbye, though, I'll take a final jaunt in the rowboat and trail my hands one last time in the waters of this small green planet. So I work the oars and strike out on black twinkling wavelets under stars, in the rowboat, for two solid hours, till the ship is just a hyphen floating free on the horizon. I pull the oars in, lie back, get comfortable and listen to the water's slosh and sway against my boat's wooden sides. A dragonfly flicks in lazy arcs across my vision. The hyphen's tiny lights shimmer subtly, when I turn my head to face the right; but over on the left, just the ocean shines, out from this boat to the edges of the world where it leaps into nothing at the calm black horizon.

I reach in my pocket for my matchbox, and sniff the soft air—salt water and the scent of unseen harmonies. I strike a match, let it flare, hold it up, then toss it out from the rowboat. It curves up and out and down, as if in slow-motion. Where it breaks the water, there erupts a soundless plume of pale flame rising curling, swaying, higher up, and higher still: although its root remains here, its tip rises in a rocket path, to lick the highest stratosphere. This signal meets the gaze of that mountain up on Mars whose side-lit contours form a face that stares across at us—you know the one. I move the boat towards the flame's root. The face winks and smiles, with an eyelid volcano and an earthquake of the mouth. Leaning from the rowboat, I whisper my reply by the flame's root. It sends my whisper upward, all the way; then the flame demurely falls, from the upper stratosphere to a point beside my rowboat, and vanishes at once with a gurgle and a puff, sending out concentric ripples through the slick black water where it fell. I breathe the night, thrilled to be escaping from the world so soon, and thrilled that my last conversation here possessed the scale and grandeur that it should have done. I take up the oars again and row at leisure, back to the beacons of the hyphen ship floating at the shiny black horizon, for two solid hours; and I climb aboard.

The aperture in each of the three lenses shrinks to a pinpoint, then disappears.

55 A SIGHTING OF THE WEASEL

I have less communication with Alaia after this *Big Bang* record-ing than I had after yesterday's, for as soon as it is finished she announces she is going out for a walk on the beach and slips away. I reflect upon this, as I enter my room upstairs, but am distracted by my mobile phone flashing on the table. Glancing through the incoming message symbols, I find a text from Kim requesting I call him. I touch his number. "Hallo," he says.

"Kim, it's Jaymi."

"Oh, hi. Yeah, I was just calling to let you know the latest weirdness with Pippa."

"What is it?"

"It was some time really late last night. I couldn't get to sleep, so I finally went out for a quick walk, and somewhere a block away from Pippa's tower I turned a corner and just stopped dead, because there she was, perched on her balcony, up near the sky, looking so spooky that I nearly cried out. For a start, it looked like she was too *big*, for the distance between us ... but I guess that must have been a trick of the light. She was lit up bright by a balcony light on one side of her. Then on the other side of her, in her shadow, was a small, darkish figure, and I swear it looked like it was in a wheelchair. I was certain it must be that weasel-eyed person I saw in the toilet cubicle—that vegetable Angel, or whatever it was. I was too far away to see any more, but then when I crept further forward, the front of their balcony would creep upward and block my view of the pair of them. I did think of shouting up at them, but then that seemed pointless and dangerous, and even ... I don't know why, but it even felt as if it would be somehow obscene. I wished I had binoculars, so I could return to the other corner of the street, further back, and see them better. I pictured all the stuff lying around the flat here waiting to be packed, to see if I could remember binoculars that I could run and fetch before she left her balcony... But I couldn't remember any binoculars, so I just went home and got back into bed and made sure I was somewhere in contact with the warmth of Shigem."

"Wow. We need to find out what's happening there—for the good of Pippa, but maybe also for the good of ... whoever that person is."

"Yeah, we need to. By the way, if you and Alaia want to swing by later this evening, you're welcome. All we're doing is packing. Just give us a call before you come over."

"OK, thanks, I will."

I'd like to see those two again this evening; I hope Alaia's on for joining me. (And nice to see these cosy reflections busying themselves to defer my thinking about that creepy figure Kim saw—oh yes, *that* figure.) I haven't heard her return to her room yet. I go down to the breakfast room, discover the silent Mexican girl playing a videogame on a handheld console in the adjoining kitchen area, and respond to her quizzical look by requesting a big round of hummus on toast. Soon I am sitting alone in the breakfast room, tucking into a meal that more than lives up to my hopes, while she returns to a furious manipulation of her console.

56 LUCAN'S AND ANGEL'S SUMPTUOUS FIGHT

Upstairs again, I lie down. Throughout my hummus on toast, I was keeping at bay the picture of Kim's Angel-like figure at Pippa's, but now it floats up through the quiet air of my bedroom, floats down on top of me here on the bed, and softly gnaws at me.

It's not going to go away, unless I deal with it. There's no choice: I had better have a tune-in to Angel himself.

So I close my eyes, conjure up a vivid blast of Angel, aim it out into town, and send my sight running after it like the obedient dog it's become. I half-expect to find myself strapped into a wheelchair on Pippa's balcony or locked behind a keyhole in a cubicle off her hallway. But no, I land at Lucan's house on Summerfield Avenue ... and straightaway I see it's not a soothing moment, Angel, for it seems you just demanded something Lucan won't allow. Your little body's angry as you jump to your feet, shrieking "How *dare* you say no? I *hate* that." Lucan launches off his chair; his left hand grabs your right wrist hard, so you yelp. He thrusts his gorgeous snarl towards your face and growls: "Where the fuck were you, here, before me, huh?" He lifts you off the floor and holds you up aloft before him. The tight supple muscles underneath your tattooed angel's wings strain to flail you upright, in vain, while the little silver crucifix dangles in mid-air beside your black vinyl brassiere. "Where would you be without me—huh? Nowhere! Dirt-poor! Dead, or good as dead. And I can send you back down there, any time I want."

An explosion of black light floods your eyes and mind: it's time to kill. It's time to kill Lucan. Instead, with a mesmerising weakness and passive spite, you mutter, "Jerk..." In a split second Lucan's hand slaps you in the face so hard, you nearly black out. As your eyes swim slowly back to focus, your left cheek stinging hard, you see his eyes above you. He pulls you up to a level with his grin, spits upon your face and lets loose a deep and wicked laugh. The spit hits your stinging left cheek and stays, hot and sticky. Hanging by your right wrist, hurt and stung and knotted up with weak rage, you start to cry. Lucan holds you up there, one long minute, with the hot tears streaming down your face, and he stares at you the whole time in deep reflective pleasure. He jerks you nearer to him and you flinch, thinking you'll be bitten now or spat at once again, but instead he moves gently in and licks the burning tears from your cheek: his tongue is slightly rough upon your flesh.

You dart your jaws leftwards and grab with your teeth the end of Lucan's tongue—not hard enough to bite through, but hard enough to kidnap it by threatening to bite through. Lucan's eyes blaze at your tear-stained face, across a gap of centimetres. He fears that he may really lose his tongue's end, and he's right to fear it. So, for one extraordinary moment, you both stay exactly there: Lucan, strongly braced like a pylon, holding you aloft, and fearing for the end of his tongue; and you hanging dizzy there, a point of reflected light shining off your earring, dripping tears and wet with sweat and emanating triumph.

Then, by degrees as gradual as if he were complying at gun-point with an order to take his hands out of his pockets very slowly, Lucan creeps his right hand up in the direction of your chest and brings his thumb to rest on the outer surface of your black vinyl bra, just above your left breast. The thumb doesn't move but just rests there, waiting five whole seconds in a new clash of wills. Then it feels what it aimed for, as your nipple starts to swell, against your will. Your teeth don't unclench but stay together, just close enough to hold Lucan's tongue where it is. Still neither of you moves at all, except for your nipple, now erect, pushing up its brown nipple-meat hard against the vinyl bra and Lucan's thumb. Felt by you alone but inferred by Lucan too, a dull throb inside the nipple grows in urgency, without Lucan's moving his thumb at all. Your eyes face each other, sharp and murderous across the tiny gap between you both, for ten whole seconds more—then at last your eyes flicker down and stay down, Angel. With his thumb still pressing in from outside, Lucan's index finger slips inside the vinyl bra and tweaks the nipple with its nail, slow and hard; then again, slow and hard; then again, slow and hard... You moan, your teeth unclench, your limbs and your bottom and your stomach unclench and all resistance in you melts.

Lucan lets you to the floor in a curled moist heap and squats beside you. He lifts your streaming face and plants a slow kiss upon it. Throughout this your eyes stay closed, but your hand reaches up to feel the big golden crucifix hanging at his chest, where his muscles are so close that you can feel their heat, here upon your face.

I zoom in on your eyelids and through them, to your grand estate: a seven-layered formal garden, planted with metal trees and cinder-chip flower-beds and black ponds of oil, around a mansion with minarets and jagged glass spires. Here in your prison-pit of decadence, you're powerful and wealthy. Your contempt is pure, aesthetically; your darkness divine, aristocratic. Around your mansion's ballroom floor, waltzing mannequins grimace, by themselves or in internecine pairs, on jerky rails, while a poisoned orange light from the setting sun blasts through the terrace doors from far beyond the lonely claustrophobic furthest end of the mile-long enclosed Linden Alley carved westward through your forestlands...

Never can you rest, even here in your estate, for Lucan always slips in, hiding on your battlements or somewhere in your corridors, behind the wooden panels, and at any time he may smash or slash with the force of a scythe or a mallet, like a dangerous unpredictable machine. But every day, when he finds you, when the mallet or the scythe hits or slashes you, it feeds you and validates you—tells you that you're loved, in the only tongue by which you are persuadable it's true. Your existence is exhausting, is it not? but you're trapped in it for life, you may be certain.

And everything you love might seem to smile at you; but inside, it's always preparing to escape you. Whatever thrill tingles in your fingertips, a death-shadow palpitates close above your head. Your vermilion-tinted eyes have the fever of a flame on a grave in the dusk, and your little pouting lips hide the kiss of death behind them where your canines sweat. Your glamour's violent to the core, my Angel Deon—and your violence in itself is a glamour unto death.

Hear Lucan stalking through the attics of your palace, up your dark wooden staircases, hunting for you, whip in hand. Crouched there beyond the heavy four-poster bed, you think he cannot see you, but he lashes out, straight in your direction, with the whip. You screech. So he saw you, or he knew you were there, and he still knows. You both wait motionless a moment, in silence... Then the whip whistles out again and bites your back and cuts it like a knife, and you feel a warm trickle down your left flank. You breathe hard; adrenalin is raging through your system now, mixed with this morning's dose of female hormones. The whiplash comes at you again, again, again—from right, from left, from overhead, and even curling up with its end from underneath you where you crouch on all fours, ready to scuttle away through the door like a dog or through the floor like a cockroach. The end of the whip streaks and zings through the air, hissing up around your slinky body, stroking at your blood-dripping black vinyl brassiere. The whip's end hits the bedside table and a glass shatters, wrenching you away from your mansion and your grand estate, and landing you back here in Lucan's house in Asbury Park. You feel you could shatter too or shrivel up and die like an insect in a flame, if you ever got too close to Lucan's lethal anger—yet you want that badly, too—to shatter and shrivel and die!

57 HOW KIM MET SHIGEM

I open my eyes, blinking. The warmest imagination I've tuned in to here has been Evelyn's. The most water-clear has been Kim's. The cloudiest has been Pippa's. The most purely beautiful, Shigem's. The most coolly passionate, Alaia's. But the most extraordinarily alive of all has been Angel's: never have I seen a greater drive to experience the full million volts that are available to any of us, did we but have the daring and the energy to conduct them. Angel's is the most addictive personality I have ever seen or heard of, allowing no insulating space between it and what presses in on it. In short, between him and Lucan, things are just as surmised by Alaia.

I get up and open my door, to go and knock on hers, but instead discover her right outside, about to knock on mine. "Hi," I say. "I was just coming round to say that Kim asked us over at any time today, if we want. They have to spend all day packing, so it won't be a proper visit, just a bit of moral support."

"You mean now? Sure."

So I call Kim to tell him we're on our way and we set out, without much conversation. Halfway there I remember: "Oh yes, I did tune in to Angel and your instincts were right. We are talking serious physical abuse of him by Lucan... I'm almost inclined to fear for his survival."

"Tell me."

We are too nearly at Shigem's for me to begin it now. "I can't really summarise it quickly. The best thing would be for you just to watch it after we do the spokes-sheep session this evening."

"OK," she says, looking troubled.

At Shigem's apartment a chaotic packing scene is in progress, ready for their move to London in a few days' time. Kim clears sitting places for us in the box-strewn main room. "How's it going?" asks Alaia.

"I don't know, I've been obsessing over when we met Lucan on the street the other night," says Shigem, returning from the kitchen with mugs of coffee. "That gesture he made. Not that I think he's going to decapitate me, but I've known him for years, so I know what he's capable of. I know what he's done to people—bad shit. I've actually been pretty stressed." Looking at him, I can believe it, and it may have something to do with why the skin on his beautiful high cheekbones isn't just cratered as always but is today marked with fresh acne. His bright brown eyes open wider: "Cos if he really has decided *I* did those wax heads, which he looked as if he had decided, then he really may hurt me, or destroy this apartment, or something terrible. I can't escape here till Sunday, so he still has time to get to me. Oh, well! It's a giggle to live life on the edge."

"Best get packing, then," says Kim.

We look around. This is not a small move. So we help: while Alaia and Shigem work on things in the kitchen, Kim and I sort books into different sizes before slotting them into boxes. As we work, I tune in ... and I see when you first met Shigem, Kim, three months ago. You'd gone to a party called Jungle, on a Monday at a club called Busby's on Charing Cross Road, with your friend Robert plus a friend of his. The three of you were sitting in an alcove on the left, when another friend of Robert's came over and greeted him. You took little notice but went to the dance-floor. A few minutes later you saw this new arrival dancing near you, glancing at you. You made recognition signs. He leaned towards your ear, but then said nothing. Flattered and amused by his shy approach, you smiled at him. "Can I buy you a drink?" he asked. You were attracted to him, no question. Everything was easy. "Yes," you replied. You felt his arm go round your waist, and his long black hair with its blond highlights spilling past your shoulder. His presence was permeated by gayness, somatically engrained—a luscious quality that spread, sleek and fluid as a dancer, through every move and every word of his, as blood pervades a body. The chemistry between you was enormous and immediate. With absolute naturalness, you both were embracing by the time you'd reached the bar. With such unholy speed did your relationship start: there never was a thing between the two of you, except it.

Later in the evening you both went back to your flat. He told you that he'd grown up in Asbury Park (you'd never heard of it), had recently come into a modest amount of money through his parents' death and had now arranged to spend a month living in a series of cheap accommodations here in London, on his first trip abroad.

The things you said aloud to him were in-control things, but the things that your mind yelped inside itself were different, as they escalated upward by the minute and the hour: "Beautiful friend," your mind said. "I long to hold your hand in the rain," said your mind to him. "Take me in your arms—we'll be silent together, as the wind through the window stirs our hair, satin-cool, and we'll kiss like velvet, please, Shigem, Shigem, Shigem..." said your mind to him.

And never before or since has your mind spoken clearer or more truly.

You weren't so easily swayed; your feet were on the ground. Yet this was it, you felt—right here. The once in a lifetime.

Later in the night, lying beside him as he slept, you looked back to the past, a day ago, when you were still alone: night after night, your fingers caressing your skin that was so fair, you'd slowly undress. But now this sleeping human body beside you, with its vulnerability and that squirly word "Virginity" on its left shoulder, was a wonder. Then with a smile to hold his penis as he slept, and feel it swell while he squirmed and faintly moaned in his sleep, caused you to search this situation for a catch or trap—for surely there was *never* such a free lunch as this?

Profusely you both sweated, lying in the hot dark. The beer-bottle sweated too, upon the bedside table. You reached for it and took a swig, he woke and you offered it, he drank from it and put it down. Lying hard against him, you whispered, "You feel beautiful..." He moved to hold you closer, then, after a second's magic, whispered "So do you!" Then thinking of a better truth, he added it: "You see through beautiful eyes." You remembered him in the club tonight, dancing right in reach of you, his cock tight-sprung, its shape clear behind the red leather, vastly aroused by the feeling of his motion as he gazed at you, very nearly ready to ejaculate without a touch. And now, warm skin and long black hair and sweat and urgency and pleasure, with absolutely nowhere else that either of you had to go or wanted to...

Memories of the very early evenings spent at your place have a golden glow already, just three months on. You kissed the brim of his glass before you handed it to him. Candle-light on bookshelves and cabinets, enchanted conversation, wine glasses filled and the evening and night ahead. Food, wine, cigarettes, the sharing of music and books, then making love, then sleep (or lying there awake as you stared at the sweep of passing headlights on the darkened bedroom ceiling, while Shigem stirred in sleep and then became still again), while the London rain pattered on outside ... simple, inevitable, joyful incunabula of this relationship.

You spent hours entwined, not only in bed but in most other places too. Wherever you went, there was a powerful pull to hold each other close, whether talking or silent, serious or giggling. You spent so long entwined, it was as if you were catching up on lost affection, making up for all that lost time when you didn't know each other. Shigem was so attracted, needing, gentle, wanting always to be with you, that you were wary sometimes of the strength of his need. But you returned it, exulting in the warmth and the comfort and the friendship and the love.

There was that graffito on the wall by the café where you used to meet: "Meanwhile a dwarf is passing out in downtown Detroit." Much excited dialogue, talking on the phone and meeting every day. Together in the photo booth in Earl's Court station, while it thundered outside; spitting rain, wet streets, wet umbrellas and the Underground. Sex on the mattress on the floor of the cold Friern

Barnet room: the curtains always drawn, the electric bar-heater and the television playing, with the chair-legs black across the screen, from where you lay.

A montage of all the bars and clubs you knew together flashes crowded through a neon-lit door in your memory: you'd both rise and step to the dance-floor, the moment that a mutually adored track was played, where you'd make as if to eat him and he'd peal with a helpless and scandalised giggle. Then there were the funny tired rides in the rear of the upper deck of night-buses leaving Trafalgar Square, with all the queens from Heaven and the other clubs. One day you each had your right ear pierced on Oxford Street, and once you hugged goodbye beside the Albery Theatre stage-door.

And there among the housing in a cramped grey corner of a stretch of the city was another room where you and he sailed away—the room where he was staying with some others, in a council estate down in Elephant & Castle. You laughed out of wonder and anxiety, wanting this emotional adventure with Shigem of course, yet fearing it. His friends were always barging through or idling in the room—except they weren't real friends, just temporary roommates who shared the same nightlife. The blond one, Fred, would flounce around, prattling on and borrowing clothes and making mugs of tea for the three of you. He'd do a fashion show with a towel for the whole room—the two of you—and you would both hold each other, there beneath the bedclothes, and squeal, to encourage him and also because, in your excitement and happiness, anything was funny if you wanted it to be. You slept on a mattress on the floor, at the head of which, right where a headboard should have been, was a scalding radiator; so you couldn't sit and lean back against anything, but had to recline on your elbows or lie upon your side on one elbow or sit cross-legged leaning forward. Through a long low window was a dim court, half-enclosed between blocks of flats in brown brick with walkways. The London spring outside was wet and cold, so near the window it was cold, but near the radiator too hot; below the duvet too hot, but too cold above it. The joints that were rolled and passed around were thin, like Shigem, but strong—they'd make your head spin, first thing in the morning with a mug of instant coffee. Crumbs of hash crackled when unevenly mixed with the tobacco and too weakly tamped down inside the Rizla; bits of it fell to the carpet and were fumbled for. The TV's on too loud—turn the news off, find some music, and did you know the singer of that group is really male? There's nothing much to do, so you'll lie around and see what happens, who appears, and then maybe start getting dolled up for Heaven later; and maybe you should eat something too, while you're out.

Some music on the TV is recognised and turned up, and starts to grab you strongly. The screen shows two men dancing on a rooftop among hanging sheets. You ask Shigem and Fred what it is; they know, between them, the names of the band and the track. A few moments later you've forgotten, ask again, are told—and not since then have you forgotten it again. Sometimes, you feel this track is sacred to you, because for you it came right at the proper birth of Love, revelatory and not in your control. It accesses happiness, anguish and fire: beautiful, vulnerable, serious and famous, it rises, is shot at, is protected, is championed, spins for years and sits at last within its little god-niche. You say not much about it, but you know that in a sense it will play within you always.

You've forgotten the address there, Kim, but I can see it buried in the trash-bin of your memory: that block of flats on Falmouth Road, Elephant & Castle. For the next few weeks until you both came to Asbury Park, Shigem stayed with friends he made in club-land, in six other flats, and I can see them too, tucked away beneath your memory, Kim: one flat on Bouverie Road, Stoke Newington; two successive rooms in that house on Dollis Hill Lane; one on Reighton Road in Upper Clapton; one in Stamford Hill; one on Hemington Avenue, Friern Barnet; and one on Craven Walk, Stamford Hill. Remember?...

58 HOW SHIGEM MET KIM

Kim and I have now filled up a couple of boxes with books. "By the way," I ask, "did you ever find any binoculars here?"

Returning to the room from the kitchen, Shigem hears my question. "I know what you're thinking of," he says. "Pippa's little mystery friend. Yeah, that freaked me out! I don't have binoculars, but a friend of mine has a pair of antique opera-glasses that'll work. She's back in Asbury on Thursday, so I'll get them from her then. Looking through them at night, though—I think I'll leave that to Kim."

"How well d'you know Pippa?" I ask.

"I've seen her around for years. Sometimes we've said hi. I've always felt kind of sorry for her. She seems so alone, and ever since she was a teenager those big green eyes of hers have always looked like they were just crying. I never saw her apartment till the other night. It was a bit creepy in there, didn't you think?"

"Yes," says Alaia. "The space was all wrong, somehow. Can I pack anything else?"

Shigem looks around, considering this. While he does so, I have an interesting idea ... and as you stand in thought, Shigem, I take a look at *your* memories of first meeting Kim. To my surprise, though, I find that your first sight of him was not inside the club where he first saw you; for your memory is instead from a week before that club night, downstairs in the First Out Café, where he never noticed you but you most surely noticed him. In the corner, there he was: a handsome masculine blond boy, slightly sad-eyed, deep in thought, biting his nails as he read the menu. You were startled, as you watched him, to sense across the café the erection of his penis and his nipples, as their heat spread towards you—*no* it didn't, you correct yourself whenever you remember this scene—*that* couldn't happen! Anyway, then he ordered a veggie-burger, nothing else, and his voice was deep but also tinged with a blush of immaturity, as if newly broken. You started to realise you were not going to be able to get out of summoning up the guts to approach him (such approaches not being something you did often), and this prospect straightaway made you feel so young and vulnerable that you laughed at yourself inside. "Get it together," you thought, as you got up, but already your body had that tight invisible all-over quivering it gets when emotionally naked, as if pressed close under your skin against your clothes. Your throat drily gulped and clunked. "For *fuck's* sake," you shouted within yourself, "enough with this nerviness, you're not fifteen. You are *not* going to faint, you are *not* going to faint," and you frowned and walked purposefully towards Kim's table and towards it some more ... and then straight past his table and upstairs and out through the door of the café while you slapped yourself inside and then carried on slapping all the way around the corner to Charing Cross Road.

But you saw him a second time, by chance, in the nightclub one week later, on the occasion of Kim's first memory of you; and then for you, just as for him, a new continent inside you began to unfurl while you watched it.

One night, early on at the Elephant & Castle place, you dreamed that you and Kim would have to split up soon, because for some stupid reason the two of you just weren't going to work. You groaned in your dream: was yet another incipient relationship over, too soon? Had you flamed, for a moment, with another blond boy—had you danced as a pair, for an instant, in a daydream? So bright you'd been, the two of you, together for a brief spell. You'd crackled and you'd shone with possibility and hope against the usual grey backdrop of everyday life. There'd been magic in the air around you, visible to all: the promise of a new and rich adventure! Circling each other, you'd been flaming creatures, butterfly-lions, but it seemed that the flat winds had blown you apart now. What a drag, if so. Once again, not your fault, but how commonplace, predictable—and didn't you feel the temperature descend again, the lights dim to grey as they had been before he came along? Would you not see Kim again?... Oh well, how sad. You would always remember him, at least. "Turn and walk away, Shigem," you thought, "and dance alone tonight. Tomorrow it will hit you and you'll suffer. Then you'll mend, for sure, for you'll have no other choice—but once again, what a drag. Shigem, you'll not forget Kim, but turn and walk away now, and dance alone tonight..."

But later that same night, you had a much better dream: you both were alone on some deserted level of a multiplex cinema, trying to find the exit. You came across an older gentleman, who stood in silence holding out a tray of mints. "Oh look—we get a mint!" you cried, and grabbed Kim's hand. You scampered up to the man and both curtseyed and both took a mint. The man smiled, then with just a trace of irony he watched you both running off away down the escalator giggling and whispering in unison, "*My god, I think we've just met the Mint Man! Tee-hee-hee!...*"

My attention shoots back west across the Atlantic, back to the present and this packing scene. "No, I don't think there's anything else you can do here," Shigem replies to Alaia. "So I'll let you both go and do something more interesting—it shouldn't be difficult to find something. Thanks for your help."

59 THEFT THREE, AND ALAIA LANDS ANGEL IN THE SHIT

As Alaia and I step off Shigem's front path onto the pavement, she says "How about seeing if Rik can move today's secret recording a bit earlier?"

She must be impatient to investigate the truth of her concerns for Angel's safety, as we were talking about on the way here. "Sure, we can ask." I start to realise she's probably not going to enjoy tonight's recording session much. I need to start gearing myself into the mode of projectionist, not film critic, however, so I let this topic hang in the air.

Back at the Metropolitan we find Rik alone in the studio. Alaia asks him if we can bring our recording forward a bit tonight and suggests we view the material straight afterwards.

"How about half past three in the morning, like last night?" suggests Rik. But it's cleared with Evelyn on the phone that we shall instead do it next-ish. I go upstairs to freshen up, then back to the studio to find Evelyn has joined us; and before long I'm in front of the camera, projecting what I'm relieved to count is only four tune-ins since our marathon spokes-sheep session last night…

First off, here comes Pippa last night: her emotional machinery filling half her bedroom; her fire-escape in the sky, a stair to death; and the demon in her abdomen.

Then from today comes Angel being beaten up, his hijacking Lucan's tongue but losing anyway; his aristocratic darkness, but no rest from Lucan.

Here's Kim's first meeting Shigem in a nightclub, their romance and nightlife, their London rooms, the music of their early days.

And here is Shigem's first seeing Kim, in a café; his fear, early on, that such romance must surely end … and the Mint Man.

It's a work-out for me emotionally, as both times before. During the Angel material I become aware, however, that I am not alone in this emotional involvement, as I can sense from across the studio that Alaia is also becoming very much other than cool despite her taking care not to move. (I'm pleased to find this awareness of mine doesn't affect my focus as projectionist.) As soon as the camera is turned off, she gets up, muttering "Lucan is *disgusting*," and heads for the studio door.

"Where you going, girl?" says Evelyn.

"I'll be right back," she replies and then is gone.

We all stare after her. "Do I sense she failed to pay the closing Kim and Shigem material the full attention it deserved?" I ask.

"Well, that Angel footage was quite something," says Evelyn. "I knew that that was basically the scene there, but it's another thing seeing it."

"Maybe we should help Angel?" wonders Rik.

"I think if someone wants to be in that kind of relationship," I say, "then they should be left to make their own decision."

"Anyway, Angel doesn't want to leave Lucan," agrees Evelyn. "I know what he's like."

After a few more minutes, I say, "Isn't Alaia being rather a long time?"

At this moment Alaia comes back in. "I've just called Lucan," she announces. "I told him I know about the abuse and I appealed to his better nature to stop it."

Evelyn claps her hands to her mouth. "You did *what?*" she hollers… "Oh shit, you don't know what you've done. 'Lucan's better nature'! What better nature?… Why didn't you say you were going to go and do that? Now the shit's gonna hit the fan."

Alaia looks down. "OK, I know I should have said. I was just in the heat of the moment, doing what I thought was right."

"That's all we need," says Evelyn. "What did he say?"

"Well … at first he laughed and said something dismissive about me being an out-of-touch bitch from Manhattan or something. Then he said I was talking bullshit—how could I know what he did at home? So I said that I wished he had lost the end of his tongue, as it would have been an appropriate price to pay for half-killing Angel like that—"

"Oh fuck," groans Evelyn.

"Then he became a lot quieter, and before long he just hung up on me."

Evelyn sighs. "Alaia … Lucan will now assume Angel must have gossiped to you about their home life. How else would you know about the tongue?… He won't like that! He'll punish Angel for it. You've probably landed Angel in deeper shit than we saw tonight."

Alaia sinks to a chair. And so a war council begins, seeking what we can do in the way of damage control. Calling Lucan back right now is quickly ruled out by Evelyn as being likely to inflame any anger Lucan may already be venting on Angel. Yet we feel we have to do something, because the victimisation that I've just projected, though wrapped up with love, was great enough to cause concern for Angel's safety, even before Alaia's phone call—Lucan being not unaccustomed to murder, after all.

"I'm sorry to have brought us to this," says Alaia, "but I don't want anybody's death on my conscience: I think we have no choice but to show Lucan we've been spying on Angel."

Evelyn, Rik and I glance at one another. "We'd be risking the spokes-sheep deal with Jason," I say.

Alaia looks at me. "Yes, I'm sorry, Jaymi. But which is more important: the corporate sheep, or maybe saving a life?"

Oh, fuck it. "Thanks for putting it that way. Well, I suppose it's the second one."

"There you go. And the only way Lucan's going to believe it's our spying and not Angel's gossip that's to blame for me knowing about his tongue is if we give Lucan a copy of the Angel footage we just watched—then he'll see where I got it from."

"Can't we just *tell* him?" I ask.

"I wish Alaia was wrong here," says Evelyn, "but she's right: once Lucan thinks someone's guilty, he's hard to budge. We can't just tell him, we have to prove it. We need to show him the footage. We'd better give him a DVD of that Angel stuff."

Rik draws his breath in. "Giving that stuff out is so dodgy. We don't know where it might end up, and we all have confidentiality agreements with Jason … except Alaia."

"So our jobs are kind of on the line here," says Evelyn.

"I'm sorry," says Alaia. "But we don't have any choice, do we?"

"Here's an idea," says Rik. "We could just ask Lucan to pop round here for tea and stickies, and have a peek at the footage, without taking a copy away with him."

Evelyn shakes her head. "Nice idea, but can you really see Lucan just 'popping round'? He's incapable of popping, trust me. We can't have him in here. For one thing, you don't want him seeing all this equipment. Don't forget he's running an operation. He may start seeing dollar signs here."

A warning thought stirs in me. "You said he wanted revenge against me because I may have lost him some face on the street," I address Evelyn. "Won't he want even more revenge, if he knows I've also been spying on him?"

Evelyn thinks carefully. "No. I know Lucan. It's funny but that's not really an issue. He's too vain—he'll think of it as starring in his own movie."

"But wouldn't he at least be sorry that his abuse of Angel had been uncovered?" asks Alaia.

Evelyn considers this, then shakes her head. "This is gonna sound strange, but he'd probably be OK with being seen to be abusing such a cute slave."

"Then wouldn't he still feel OK in that way," asks Alaia, "whatever the source of the leaked info? I mean, whether that source had been Angel or someone else or something else?"

"No," says Evelyn. "It wouldn't really be the information getting out, that Lucan would mind—it would be the fact that it was spread by Angel gossiping. 'Cos that would turn their power relationship around. Lucan's addicted to his power over Angel. Lucan's only been beaten once, by anybody—when he first met Jaymi and Jaymi took control of him—and he didn't like that. So there's no way in hell that he would like it, if he found out that Angel took any kind of control. So I really think we need to give Lucan a copy of the Angel tune-in." She looks at the clock. "Damn, where did the time go? It's too late to call him now. And I'm not knocking on his front door tonight, or even just putting a DVD through the letterbox—he'd probably hear something anyway and it would just be too late and strange. We'll give him a copy tomorrow morning. I just hope Angel will be all right tonight."

So, tired but resigned to it, Rik switches on a multiple-DVD-burner and starts burning discs. Yawning, he scribbles the names of the targets on the top of the discs as they emerge. "Are you two still coming upstairs for a while, when we're done in here?" he asks.

"Oh, sure," I say. I'd forgotten we had arranged this.

"Thanks Rik, but I'm going to pass," says Alaia. "I need to sleep. Plus I want to get up early and call Lucan about giving him the DVD. It's my job to do it, and I'd like to do it sooner rather than later."

"Early?" says Rik, turning off the DVD-burner. "Rather you than me." He crosses the studio to the door and holds it open for us. "That's fine, you get some sleep. Oh, don't forget the DVD—look in the pile by the burner there. There's a few copies of all the footage together, plus a few copies of each target by itself—I forget how many of which, but they're all labelled."

As Alaia looks through the discs, I gather my things. "I've got a Camberwell Carrot ready-rolled upstairs," says Evelyn.

"Sorted," says Rik, giving her a kiss on the lips and then a slap on the bottom. "What a woman."

Alaia seems to be taking a while by the DVD-burner, but she now has her disc at last and follows us out of the studio. Outside the door, the three of us say goodnight to her. While I follow Rik and Evelyn towards the back stairs, I look back over my shoulder to watch her receding quickly alone, in the opposite direction down the long dim corridor. Near the very end, she wheels around without warning, sees me watching her, doesn't smile, then wheels back around again and vanishes into the marble hallway, sending a chill up the back of my neck.

60 RIK'S AND EVELYN'S GENIUS AT HANG-OUTS

Upstairs we make good use of Rik's and Evelyn's comfortable leather sofas and armchairs. Drinks and snacks appear and the promised Camberwell Carrot is lit, handed round and drawn in deep.

Some oozingly atmospheric dubstep echoes and drips from the bass-bins of a set of high-end speakers positioned around the room. Of course: what better soundtrack could there possibly be, especially at night, for this wrecked but enchanted little wasteland of a town? It's almost as if this deep and spooky sound were made specifically for Asbury Park—a place that I've already begun to love, oddly, with something of the love Evelyn has for it. Her love will be more authentic, since she grew up here. But neither is my own love inauthentic, for this fractured and unique corner of the world—half quiet town, half slum by the sea.

"Where did you two meet?" I ask.

"In a bar just down the road here," he says. "Now demolished. It was soon after I moved here from New York. I was wandering round one night, to see what was here, and looked through the door and saw this one behind the bar."

"I only worked there two weeks, so it was lucky timing," she says. "The place was nearly empty and he just came in and parked himself at the bar right in front of me. He was tipsy already and I was thinking, I have to get rid of this one somehow! But there wasn't much I could pretend I had to be doing, so I was kind of stuck with him. I thought, not long till closing time, I'll survive till then. But then he started telling me the stupidest jokes—"

"Two pretzels were walking down the street," says Rik. "One was a salted."

"Yeah, that was one of them."

"A horse walks into a bar," says Rik. "Bartender says, 'Hi there, why the long face?'"

She throws a pillow at him. "So I had a couple of drinks, to help me make it through the jokes. Then by closing time I just found I was nearly on the floor laughing, even though the jokes hadn't improved at all—including mine. So we locked up and turned the lights lower and just kept pouring drinks and got slammed. We could hardly stand up by the end of it. For some strange reason it was just the funniest night." She chuckles long and loud at the memory.

"When I first came in, I was pretty desperate for a drink," says Rik, "but I was out of money by this point, so I was down to sponge shots."

"What are they?" I ask.

"You know, those squeezes of juice from the sponge they use to wipe off the bar, when you can't afford anything else? Well, maybe I wasn't that desperate. But this place we're talking about, it was hardly even a real bar, it just about had wall-to-wall floors. I was scraping the barrel, going in there, because what I was really looking for was some rich chick to snog and then maybe shack up with. Instead of which..." He looks at her.

She throws another pillow at him. "I'm running out of pillows. So yeah, at last we left the bar and he took me back to his place, which turned out to be a tiny, half-renovated apartment here."

"I could hardly get it up."

She nods. "But before that, he poured us a nightcap, but the sitting room was so ridiculously small that there was only space for one single wooden chair—which he went and sat in! Leaving me to sit on the floor, excuse me. 'You OK?' he asked me. And I said, 'Well if you've got an enormous ass like I have, the floor's quite comfortable, thank you very much.' Then he remembered his manners and dragged me into the bedroom. Then later I got all serious and asked, 'Who *are* you?' And you said—"

"I said, 'I am the fleck of beefburger on the mirror of humanity.'" He gets up to change the music. "Here's an oldie but goodie, *Chill Out*. Reminds me of hearing it in Glasgow."

"Happy memories?" I ask.

"Oh yeah… Sometimes the smallest snippets of a place are the most flavoursome. Like at school there, there was this thicket beside a pond—"

"How thick was the thicket?" asks Evelyn.

"—Where we used to smoke in break, to avoid getting caught, though the teachers always knew we were there of course. It was all 'Let's spark up' and 'Flash us a cigarette' and the fag-packets tossed down among the roots in the banks of the pond… Nothing special really, just a keen little scene for a while there, which I shan't forget. I used to go there with Florinda, my girlfriend at the time. She had a face like a well-smacked arse—they used to call her the blonde bombsite. She used to play these CDs of nature recordings all the time, like ninety minutes of whales moaning or *The Sound of Hippos Belching* volume 3. She wore tons of scent, I have to say. Always smelt like a hooker's handbag, but I liked her, she was cool… Talk about loose, though, man: it was like throwing a sausage up a close."

He dodges as a third pillow is hurled at him.

So we chat and laugh, and smoke another joint and sink further down into the deep-purple sofa and armchairs, as Rik regularly nudges the music in a different direction to suit the shifting mood; and such is their understated genius as informal hosts, that when at last I take a leisurely float through the Metropolitan's stairways and corridors to my room, I feel I have known them my entire life.

PART V

WEDNESDAY:
I LEARN ALAIA'S SUBTERFUGE

61 ALAIA BITES THE BULLET AND CALLS LUCAN

Next day in my room at noon, Alaia sits at the table to phone Lucan from the landline, while I perch on the table beside her and Evelyn stands by. "I just have to bite the bullet and do this," she says, dialling. "How do I phrase it?" she asks us. "Oh, I'll just blurt it out... Hi Lucan, it's Alaia, about my phone call to you last night, I just meant to add that I didn't hear anything from anybody else about what we were talking about—nothing at all. I knew about that thing, only because we were just tuning in to Angel a bit, through Jaymi's psychic sight, you know, just to test that sight—" She pauses. "It's not bullshit and I'm going to prove it: I'm going to lend you a copy of what he tuned in to, on DVD... Good, I'm going to deliver it to you today, what time d'you want me to come and deliver it?... *What time*, Lucan, I'm going to come and deliver it. OK, I'll come to your front door at one o'clock and just give it to you. Goodbye..." She carries on listening to the receiver, glancing up at us. "No, just Angel. Bye then. What?... Oh, really? Tonight at your place? What time?... Oh, well, I don't know, maybe... OK bye, thanks, yeah, bye." She hangs up and stares at us. "I didn't sound very cool and collected, did I? So much for the *Sound & Vision* ice-goddess. Anyway, I think that went OK, maybe. But then the funny thing was, he invited us to a party."

"I half-heard he was having one," says Evelyn. "Did he invite all of us?"

"Yeah. Is it some kind of trap? It must be a trap."

Evelyn considers this, then grins. "No, girl, I think it's just a party!" She shrugs. "Well OK then, we should go. But we should go early and not stay so long and not have too much fun, because we need to keep it together and not get too involved over there—we're still under contract with Jason and we're meant to carry on keeping a low profile."

Alaia's phone vibrates. "That's my new therapist," she says, peering at the incoming number. "I'm going to take this outside, I'll be right back," and heads for the door.

Evelyn stares after her, then back at me. "She is *so* New York... But yeah, I've been to a few parties at Lucan's."

"Fun?" I ask, casually picking up the brown envelope I've been noticing beside Alaia's bag on the table beside me. It is unsealed and bears Lucan's name. I glance inside.

"Sure." Evelyn grins: "Just go easy on the weed there, it's Humboldt County... We may find out if he still thinks Shigem left those heads."

I nod thoughtfully, only half-attending to her words because I'm seeing something interesting here in my hands. Half-pulling the DVD from its envelope, I'm struck by its labelling, in Rik's scrawl: it reads not "Angel", as it should have read, but rather "All 4"...

"I'm due to call Jason and Marc now," Evelyn is saying. "D'you want a word with them?"

I replace the disc and the envelope on the table, just as they were before. "Oh, yes please."

Alaia re-enters the room, looking tense. "How was the therapist?" I ask.

"Fine. I told her about my call with Lucan just now."

"You what?" says Evelyn. "You told some stranger out there about our dealings with Lucan?"

"I didn't give anything away that I shouldn't have. I only said I'd just had to make a demanding phone-call, which had taken it out of me. She said I should lie down and take a rest."

Evelyn raises her eyes. "Jesus, and you pay her for *that*? Anyway, I didn't think starving artists could afford therapists."

"I finished starving last month. Now I'm well-fed. But I still have the same issues. Believe it or not, I'm actually quite high-tension."

"*Surely* not," says Evelyn. She shakes her head, as if to clear it. "All right. Now I have to call Marc—d'you want a word with him?" Alaia nods. "OK, you speak with him first, then Jaymi, then me." Evelyn dials a number on the landline and hands the receiver over to her.

I lose myself in puzzling over the scribbled label on the DVD, until I see Alaia holding the receiver out to me.

I take it. "Hallo Marc."

"Jaymi. I can't speak for long, but just to say that tomorrow or the next day I'll know whether we're doing a third broadcast and when we'll be bringing you out of hiding. I'll let you know. Meanwhile, I'm sorry you're a prisoner of the Metropolitan. You must have wanted to go out, but I'm grateful you haven't—there's just too much at stake for us to risk introducing any loose variables into the equation, and I'm told Asbury Park is full of those!"

"Well, if this is a prison, it's certainly a luxurious one."

"Good, good. Do make yourselves at home, no expense spared. You can order food down from Manhattan if you like—they can bike it down, 24/7. Ask Evelyn for the folder of menus, it has all the best places in it. Alaia sounded relaxed?"

"Oh, yes, very relaxed," I say, glancing at her where she stands grinding her teeth beside me, probably still chewing over her call to Lucan.

"Excellent. Jaymi, there's another call coming in, that I have to take. Tell Evelyn to call me later, if you would."

"Shall do. Bye!" I hang up. "He wants you to call him later," I tell her.

"OK." She points at the window. "The sun's out, and I'm going for a walk. Wanna come, you two?"

"I shan't, thanks," says Alaia, "I need to go to Lucan's, then I must practise some vocals in the studio."

"Good girl," says Evelyn, then turns to me, enquiring.

I'm not sure what I want to do, now I've seen that DVD. *Why* did Alaia pick up one of the copies containing all four targets from all three sessions, instead of one of the copies of just Angel as we'd agreed? Should I say anything about this to her? Maybe. But if so, should I do so in front of Evelyn? I can't think it all through, quite this fast, but here is Evelyn staring at me... "Yeah, why not," I tell her.

62 PLEASURE TO BE YOU

Alaia picks up the envelope and goes to her room, therefore, while Evelyn and I leave the building and turn left on Bergh Street. As we walk, my mind is working. Alaia must surely have seen it was the wrong disc when she picked it up. I remember, too, her slight hesitation when choosing it from the heap beside the DVD-burner, while Rik was across the studio holding the door open for us... So it was deliberate on her part, no question! But why?

My reflections are interrupted by the sight of Flames ahead across Third Avenue, standing beside a ruined hotel. When we reach him he joins us and starts to tag along, on the other side of her from me, sneaking glances at her while they make small talk. I tune in to her ... and as you walk with your gentle self-contained swing, Evelyn, I feel the easy sway and liberation of your limbs. I'm there for a second in your fingertips, stroking the arch of your brows up and round. I know the need to flick your hair back past your ears and down your shoulders. I feel the breeze bring a sudden drying cool to the smoothness of the side of your neck, where the skin is faintly moist. I see how centred you are feeling when you glance at your breasts and the curves of your thighs, with your hands on your hips in your chocolate-brown jeans, full of love for and pleasure at your own body: now and here and this is what you want to be. Through the sparkle of your eyes, slick and fine, it always seems you are sticking up two rude fingers at the world, while you kiss the world. You love being a girl and you know what a cute little number you are, with your smooth pale-brown skin warm and irresistible. A flock of white birds wheels high above the ocean; and way above them, too high to hear, a plane slides silver in the sky, like a capsule. It won't be landing here on the torn asphalt airstrip of Kingsley Street, you think. It can't see you, but you see it—a mirage of the elsewhere. "Elsewhere": but you prefer here. You may go there in future, but not yet. Within you, it's as if there lives a stadium of raised hands, swaying to the currents of the vocals in your mind. There is no elsewhere, in a general sense;

there's only what's before you and you love this very much. You could do many things, but all you really have to do, my Evelyn, is just be you—and that's a pleasure!

She lets Flames stay with us for a block, before her body language nudges him cheerfully away. I feel a momentary temptation to hit him with a chummy, man-to-man statement about lesbians being the only women allowed to have ideas of their own, just as I yesterday learned that his own opinion once was; but I resist this and merely echo his goodbye salute to me.

63 I PUZZLE OUT ALAIA'S SUBTERFUGE

She and I turn right on Fourth Avenue and pass the bowling alley. "My parents' first assignation was at a bowling alley out in Omaha, Nebraska," I muse aloud.

"Very fitting! So, this evening is our last recording session for *Big Bang*. What are you dishing up for us tonight?" We wander past the Fast Lane, a music venue, then past the closed Baronet Theater.

"It'll just be a short one. It'll be something about how I'd like to get away."

"On a vacation?"

"No, off the planet. It's overrated here, don't you think?"

"No, I can't say I do. You just have to run at it."

"And if you don't like running, you're out of luck?"

She stands still and smiles up at me. "Yeah," she says. "You see, not all of your analyses are cuckoo! Anyway, I should head home now, I've got stuff to do." So we turn right on Kingsley Street and wend back towards the Metropolitan.

Lucan, Kev, Flames and Angel are standing beside the Cadillac on Saint James Place. "What a car," Kev is crowing. "The only trouble Cadillacs have around here is the kids. They scratch Cadillacs, all down the sides. But not mine, oh no, 'cos they know I'd break their legs—'cos I've done it twice already."

Angel stares at Kev, and through his stare seeps a breath of night into the sunny afternoon. He despises Kev, I can tell, as a crass and brainless brute lacking mind, style or finer feelings altogether. Though he tries not to make this obvious, it spills from his eyes. It is even understood between Kev and him. Lucan knows it, of course, and I can see it amuses him. To Angel, Kev's bulky machismo, piggy eyes and chewing-gum are all so ugly; everything about him is stupid and clunky. As Angel's eyes reveal: if Angel Deon ran the world, Kev Banton's death would be very soon indeed. For his part, Kev hates Angel less than he's hated, but he is always wary of Angel—a lot because Angel is obviously Lucan's bitch and so cannot be mistreated by anyone other than Lucan, but also because Kev is unnerved by what's foreign to him.

Lucan is about to call across the road to me and Evelyn when he is distracted by Pippa, who appears around the corner ahead of us with her head down. To my surprise she is dressed not in her signature sweatshirt and sweatpants, but in a chic purple blouse and a short black skirt, revealing extremely attractive legs. "She's so fine," mutters Kev. "That's a bitchin' skirt, Pippa," he blurts out, with a genuine admiration.

"*Don't* come near me," she says, immediately blushing, and quickens her pace.

"Been crying again, Pippa?" says Kev. "I'm sorry, honey. Bet you got a weeping pussy too—well, I could stop the leaks, sugar!"

She stops in her tracks and glares at him with anger and hatred. She spits in his direction, then turns away and runs off.

Kev looks stung. "Come and get it, bitch!"

There's a silence, as the group stares after her, then we all stare at Kev.

"I think you just won her heart," mocks Lucan.

"Classy, Kev," calls Evelyn, and Angel smirks at her across the street.

Flames pats Kev on the shoulder: "Yeah, smooth, man! Those charm school lessons are really working."

Kev looks from person to person with vague uncertainty. He wipes his mouth with the back of his hand. "Some people..." he states, shifting from foot to foot and frowning. "Some people just can't stand the heat from my flame."

Lucan and Flames crack up together, slapping their thighs with laughter at him.

"Well, this is edifying," I murmur. Evelyn raises her eyes to the sky and we resume our walk towards the Metropolitan, saying nothing.

As the hooting and caterwauling of Lucan's crew recedes behind us, I resume pondering over the DVD. I think I can now see why Alaia chose the wrong one. I think she is still secretly resentful that we were keeping her ignorant of the imagination-cloning deal, which she disapproves of in itself. And I think she picked up one of the four-target discs because she reckoned that if Lucan sees the full extent of the spying and recording, then he'll react in some unpredictable way that'll sabotage the project. Then if it emerges that she picked up the wrong DVD, she'll probably just claim it was an accident. And if I were ever to tune in to her and see this was untrue, then I couldn't even tell her so, because of the solemn promises I've made not to snoop on her.

Very clever. But I don't want the imagination-thieving sabotaged, because—well, because my targets deserve to have their internal beauties preserved. So what can I do about Alaia's skulduggery?

I check the time. Five to one. Too late to stop Alaia's delivery.

I wonder whether Evelyn knows. "So I guess Alaia will be delivering that DVD any minute now," I say, watching her eyes from the side.

"Yeah. It was the right thing to do, I think. I hope Angel's OK."

No, she doesn't know. "He looked OK back there," I say.

"That doesn't really tell us much, though, does it?"

"No, I suppose it doesn't."

A block more, and we reach the Metropolitan. "Bye, sweetie!" she pecks me on the cheek and steps up into her van.

64 *BIG BANG*: RUN TO THE SUN

During the afternoon I toy with the idea of tuning in to Alaia, to confirm her trying to sabotage Jason's deal with me; but I don't. This is because she is still my best friend and I don't want to snoop into her, but it's also because I don't want to see the resentment that I fear must have contributed to her sabotage effort.

She returns to the Metropolitan late in the afternoon. "Mission accomplished at Lucan's?" I ask.

"Yes, he took the DVD of Angel. He even seemed in quite a good mood, so I took advantage of that to ask him very gently if he hasn't any compassion for the addicts he caters to."

"Alaia! Your stern moral compass makes me feel louche and weak, and I love feeling louche and weak, so please keep it up."

"You do need emotional guidance, Jaymi, yes. I think you may also benefit from a little therapy, and as soon as you're ready to ask me, I have a recommendation or two in that direction."

I'm never quite sure how much she's kidding when she says things like that. Nor am I quite certain she's wrong. "What did Lucan say?"

"He laughed rudely, said I was a bleeding heart from New York who's out of touch with the real world, and asked if I'd ever tried to earn a living here myself. To which I said, 'Actually, Lucan, I have been employed, right here in Asbury Park, as a singer—perhaps you've heard about it.'"

"*Touché*! What did he say to that?"

She laughs. "He said, 'Fuck you, sister, I'll see you at the party!' and shut the door on me."

"Are you going to go?"

"I think we should show our faces for a while, with Evelyn, yes, because it might help us to help Angel and I want to know if Lucan's watched the disc. But I don't want to stay long, because I don't want to start getting pally with Lucan—no way."

She's not coming across as someone who'd be likely to admit to the subterfuge that I think I've fathomed, but I shan't probe her because it's not the moment most conducive to her openness: that moment will occur in the context of the euphoria we shall inevitably share after our seven o'clock recording for the broadcast.

Before long, then, I am back in my *Big Bang* black, standing alone at the window of my room for a few minutes, letting the sound of the ocean seep into me, until the bells across town chime seven. Then she and I are back in the studio with Rik and Evelyn for our third and last official recording session, so that Rik can spend tonight and tomorrow combining the fruits of all three sessions in post-production, ready for airing tomorrow evening. He has spent today reprocessing our recording yesterday evening featuring the return of the giant ship, and he's clearly eager to see what final helping we have for him now.

Today Alaia and I are not sparking with each other, after the technical checks, as much as we were yesterday, so Rik doesn't repeat his trick of throwing us in at the deep end but returns to the established drill of a silent focus period before the countdown. Then the cameras roll and *bam*—time to go! The stadium balloons out around me ... *and are you all ready out there in the stadium now, for the last time? Hallo America, and hallo world!*—and the audience roars in the distance, gigantic. *This is just a little song I wrote while we were on the road (I think it was in a run-down motel in Phoenix, but those run-down motels all run together when you've been on the road as long as we have), a song about how I'd like to get away from here... D'you all ever feel like that, out there? I'm sure you do! Well, just so you all know, I feel your pain, yes I do, I do, I do...* So now at last we fly away and unfurl, from body-form to something grander, freer, lighter, stronger. I don't want the eating and the fighting and the struggle down here—I was made to be aloft and to fling silver rainbows and fly in a wide curve out past Jupiter, a comet's light for food and the music of the spheres beneath my wings. I'm unimpressed that this has taken until now. How natural to expand by a quantum leap, exult between the planets and the quasars, and travel at the speed of light!

So I get into the plane parked here on the ship's deck, and lay the stadium down in the cockpit beside me. Up we fly, close beneath the sky's giant dome, over mountains and forests and seas, and there appears far below, through clouds and sunset light, a city dancing wickedly as night falls. A night-time rainbow flickers up, connected via multi-coloured lightning to the city, which is spraying up light and heat as harp-strings sound—every *plink* a highlight on a champagne drip. Zooming in to the city, we descry queen-palms among the street-lights and freeways, and the harp-plinks are heard to be the chirping of crickets. The plane dips low and veers out from the city, down a valley, in between coloured mountains. The plane's roof is down but there's no wind in my hair.

I twirl a dial, and as the aeroplane spins around its fuselage's axis, the horizon spins slowly round a point upon its length, like a double-headed compass needle. Continents unroll on either side. We fly above a golden country far away, a country of colours all different from the earthly ones, where stately masked figures walk in poppy fields. The tips of two golden clouds pass by each other, while a golden moon behind them blinks soft through their vapours, like a gong's bronze clang. A river of light flows around a chateau of air, reflecting a magenta-crystal sky upon its ripples. Flowers burst aflame in a pale space of foliage where white lions roar under fountains of light, as we fly through a tunnel, disappear in a sunburst and land upon the centre of an opened tangerine, pierced through with the howl of the beauty of its segments!

Tangerine magma rises under us; we soar through the clouds and up and out from the atmosphere and curve toward the sun, which hangs in a black sky. As earth recedes, we hurtle with the sun-blast pulling us, up to a mad speed. Specks of dust streak past, in thin cutting lines. The surface of the sun is rippled, raging and lethal. Streaming solar wind and shafts of light from other stars slash down through infinities of space, with a cold perfect cosmic enormity of scale. The disc of the sun has grown already somewhat bigger; I feel its hidden roar and its engines of destruction. A huge solar flame arcs out from it in ragged shreds, and rays of something shoot from some explosion at the flame's tip, receding at the speed of light in straight lines splayed in all directions to the ends of space. Exultation pumps in me—I scream, and my scream stabs out from the open-roofed cockpit, faster than the speed of sound. I scream again, tears stream out from my eyes, streaking back—

Across the solar system, a choir of sprites sings on Saturn (icy cold and deep black and acid-green chartreuse), ranged on a cloudscape, shooting out strains of a song in high soprano, sharp and ethereal. Above their little pointy ears and sharky shaped eyebrows, the giant planet's rings curve divine across the blackness of space.

And there I shall leave us: running to the sun, with the sprites for a soundtrack. *Oh, you know you want it!* My face fades to black on screen, Alaia's voice fades out, and *Big Bang* glides to the smoothest of halts.

65 HOME IN A NOWHERE TOWN

"Cut," says a quiet voice.

Dark, quiet. Where is this? A fluorescent light flickers on. *A squint at different great events, slanting through the windows of this same narrow room...*

There's a whoop, in Evelyn's voice. The lights around the lenses, which have been cocooning me in my own space by obscuring what is behind them, are turned off and Rik is revealed in that small corner of the studio, behind the camera on my right which has been capturing my right half-profile.

"Fuck me, what a trip!" says Alaia, high-fiving me as she bubbles up out of the sound booth in that noisy black silk dress, and the two of us caper around the studio together.

As a big-stadium performance, this *Big Bang* climax felt just as electrifying as the climax of the international broadcast of *Sound & Vision*. It's a little strange, however, because of course this wasn't live: there weren't the tens or hundreds of millions watching in real time around the world; there weren't the tens or hundreds of thousands watching around the stadium (well, their level of attentiveness was debatable, at best, for *Sound & Vision* too, I remind myself); there weren't the New York broadcast crew watching it just a fraction before the TV viewers did; and once again there weren't even Evelyn and Rik watching it right here in the studio, because he was averting his gaze through the cameras and she was crouching behind me watching Rik's face and my rear end... Not for the first time, I feel gloriously ignored here.

Once Alaia and I have taken our leave of the other two and left the studio, I try, as planned, to take advantage of our euphoria to probe her subtly in order to get a feel about whether she'll be admitting to the subterfuge I fathomed: "You know, I was thinking earlier, it's possible Lucan may actually enjoy all the stuff on the DVD! D'you think he will?"

An element of propriety enters her manner as she replies, "I'm afraid he may, yes. Still, I doubt it'll occur to him that you might be testing out your sight on anyone other than Angel."

OK, so not a chink in the armour there.

"I meant to tell you," she says, "I spoke to Kim and Shigem on the phone earlier and I kind of promised that the two of us would go visit them now to say hallo, and then we'll meet Evelyn and go to Lucan's party."

"Oh, OK, sure—let's go."

So we set off, still bubbling about *Big Bang*. Nearing Shigem's front gate, we see him and Kim approaching from a block away with Pizza Plus bags.

"What a mess," says Alaia inside the apartment.

"I know," says Shigem, "and three days ago it was so tidy. Not that I'm super-particular about where everything goes in my life—just mildly tyrannical."

"I'd noticed," says Kim. "Which bodes well for our place in London, because I like to live in a creative compost."

"A pig-sty, you mean. Yes, it's going to be such fun. This is pizza for everyone, so jump in." We grab slices, perch on boxes and eat. "I tell you, I am so not going to miss that old trout who lives across the landing over there. It's so buttock-clenching, the way she makes this big production number out of me playing music even the teensiest bit louder than we're talking right now. Which gets really old, really fast. When she first complained, I thought I'd ask her round here, to win her over and break the ice: you know, 'Hallo, fancy coming over for stiff conversation, you old bag? We could have sherry and a selection of cheeses, and maybe I'll break out the cyanide cookies.' But somehow, going to the dentist always sounded like more fun than having her over, so I never asked her."

"Bye bye!" Kim waves, in the direction of the woman's apartment. "Keep in touch, you old bag."

Shigem reaches down to retrieve three teddy-bears from the floor where they have been getting unceremoniously trampled, and introduces them: "The small pink one is Kum-kum, the smaller white one is Jason (he glows in the dark) and the bigger white one is Zéphire. Coffee?"

"Yes," says Alaia. "I'm impressed you can still find the tea-spoons."

"Weeks of planning," says Shigem. "You know, I used to be really into kitchen utensils, but I've calmed down about them a bit, in recent years."

"What a strange town this is," says Alaia, looking out of the window.

"Yeah, it's not the kind of boring bland suburbia where I grew up," says Kim. "It's interestingly fucked-up instead."

"It's fucked-up for sure," says Shigem, "but in a funny kind of way I love it, although it battered me into the car-wreck I am."

"You're not a car-wreck," says Kim.

"No? Maybe I just look like one: I look in the mirror and I think, 'What a car-wreck, but I still love you!'"

"You're beautiful," says Kim.

"Charmed, I'm sure."

"You two are going to have a fabulous time living in London," says Alaia.

"Unless the plane crashes," says Shigem. "Then we'd probably have less of a good time. Oh well, that's just a risk we'll have to take. Who wants to be safe and contrived and always know everything's going to work out nicely? It's never too late for a nice little plane-crash, just like it's never too late to start smoking... Which reminds me, last night Lucan's Cadillac passed by us. The window was open and Lucan was in the passenger's seat staring out and he made that sign at me again, even more aggressive than he did on Sunday night"— and here he does a very Shigem version of Lucan's brutally eloquent self-decapitation gesture—"which has left me fucking stressed."

His bright brown eyes confirm this fear. "I'm not surprised," I say; and as if in confirmation of the stress, I only now register that the acne I saw on him last night is considerably worse today. "By the way," I ask, "why did smoking remind you of Lucan, just then?"

"Because Lucan makes me want to smoke."

"They should use him in smoking commercials," says Kim.

"Those would be commercials that only worked on me, though," says Shigem. "Not that I'd need them, because I've got him living here just a few blocks away, making gestures out of Cadillacs wherever I go. I go round a corner and wham—there he is again, in a different Cadillac, making this week's style of decapitation gesture. So they wouldn't be very cost-effective commercials. Mr Smoking and Mr Cigarette and all those other rich smoky fucks wouldn't have that warm glow of money well-spent."

"I visited Lucan today," Alaia tells him, "and I gave him a glowing character reference for you, and I swore I saw you myself in Paradise on Sunday night at the exact time the first head would have been taken to Downstairs."

"*Did you?* Thank you, Alaia, that was very sweet and brave of you! You're an absolute doll. How did he react?"

"He didn't give anything away, I'm afraid ... but he's got to take the heat off you. It's so stupid if he doesn't."

I think back a couple of nights, to see whether any similar alibi will also be available to cover Shigem for the discovery of the waxwork head of Kev on the following evening, Monday; but I abandon this when I recall tuning in to him and Kim at that time, after the gathering at Evelyn's place, to find them simply going to bed here with no other witnesses than me.

After more cheap pizza and another hour of nattering, the doorbell rings. "That'll be Evelyn," I say. "Believe it or not, the three of us are actually going to a party at Lucan's tonight, though I'm not sure why. Would you like to join us, Shigem?"

"I'll think I'll pass, thanks, but give him a big kiss from me and ask him not to kill me, please."

66 RAIN ON CORRUGATED IRON

"OK," says Evelyn as we come within earshot of the music spilling out of Lucan's house, "we don't want to get too involved here, we don't want to get too chummy or stick around too long, because you two are still meant to be keeping a low profile. So let's head straight across the front hallway and downstairs to the den, because then the lighting will be low. Also, down there it'll be more about music than talk, and half the people will be dancing or stoned—so even if they do recognise Jaymi, they probably won't care. Plus Lucan'll be down there."

"I want to know if he watched the DVD," says Alaia. "It might help us to help Angel."

A couple of guys are stationed on the front porch, flanking the open door. They nod to Evelyn and we pass inside, straight across the hallway where a few people are milling around, and down a steep flight of wooden steps to the source of some fast, dirty drum and bass. At the bottom is a capacious smoky basement den, half-filled with a couple of dozen figures I can barely see, so dimly is the space lit by various red and yellow lights. I can make out Flames nearby, talking with someone and holding a bass saxophone by his side; he sees us and greets us amiably, giving Evelyn a kiss on the cheek. I'm pleased to be able to see no sign at all of Kev, who must be upstairs; but I do spot Damian sitting alone on the other side of the room, glowering on a bean-bag and nursing a tall glass of what I suspect may be grapefruit juice. I give him a wave and he nods back with respectful gruffness.

And what an upbeat but mellow party it is. I was half-expecting some new and gruesome wax dummy head to unveil itself, but no. Soon the drum and bass gives way to some booming old dub track full of basement chat and slow echoes, to which Flames improvises artfully and softly on his saxophone, leaning against a wall. The combination of sounds is like a rich thick whisky running over elephant hide, somewhere in a cavernous dance-hall, with the rain splattering down onto a corrugated iron roof high above.

As this segues into a dance-hall track, Flames keeps pace with it. A group of people near us drift away, so for the first time I see Angel where he dances in a corner by himself, and very much for himself, stoned and beautiful … and for the room too, you must admit, my little Angel, for several here are watching you with warmth while they talk and dance and sway. Lucan is among them, grinning as his eyes track your movements. He banters with the others all the while, taps his feet and dips his head in time with the beat. He's so genial tonight that you almost forget his dictatorship and the tyranny he exercises over you—different as it is from the other tyrannies he exercises over many others here. So you just let go and bliss out, while in your mind you lie in comfort on the warm bouncy surface of an elevated roadway made from the horizontal stiff cocks, rooted alternately on left and right, of two lines of Lucans standing shoulder to shoulder who face one another just to hold you off the ground! You're making subtle love with this music and this moment and the watching of the others, while you dance, with a pinpoint of red light reflected in the silver of your earring. Music never does harm, you tell yourself. So tonight you will dance, transcending all that needs transcending, till your stark black Angel's wings will lift this whole smoky den up over Asbury Park and out across the USA. Lucan smiles and winks at you across the red and yellow space; you smile back weakly, hot and swirling in the dimness, wishing it could always be as now and never change…

67 OVERHEARD THROUGH THE CORN-CHIPS

A joint obtrudes itself into my sightline, proffered by Evelyn. "All the way from Humboldt County," she reminds me. I take two or three good tokes and hand it on to Alaia: strong, for sure, and very nice, though it doesn't feel like anything so unusual.

I glimpse a kitchen down a corridor at the back, where I think I can see glass bowls of corn-chips on a counter-top. "I'm going to the kitchen," I tell the other two and wander off across the den to the start of the corridor. Then swiftly but smoothly over the next few seconds, I come to a point where I cannot feel my feet on the floor at all. I stop and peer down: I am not levitating, but I have no sensory evidence of this, except through my eyes. I reach out and touch the corridor walls on either side of me, to guide myself, and set off again. There's a problem, though: my ability to feel my hands on the walls is also disappearing. At this moment, out of the track that just came onto the sound system, there erupts the single-word lyric, *BABYLON!* in a voice of thunderous charismatic depth and power, resonating with fantastic volume and sensuality, welling up out of driving drumbeats that seem first to belch the word out and then to be flattened by it… I come to a halt again: I wasn't expecting that. Now the word returns, thrown up by that driving beat, surging up the short corridor from behind me like the deep-bass explosion of a volcano: *BABYLON!* I realise I don't want or need to move anywhere, if this sound will be coming back to me again here (as I suspect it will be), because it contains everything I need. Yes indeed, here it comes: *BABYLON!*… I feel I could listen to this, repeated, for hours straight—but I also begin to wish that this explosive aural feast had chosen a more convenient moment to visit itself upon me, for all I have here, pretty much, is visual data: proprioception has gone out of the window, leaving just a conscious head floating in a hallway above an unrelated torso.

This head decides it had better press on nonetheless, guiding itself by looking at where those fingers appear to be pressing into those walls on either side and somewhat below it … and somehow, after a few more *BABYLON!*s, the head reaches the door of an empty kitchen. I see a bathroom doorway on the other side of the kitchen, sway across towards it, disembodied, as if watching myself in a movie, float through the bathroom doorway with a good bit of guesswork, plonk myself down onto the toilet just inside it and pull the door closed beside me. Over the course of some long number of minutes, I'm not sure how many, the feeling creeps back into my hands, then into my feet, while a good number of further *BABYLON!*s erupt.

Evelyn was right about the weed here—I should've gone easier on those tokes.

As I return to earth with the bathroom gently spinning, I hear someone enter the kitchen, humming to himself. I make out the oily-dry scrape and muffled ring of a handful of corn-chips being clawed up from a glass bowl on the counter, then the snap-crunch-chomp of their ingestion and mastication. "Hey, baby Angel," comes Lucan's unmistakable deep brown voice through the corn-chips, as another much lighter step comes into the kitchen.

"Hey," says Angel's voice.

"That DVD was sexy," murmurs Lucan through a mouthful of chips.

"Mmm," comes the answer, in a tone I can't decipher.

With surprise I find I am tuning in to Lucan, as he contemplates Angel on the other side of this door. This is happening without my having intended it at all—the only time I've tuned in to anyone by mistake. Maybe I'm stoned? Yes, perhaps I am! Before I can think about whether and how to extricate myself from the tune-in, I see that I'm looking at Lucan's memory of first meeting Angel, two or three years ago on Kingsley Street, and I cannot look away … for he seemed to you, Lucan, like a sexy little fly. You saw him as a creature whose natural habitat would be hovering above a steaming-hot pool of blood and honey, sending his feelers down into it like the snouts of a voracious alien. And those *killer* eyes on him—so startling in close-up! Those big, brown, vital eyes, so dark and alive and dangerous and watchful, beneath long black eyelashes; the curve of the eyes echoed and magnified underneath by the fuller convexity of pale brown-olive skin curving outward over his cheekbones, then quickly back in and down in slanting arcs to the reticent mouth and smooth sharp chin; and the delicate jaw-line rising around behind, past small ears to the flame of black hair above a round intelligent forehead. That animal immediacy, that play of flesh and electricity combined, that scything sharpness and tang within a wrapping of organic yield and warmth, which knew that it grabbed your own gaze and licked it back. Here was an urgent, self-evident truth for you, Lucan, discovered at a moment and in a human vehicle where you would never have expected to find it. For you'd only ever had girlfriends—yet how *beautiful* this boy would look, raped and crying! No, there was no way to move away and leave this one behind, without the stale and dreary guilt of loss, and you weren't that stupid, were you, Lucan?

"Can you believe that stuck-up bitch fucked up and gave us the wrong disc?" says Lucan, jolting me out of him, so I find myself looking once again at the inside of the bathroom door. A slap resounds around the kitchen, which sounds very like the sound of two powerful hands clapping gleefully together. I hear him take another almighty fistful of corn-chips.

"Can you believe Shigem and Kim! Can we say *insipid?*" replies Angel with a sensual acidic malevolence, like a lisping snake.

"Vanilla essence, yummy-yum," murmurs Lucan, buried in his chips.

"I still can't believe you thought I'd gossiped about us," Angel accuses him. "How are you going to make it up to me?"

The only reply is a loud, leisurely, nonchalant crunch.

"*Answer me!*" lisps Angel, insistent, but is answered by nothing more than another big, slow crunch, doubtless with an insolent grin to match it. "Whatever it is, it had better be good..."

I should probably get up and return to Alaia and Evelyn, before they wonder whether I've crashed out somewhere; but having just seen Lucan's memory of first meeting Angel, I decide to sneak the quickest of peeks at Angel's first memory of meeting Lucan, as I did yesterday evening with Kim's and Shigem's memories ... and you'd seen Lucan here and there around town, Angel, but never from as close as when he stopped on Kingsley Street and looked you up and down. Planted there in front of you, surrounded by his entourage, he struck you as a drummer on a stage in a cone of light, with all the band beneath him and the curves of his biceps drumming with a slow aggression, face remaining shaded till he tossed up his head with sexy arrogance, flinging up droplets of sweat in slow motion through the spotlight.

You saw him, all in all, as a vision of perfection. You dreamed that he would sweep you off your feet and that you'd lie draped lasciviously across his powerful arms, like a fairy princess swooning when she's rescued by a prince. In blunter terms, while assuming he was straight (but more especially if he was), you were desperate to be fucked.

Then, to your shock, this all occurred, for many months.

Then during its occurrence, Lucan's laughter in the dark welled up behind the air and echoed all across the sky, deep and wicked. And along with his laughter came your first intimation that your new position here with him, despite its nightly ecstasy, provided scant protection from the murderous dangers inherent in associating with him.

68 MOVEMENTS THROUGH THE WALL

Hearing Angel and Lucan leave the kitchen, I open the bathroom door, slip across the room into the corridor and follow them back into the music and babble of the den. As I slide through the surface of the revolving-door image of people all around me, Alaia swims up from somewhere. "Hi!" I say, then speak low into her ear: "I just overheard Lucan and Angel talking about what they saw on the DVD."

Her eyes flick to mine, then away again. "Oh, really?"

"I only overheard them for a moment. They didn't know I could hear. But they seem to be getting on fine with each other."

"Thank goodness. I just never found any opportunity here to ask Lucan if he'd watched it, he was always with other people."

I refrain from speaking. Is she going to ask me, I wonder, whether I overheard Lucan and Angel revealing what they saw on the DVD—*whom* they saw on the DVD?...

No, she's not. Maybe she'd ask this if we were outside? "Shall we leave, since we planned not to stay late?" I ask.

"Um, I think I'm going to stay a bit longer. But if you want to head out, that's fine, I'll see you tomorrow morning. Evelyn left a few minutes ago."

"OK, sure. Have fun."

"You'll get back OK?"

I nod, float upstairs and out onto the Avenue. No sign of any confession from Alaia, then.

Back in the Metropolitan, I sprawl on my bed with the light off and my sense of space revolving. From throughout the last four roller-coaster days, the disparate voices of Marc, Alaia, Jason, Evelyn, Rik, Flames, Lucan, Kev, Damian, Angel, Shigem, Kim and Pippa all chatter at once in grand cacophony, each voice emanating from inside its own densely specific human life and all bubbling up around me in the spume of a million overwhelming details, until a most welcome sleep hits the "mute" button.

I surface when a late and unsteady footfall comes down the corridor—Alaia. She hesitates outside and I lie still, listening to the silence of her listening for me. At last she gets her key out, turns it fumbling in her door-lock, enters and shuts her door. Does she think I'm tuning in to her? Does she know I know about her subterfuge? I've told her that I don't tune in to her. Does she disbelieve me? I'm tempted to find that out right now by tuning in, but I don't. I listen to her moving around next door while I drift back towards sleep, conscious of a chill of subterfuge and uncertainty hanging in the air of my room, seeping in through the wall right beside me here, from wherever she may happen to be positioned in relation to this bed...

PART VI

THURSDAY: SECOND
SPOTLIGHT WITH ALAIA

69 ALAIA FAKES FOR TWO
AUDIENCES AT ONCE

On waking next morning, I decide I shan't yet tell Alaia I know about her subterfuge but shall see how the situation plays out. We meet mid-morning when she knocks and comes into my room. She plays it "natural" and I play along, but I'm not feeling it. We call Rik's and Evelyn's home number, to see if we need to do anything more for tonight's *Big Bang* broadcast. "Rik's gone out, but why not come round and we'll call him and ask," says Evelyn. "I'm just getting into the shower but I'll leave the front door open, so just come on in and make yourselves at home and make us an instant coffee and I'll be out in a few minutes." So Alaia and I go round to their place and make three mugs of coffee and lounge on the sofa in the sitting room, with the splash of the shower coming from behind the bathroom door. The landline rings. "See who that is," calls Evelyn.

"OK," calls Alaia and picks up the phone. "Hallo, this is Evelyn's apartment... Lucan!" she says in a lowered voice, glancing at the bathroom door. "This is Alaia, I'm just visiting Evelyn, she's in the shower right now; can I take a mess— You wanted *me*? You don't have my number..." She listens, casting anxious looks at me. "You've seen it? Yes, I didn't get a chance to ask you last night. Thanks for the party, by the way... Yes... Good, you'll make it up to..." She smiles and looks down, embarrassed. Next moment her smile is gone, however, and I monitor my own reactions carefully while I am treated to the sight of her putting on a plausible act for two different audiences—me and Lucan, only one of whom she believes to have knowledge that all four targets were on the DVD, but both of whom she believes to have no knowledge of her deliberation in delivering that wrong DVD. And she does a damn good job of this delicate task, serving up a sequence of three well-judged effects: first, more for Lucan's benefit, comes a brief pretence of disbelief that any other footage than Angel's is on the DVD; then secondly, more for my benefit, comes the pretence of reluctant but growing belief that what he says must be true, as he doubtless informs her of some detail from one of the other three targets that he couldn't have known without seeing a disc containing it; then thirdly, for both of us, she dishes up the requisite embarrassment at having made such a foolish and indiscreet error. Yes, she admits, the wrong disc must have been sent—oh dear. I feel like clapping, but must instead begin my own feint, in the form of raised eyebrows, worried glances, disappoint-ment, head-shakings and half-forgiving looks. She sits listening awhile, as Lucan says something I can't guess. "Very civic-minded of you, I'm sure," she says dryly. "OK Lucan, I'll relay the message," and she hangs up.

Evelyn enters from the bathroom, dressed, with damp hair. "Did you just say 'Lucan'?" she asks. "What did he want—what 'message'?"

"Oh ... he called to say the footage is 'really hot', he sees now that Angel wasn't gossiping to me, and he'll make it up to Angel, probably with some 'extra-hot loving'."

"Jesus, any more of that and Angel will expire from it," says Evelyn. "Not that we should underestimate him: I've always said that if he were a computer peripheral, he'd be hot-pluggable. But anyway, I'm happy the DVD worked—you're a genius, girl!" She picks up the phone. "Now let's call Rik."

"Yeah, well handled," I tell Alaia. "Sounds like it was easier than we expected."

She gives a small smile.

70 COLDNESS ON THE BEACH

"Rik says there's nothing more for us to do for the *Big Bang* broadcast tonight," says Evelyn. "He was up super-late last night, processing your run to the sun. Then he was up at dawn today, putting the three sessions together."

Twenty minutes later, the three of us are strolling up the Boardwalk in the sun. There are one or two other people around, but the sand is deserted. "Strange there's no one lying on the beach or swimming," I say.

Evelyn laughs. "You'd have been looking at hundreds of them, back in the 'twenties. You can see them in the old photos on the wall in the hotel there. Even just a few years ago there'd have been a handful of people sunbathing. I used to see them, growing up. Pippa was one of them. But hardly ever since then."

"Today was when Shigem was going to borrow those opera-glasses, for Kim to look up at her balcony," I say. "Should we call and remind him?"

"No, let's not. Of course he won't forget," says Alaia with a rather cold dismissiveness, as if her understanding of Shigem were as well-honed as Evelyn's is from years of knowing him. This I find annoying. And her cold, hurtful manner certainly belies the "natural" effect that she was cloaking her conversation in this morning: I knew there was something wrong with that, while it was happening. I muse upon the subtle change there seems to have been, between us, since we got here. Maybe there's just been too much going on. It's easy enough while we're actually working together, when it's all about the project at hand; but at other times there has started to be an odd undercurrent from her that I can't quite make sense of.

We duck beneath yellow tape and set off across the sand. I watch Evelyn while she hurls pebbles out to sea, competing with Alaia to throw further … and a faint music wafts on the breeze, Evelyn. It has the magic of the song in *Sound & Vision*; but you know it is a lie, because it's mixed with the lies from Alaia's song of death. You hear it as a song of some unreachable perfection—a thing from which this world has fallen short and for which this world yearns from its gutters of disease and dirt. There's lifting-up and flowering and bursts of sunlit glory in this music, with angel choirs piercing and soft (maybe lies?). The music carries ancient things and future evolution, outside time (another lie?). Out above the ocean we half-see mountains in celestial mist and valleys inaccessible, or is this just a cloudscape? I suppose that if you'd not been so behind the scenes with us, so much "behind the curtain", you might have been more taken in by the pair of us.

In your eyes, behind the watermarks of Asbury Park, are flickers of another world you carry inside. As you laugh with Alaia in your pebble-throwing contest, I tune deeper in, to see the flowers in your looking-glass. And there in the palace garden's scented dusk, I see them: flowers, in a more literal sense than I'd expected, mauve petals dripping scented tears onto humus. You've caught a peacock butterfly somewhere in the palace and have cupped your hands around it to bring it out here, where you now toss it up into the night—whereupon a dark bird swoops from the roof, snaps the peacock up, wheels with a rip of feathers flapping through the air, and is gone. You cry out and set off at a run through the grounds—a sweep of yellow silk down a twilit colonnade, where a frieze on the wall shows black human figures flitting delicate and sharp through a pale gold field. Your skirt is like a fluted column, coloured pale celadon beneath the yellow silk sash, running, turning back to me. (Celadon and yellow—a combo that you'd probably once have judged too fresh for Kingsley Street.) "I once collected tears in a glass!" you call. Your laughter ripples out from you, fluid as the image of the moon ahead reflected on the lanes of water running up the fields in our direction through a valley full of dripping mist. Soft weather, lilac-tide: we'd hear a feather float, just assuming that there were a feather, carried on the air where the samphire blooms under trees whose golden autumn leaves tremble on their branches. This cartoon candy-pastoral is undermined, however, by the final thing I see. Through your palace garden gate is the sea, but de-classicised by certain shoreline details: "Evelyn, it's a mushroom bay," I say. And it's true: for the only things growing on the curve of this enchanted shore are mushrooms, some a metre high. As you nod in solemn pride at this, a line of dolphins leap from the water far across the bay, then dive beneath the surface once again, without a ripple. We hear a magic interval between two notes, several times—bewitching, as if an angel lives between them—and I know that I should now leave your mushroom bay. I shan't intrude again here, so never shall I hear again that magic angel interval; but never will it leave me.

71 ALAIA SWIRLS IN DECREASING CIRCLES

The pebble-throwing contest is a tie. Alaia and Evelyn want to head home, but I'm in the mood to walk further, so we split. Alaia continues her coldness in taking her leave of me, with a kind of guarded cordiality. I wonder what Evelyn will have made of this? I doubt she'll have missed it.

I head inland along the grassy further edge of Sunset Lake, turn right on Main Street, get a coffee from Frank's Deli and wander into a bric-a-brac store named Zebra. A middle-aged black woman appears at the back and looks at me with kind, perceptive eyes. "See anything you like?"

"Yes," I say, on a whim, holding up a small, grey, plastic elephant. "How much?"

"You can have that for free."

"Really? Thank you! What's your name?"

"Dotty."

"Jaymi."

"How long you staying in Asbury?"

"Not long. But I may be back."

She shakes her head.

I laugh. "Why d'you shake your head?"

"You'll never return here." Witnessing my surprise at this impromptu psychic reading, she adds, "Don't worry, it's nothing bad." She turns away, into a hidden room. "You did good here," she calls back over her shoulder. "Remember that."

Does she recognise me? "Anything else you can tell me?"

She pauses in the doorway, holds my inquisitive look with a glance of knowledge, humour and compassion, and shakes her head.

"Thank you, Dotty," I say, holding the elephant up beside my face. She inclines her head a fraction, then is gone.

I step out, head back towards the ocean and look at the elephant. "Hallo Dotty," I whisper, give her a kiss and put her in my pocket.

Halfway across the Sunset Lake footbridge, I go down the steps onto the island and up to its inland end and recline on the grass against a tree-trunk, near some ducks.

My phone vibrates—Alaia. "Jaymi, I need to make confession. I've got myself in a mix. Don't hate me, please. When I was on the phone at Evelyn's, Lucan gave me an ultimatum: he said I'd better get the General Network to call him and offer him some money for his discretion, or else he'd go public about us spying into people. I told him that was very civic-minded of him. That was his real message, not just the bit about making it up to Angel."

"Why didn't you say so, when Evelyn asked what his message was?"

"Because I thought that if I told her straightaway, then Jason would have to be told and would probably just buy Lucan's silence, so the spying would stay secret. But if I waited before passing along his ultimatum, then Lucan would go public and our spying project would be sabotaged."

"And that was a reason to *wait*? ... Why?"

"Because ... I didn't like your going behind my back with that spying deal, though I do understand the reasons. I'm sorry, I'm just not good at dealing with being left out. I know it's dysfunctional, but there it is. So there. I've drummed up the courage to confess to you—but how can I go through this with Evelyn too? She wouldn't understand this. She'd never get herself caught up like this. And here am I, this 'goddess of the airwaves'. Then I'd have to go through it with Rik too—no, I can't! But then, part of me feels that although Evelyn and Rik are great ... still, when you get down to it, they're General Network people and they've colluded in Jason's blackmail of you. Very principled, I'm sure. Because don't forget, Jason *is* manipulating you for cynical and greedy ends. Am I dysfunctional?"

"You're a complete mess. No, scrub that: you're just very hightension with an over-developed moral sense. But do carry on."

"The trouble is, maybe it was dangerous not to tell Evelyn there and then, because if it comes out in future that Lucan gave us his ultimatum today, then why didn't I immediately relay it to her? And it gets worse: because I decided not to tell her about the ultimatum, I couldn't even tell her that I'd given Lucan the wrong disc, because if she knew about the wrongness of the disc, she'd raise it with him and then find out about the ultimatum he gave me… Oh yes, I forgot—as you overheard while I was on the phone with him, I gave Lucan the wrong disc. Sorry about that."

"Oh, yes. Human error?"

"I don't know what to do. I guess I could call Evelyn and say that Lucan called me just now and delivered the ultimatum. Then she'd probably never know that I waited for this hour or two… He'd have had to call me just now on my mobile, though, because if I told Evelyn he called the Metropolitan office and asked for me, then she might find out that he hadn't really done so. And would Evelyn really believe that I would have given Lucan my mobile number? She knows he's the last person I'd give it to. I guess I could call him from my mobile right now, so then he *would* have my number … but then I'd first need to ask Evelyn for *his* number, which would excite her suspicion. Would anyone else here have his number, aside from her? Could I ask Rik, without her knowing? No. Would Shigem have it? He might: he's from the town … but how could I just casually ask him for Lucan's number without making him suspicious, especially when he's one of our targets?… Would Pippa have it? Probably not… Hey! I could look him up online or in the phone book—but *damn*, Jaymi, we don't know his surname."

I rub my eyes: I'm getting a headache here. "Abayomi," I say wearily.

"But then, there's no point looking in phone listings, because of course he'll be ex-directory—how could he not be?"

"Abayomi."

"What?… Oh. How d'you know?"

"I saw it written on a cardboard box in the corner of his hallway. Alaia, you're just swirling around in decreasing circles here. Look, I shan't tell Jason about Lucan's ultimatum… So long as you don't say you told me. You see, this is making it complicated for me already."

"But how do I let Evelyn know about it?"

"I don't think you can, by now, or she'll think you're duplicitous. We'll just have to cross our fingers and hope it works out all right. I know you're not duplicitous."

She sighs. "OK."

"See you later."

72 THE WEASEL AT THE WINDOW

I groan. I have no stomach for disentangling all these permutations of hers. Her confession of her mess just now is an improvement on the coldness she was displaying earlier, and I feel some relief to realise the mess partly explains the coldness—but only partly. As for Lucan, I'd like to think his ultimatum for the General Network suggests he has become distracted from any feelings of resentment against me, but this may not be true. My phone vibrates again. "Hi Kim," I say.

"Hello. Just to let you know I'm a couple of blocks away from Pippa's, with these old opera-glasses that Shigem's borrowed, and a few seconds ago I was looking through them at Pippa's balcony and there *did* seem to be a figure in the shadows, just behind her window. It was the same weaselly size as the figure I saw on the balcony with her the other night—and of course, the one through the keyhole."

"Were they talking to each other?"

"Hard to tell. I think so, yes."

"We have to do something about this—don't you think?"

"Yeah, we do. Not for the next couple of hours, though, because Shigem and I are gonna turn our phones off and go sunbathing, so we'll be out of the loop! But come join us at Paradise tonight, and we can talk. It's the last time he'll be hosting there."

"OK, sure. See you later, then."

I close my eyes, lying here on my island, and throw my attention out to Pippa, hoping she'll be in her sitting room so that I can see through her eyes the figure Kim just glimpsed from a couple of blocks away beyond the glass. As I tune in to her perceptions, however, I see she's gone into her bedroom now. I wish I could simply see through these bedroom walls into her sitting room, in addition to just seeing through her eyes and around her mind right now; though my ability to see around minds has begun to be revealed as being less complete and less under my control than I believed ... and there you are, Pippa. The clock says it's lunchtime (and what clement weather!)—but to you of course it already feels like an evening.

Time to return to your balcony, you feel. Good: this will show me your sitting room and perhaps also ... but no, in fact it won't, for now you part your curtains and uncover a door giving onto your balcony directly from this bedroom, of which I have been unaware until now.

You take your accustomed seat on the balcony, with the back of your head touching the sitting room window-pane right behind us, which I'd guess is in shadow, as Kim said it was just now. From your perch here you look across the grid of streets, beyond the edge of town, to another high-rise, where a young man undresses in the evenings and stands at his window and looks across the space above this town, at you—or seems to. As he ages, year by year, so do you. You never go to seek his building out at ground level, though you're not sure why you don't. Has he ever come to your building, down at ground level, seeking out its address? You guess that he hasn't, and you're most likely right, and yet... Sometimes in the dusk air, precisely between you both, flocks of birds alight on wires, silhouetted hard and small against the fading light that's reflected on his windows; then they fly away. You know him, in a small way. You watched him yesterday, with his light on and yours off. Your bird-seed packet hung here at your balcony, unpecked, while the birds sat over there on the telephone wires. Behind you a game-show flickered, with the sound off. A jet plane buzzed through the sky above his high-rise; you got slowly older while you watched him undress; and he got older too, while he didn't know you watched. What does he do when you can't see him there at his window? you wondered. Does he watch for you inside his unlit room, like you in yours? You heated up a tin of food and ate it from the pan with a spoon, at your window. The clock ticked. The birds on the wire flew away, one by one. The last bird lingered, as if deciding whether it would try your bird-seed packet, but then joined its companions. You lit a Lucky Strike and slowly smoked it in the shadows, down to the end. The man's light went off. Had he gone somewhere, or was he sitting there? Was he smoking, in the flicker of a game-show with muted sound, like you? The hourly bus passed below, empty, and turned right to trundle up Main Street towards the other high-rise. Suddenly you think you see, there in the high-rise nestled at the skyline, the shape of the man in the shadows of his window. You wave ... but he doesn't wave back, because the view between the two of you is only one-way. His shape behind the window is yours to enjoy, but his view of you is blocked, for he never has thought about the mile of air between you; and the traffic-lights are lonely where you live.

You should leave this town and start again, but that would be so tiring and large and complicated. You should have done this and that and made other moves, but you didn't. "Those who lag behind will be beaten," said the big man.

Have you seen your stars in the papers today? You'll forget them by tomorrow, but you may as well look. So you do look. And you know what? They aren't bad at all, Pippa Vail!

73 A NAKED ANGEL ON THE FRONT PATH

Sunset Lake returns to me. How terrible her sadness is. I feel in danger of being drawn into it. However, it is not mine, I remind myself, so I'm entitled to resist this. She certainly makes a good point or two, I must say. She speaks the truth.

And one thing's for sure: what a deep spokes-sheep it's going to be.

I'm restless. I rise and a goose gives a loud honk, startling me. I wander between the trees, turn right along the rest of the footbridge, over swimming ducks to the grassy lake-bank, and head on down Emory Street. I zigzag through the street grid to the width and quiet of Second Avenue, where the large, ramshackle houses look forlorn and somewhat spooky. I see that I'm about to pass Damian's house, and I look ahead to locate it. It contrives to look haunted even in this summer sun. As I approach along the pavement across from it, a glimpse of something in front of his porch twangs inside me and makes me stare across this considerable distance. The old elm branches sway in a sudden cool wind from the sea behind me. That looks like a little figure, sitting in front of Damian's door... It is a figure. It's Angel! But something is wrong with him. It looked for a moment as if he was naked... *Is* he? I still cannot quite tell from this far away but I can see Damian's guard-dogs pacing in agitation up and down the alleyway beside him, their tails out horizontally in the air like stiffened whiplashes. I cut across the empty street, at a trot—nearer, swaying as I go—and the dogs turn their attention to me, their eyes like pinpoints through the air. Angel is hidden behind a shrub which is swaying in the breeze, but now I come into view of him and there he is, rigid and staring and skinny and nude on the front path, staring right at me with creepy big beautiful eyes … but within a second, the penny drops and I see he's a waxwork. (Is he?) Yes! A life-size, full-body wax Angel, rendered exquisitely in face and limb, complete with accurate black angel's wing tattoos and modest male genitals tucked demurely between his thighs, beneath a small and lovely pair of female breasts—all of him modelled with taste, care and an all-too-evident love.

Damian's lights are off. He'd never let this sit out here, in full view; he must be out. I walk on past his house, inland down the Avenue, as if I haven't noticed Angel. Then at the next street I double-back, return to my island nook and lie down again in my previous place. And only now do I realise: this wax model is quite probably the figure that Kim has been seeing these last few days at Pippa's…

So did Pippa make this beautiful object?

I smile, as it occurs to me that if she did make it and I include this in my next spokes-sheep recording, then there'll be a dimension Jason won't have been expecting: one of his four target imaginations fashioning a faithful copy of one of the other three target imaginations. That's surely a bit more thought-provoking than he and his client company had a right to expect, for their silly sheep. Which means, of course, that the company will probably hate it and cut it out straightaway.

In any case, if Pippa made this model, then it's looking as if she was probably also the elusive culprit responsible for those two waxwork heads, of Lucan and Kev!

I'm glad, for her, that her sinister weasel has turned out to be something so innocent … kind of. Yet why on earth would she be playing so dangerous a game as to goad Lucan and his gang like this? She should be warned not to be so stupid. Evelyn needs to warn her, now, this very afternoon.

74 GOLDEN ON THE BEACH FOR THE LAST TIME

I wonder whether Kim and Shigem know about this wax Angel yet. I throw my attention out in search of them both and feel it dragged five or six blocks eastward from where I'm lying here, to the beach where they are also sprawled flat, in disobedience of the yellow tape stretched across the steps from the Boardwalk to the sand. Presumably for privacy, they have avoided the main stretch between the Convention Hall and the Casino, and have settled on this lonelier beach further north, across from the fields of concrete and grass at Seventh Avenue. They are clearly set to stay a while here, knowing they'll be moving away in a couple of days and won't have time to do this again. So calm and idyllic is the scene, that I cannot resist prolonging my shared tune-in to them. In fact, I'm so very comfortable that I drift to sleep, as I discover at least a couple of hours later.

On waking, I can feel that for those two lovers this has grown into a golden, classic day, an epic piece of sun-worship, as there is an almost mythical aura of closeness and childlike enchantment between them. Ignoring the "No Swimming" signs along the Boardwalk fence, they make regular trips into the water, then cover each other's body in suntan lotion again after each trip, as the sun breathes Arabian fire without relent. With every splash into the waves, it's as if they are diving deeper into an ever-more-vivid, not-quite-visible water—a pool both invisible and ultramarine, somewhere behind the appearance of the sea-water here, of an absolutely perfect temperature, that seals them off from the glare and splash of waves above their heads where the gulls cast shadows on the surface. Even when they have both returned to lie on the sand with their eyes closed, it's as if they are diving together, holding hands, into this mirage of a pool, this lagoon beside a desert palace flanked with skinny palm trees.

Shigem lies on his side, staring gently into Kim's eyes and holding his hand. "Love you, boy," he whispers, "my diffident boy." And they roll together again and hold each other close and stroke each other's head and face and body, deep in love—two boys together alone, unseen upon this blasted and beautiful beach. Soon they are making love. Each gives the other and himself much pleasure, in a wordless, joyful, animal union, healthy and beautiful, simple and complex, till each of them ejaculates long and hard, crests out of tension and sinks back down again, to peace and limpidity.

"I feel like a lion under a tree on the Serengeti," says Kim after a while.

"More blond than brunet," Shigem murmurs.

Weightless and barely moving, my attention floats for another hour or two in their company, while they say hardly a word more.

At last I watch them rise, gather up their things and stand looking out across this sea beside which Shigem has lived throughout his life. Then they turn and meander up the beach. When they reach Ocean Avenue and turn left, walking down the middle of it, Kim says, "It's funny, but it feels like a story's being played out here—as if some tale were being spun, involving me. As if all this Asbury Park backdrop (except for you, my love) were some movie being projected onto the air around me, while I walk through it. But who's projecting it for me? Who's bringing me into it, and why?"

As he speaks, Ocean Avenue seems for a moment to be much longer than they've known it. It is heavy with a furnace heat, wide and deserted. Façades recede in both directions, matte brown and grey, flat as scenery or movie screens. A breath of wind in the dust stirs a cellophane wrapper on the road. Tiny in the distance, the street vista vanishes in glare: where it wets the horizon a shimmer hides the buildings, so the roadway punctures the smudgy blue sky. Shreds of air undulate thickly in the heat...

And there I shall leave them for this afternoon: ambling down the road's yellow centre-line, each with a bag in his hand and an arm around the other's shoulders, bodies touching all the way down to the hip, both leisurely and in-step, into the distance.

75 ATTITUDE ON THE PHONE

My phone vibrates and I jump, startling a nearby flotilla of ducks, before I am plunged once more into the urgent world of Alaia.

"Hey, Jaymi!"

"*Now* what."

"There's been a third waxwork," she announces.

"A full-body model this time," glosses Evelyn's voice in the background.

"A full-body model this time," echoes Alaia.

Perhaps because of the lyrical space I was in while tuning in to Kim and Shigem, before it was trampled by all this drama, I find myself irresistibly inclined to be obstructive here. "I'm sorry, what kind of model was that?"

"A full-body one."

"Oh well, in that case, yes—I saw it. Wasn't it a stunner?"

"You saw it? How?"

"I kind of looked at it."

There is a "patient" sound at the other end of the line.

"I was walking past," I clarify, "and I saw it."

"Aha. And you didn't do anything?"

"Well, what did you want me to do, take it to bed?"

I hear a hint of clenched teeth, as she explains, "Shigem was in danger as a result of the first two waxworks."

"Which your visit to Lucan seems to have taken care of now. And if this waxwork casts suspicion on Damian, then I'm sorry for him but he's a big boy and can look after himself. He doesn't warm my heart as much as Shigem does."

"*Oh*, one has to talk so loudly and clearly. Jaymi, this doesn't suggest Damian's guilt, it suggests Pippa's: this new wax model must be the figure Kim's been seeing at Pippa's, which means she sculpted it, which means she must have sculpted the other two heads, which means Shigem is off the hook for those two, which is great news. Evelyn and I just left phone messages for Shigem and Kim, saying this."

Having seen at the start of her speech that she was about to describe the same path of reasoning that I beat out for myself earlier, I've been free, during the course of her delivery, not only to have a brand-new thought of my own but also to polish it into its most economical form, ready for delivery at the end of her speech: "So you think Shigem's going to want to shop Pippa to Lucan?"

There's a silence on the line. "Well, I don't know … maybe you can tune in to a few people and investigate."

"I was doing so, just now."

"Who was it? Did you find anything important?"

"Yes; I've been doing virtual, vicarious sunbathing with Shigem and Kim, all afternoon, and plenty hot it was!"

"Oh."

I inspect my hands and arms, which are as pale as ever. "And I didn't get a tan, but I had a lesson in love, Alaia—pure, simple love."

"Well that's all-important, of course."

"Much more important than wax dummies. It was beautiful."

"I've got it," she says, her voice lowered and all business again. "Why don't you tune in to Pippa again, to see what you can sniff out?"

In addition to my obstructiveness, I now feel oddly entitled to serve her up a serious note of bitchiness, and I do so: "I don't know, I think I'm reluctant to intrude upon her privacy."

"…All right. I'll see you in the screening-room tonight. Oh, hold on," and I hear Evelyn speaking in the background. "Evelyn says Rik has finished all the stuff he had to do for the *Big Bang* broadcast, quicker than expected, so why don't we meet in the studio in one hour for a spokes-sheep session."

"Fine for me. I'll see you there." And our miniature bitch-fest is cut short.

Then as soon as we have rung off, an uncomfortable truth begins to dawn on me: there was not enough time, between Kim's use of opera-glasses and my discovering the model, for the naked Angel to have been transported from Pippa's high-rise to Damian's front path. Kim said he'd just been using the opera-glasses, a matter of seconds before calling me; then I found Angel a mere twenty minutes later, during which time I was tuning in to Pippa in her bedroom. If the model on the path were the figure Kim saw at Pippa's window, then persons unknown would have had to be removing this model from her sitting room, just the other side of her bedroom wall, while I was doing that tune-in to her, without her or my hearing those persons or knowing they were removing it … which feels implausible. So whatever Kim saw in her window must still be right there—or elsewhere in her apartment. Furthermore, I realise I am the only one who's in a position to know this: from Alaia's call just now it is evident that she and Evelyn have not considered this possibility, not having been in a position to know how little time elapsed between the figure in the window and the figure on the path.

Who, or what, is still hiding in Pippa's apartment?

76 THE PUSSY-CATS LOST IN TRANSLATION

I flick my attention back across town and up ... and I see you, Pippa, hiding in your bed beneath the duvet, although it's only early evening—hiding in your high-rise, hiding from your life. I'm sorry for the pain in you: my gentle enjoyment, at our picnic, of the relaxing quality that comes along with your depressiveness has given way to a real sorrow in me that you should have to bear such a condition.

Happy music plays in the distance somewhere. Dead-eyed, you throw off the duvet, revealing that after yesterday's chic purple blouse you have returned to your signature outfit, in the form of a clean white sweatshirt with matching white sweatpants. You rise from your bed, float across to the curtains and out to your balcony; the window-door swings shut behind you with a faint squeak. Below you the streetlights flicker on, glow red and brighten to a yellow-white. You murmur something voiceless at a plane flying by. The blue sky dims; from your right, above the ocean in the east, creeps the night. Miles out to sea a lighted ship floats north and you want to be aboard, up the coast to the lights and the spires and the towers of New York, and then to elsewhere.

You can't feel me merely tuning in, and I can't give you any hypnotic treatment because you can't see me now. Still, let's try projecting a quick piece of fun at you, just in case you can somehow catch something of it. I wish it could be more, but here we go: can you hear the air mew, as if a thin choir sang behind the night? "Is there anybody out there?" you wonder. OK, you're not far off, there; so concentrate, Pippa, listen harder... But no, you cannot hear us. Pippa, we are cats, ranged around the space across Sewall Avenue—in trees, on the grass, on porches and balconies and chimney-stacks—a pussy-cat epiphany for you alone! I'll pretend you can hear us serenading you, a hundred pussy-mouths singing loud for you. And next, can you see us, maybe? A private light fills this space, designed just for you, and you peer down towards us, as it happens, and we watch you... But no, you cannot see us either. I wish I could report that your mouth falls open, that laughter lights your face, that your ears feel like wings and your smile warms the night; but I can't.

I haven't the heart to go snooping around in the corners of your mind and the corners of your bedroom, hunting down your mysterious weasel, even though I know it must be hidden somewhere in your mind, and probably somewhere in your apartment too, right now…

77 SNATCHING THE DIVINE ON THE CORNER OF THE STREET

Out from her balcony my gaze shoots up across the quiet town, sticky-soft as cobweb, and it curves down between the evening air molecules, towards Shigem and Kim. They're idling along beside the L-shaped building on Kingsley Street and Fourth Avenue, where they wander to a stop and stand facing each other.

My tune-in on the beach was a shared one, hovering between the two of them … but this time, Kim, my cobweb lands on you alone. With your forehead almost touching Shigem's, you observe with a tiny shock across the centimetres, more than you've ever seen before, that his eyes are the eyes of a girl—there's a beautiful girl just behind them, inside them. She's so clear, now you've come to see her. Shigem's lips kiss yours: a girl's lips, a girl's kiss, a girl's sweet breath and gentle touch. It's exquisite, beyond words.

You lift your face. Cold light stares from a dead-faced moon to the east, where the stars are emerging in the late deep dusk. A breeze whispers, stirring Shigem's long hair and carrying the faint crash of waves and scent of brine. The moonlight darkens as a ragged stab of cloud pricks the moon's disc and grows to conceal it. There murmurs a voice in your head, without warning, as if from behind the air, "The eggplants burning by the sea."

I slide my attention out of Kim and let it drift up and float in the air above the pair of them.

That was the clearest channel I've ever had into anyone—and straight through him into someone else.

78 THEFT FOUR, AND ALAIA EXTRICATES HERSELF

I shake my head gently, return to this island and check the time. My spirits lift, as it is time for something that I shall miss, once it's ended, as it'll have to end soon: the recording of raw material for Jason, as fixed with Alaia on the phone. So I high-tail it back to meet Alaia, Evelyn and Rik in the studio, where I listen with renewed respect and some befuddlement to a quick account of the wizardry that was employed today when he edited together the final presentation of *Big Bang* from our three recordings, processed it in various ways and sent it barrelling up the pipe to the General Network's playout division for airing tonight. For him, after such post-production intricacies, setting up the camera now for a quick fourth spokes-sheep recording is evidently a bagatelle and he sets to it with a weary jauntiness. As for me, my hurry to get here, combined with my knowing there will only be one or two more of these sessions, contributes to the intensity with which I now psych myself up and spew out the five tune-ins I've done since last time...

First, playing it with all the sex and joy and sadness and emotion in the subject itself, I squeeze out Angel dancing at Lucan's party last night in the smoky basement den, with Lucan's pride in watching him, as a too-brief respite for Angel.

Then from today comes Pippa's hopeless yearning for the young man in the tower, how she should leave here but won't, and her favourite stars in the newspaper.

Here comes Kim's and Shigem's beach idyll in its golden glow of early romance, and Kim's intimation of being in a story that somehow isn't real. (I've felt this too now and again in recent days, as it happens, and thus permit myself to embellish his feeling with two or three grace-notes all my own.)

Here's Pippa hiding in bed earlier this evening, the passing ship to New York and (to complicate our spokes-sheep a bit) the singing cats that she never knew were hers.

And here's Kim's moment of enchantment on the night-time street just now.

The screening we have straight afterwards on the TV monitor is moving for all of us. "Seeing those four people laid so bare on that screen—it focuses such a spotlight on them," muses Rik. "With each one, there's a small corner of human consciousness, and it's very detailed and urgent and deeply felt. And you wonder about all the influences that buffeted them around till they became just like that and not otherwise."

"I'm just glad I'm not trapped inside Pippa," says Evelyn. "Poor honey... Oh, I've just remembered, I heard from Flames that Lucan is spreading it about Shigem being responsible for all the waxworks now, including the new one of Angel. It's the same shit: Lucan doesn't have a clue who made them but he hates to look clueless."

"Then I'm worried for Shigem," I say. Now that the Angel on Damian's path has come together with the weaselly figures Kim has seen at Pippa's, thereby revealing who the wax-modeller must be, the easiest way to protect Shigem would be to tell Lucan it was Pippa and then just wait for his thugs to muscle into her apartment and lay bare the truth ... but none of us voices this option, as I think we're all aware that Pippa doesn't deserve it to be considered as an option.

"I've got it," says Evelyn. "We know Shigem was in Paradise when the first wax head appeared. Well, guess what—we have *proof* he was there. I mean we have the footage from Jaymi's first tune-in to Shigem in the club that night... Maybe we should just lend Lucan that footage too? He accepted that the stuff on the Angel DVD was genuine, so why wouldn't he accept the Shigem footage was real too?"

I don't need to look at Alaia to know she'll be squirming inside and working out permutations. I realise, doubtless at the same instant she does, that this Shigem footage was of course on the DVD Alaia gave Lucan, the DVD with "All 4" scribbled on it. Alaia must be calculating right now that if Lucan is next given the Shigem footage, then he'll tell Evelyn he's already seen it, so Alaia's secret will be out. "Oh," says Alaia, "I don't think there's any point in that, Evelyn. There's no proof that the footage showing Shigem at Paradise is from the same time the head was left. Jaymi could have absorbed it at any time in the evening. Not much of an alibi."

"It shows Shigem on a full dance-floor," says Evelyn. There wasn't a full dance-floor all evening. People could corroborate what time it was, they could verify he was there. Maybe the DJ—"

"We can't start bringing other people into this," says Alaia. "The aim here is to stop this getting out, not spread the news. So, no witnesses—no proof. Plus, frankly, I'm a little uncomfortable giving out footage of Shigem without his permission."

Evelyn raises her eyes to the ceiling. Feeling obliged to give Alaia some help, I add, "Giving out footage of other people aside from Angel—it's a bit risky for the cloning deal. Just giving Lucan the Angel footage was risky enough."

"And anyway," closes Alaia in triumph, "even if Lucan did see the stuff with Shigem in Paradise during the first head, *and* the timing was proved—still, as you pointed out before, Lucan could always say Shigem simply delegated the actual placing of the head."

I'll be impressed if Evelyn overcomes that triple-whammy of objections; and indeed she doesn't. "I'm just worried for him," she replies. "If we're not careful, someone's going to die here."

Alaia frowns and turns to me. "Jaymi, can you see that happening?"

I raise my hands in surrender. "You mean in *future*? Now the future's one thing I can't see, thank goodness! That would feel entirely different... By the way, would Shigem ever snitch on Pippa, to protect himself?"

"I very much doubt it," says Evelyn.

I'm about to ask whether she thinks Kim would ever snitch on Pippa to protect Shigem, but at the last moment I refrain, prompted by an instinct to keep this notion to myself, for whatever options it may provide.

79 HIGH VOLTAGE FOR ANGEL

We split and I go to my room. There's only half an hour before I need to go see *Big Bang*, so I really don't have the time or opportunity to decide on any course of action in any direction. There's no point in even thinking about it now, in fact ... so I zero in upon you, Angel, all by yourself in the bedroom. You have a new addiction, to add to alcohol, cigarettes, sex and female hormones: it is looking at this bewitching full-length wax self, which you've lovingly seated against the wall by your side of the wide double-bed. Lucan's real fury that he has been anonymously provoked in public on a third occasion has now transmuted, here at home, into a subtly amused promise to not to abuse the waxen provocation itself. This you are most glad of, for your initial shock upon being shown the model by a grimly bemused Damian has become an adoration that you're careful to conceal from Lucan, lest he grow jealous. (Such jealousy I myself could understand, incidentally, since it's with some pique that I observe this wax self-adoration has already surpassed the adoration I implanted in you for Alaia and me—which survives in you now at only half-strength and upon a basis of memories that I sheepishly observe are still oddly confusing to you.)

Coiled on the floor beneath the open turret window in the corner of the bedroom, you watch the distant white waves hiss and suck the sand, which you can see through a gap between two other pointed roofs, and you wonder why these things are happening to you. Catching a glimpse of yourself from above, you see a dark elf curled up inside a turret, with the shadow of a dagger clutched tightly in your left hand, the shadow of another dagger stuck into your chest— and your right hand diving to your chest right now, to flap in horror at the surface of your bright red T-shirt, feeling for this unfamiliar dagger in your chest that you've just seen. But your hand finds only your little silver cross, while your left hand clenches the handle of its shadow-dagger harder, harder, harder now than ever; and the sea sighs on, and a clump of old leaves rustle brittly in the gutter just beneath you.

What's with those shadow-daggers, Angel? Are they part of that luscious fierce anguished little body you're imprisoned in? Your red fingernails are like spray-painted petals broken sharp through your finger flesh. Did you ever feel as average people feel, or were you gorgeously twisted from the start? Tell me, do. You turn as if to camera (though I know you cannot see me), mouth "You'll never know" and turn away. What went so wrong with you?—or went so right, perhaps. You want to kill most human beings that you see: twenty times a day you think of stabbing with your shadow-dagger, through someone's forehead and deep into their brain, and this picture gives you peace and liberation. Under the dictatorship of Lucan you inhabit a delirium of the senses, yet at the same time you've always felt somehow that you were buried alive. The black sky inside your head oppresses, claustrophobically immense; and rest assured, you will stay buried there, alive inside your poisoned night of dagger-skewered self, until you die... And yet there's one problem, Angel, I'm afraid: you see, you can't die. You'll stay buried there, still alive, inside yourself, forever more, without dying. Why? Because I like you there! Yes, I like to watch you, have you noticed? Oh I see you, Angel Deon—I see every twist inside you.

Yet again recently Lucan upped your dose of hormones, so you yearn to feel his body pressed against you, when it's not. Focused thought is hard, because throughout the days and hours you are with him, you're erect at all times, except for a short while after you ejaculate. And then, once apart, you're erect from even half-thinking on him: on his smile and his wicked eyes, his masculine chest and his deep brown voice, on his muscles and his heat, then up inside you deep for hours, till he comes, long and hard and powerful and pulsing and desperate up the hungry wet centre of your torso. Being penetrated by him is like being fisted by an entire forearm—unlike your own erection which, though permanent, is somewhere between the size of Lucan's middle-finger and that of his ring-finger. Obviously he stretched even you, when you first met, and carried on stretching you throughout the first weeks, despite your ramping up the size of the toys you used daily as your training for the nights to come; and yet, to your surprise, he was somehow less challenging to take than other smaller ones you'd taken in the past now and then, whose first look had made you doubt you'd ever find room for them.

In Lucan's presence and his absence you are hard for so long that it feels as if your mind itself has grown an erection, sticking up from your forehead like a unicorn's horn. The whole of your aura is scarlet and black, pulsing around you in the air, while your body looks horny and tense as if your hard-on is so tight that it's tying you in knots. Sore from the constant masturbation during sex, your penis aches, as if erect for such an age that it's bruised from inside; and yet without relief it stays always tighter than a bone. Although you're always clean, you have the faint scent of sex, and you sweat sex even in the coldest of weather. It's exhausting, exhilarating, almost unto illness... So in conclusion, yes; it could perhaps be said the hormones he feeds you are measured out in doses that are somewhat on the high side.

Curled in your turret there, your system in overdrive, you glance at the bedroom clock, as very well you might: after all, as a lifelong fan of ours, you mustn't miss *Big Bang*!

80 WHO COULD ASK FOR MORE?

I surface from Angel, like an astronaut departing the down-bent light and acid clouds of Venus, at ten to nine. I fetch Alaia, head downstairs with her, find the screening-room and settle down in front of a large wall-mounted television screen. "Jason just called to say he and Marc are watching in New York," says Rik, lounging back in his seat and operating a remote control. The start of the main GN channel ident appears, with the sound muted. "I tell you, having been up all night on this edit, I am seriously glad just to kick back and watch TV!" He dims the house lights with the same remote. "Nine o'clock, on the nose." He fades the sound up during the moment of silent black after the ident, and it begins.

Throughout the whole of *Big Bang*—from the anticipation of the stadium audience before the first notes of Alaia's song of death, until we disappear into space on our run to the sun—I feel as if Alaia and I are sitting here in a small bubble together, sealed off from the rest of humanity, including from Rik and Evelyn.

Any viewer's awareness of the commercial undertones attaching to sequels is likely to have dissipated not long after the opening, as it is a truly hypnotic and sumptuous presentation. Compared with *Sound & Vision* it has a somewhat slicker feel, owing to the effects Rik has inserted in post, whereby snatches of music or imagery are plucked from the rest, sampled and repeated amid our continued input. For example, in time with a cadence of four deep-twanging notes of Alaia's, the angle from which my face is viewed travels from camera one to camera three, right to left, insulated cleanly in the notes' elastic looseness; then it flicks back to where it was, travels again in time with the notes' repetition; flicks back, travels again with the notes; and again; and again, periodic and addictive. The effects have not been drastic or intrusive: they have simply made *Big Bang* a bit more flashy and (this is the most accurate term) *slinky* than the first broadcast. In fact, I decide—this is probably the slinkiest thing I have ever watched!

Just as when she and I watched *Sound & Vision*, what can I say except how lucky we have been? By the end credits, so much of the landscape of my own internal life has been channelled through lenses, entwined with a magical voice, enhanced through high-end software and beamed around the world for a planet-ful of people, that I could almost be content to die tomorrow—because these two monster broadcasts feel to me, right now, like the reason I was born.

Who could ask for more?

81 A FARCICAL AUDITION FOR RIK

Afterwards I am walking on air. "So, will *Big Bang* give you as good a shag as *Sound & Vision* did?" I ask Evelyn and Rik.

"*Yeah*, baby," says Evelyn.

"Mmm, pretty good," says Rik. "A bit more predictable for me."

My phone vibrates. "Yay!" says Jason down the line. "That was the just the fiercest!"

"Was it fierce for you?" I ask. "For me it was more slinky than fierce."

"Sure, I can see slinky in there too. 'Cos this wasn't just fierce, this was *fiieeerce*—and that means there's always gonna be some slinky there somewhere, right from the get-go. Anyway, I gotta run now. Congratulate Alaia and Rik from me. Marc says give him a call tomorrow as soon as you're both up."

"OK, will do."

Before long, the four of us are reclining on those deep-purple-leather-covered armchairs and sofa in Rik's and Evelyn's place, as Rik takes a drag from a joint and hands it on to Evelyn. "Reminds me," he is saying, "only once did I ever try out for a part in a play. Fuckin' disaster. I was about eighteen. It was at this theatre in Glasgow where they normally did variety acts, like Sweaty Albert and his Performing Dog, or whoever, but this time it was a new play with lots of parts. Someone had called me in, but I never got their name, so when I got there and nobody knew who the fuck I was, or what I was meant to be auditioning for, I couldn't say the name of anyone who actually wanted me to be there. It became a hilarious kind of non-event. Eventually some prissy thespian guy with a face like a cantankerous ferret took pity and said, 'Well, I suppose you may as well audition for something, since you do seem to be here,' about as enthusiastic as if he was going to get a tooth extracted. He had one of those half-assed moustaches, like he'd just sneezed in an ashtray. Sanctimonious little wanker, real nuttable material—I wanted to head-bang him, just on sight, but I thought maybe that wouldn't help me with the audition, so I didn't. He gave me some long pages of script and I sat on this scabby staircase and read them... Man, I know fuck-all about the well-made play, but even I could tell that this play was a sack of shit! Then the ferrety guy said, 'Oh yes, by the way, you'll have to do your part in a French accent.' Which is an accent I've used for a total of about ten seconds in my life, probably when I was six years old and drunk. Then he paired me up to read with some really mousy-looking girl that you could tell he just wanted to get rid of. One look at this girl and you knew she was gonna be terrible in the audition. So, she and I read it out loud once, on the staircase, and she was worse than terrible—even worse than my toolish French accent, which was painful in itself. Then it was our turn, so we go through a door, straight onto the stage under harsh spotlights. And this woman we're auditioning for, the director, is sitting way up at the back of the auditorium, high up on the bleachers, as far away as possible. 'Er—*when* you're ready,' she says in this hoity-toity voice, like she'd had a lemon enema at birth: '*When* you're ready...' So the two of us start the script, and the mousy girl was so quiet that even I could barely hear her, and I was standing next to her. 'Er—*could* you speak up please?—*could* you speak up?' said the annoying lemon-up-the-ass woman, who was really starting to get on my tits. 'Er—I'm thirty per cent deaf, you know, so you'll *have* to speak up, you'll *have* to speak up!' I sounded like a bad parody of Inspector Clouseau to begin with, and now I had to shout too."

The joint has come back around the circle to Rik. "Cheers," he murmurs, inspects it and takes a long, cool drag. The candles flicker, the dubstep echoes and booms quietly onwards out of the speakers and the entire warm stoned attention of the room is upon him.

"Anyway, sometimes I glanced up from the script, while the girl was whispering it and I was shouting it, and my eyes had now adjusted to the spotlights, so I could see that sourpuss up there on the bleachers was smoking this ridiculous big cigar the whole time." He hands the joint on to Evelyn. "The smoke was wreathing up all around her, like the mushroom cloud of a bomb. Also, bizarrely, her hair hung right down, across the front of her, so I couldn't see her face at all. That made me curious, so I kept sneaking peeks at her during this interminable dirge of a scene. And every time I looked, the more it seemed her hair hung thicker than ever and further down over her face—and boy, was that off-putting, so I started buggering up the script, so the mousy girl started giving me these distraught looks and sounded like she was about to burst into tears. But it was too late, I was hooked, I couldn't stop sneaking peeks at sourpuss up there, and with every peek I became more certain: no two ways about it, her hair was all the way down to her chin in a solid curtain, bushier than anybody's hair should be, even at the back of their head... And while I was reading I was thinking, what a silly cow! What kind of doofus requests a haircut like that at the barber's? 'Yeah, I'll have it right down over my *entire* face, please, extra-thick and extra-bushy, so I can't see *anything*, and long around at the back and maybe just casual at the sides, thank you.' So, being thirty per cent deaf, she'd chosen a nice seat about half a mile away from us, trying to hear me through her bushy hair-curtain, while I did a *dire* French accent that was regularly shading into Russian and Welsh and Indian and Norwegian, in a play that was a chunk of sludge to begin with. There were still several dense pages of the script left. Why was she letting us go on so long? Why *were* we going on? Why were we *here*, in every sense of the question? Then I thought, maybe I should sneak up the bleachers without her hearing me—she certainly wouldn't see me—and then I could reach forward and part those curtains of hair without her expecting it, just to see what was behind ... and I suddenly knew the awful truth: that if I did so, then I'd see the back of her head; and if I went round to the far side of her and parted the curtains there, then I'd also see the back of her head; and if I went to either side of her and parted the curtains, all I would ever see would be the back of her head, because she was *all* back-of-the-head... Well, that did it for me. I stopped in mid-dirge. I put the script down, and I just headed back to the door. And right before I disappeared, I called up at sourpuss, 'Keep in touch!...' and I was out of there."

82 THE SUPREME RULER AND HER SPACE-CAT

Three effortless hours later, we are all four stoned as we wander the three blocks to Paradise, which is packed. Shigem is much in demand, this being his last occasion hosting, and is looking divinely flamboyant, wearing a lot of make-up both glamorous and subtle, plus a soft-edged but extensive application of silver body-paint.

As soon as he and I greet each other, there's a mute agreement similar to the one we reached here after *Sound & Vision*, though this time it is mutually arrived at rather than being imposed by me: namely, that we shan't bother talking about what he experienced earlier tonight through *Big Bang*, so personal and self-sufficiently complete were the beauties it will have caused to flower in him.

I see, too, that so close are we without words, he has also come to know about my passive tuning-in. He can't directly feel it happening, but he knows or at least assumes that I do it. The other member of my target group who must know I do it is Angel, but only because we gave Lucan the DVD. Shigem knows it just within himself. So he knows I'll have access to the beauties that *Big Bang* elicited in him; he knows I'll respect these and love them, if I seek them; and the rest will stay between us.

Unlike after *Sound & Vision*, however, I shan't tune in here to his experience of tonight's broadcast. Although I can sense that this one's effect on him was of comparable emotional depth, I can also sense he hasn't yet made sense of it—partly because this one lacked the simplifying effect of surprise, and partly because he'll have watched this one in the company of Kim, which will have introduced a new complexity and mediation into the experience.

Yet my stoned state is tipping me into tuning in to Shigem, as when I was tipped into tuning in to Lucan in his kitchen and picked up his memory of first meeting Angel. I allow this to happen, but turn myself to face away from the churning of *Big Bang* and steer instead towards something much easier—just his memory of when he arrived here in the club tonight. But in my current state, even this factual memory of Shigem's is less simple than I expected ... for the first thing I see, Shigem, from when you and Kim first walked in here, is that a stylish woman in her thirties was perched on a bar-stool: the skin of her entire shoulders and arms was covered in a tattooed leopard-skin design, while in her lap sat a rabbit with leopard-skin fur and busy ears, and by her side squatted a sleek, disturbing space-cat. There she sat, callipygous and elfin, sucking down a tall blue drink through a straw—an Electric Lemonade, you guessed. I see that you recognised her as one of the club's owners and its Supreme Ruler, and that she was about to make an announcement to the staff, right before the club doors opened. The bar was stocked with rare and mischievous drinks: the yellow and the green Chartreuses enjoyed a passionate celibacy, alongside violet champagne, moon-wine and a pointed flask of Sweet Spirits of Night. Spaced behind the bar's length, five exotic bartenders listened as she rapped out their names in an upscale electronic voice: "Tapette, Twinky, Chi-chi, Maiden-boy, Chiaroscuro Queen—hear me well. No fuck-ups, please, tonight of all nights, our special friend Shigem's very last!" Dead silence—she was Supreme Ruler here, after all. "A Joan Collins is a Tom Collins made with vodka instead of gin, but the sour-mix, the soda and the cherry are otherwise quite unchanged. I shall refrain from describing the dog's dinner I saw being made of a Joan Collins by one of you here last week—I say not by whom. Make no mistake, I've commanded boys behind bars around the world, of every hue, from disco to disco: painted boys in neon bars, muscled brutes in smoky dives, fey boys with high-pitched lisps, and parrot-wearing bartenders training as pirates, so I know whereof I speak… Think about the dry vermouth very hard, before you add a dash or a drop of it or even just walk past the glass with it: if you don't, it will feel insulted. Don't pout, Tapette. I'm a sensitive boss—moonlight through dark glasses sometimes hurts my eyes—but I shall slap your impudent little bottoms that wiggle so pertly, if any of you fucks up a drink tonight, because this is Shigem's swan-song." With her hands on her hips, she concluded her harangue with a slick, swishy, tightly-timed sass: "*And that's that, as far as I'm concerned!*" before picking up her leopard-skin rabbit and sweeping across the dance-floor to the management office, followed slinkily by the space-cat emanating a regal felinity that purred *Learn it, bitches!* to all assembled.

Half an hour after you saw the club doors opened, the DJ was already in top gear, though only a small crowd had yet arrived. There was a huge build-up of lighting effects and increasingly manic, dirty, twisted, even *chunky* house music ... but at the centre of this spectacular whirl and bombast the dance-floor was as empty and still as the centre of a tornado. On the video screens above, there appeared some footage of that Supreme Ruler's arms with their distinctive leopard-skin artwork: one hand stroked with long golden nails the white fur of a long-haired cat, while the other hand limply held a peeled banana.

"Remember that really chunderous décor that used to be here?" the bartender Tapette tittered at you from behind the bar. "Those pink fur walls..."

"Oh I used to love those walls," you said. "I used to writhe against them. I miss that."

"But they kept getting bits of chewing-gum caught in them," objected Tapette.

"True, but I used to writhe against the bits without chewing-gum. Anyway, sweetie, I'll have a Parfait Amour liqueur and cream soda, please." You turned to Kim beside you. "Kim, did you know that our luscious bartender Tapette here colours the wine artificially—even the good stuff—just to jazz it up a bit, 'cos he thinks wine gets to be a boring colour after a while."

"I do *not!*" shrilled Tapette at you, taking offence and stamping his foot. "I'd *never* commit such a sacrilege," and he whipped out a diminutive cauliflower from beneath the bar and started peevishly trimming off miniature florets of it into the garnish trays...

83 LOW-BUDGET SNARLS IN THE NIGHTCLUB

I slap my cheek, to bring myself back to the present, standing here with Shigem, and become aware that I have been chatting with him for many minutes—about what, I have no idea. I glance around, seeking the personnel I was just seeing in his memory of tonight, and I have to conclude that not every stoned tune-in should be relied upon for accuracy, for it seems I was conjuring up a mixture of truth and fabrication. Although none of the five exotic bartenders was real, I can indeed see the female club-owner, whom Shigem must have identified as such to me: I recognise her in the crowd nearby, with a leopard-skin design painted in make-up across her shoulders and down her arms, albeit sans rabbit and space-cat. "What's she like as a boss to work for?" I ask him, nodding towards her.

"She pretends to be a holy terror but in reality she's a sweetie-pie. Certainly a great improvement on the guy she replaced."

"What was he like?"

"Very pantsy and high-maintenance. He had a tweezy poise and a ferny fragility, don't you know, and really he was a bitch on a stick, though we couldn't tell him that. I'd try and give the situation a spasmodic tweeze now and then, but nothing was going to change till he was gone."

I see Shigem has had the name "Kim" added to the bracelet that I observed when I very first saw him on the street, just above the already-engraved "Shigem" and entwined with it, in the same slick swirly lettering. "Just adorable!" I comment, pointing at it.

"Cheesy and adorable," he qualifies.

"This one's for Shigem," says the DJ through the sound system. Shigem turns to him and takes a bow. We drift towards the dance-floor. The track's opening sounds like a fine slice of dance music, but quickly reveals itself to have been produced with a hilarious profusion and excess of faux-feral and faux-Oriental sound effects, as if from a child's keyboard. Shigem swoops to the DJ booth and stands there with his hands on his hips. The DJ blows a kiss at him and Shigem raises his eyes and flounces back to me. The track is a cut-price version of something wild and Far Eastern, made in Taiwan to be sold in Las Vegas. There are heroically weedy "Oriental" intervals, low-budget snarls and cats' growls, as the anonymous diva phones in her lyrics with brio. I picture a likely video for it: fake coloured animal fur, hookahs and pagodas, with a big plastic pineapple for a touch of incongruity; the caged-animal extras, between the twelfth and thirteenth takes of the "writhing" shot, raising limp claws as that falsetto background chorus warbles "Caged!"; and Pearl the wardrobe mistress picking her teeth while distributing plastic fangs. Alaia shimmers up, bringing drinks for us. She looks stunning. Evelyn and Rik bubble up behind her. "Alaia," says Shigem, "if you want to start a wail over the music, just go up there and take the mic—for real."

"I'd empty the club," she says with dry affection.

Some nerdy drunken frat-boy appears, looks Shigem up and down and asks, "Who are *you?*"

"I'm a little Myth," Shigem replies. The guy just stands staring like a dumb bunny. "*Which means* that I don't hoi-polloi with the willy-nillies—so here's a drink-ticket. Run along and have a Shirley Temple, there's a good boy."

Things are getting squirly in my head once again, after this spell of relative clarity. Soon afterwards, Kim, Shigem, I, Alaia, Rik and Evelyn are heading in a line across the dance-floor from somewhere to somewhere, with a landscape of heads and drinks and shoulders and hands and eyes billowing out in all directions, and Shigem's "Virginity" grinning through his silver body-paint close in front of me. While we travel thus, this landscape streaks by, too fast to result solely from my own movement: I've only to walk at a regular pace to be treated to a rush and slant and sway of gibbering faces, as if I were speeding past them on a curving, hilly road. The music tickles, meanwhile. I speak with certain faces, when I pass them, an automatic chatter that I cannot quite hear...

PART VII

FRIDAY: ALAIA RECEDING

84 ANGEL TRIES TO USE ME

I wake in my bed to the sound of the gulls in the wooden eaves, return foggily to consciousness and make a decision: to clarify our options for helping protect Shigem from Lucan's blame, I really must take action today, in light of my being the only one who knows that the weaselly figure glimpsed behind Pippa's window is probably still in Pippa's apartment. I must bite the bullet, visit Pippa and find out just what's happening, up in that high-rise.

I find Alaia in the breakfast room, where we both try to clear our heads with coffee. She's emitting none of the cold energy of yesterday morning on the beach, but there is something in her presence that makes me feel as if she's behind a wall from me and receding into the distance.

After breakfast we call Marc, as I promised Jason yesterday evening. "Jaymi!" he booms. "Congratulations. An absolute triumph last night. By the end of the broadcast we had a viewership of fifty million in the U.S. alone. That's way up on *Sound & Vision's* thirty-three million. Here's *Variety*: 'The nation is now agog to know more of this hypnotic face and its wailing accompanist, whose identities the General Network continues to keep enticingly enigmatic...' I'm very happy, Jaymi."

"I'm deliriously happy with it, Marc. Not to mention quite hung-over."

"I'm glad to hear both those things!"

"You're not going to trot us out a third time, are you?"

"Well, here's the plan. Today's Friday. By Monday I'll know whether there'll be a third one, and if so, when. But either way, I shall come down there on Monday afternoon, so you and Alaia and I can talk about plans, going forward—because the broadcasts themselves were just the curtain-raiser on an orgy of content-repurposings, scads of innovative on-demand download options, and even a smattering of some good old-fashioned ejectable media. All confidential, of course. Can you both hold on for three more days, down there?"

"Oh, sure. I'll think we'll cope."

After Alaia and I have both finished speaking with him, she says, "I need to work alone on some new vocals in the studio today. I'll see you later. We'll go to Shigem's together."

"I admire your discipline. Are you OK?"

"Yes, fine. See you later."

I watch her recede up the white marble staircase and out of sight. I remember how she looked in the club last night when she brought us drinks on the dance-floor. I wish I could go with her to the studio today, but she clearly doesn't want me there.

In any case, I've promised Evelyn that today I shall find out what I can about the three waxworks, by seeing what severed heads I can nose up inside our targets' minds. The trouble is that my sight doesn't really work in this search-engine-like way, because it is an incomplete sight: I'm restricted to the parts of people's memories and imaginations that present themselves, voluminous though these are. There are swathes of their internal landscapes I just can't see, or haven't learned to see. I must give it a whirl, though. Plus, tonight is the last spokes-sheep session and therefore my last chance to make sure I do justice to the recording of our four targets for posterity, whatever posterity may make of them. I shall therefore go one last time to my island hideaway for a while. Before I leave my room, an idea strikes me; I pick up a DVD case containing a copy of *Sound & Vision* and put it in my pocket.

"Hiya! Where you going?" says Evelyn from her van when I step through the Metropolitan's inconspicuous door.

"Sunset Lake."

"Jump in the van and I'll give you a lift, I'm going to the lock-smith's."

"Don't tell me," I say, climbing in. "Jason wants the Metropolitan's door-locks changed as soon as Alaia and I have gone?"

She grins. "I'm sayin' nothin'! How's the head today?"

"A bit foggy. Yours?"

"Fresh as a cucumber, cool as a daisy," she coos … and as you speak, Evelyn, I perceive how you are when you drive this van alone: there's affection in your eyes for the people on the street, who have usually done their best with their clothes and hair and make-up; for those things take effort. Just to leave their house on time for work, morning after morning—you'd call that deserving of respect. For their relationships, their crappy jobs, their alcohol and drugs to spark their lives up, their over-numerous children and their interfering relatives, you feel a simple love, though you see them all too clearly. Through years here, you've seen so many people and their violence and their hassles and their dumb misunderstandings; and yet if there was love in them, you've seen that as well. You've seen them when they partied till they passed out, in bars, clubs, sitting rooms and doorways. You've seen them watching TV with their mouths hanging open, hundreds of channels piped raucous into cramped sitting rooms, and you've even loved them then—

My phone vibrates. I don't recognise the number, but it does have a local 732 area code, so I pick up. "Jaymi, hi! *Big Bang* was *so* amazing last night" comes Angel's lisping-snake voice. "*So* amazing."

"Thanks…"

"Listen, I need your help. I just need you to help me find out something about Lucan. He's treating me like shit. All I need is for you to do a tuning, or whatever you call it, and find out—"

"Angel, no. I can't start getting involved in that way. Spying on people—"

"You spied on me and those other three," he shoots back.

I glance at Evelyn, whose eyes are on the road. "Yes, just to test out my sight, but this is different."

"How?"

"Because this would be altering people's dealings with one another, not just passive spying."

"I can't take Lucan's abuse any more."

"Angel, I can't get involved like this."

"*Shit!*" he spits. "OK, thanks for nothing. I'll see you round."

"Sorry, bye." I put the phone away. "He wanted me to help him spy on Lucan."

Evelyn nods. "The temperature's rising there."

"Any gossip on the wax Angel?"

"No, just noise. I have no idea who could be making those things." She smiles. "I was talking about it with a friend of mine and she said Lucan should be suspecting Damian and me, because we're the only ones who like Angel enough to flatter him like that model did."

"Huh! Well ... she should look at the model again, because it didn't actually flatter him."

"True! Anyway, I'm beginning to suspect *you*, Jaymi," she deadpans. "I mean, you were the one who discovered the Angel model first, right?"

"OK. You've seen through me."

"But seriously, we need to find a way to stop Lucan blaming Shigem, because he's still stirring that shit around more than ever. We'll work on it." She pulls up beside Sunset Lake. "See you at Shigem's later. Toodles."

85 LUCAN SPREADS POISON IN THE MORNING

The air is humid today and grey clouds are visible far across the Atlantic, but here on the shore the sun still beats down. I cross the footbridge to my island and settle down with my back to the trunk of my tree. The sunlight dapples my arms through the foliage above, which stirs in a faint breeze. No one is around. I breathe in and let my eyes close.

Picturing Shigem, I feel my sight dragged sideways and very slightly up, to his apartment on First Avenue ... and there you lie, Shigem, half-awake beside a sleeping Kim. It's clear why you went heavy on the glamour make-up last night in the strobe-lights of Paradise, as your stress at being targeted by Lucan has made your face erupt more than ever now, resembling what I saw in your memories of your adolescence and early twenties. Your phone vibrates on the floor. You reach down, grab the phone, inspect it, frown, roll yourself out of bed, dart to the doorway, pull the door shut and answer in the next room, "Hallo?"

"It's Lucan."

You stop dead. "Oh… Hi."

"Thought you'd wanna know Jaymi and Alaia are spying on you, with his sight… Jaymi paid Kim, to get his permission to spy on you. Maybe Kim wants power over you…"

"Lucan—that's not true."

"'Oh look—we get a mint!'" he simpers, mimicking your voice. "And you two scamper up and curtsey like bitches and you take a mint and run away down the escalator, giggling cuntily: *'My god, I think we've just met the Mint Man! Tee-hee-hee!…'*" Hearing this, you freeze in horror. "You better watch out, petal—you got a man there who makes deals behind your back, spills out the family secrets… Still, better to make deals than wax models. Mm-hm. Have a nice day, Shigem, it may be your last." The line goes dead.

You sink to a chair. "OK, be rational," you think. "Lucan's spreading shit here, trying to poison me against Kim and Jaymi. Kim would never make a spying deal like that. But how did Lucan know the dream with the Mint Man? Kim's the only person I've told that to…"

You rise, return to bed and drift back towards a fitful sleep.

As Shigem's sleep arrives, I pull myself from inside him and hover just above the bed, concerned at Lucan's call myself. Before I can puzzle through its implications, however, Kim stirs and wakes up, nudging me into a shared tune-in to the pair of them. He gazes at Shigem's face beside him on the pillow, then enwraps him in his arms, without waking him. They lie there a few minutes in peace, until Shigem convulses in Kim's embrace, yelps, ejaculates voluminously and slants awake into confusion. He stares at Kim, discombobulated in close-up. "I dreamed you were holding me," he blinks.

"I am," laughs Kim, and despite the rather surface-level nature of a shared tune-in, one internal thought of Kim's alone is so powerful that I catch it in any case when it leaps up inside him: *I would kill someone, to protect him.*

"Oh god… You know, this reminds me, I once sneezed and came at the same time."

"Can you recommend it?" asks Kim.

"Yes! It was beautiful. But it was also exhausting—to be so pent-up, then suddenly so un-pent." He looks around the bedroom, whose objects are mostly in boxes. "I'm feeling fresher than I expected," he yawns, "considering last night."

"I'm not."

The sun streams in through the windows. Shigem brushes his hair out of his face, then back in front of it again. "I'd like to be a bird in a cage," he muses, stretching luxuriously.

Kim reflects. "Would you? In a cage?"

Shigem squirms around to face Kim, buries his face against him, and qualifies this: "Well, I mean a golden cage. With the door always open, of course."

"You're the loveliest thing in the world. I don't have a golden cage in London, but I do have an old rabbit-hutch. Would that work?"

"Only if it's a golden rabbit-hutch."

"It was for golden rabbits, but the hutch itself isn't golden. We could paint it."

They make love, then Shigem says, "What most turns me on is being loved and having someone to love. It's so sexy, so gay, so beautiful. For years I daydreamed about it."

"Oh, hold on—I had a fun dream while I was asleep," says Kim, closing his eyes. "What was it… Yeah, I remember. I was a little blue animated elephant, being grilled across a desk by a scary officious woman with glasses, about what on earth I was good for. I felt quite hot inside while I explained to her all the things I could do with my blue trunk and pushed the general idea that I had a valid place in the world. Then later on a beach, I saw the scary woman again and she stared at me through her glasses and said, 'But I never knew little blue elephants liked the sea?' 'Yes!' I trumpeted. 'But—that changes everything,' she said, 'I shall have to go and think about this.' And she beetled off, and I was so proud and squirted seawater up from my trunk, in case she was going to turn around and look, which of course she didn't."

Shigem makes his arm into a substitute for an elephant's trunk and pretends to squirt seawater around the bed. Kim joins him and the bed becomes a small blue elephants' beach party.

"I just had a call from Lucan," says Shigem, when this is over. "While you were asleep. He said, 'Have a nice day, Shigem, it may be your last.'"

Kim considers this. "You know, we have the option to cause Lucan to find out that those waxworks were Pippa's. What do we think of this option?"

"...Snitching on Pippa."

"It might put her in danger, yes. But your two days left here are quite long enough for Lucan to hurt you instead. Evelyn says he seems to be deciding it was you who did it."

"*Why* does he think it was me?"

"I don't know, but that doesn't really matter. And if he knows you're only here for only a couple more days, which he probably does, then he may hurt you sooner rather than later. Can we leave any sooner than planned?"

"I don't think so, because look at this place: there's still at least two days' essential stuff I need to sort out here before Sunday evening, when my whole life has to be out of here because I have to give the key to the landlord."

"Would Lucan really hurt you?"

"All I know is, he's done it before, to other people, for smaller crimes than those wax models."

"But we're still not letting him know it was Pippa?"

"For two days' safety for me, he might do something to her that lasts her whole life. I couldn't do that."

"I guess not. Could we call the cops?"

"Call the *cops* on Lucan? If I was already at the airport, and about to step onto the plane, and wearing that little bullet-proof number I keep forgetting to buy, then I might just think about it—but by that point, there'd be no need to call them. Anyway, what could they do? He hasn't done anything yet. And I bet he would guess it was me who called them, freaked out by his threat on the phone this morning."

"In that case, from now on, only one of us sleeps at a time. And we move everything we possibly can out of here, today. And let's set things up here so that if we need to run out the back door and through the back gate, then we can do that: I mean we keep a bag hidden, very near the back door, with everything essential inside it that we would need if we had to run." Shigem groans. "I'm serious. We could do all that. It's all possible and none of it's difficult. We'd be stupid not to do it. So obviously we should do it, now, as soon as we get up. Yes?" Shigem nods wearily. "OK then, so let's hit it," says Kim, getting out of bed and pulling Shigem slowly up after him.

"Oh…" murmurs Shigem at the mirror. "Thanks, Lucan. And even worse, it's a bad hair day: look at that fright-wig. The moon must be doing press-ups in my chart today. I need a Hair Supervisor. Maybe even a Hair Theatrix."

"We're both wearing combat boots today," says Kim, once they're dressed.

"Well aren't we tough. We'd better play footsie over lunch, so as to live up to them."

"They should make a film, *Footsie in Combat Boots*, 'a love story from the mean streets of Asbury Park'. Is there any pizza left?"

Shigem opens the fridge. "No. Let's go get some take-away something and bring it back here."

So they go out, turn up the Avenue and hang a right on Main Street to the Diamond Chinese take-out. On the way back they see Evelyn's van at a red light, perhaps returning with the new locks. "Hi gal-pal," says Shigem through the van window.

"Hi Flowerpot." The light goes green and she steps on the gas and zooms off.

"How long have you known her?" asks Kim.

"Forever. We shared an apartment for a short while, years ago. She's so sweet, we used to have girly chats in the morning—she'd be there for me if the shit hit the fan, and I'd be there for her."

"Seems like she knows everyone."

"Yeah. No one dislikes her, either. That's unique."

When they've eaten in the kitchen, Shigem says, "I have to be here between two and five, to let the guys in from the moving company, to pick up the full boxes so far. They'll pick up the rest tomorrow. But you don't have to be here the whole time, so if you want to wander out somewhere, go."

"I should be here as much as possible, just in case. But yeah, a wander would be good. OK, I'll do it now. Back soon."

86 STARED AT ON AN EMPTY BEACH

As Kim heads for the door, I realise I've stuck around with these two for much longer than I was intending when I sat back against this tree and started what I thought would be a quick tune-in to Shigem alone. I've been with them for an hour or two, as if I were just zoning out in front of some reality TV show with my mouth hanging open.

I shall now get back on track with a quick look around Kim, but this time on a properly-focused, single-tune-in basis … and in no time, Kim, you are wandering the bank of Wesley Lake towards the sea, past the Heck Street footbridge. The low-growing pines by the lake jog a memory: alone on the platform, the wind and the rain on your sad and lonely face, at the station in Southport, with a little black case in your hand, to move to London. There were low-growing pines there too, across the tracks while you waited on the platform. The train came; you went, and you never thought again about the pines, till now. Then alone in London at the window of your bed-sit, you watched the lights reflected on the surface of the wet streets. You met friends and others, and you partied and ran around, but still in many ways you were alone, as you liked to be. Then, by and by, you met Shigem, loved Shigem, came here in a dream and are together now. Yet in many ways you're alone inside, as before; and that aloneness is a rich, peaceful place. Moving on, you run your right hand gently through the pines, while your left hand makes to clutch a little black case.

Soon you reach the Boardwalk and sit halfway down it. Away to your left, amid the pastel terracotta on the walls of the Convention Hall, are green copper sculptures of winged seahorses and lanterns; away to your right upon the shell of the Casino are reliefs of ships and seashells; and there on the windows of the shuttered Carousel house, Medusa faces. All these were designed, produced and fixed up in a flurry of labour and care, then left there immobile for seventy or a hundred years, while swathes of people were born, grew up, ran around, fought, laughed, fell ill and died. The Medusa faces look at you, impassive. Soon enough, you will die too, perhaps from illness or suicide, murder or old age or accident. Maybe then they'll still be here, staring out, or maybe they'll have been pulled down, crushed and buried somewhere. Either way—for what?

You rise to your feet. "Maybe," you think, "just maybe I should tell Lucan myself, that Pippa made the waxworks." You turn inland, hesitating. Directly behind you the waves lap and sigh; while behind you on your left, those Medusa faces watch you go, swivelling their empty gaze to bore into your neck.

87 FIXING THE WEASEL HUNT

I can feel the working voltages of decision-making in the collaboration between Kim's mind and his will, hovering evenly—whether to snitch on Pippa to Lucan, or not. Kim's choice may cast a shadow, both long in shape and deep in colour, upon either or both of the lives of Pippa and Shigem. There's an unusual clarity and moment in this particular glimpse into the process of free will in action. Rather than just savouring it, however, I feel prompted to influence Kim, because I have an opinion as to which he should choose and because I'm the only one who can see and influence his choice. If there were time, I might consider whether my entitlement to act here is undercut by the fortuitousness of my power to act, but as it happens there isn't time: if Kim is going to tell Lucan, he's likely to do it next, during this walk, because this'll probably be his only time away from Shigem today. He may visit Lucan on the way home, or he may have Lucan's number and be about to call him...

I confess: I don't think Kim should make this move. At least not before I've been back to Pippa's place. Should I go to stop him? I lie here, deciding. I reach into my pocket, take out the *Sound & Vision* DVD and contemplate it. I picked it up this morning as a possible passport for me into Pippa's apartment. Well, perhaps it can now be a passport for both me and Kim? I check the time; half past one. OK, then—here goes.

I get up, leave the island and the lake, go to the Boardwalk, walk briskly along it until I come into sight of Kim, then slow down to a wander. He notices me, I notice him and we join each other. "Hey, how's it going?" I say.

"It's happening... By the way, I never had time to say last night that *Big Bang* was just as amazing as the first one. It was like the same drug, except that this time, with those special effects, it felt as if the drug was rolled up in coloured papers with golden filters, like those Sobranie Cocktail cigarettes—do they sell those over here?"

"I don't know, I don't smoke. But if I did, I'm sure I'd choose those."

"They taste normal but they don't look it. Anyway, this time I don't really want to know how you made it, so I won't ask what you did in the studio: I'd rather just savour the memory."

"Thank you very much. I shan't tell you, then..." I look around. "You know, I was wondering this morning: just as a possibility, have you thought about the option of letting Lucan know who really made those models, now that we know who it was? For Shigem's protection, I mean."

"Shigem doesn't want to do that. But I admit, it's crossed my mind to do it anyway. I don't know if I should. What d'you think?"

"It's a tough call," I say. "But I think we owe it to Pippa to pay her at least one more visit before telling Lucan, just to see if we can find any kind of confirmation she made those models. We think she did, but you know we could be wrong."

"I guess we could..."

"Well, I've actually been meaning to take something round to her—just a copy of *Sound & Vision*, since she missed it. So why don't I give her a call right now and see if we can pop round?"

He considers, then nods. "OK, sure. Let's try it."

I dial her number. "Hallo?" comes her flat voice.

"Hi Pippa, it's Jaymi."

"Oh, hi..."

"Hi. Look, I was just passing and I thought, why don't I swing by and show you a bit of that *Sound & Vision* broadcast, like I promised at our picnic."

"Oh... OK. Not right now but ... in an hour? Come at three." I can almost hear her blushing in the shadows of that hallway.

"Three o'clock?" I look at Kim, who nods. "All right. I'm going to be with Kim at three, as it happens, just running a few errands, but that's fine, maybe I'll see if he wants to tag along and come upstairs and watch a bit of it with us?"

"OK," says Pippa.

"Good! See you then."

"OK, bye…" her faint voice trails away.

I look at Kim, who shrugs and smiles. "Well, fingers crossed," he says. "I should go back and help Shigem now, but I'll see you outside hers at three. I'm glad I happened to bump into you."

88 AN INTERRUPTED DRAMA AND A DUBIOUS PORTENT

He heads off inland and I turn back to the beach. So, I have an hour to spare. I should keep an eye on Lucan and Angel, in case there's any mischief being hatched there against Shigem. I set my phone's alarm, head down to the old Casino and perch in seclusion on the wide ledge behind it, facing out across the water.

I fire out a quick picture of Angel, lob my attention after it and feel this pulled over towards him … and to the extent I find myself landing inside you, Angel, I suddenly find myself squatting down naked, licking Lucan's prodigious cock, in something like heaven—which wasn't what I was expecting and for which I haven't quite prepared.

Still, I stick with it, for research's sake, till Lucan at last lets your head away. By gesture you suggest that Lucan reciprocate, which I'm sensing is a rare suggestion—and perhaps I'm right, as straightaway a hand wraps itself around your throat and shoves you up hard against the headboard. "I don't suck cock, faggot," he whispers with half-ironic menace. "Why are your breasts still small? Double hormones from now on—four pills a day. That could be a boy's chest, almost. Cover it up, we're going out."

"*Out?* But we haven't—I was just getting started and I need closure and I'm gonna *kill* someone—I *HATE* that—"

"Later. Shut the fuck up now. We're meeting the others for lunch and we're late," says Lucan, zipping his black jeans back up, lounging back onto a divan by the bed and lighting a cigarette. "And cover up your love-bites, or the model gets it," and he pulls out a flick-knife and deftly slices the blade up through the air to rest against the neck of the wax Angel from Damian's path, which sits coquettishly posed on the divan beside him, naked except for mirrored sunglasses and a whip around its neck.

It's not a moment when I'm expecting a make-up tip, but this is in fact what I get, as you smother your anger, sit at the vanity mirror and start applying Angel-coloured concealer, at high speed and with the blitheness of practice, to what I should hope is an unusually violent night's worth of whip-marks, bruises, love-bites and noose-marks, new and old, around your neck and shoulders. The mention of food reminds you you've not eaten for nearly twenty-four hours.

"No time for make-up," says Lucan, "put something over it, cover it up—quick, Flames and Kev and Damian are waiting."

"But it's a hot-ass day."

"Quit moaning or I'll bitch-slap you and the model to hell," says Lucan, lounging back easily with the cigarette hanging out of his mouth, while you put down the make-up, flounce to your feet and start hunting through a wardrobe, wings aquiver.

Lucan's phone rings. "Yeah… Evelyn baby, what do *you* want. Did Alaia give you my message I gave her on the phone? Good… Oh, you bet I'll give him some special treatment, mm-hm… What?… *Oh?* And why couldn't it be Shigem?… How do I know he was in Paradise that night? Prove it! I mean, I know he was in there with Jaymi, but *prove*… Hold on, why are you just giving me a character ass-lick for him?… If you tell me how 'sweet' he is again, I'm going to throw up on the phone… Fuck eye-witness accounts, that's not the best you have … that *is* the best—? Wait, wait… No, wait—Evelyn, shut the fuck up and listen to me. So you're giving me a character ass-lick for Shigem and you're saying people could swear he was in Paradise that night—and this is the *best* proof I can get that he was there?… There's nothing else you could give me, to prove the little cock-sucker was in Paradise? You have *no* proof, more than that, to persuade me to promise you some protection for him?… OK! OK, Evelyn—very interesting… No, no, nothing. All I'm saying is, you know, he still coulda got someone else to plant the head, or it still coulda been his idea—I can't rule these things out… Well I dunno, maybe Paradise paid him to scare business away from Downstairs, why not. OK, gotta go now Evelyn, kiss kiss," and he cuts her off.

Lucan pockets his phone with a slow-growing shine of thought in his eyes and turns towards you, who have quickly pulled on your black vinyl bra and a skinny black polo-neck and are climbing into a pair of black leather trousers, looking heated, still horny and seethingly hassled. "She never mentioned the video of Shigem on the DVD!" crows Lucan. "The video of him and Jaymi at Paradise, the night when the first wax head showed up. That video shoulda been her proof that he never came to Downstairs then… She's busting her head on the phone trying to prove he's innocent, and she never even *mentions* that video? I pushed her, you heard—and she still didn't. Why not? All she could say was, *oh* he'd never have done it, and *oh* people could swear he was in Paradise…" In his enthusiasm Lucan has been absent-mindedly flicking the wax Angel's nipples with his fingernail throughout this speech, until you notice this in the mirror where you're brushing your hair. Hairbrush in hand, you flit across the room in renewed anger, bat his hand away from the nipples and slide the model along the divan away from danger. "And you know what that tells me?" continues Lucan, hardly noticing this. "*Evelyn doesn't know we got the wrong disc!*" He claps his big hands together and rubs them in glee. "She still thinks we got a disc with only you and me on, like Alaia promised."

You pull your mind reluctantly away from the flicked wax nipples and force it to wrap itself instead around these elusive abstract hypotheses, whose very slipperiness reminds you immediately of nipples again. You stare at Lucan for several seconds, trying to focus through your hassled state, and your anus twitches hungrily. "Has Alaia passed your message along to Evelyn?" you manage at last. "I mean the money demand?"

"Evelyn just said yeah Alaia gave her my message. But Alaia could have given her any old bullshit message. Maybe Evelyn doesn't know about the money demand, 'cos Alaia didn't even tell her we got the wrong disc."

"Why didn't you ask Evelyn about all this just now?"

As Lucan gives one of his deep, wicked laughs, I feel you wince with an unsated desire that's almost like pain, and fleetingly I glimpse the clearest view I've had down that avenue where you live every day, a sexual and emotional slave to one man's all-dominating physicality. "*Because*," says Lucan, "I'm gonna use what I know, to make Miss Danielle do a little something for me…" He jumps up and heads for the door, stopping on the way to pick up from the dressing-table your crucifix pendant, whose thin chain he gently fixes high upon your chest in a delicate silver echo of the large golden one hanging halfway down his own. "OK, we gotta meet the others, so move your faggot ass or I'll kick it."

Seeing you both outside on Summerfield Avenue, I'm struck by what a stunning pair you make: Lucan striding fast through the bright summer sunlight, shirtless in black jeans, whistling a lazy tune; and you, Angel, half-running after him, breathing onto and polishing the lenses of the mirrored sunglasses you've just snatched off the waxwork.

As you approach Main Street where Damian, Flames and Kev are waiting, a trace of affection flickers somewhere behind the hardness of Damian's eyes—some fossil of wistful gallantry attaching to his memory of your renting a room in his house, once upon a time.

"I was just telling the others about Huntsville, Texas," says Damian, when you and Lucan reach him. "My kind of town. Every man, woman and child there knows: when the electric chair is used in the great prison there in Huntsville, every electric light in town flickers when the switch is pulled, and every TV picture shakes, and every fridge gives a quiver. And folks remember to trust no one, because they're all on their own!"

The light dims and you all look up. The bank of clouds I saw this morning across the ocean has rolled westwards across the summer sky towards us, so that its dense upper billows are just now moving across the sun's disc overhead. And as you all stare up, it seems remarkably as if there is an entire nativity scene piled on the clouds behind the billows—ass, ox, Mary, three wise men etc., with a halo round the whole group and shafts of Jesus-light fanning out in all directions. The five of you stand by the wayside a moment, your mouths hanging open to varying degrees, before you lower your gazes to one another, shifting slightly on your feet. Then you all turn towards a miniature blaze of golden light in your midst, emanating from where a dedicated beam of sun strikes Lucan's crucifix pendant. Damian turns his eyes to the ground—hunted, humble. Lucan's face assumes a hint of the messianic; Flames looks earnest; Kev picks his teeth. You meanwhile, Angel, see yourself fixed on that golden crucifix like a little twist of crackling, impaled by your wearer on the nail of the metal dildo sticking out halfway up the cross's vertical shaft, howling in religious ecstasy forever, against the gorgeous deep-brown smoothness of Lucan's intensely lickable chest and stomach muscles.

"I'm fucking starving, where we gonna eat?" says Kev.

Lucan looks around and shrugs. "What d'you think, Angel?" he asks.

Still on too transcendent a plane for such logistics, you flick your eyes up to Lucan's face, only half-sure what has been asked, while sex-hunger stretches through your sharp and pretty face, tightly wound throughout its lineaments. One look at him and you are Angel's Baby Doll inside, constantly receptive, experiencing his and by extension other men's physicality as you assume she would—with a hunger to complete it. You're about ready to fall over, from no food and from the usual cocktail of drugs and female hormones in your system from last night and this morning. Your anus contracts hard against the black rubber dildo you're still wearing, and your upper lip rides up slightly as it sweats, so your teeth are bared. "What about that Caribbean place?" you manage, in a level voice. "You know, up there around Second or Third." Lucan grins down, seeing everything, while the others peer up Main Street. You bite back a squeak, as he reaches unobtrusively and tweaks the nipple of your budding right breast: you feel it swell hard against the smooth black bra beneath your polo-neck, but you take your dark glasses from your pocket and get them onto your face before your eyes tear up. Exhausted by this permanent exposure and scrutiny, your head swims and you swallow—you need to eat, before you fall over. Fortunately, though, you hear the Caribbean place meet with general assent and the group now meanders to the north where you pointed.

89 HUNTING THE WEASEL

My mobile's alarm breaks in upon this idyll. Ten to three: I should set off for Pippa's, or I'll keep Kim waiting there. I step down from the Casino ledge onto the beach and set off inland along the bank of Wesley Lake. I reflect on what I've learned so far today from the spying homework assigned to me by Evelyn: Lucan now knows that Alaia kept her DVD misdelivery a secret from Evelyn, and Lucan is about to use this knowledge to force Alaia to do something for him.

Which is not, unfortunately, a piece of homework I can hand back to the homework-assigner.

I find Kim waiting outside the high-rise. "I told Shigem I was just going for another walk," he says, "so I probably shouldn't stay too long here."

"OK." Pippa's buzzer buzzes, to let us in. "Where in Pippa's hallway is that narrow door?" I ask Kim while we are in the lift.

"Halfway between the front door and her bedroom."

She opens her door dressed in a grey sweatshirt with matching grey sweatpants and gestures us inside in a friendly but distracted manner. Soon Kim is sitting with her in front of her TV, flicking through the DVD menu to find some of the best and loudest bits. "Is the TV muted?" he asks.

"I always have the volume down on the TV. Low or silent."

"I think we need a bit of volume for this one," I say. "Alaia does contribute significantly to the mix."

"What does she do?" asks Pippa.

"She wails," says Kim, unmuting it.

So here we all are on her sofa, he and I flanking Pippa, as he picks out the bits of *Sound & Vision* he liked best. After a couple of minutes of Alaia's and my respective wailing and staring, Pippa's eyes open promisingly wide and glassy, and I see that Alaia and I have a new fan. Whether she'll be as hardcore a fan as Angel, I cannot predict, so very cloudy are her truths: her fandom may last no longer than these edited highlights Kim is showing her, and possibly not even that long. Still, if we can give her any pleasure, I'm happy for it. As I realised yesterday afternoon on my island, I do feel a real sorrow that she should have to bear such permanent depression. As I glance at her wide eyes now, however, this sorrow for her becomes softened by the feeling that this depression is simply part of the flesh-and-blood Pippa who sits beside me. There it is—and there she is, being herself. Her damage and sweetness, depression and whimsicality go together to make up a sad and beautiful package of Pippa-ness. Yesterday she was dressed in a white sweatshirt, today she's dressed in a grey one, tomorrow she'll be dressed in a sweatshirt of a different colour best known to her upon waking (or maybe even known by her already now, which might be a curious thing to investigate next time I tune in to her), and so she will carry on.

In fact, something about this whole scene makes me smile: it's a subterfuge, because we're really here in order for me to slip out of this room in a minute and go weaselling in her hallway, but it's still rather sweet that we're genuinely guiding her towards what we judge to be the most Pippa-friendly morsels of a real monster-event that she was hardly aware of. And even if this is a bit of a movie scene, Kim is playing the part he was cast for with great professionalism: I have no doubt of his sincerity when he specifies that one of his favourite bits was the eyes and lips of the flame girl, with lashes as long as constellations and brows sweeping across the sky. (This interests me, as I'd have guessed he might prefer the monolithic slabs of grey longing as big as mountains and the skeleton of girders with the strength to march around the world. It just goes to show that even with these perceptive abilities, my understanding of the complexities of his mind goes only so far. Or perhaps it shows that Kim's understanding of the complexities of his own mind goes only so far, failing to achieve the greater clarity or objectivity that I can bring to bear upon it as an outsider? Then again, who am I to—but enough of this! I'm here at Pippa's for a reason.)

So I nod to Kim, adopt a "just-going-down-the-corridor" manner and slip out, letting the sitting room door close gently behind me. I stand on the other side of it for a moment, letting my eyes adjust to the gloom. There ahead of me is the hallway—and a cold chill runs through me as I see a horrible figure halfway down it, staring right back at me, with arms rigidly at its sides and a spiky hairdo that's both creepy and goofy.

I see the hairdo is really the leaves of a pot-plant sitting on a bookcase whose tall white side-end faces me, and the rigid arms are really black folder-ends that protrude to right and left of that tall white shape on two successive shelves ... but it's set the scene nicely, nonetheless.

I set off with a certain grimness down the long, dim, narrow space.

I glance into the kitchen door as I pass it, for the first time noticing an array of carving knives hanging on the wall, and several bulky old fridge-freezers...

I reach the bathroom and glance into it, knowing that within its shadows hangs the large blue toothbrush and then, half-hidden behind it, the smaller black toothbrush...

I pass the front door, glancing at the spy-hole through which Pippa peered so long in vain for her gentleman caller. (Did I just see the little spyhole-cover swing and slither around a bit, on its tiny hinge?)

Then I start to slow down, approaching her closed bedroom door ahead of me at the end of the corridor, because I know that very soon I shall spot the thing I do indeed now spot—the narrow door Kim described.

I slow right down, as I near it, then come to a halt just this side of it. I run my eyes comprehensively over it, skewering my gaze into the black crack that borders its tall rectangular outline. No light glimmers through the hinges, which are nearer to me. It is too dim in this hallway to see if there are any marks on the carpet, from movement in or out of the door. I cannot make out anything red and sticky on the handle ... and there's the large keyhole. I bend downward slowly, moving my face to a level with it. I'm not sure how wide the aperture within the keyhole is, so I narrow my eyes as I approach it with one eye, pushing aside thoughts of something long and sharp jabbing out of it without warning. By slow degrees I get close enough, and stay there motionless for long enough, to conclude that I am not going to be able to see or hear anything through the blackness of the keyhole.

What *is* it, sitting there right in front of me, that I can't see through that little keyhole-shaped piece of blackness there?

A distant Alaia wails somewhere far down the hallway through the sitting room door, while I scrutinise. I straighten up, brace myself for the unexpected, and gently turn the handle...

Locked. I give a quiet knock. No reaction. "Hallo?" I murmur into the black crack. "Is there anybody in there? Please answer..."

I listen acutely for any vegetable Angel sigh, moan, grunt or shriek—but there is silence.

90 PIPPA ON THE BRINK OF NO RETURN

As soon as the lift-doors enclose us, Kim says, "I tell you, when you came back into the room shaking your head, I just wanted to say, 'OK, Pippa, you made those waxworks, didn't you?' But I chickened out, because then it would have had to come out, about me snooping through keyholes and spying on her with opera-glasses, and anyway, if she's kept it a secret so far, why would she admit it now?"

"You were right to keep quiet. Don't worry, we'll get to the bottom of this. Are you going back home now?"

"Yes. But again, if you and Alaia want to come over later, do. We'll be gone the day after tomorrow."

"OK, thanks. I'll call you." We shake hands and he sets off.

The clouds are darkening and the wind is rising. It's going to pour down any minute. I could head back to the Metropolitan right now, but on a whim I consider: how often do I sit outside, in what I know is going to be a warm rain, with no particular place to go, just getting soaked for the sheer hell of it? Not enough! Neither law nor regulation requires dryness. So I walk back down Wesley Lake to the very same secluded nook I occupied before on the ledge between the ruined Casino and the beach. The afternoon light dims to grey, the gulls fall silent and the wind picks up more, rippling the Atlantic; till here the rain comes indeed, growing quickly in strength, pelting my head with tepid drops and splattering down onto the sand-blown ledge beside me.

I conjure up my hostess this afternoon, lob her outwards and send my attention after her, to see just what she's doing, up there in her high-rise, now that Kim and I have left … and I find you, Pippa, descending the building's concrete stairwell, where the wind pushes in through the cracks around a rusty window frame beside you. You peer out and down into a small garden that no one ever visits, where a few tired leaves flap limply on stunted shrubs. You emerge from your tower through the back door and drift down the empty street, without an umbrella: glazed dim sky, grey rain. You're sinking, Pippa Vail, and I wish that I could help you, but I can't. A woman and a small child are coming down the pavement towards you. You could say hallo when she reaches you—but she would either just look at you funnily or, if she were polite enough to greet you in return, she would still think there was something odd about you and would want to hurry on, and what would be the point of that? So you don't meet her eyes and she doesn't meet yours, while the rain streams down over your furious blushing and the child stares at you rudely; and you never liked children (even and especially when you were one in Arverne) but you manage a weak half-grin at it, like thin porridge, and of course then the idiot child looks frightened and stares all the harder and more rudely, and they both scurry on, away down Sewall Avenue. Then a curtain twitches in a window, of course, and you know that there too will be a hard, curious stare at you, cutting through the thin rain sliding down the air on its way to the gutter. You look through the sad scene ahead of you, which might as well be behind you, and you move your legs forward—left foot, right foot, left foot. Yes, you're one of the lonely girls. You've seen all this before, and you'll see it all again.

The only bright thing is Lucan's phone call this morning, the first time he's phoned you for years. He told you that I, Jaymi, was spying on you; and this made you happy. To be spied on! A human connection. *Please keep spying on me*, you thought. *Stay with me, please.* "Oh, thank you!" you replied, to a nonplussed Lucan, and then by mistake you did what nobody does—cut him off. Oops. Oh well, too late to mend that.

But otherwise, it's not good, especially the other phone call. That friend of yours served you up a silence on the phone—unmistakable, the truth of his dislike carried plainly in the silence and deliberately implied. The last look he gave you was cold, too, the other week. That silence on the phone, and the last look he gave you was cold; silence and cold… A small strangled screech wriggles out through your windpipe by force and stabs up Cookman Avenue, unheard.

At the end of Wesley Lake, behind the boarded-up Carousel, you stumble round the colonnade beneath the tall chimney of the little dead power station. "Hail Satan," says a graffito on one of the pillars, scrawled in unSatanic felt-tip pen. You wander down the Boardwalk to the old Howard Johnson's diner, closed and dark today as it almost always is nowadays, where a wall-mounted radio has nevertheless been left on, aiming a small tinny music out across the ocean.

You drift onwards, anti-clockwise around the edges of the entire town, with wastes of empty space to your right and cars hissing away through the slosh to somewhere else. Grey sky hangs over wire-netting alley-ways around a corner shop, where the wind blows litter along. You come to a bus-stop where an old man sits talking to himself, a beer in his hand and his face full of fear and endless loss.

By the time you've wandered inland and some way out of town to a highway intersection where only cars move, the light is dimming into evening. In among the slip-roads you find a slip of grass, and there you sit and smoke, where nobody has ever sat and smoked before—and nobody will ever sit and smoke again, most likely.

This is the last game of all, Pippa, here among the slip-roads. The rain upon a bandstand that only you can see thaws out a music that was played here and frozen in a silent ring, awaiting your arrival now—notes rubbed thin by the ghosts of many tears. "What a nice day," you say, and wish that it were so.

Here is the border of reality, the boundary fence, before you reach the rest outside. The fence is broken, here and there, where other lone wolves have pushed holes through it, setting off on journeys where the rest of us can't follow. The air above the highway becomes arched over like a tunnel ceiling, with the wider environment merely an optical effect projected onto the tunnel walls—and this is when I know that you are really in trouble.

91 MY LIES ABOUT THE MINT MAN

If only I could help her, but I don't see how I can. I can't take her pain on board, as I could with a piece of her knowledge, but even if I could do this, it probably wouldn't do any good, as I suspect that there would then just be two people who felt it, instead of one person. The pain isn't mine, but hers specifically, it seems.

I see also that in her current state she will yield nothing coherent or useful about her mysterious weasel Angel. I return fully to my wet ledge, therefore, drop down off it to the sand and return to the Metropolitan.

In my room I change into dry clothes, then call Alaia. "Hallo," she says from the other side of the wall.

"Hi. Just to let you know Kim said we can go round to Shigem's place again this evening if we want. I'm thinking maybe we could take the pizza round this time. How does that sound?"

"I don't think I'll join you tonight. I'm going to the studio again. I still have vocals to practise."

"Once again, I admire your discipline. But just so you know: *Big Bang* was yesterday."

"Yeah but don't forget Marc's coming down here on Monday to meet us. He may tell us he's fixed a third broadcast. And knowing him, it'll probably be the following night."

"I've been postponing that thought myself, I admit."

"I have to come up with stuff. I don't have the luxury of just showing up and staring at the camera."

"I'm not going to rise to that." It's good to hear a bit of humour from her; but despite the humour, there's still that strange distance in her, that newfound wall between us ... and I lay my palm against that wall's bricks-and-mortar equivalent beside me.

"I only need half an evening, though," she continues, "so let's meet at Downstairs at nine-thirty. I'm suggesting it because we should continue to keep our ears to the ground, for Shigem."

No other reason, then. "OK, good idea—I'll see you then." So it's agreed. I call Shigem's home, hear his voice and report Kim's invitation, saying Alaia cannot make it but offering to bring pizza. He says he was about to call us and I should just come straight over, because enough pizza has just been brought by Evelyn who is already there.

Within twenty minutes he's opening his front door to me. "Come on in, there's all the food you can eat," he says. "Coffee?"

"Yes please."

He goes off to the kitchen, while I find Evelyn sitting on a box in the main room. "Kim's just out buying booze," she says through a mouthful of pizza.

As I tuck in, wondering whether that booze-buying was a handy pretence for Kim to make a private phone call to Lucan outside, Shigem enters the room, hands us mugs of coffee and sits on a box, sipping his own. His long black hair with its platinum-blond highlights has been restyled to hang down in front of his cheeks. "You know, I got the funniest call from Lucan," he says, awkwardly. "Well, not so funny, because he ended it by saying, 'Have a nice day, Shigem, it may be your last.' But before that little gem, he said that you, Jaymi, offered money to Kim for his permission to spy into me and him."

Woops, here we go... I shake my head, smiling.

"Well, I knew it must have been bullshit, of course," continues Shigem, "and I told him so. But then he described a scene from a dream I had recently, about Kim and me meeting someone called the Mint Man, and I know that the only person I've ever told that dream to was Kim. Lucan described it precisely and he even quoted something I said in the dream; it was pretty creepy. So of course it's made me a bit insecure about Kim, but I haven't said anything about it to him and I don't think I shall. I just want to forget it."

Last night in Paradise I saw that his and my unverbalised but powerful bond has brought him to a half-knowledge, or at least an assumption, that I passively tune in to him, even though he's never been told I have such an ability. He'll now be assuming, then, that I must have been the source of Lucan's knowledge about the Mint Man. This anguishes me, because my telling Lucan about something in Shigem's imagination would of course have been a considerable and possibly dangerous betrayal of Shigem. I wish I could tell him now that the way Lucan found out about the Mint Man was through a wrong DVD that was deliberately given to him by Alaia; but I can't, because Evelyn is sitting beside me and she has been kept ignorant of this. I feel a stab of sudden hatred for Alaia, for putting me in this position.

"That is so strange," says Evelyn, before I can think how to play this. She looks at me, then him. "Because—can you keep a secret, Shigem?" He nods avidly. "The Metropolitan *did* have a little project where Jaymi did some spying into Angel, just passive spying without Angel knowing, to kind of test out Jaymi's sight. We actually told Lucan and Angel about it, and it turned out they didn't really mind! So you see, Lucan knows about Jaymi spying on Angel, but not—I mean we're not spying on anyone else, so how would he—I mean why would he say we were spying on you?" She frowns at me uncertainly.

"Huh," says Shigem. "Well, I guess the Angel spying must have given Lucan the idea. So he told me I was getting spied on too, just to stir up shit. But still ... how did he know about the Mint Man?"

I have to start saying something here. Gentle but questioning,

Shigem's eyes are staring directly out at me from behind the front-most strands of his restyled hair, and this very arrangement itself gives me an idea. Our positions are such that I know Evelyn can't see his eyes if he's looking in my specific direction through just that narrow gap between hair, so I can risk causing a flash of surprise in his eyes, and so I do exactly that: I give him a sudden, clear wink with the eye further away from Evelyn, and then a split-second later I gesture towards her with an almost imperceptible but precise head movement, all while I'm half turned away from her. "I know," I say, "maybe you told someone about this Mint Man one night when you were drunk, and you don't remember doing so! It must have been relayed somehow to Lucan—you know how rumours travel—and he thought that feeding it back to you was a good way to fuck with your head. He enjoys doing that, have you noticed? He may even have overheard your actual drunken telling of it... Ever been tipsy in Downstairs?"

I remember, too late, that he doesn't go to Downstairs. But bless him, I love him, because he's running with this: "Once or twice, yeah," he says, and he may as well have said *OK, so Lucan's knowledge did originate from you, but I trust you that there was a reason you can't say right now.*

"Well there you go," I say.

"Yeah, I guess so," he says.

"But the dream scene and the dream words were so accurate," says Evelyn.

"Then Lucan must have overheard Shigem's original drunken blurting of it," I tell her. "And this morning on the phone Lucan must have just hoped Shigem wouldn't remember having blurted it."

Kim enters, holding a dripping umbrella. "This rain is good practice for London," he says. "Reminds me of that storm when we were there—remember, when we both met what's-her-name?"

"Yeah," says Shigem, "we met her in that pub, what was it called? They have such funny pub names over there. Was it called the Beige Hermaphrodite?"

"Er, I doubt it," says Kim.

"Oh, no, you're right, that wasn't it. Anyway, it was the same place where you invented a whole history of a pop group that never existed."

"Josie & the Fat Slags from Basildon?" says Kim.

"That was them, yeah. I'm still a fan of them, though I never made it to Basildon."

"Well, there's a treat in store. Plus we invented a group from ancient Rome, called Ephebe and the Romanettes."

"That's right. Yeah, that storm was wet and freezing, I remember. I have no padding, you see. I was all dressed up, though—smoulders in magenta it was, that night. Then later it was all about Mildred's missing mini-van. Remember we ended up having to go and pick it up?"

"Yeah, in Southall," says Kim. "The police found it there and it didn't work."

"That cop said it sounded like there was something wrong with the cam-shaft. He said I should open up the hood and take a look, but I wouldn't know a cam-shaft if it was decked out with cupcakes."

"I kind of prodded the engine a bit."

"Yeah, very gruff work that was, in your rubber gloves."

"Anyway, in Britain it's called a bonnet, not a hood," says Kim.

They both hoot with sudden laughter. "And what d'you call the trunk?" giggles Shigem.

Kim can barely confess, "A boot", before joining him in a puddle of mirth.

Evelyn's mouth has fallen open. Shigem has recovered, however, and continues, "Mildred got over it, though. At least, she was wearing an orange puffy-scrunchy on one wrist, when we met her later, so she must have regained some sense of style and self-worth. It was actually my puffy-scrunchy, you know, I never did get it back from her. Ah, Claire's 'Girlheaven'—where getting ready is half the fun…"

"What the *hell* are you two on about?" demands Evelyn. "Is this how they talk in England?"

"Yep," says Kim. "Every last person."

"*Cuckoo!*" she calls.

And so we all prattle on, until I notice it's getting on for half past nine. "I've fixed to meet Alaia at Downstairs now," I say. "Anyone want to come along?"

"I'm on," says Evelyn.

"No way," says Shigem. "I'm not in the mood for running into Lucan. I'll be very happy if I never see him again."

"The day after tomorrow, you'll be walking out of here," I say.

"Below this cucumber-like exterior, I am *so* stressed right now," says Shigem. "I keep expecting a knock on the door from Lucan or Damian. Still, I couldn't live with myself if I'd snitched on Pippa to Lucan, because they'd go and knock on her door instead." I'm about to look at Kim to see if he appears guilty of having just shopped Pippa to Lucan on the phone outside, but am sideswiped from this endeavour by the flash of a joyful told-you-so expression directed at me by Evelyn.

In the hallway as we all hug goodbye, I whisper into Shigem's ear, *I can explain!*

As his beautiful warm brown eyes smile into mine from close up, there flickers something of our magical communion on the dance-floor, before he contrives a moment later to whisper with equal quietness back into my ear, *You don't have to, Jaymi—I totally trust you.*

We disengage from our embrace and look away from each other, both sharply conscious of our unspoken knowledge that this may, suddenly, be our last moment together for many years—or even perhaps forever.

I follow Evelyn out through the front door, turn to wave to both of them together, and turn away again.

92 ALAIA SLITHERS OUT OF LUCAN'S GRIP

As Evelyn and I reach the pavement and set off towards Downstairs, she says, "I hate having to lie and hide things from my friends like that."

I bet you do, I think, *and is that why you chose three of your friends for me to spy on?* "Oh, I know, yes. Me too."

"I wonder," she says. "Could anyone on our team be leaking raw material, d'you think?"

Woops—I thought this would be coming. "How d'you mean?"

"Well ... what was it Alaia said the other day, that made me wonder if she's really being discreet about our spokes-sheep recording? Something struck me as odd, though I couldn't quite put my finger on it..." She thinks hard, then shakes her head. "No, it's gone. Damn. Oh well, it'll come back. Anyway, d'you remember this Mint Man character? Was he in your Shigem footage?"

Aha. I was wondering whether she remembered it. It seems she doesn't. Or is she just pretending not to remember it, to test me out? There go those permutations again. I must remember here, she can always watch the Shigem footage again by herself and find the Mint Man in it once again: I'd better sit on the fence here, then. "Hmm," I muse. "There's been such an orgy of imagery over the last week, I can't quite be certain. It may ring a vague bell, but I'm not sure."

"Huh..." And we walk on in silence.

The dive-bar approaches, and there's Alaia waiting outside.

As we enter, nodding our greetings to Lucan, Angel and Flames, Kev is boasting, "That night last week, I had five Long Island Ice Teas here, and I only had to drain the lizard once."

"You were draining it down your leg and never noticed," says Damian.

"I fucking wasn't."

"Damian's right," says Flames. "I should know, I had to mop it up, right there on the floor."

"You are all *so* full of shit—"

"And to think," says Flames, shaking his head sadly, "I even made the drinks weak, just for you."

"You did not—they were full-strength and you know it!" Kev remonstrates. "I'm warning you, Flames..." His piggy eyes fall on Evelyn, as she leads Alaia and me towards the back of the room. "Hey Evelyn, wanna go halves on a bastard?"

"I'd rather suck on a urinal cake," she calls, without looking back.

"She sounds like a beautiful sister, to me," says Flames, watching her walk.

"I got the woofers in *my* jeep!" calls Kev.

Evelyn raises one finger at him without turning around.

"Damn, you have a way with women, Kev," says Lucan.

"Damn straight," says Kev. "Unleash the beast."

"An incontinent Chihuahua?" says Angel with fatigue.

Ignoring him, Kev continues, "I have to store my briefs in the freezer overnight before I wear 'em, or else I just burn 'em off me."

"I *thought* that frozen dinner tasted like cloth, last time we were at your place," says Flames. "Now I know what I was eating..."

As we reach the back wall, Evelyn's phone rings and she starts a conversation on it. We all sit, with me facing across the table towards the corner of the room, then she shuts her phone off and says, "I have to go. Rik needs me in the studio, to help him set up for us tonight—for the next you-know-what. So I'll just see you there, around eleven-fifteen?"

"There's just no peace for me," I moan.

"OK sure," Alaia tells her, "we'll see you then." Evelyn leaves us. "Wine?" Alaia asks me.

As soon as Alaia is back from the bar with the drinks, Lucan makes a leisurely but single-minded bee-line for us. "Hi Lucan," I breeze.

"Hey," he grins down insolently, then leans in towards us with one hand at each end of our table, his face close in to us. "Alaia, honey," he croons, with a soft malevolence.

"Yes, Lucan?"

"I was talking to Evelyn on the phone."

"Oh?"

"Mm-hm." He gives one of his wicked, deep-voiced laughs—the kind that always make Angel melt into a weak pool of hungry moisture. "And *I* worked something out!..."

"...Oh yeah?" she counters.

"Oh yeah. And I think you know what that is."

"No, I can't imagine."

"You *lie*, Alaia, A-liar, you lie!... Well, I'll tell you what it was, then, yeah? Shall I tell you what it was?"

She clears her throat. "I really don't care either way, Lucan."

"Mm-hm—oh, I'm sure!" Another deep wicked laugh, as he rubs his stomach in a slow, sinister fashion. "Oh, I see you *squirm*, Alaia! Well ... I didn't tell Evelyn this, but I worked out, from how she talked, that *you* didn't tell her about that wrong DVD. Now: why didn't you tell her about that wrong DVD, Alaia?"

Oh god, I can almost see her thinking, *if Evelyn finds out I didn't tell her about Lucan's ultimatum asking the GN for a bribe, then she'll know that I wanted to sabotage the spying deal by deliberately waiting long enough for Lucan to carry out his threat of going public about it—and she'll know I wanted to sabotage it just because of my petty jealousy that I was originally left out of the deal. I can't have her seeing that far into me... What do I say to stop Lucan telling her he gave me an ultimatum?* "OK," she says coolly, "I confess it, I didn't want Evelyn to think I was a dumb-ass, and I figured she'd clock me for a dumb-ass if I told her I gave you the wrong DVD. *OK now?*—what a big deal, huh? But don't worry: I passed your ultimatum right on up the chain in the General Network, to the management guys in New York, the ones who really matter. I gave them your number, Lucan, and it's them who'll decide whether to offer you a pay-off like they should—or diss you by not calling you. And if they diss you, then I wouldn't blame you for going public. But don't ask *us* how the big guys are going to respond to you, because they probably won't even tell us little people at all..."

Not bad! I think. What a cool chick she is. And it seems to work: "So you did pass it on," he says, and partly straightens up from where he was leaning down at us. "OK then. The guys in New York have till Monday night to call me."

"It needs to be longer."

"Tough shit—you better kick their ass, then. Monday night."

"They need till the end of the week, Lucan."

"Wednesday night, on one condition: you get into Evelyn's place, you hunt everywhere for wax-modelling stuff and you tell me what you find—plus the call from New York, both by Wednesday night. Or I'm gonna hurt you, Alaia. D'you understand?"

"I understand."

"I'm expecting your call."

"What's your number?"

"It's listed: Abayomi." He moves his face up and away from us. Then he holds my eye a moment, unspeaking, before suddenly moving his hands apart with a soft plosive out-take of breath, in a casual but powerful imitation of an explosion. I guess it to be a positive acknowledgement of *Big Bang*, though I don't feel at all certain of this.

Then he's gone. Alaia lets out a breath. "That calls for another drink," I say, giving her some cash.

She gets up to go to the bar, which I can hear has become busy. A minute later she is back, without drinks. "You know, I think we should go now," she says in a low voice. "Let's quit while we're winning. The bar was really busy, so Lucan's crew didn't see me waiting, but I overheard snippets of what they were talking about. I heard that Kev's going to drive Angel home, but then there was also something about Kev coming back here afterwards to pick up Damian and then going off with Lucan to Red Bank, and I couldn't hear the rest but I could tell I really didn't want to know any more about it anyway—it sounded like some heavy shit, whatever it was."

93 ANGEL'S BABY DOLL

We rise and slip through the crowd towards the front door, where I see Angel following Kev out ahead of us. She and I linger in the porch, while I watch them get into the Cadillac; then we emerge and head swiftly away down the block. "I'm going to tune in to Angel while we walk," I murmur. "I think we should keep an eye on the Abayomi-Deon household." She nods and we lapse into quiet.

I zoom in on the figure in the Cadillac's back seat ... and there you are, Angel, exhausted and sleep-deprived, in need of rest from everything. You wail in yourself, *I need to sleep! I need to sleep for a hundred years*, and you close your eyes and rest your head on the open window frame. But Lucan sees you do this, having wandered out from the bar, and he leans his grinning head down close to your ear, so you jump when he murmurs in his sexy deep-brown voice, "Don't go to sleep, little Angel! 'Cos when we get home, I'm going to work you over hard for half the night—you'll be screaming like a female, and you'd better be nice and sweet and cunty, or you know what." And you open up your eyes and weakly smile, and your penis stirs and jumps through your tiredness again and pushes hard in its cock-ring at your black leather trousers. The Cadillac draws away.

At home you climb the front staircase, clutching the banisters. You stumble to the big double bed and flop down fully clothed, your mind churning luridly from horniness and hormones, and you picture her again, the Baby Doll: her long straight platinum-blonde hair writhes and sprays against the blackness as she strenuously swings on her trapeze, wrenching at the ropes to send herself back down with adequate swing to push her further up at the opposite end of the arc. Her smile is a grimace and her white flesh streams tepid moisture. Her motion for an instant seems to slow, so her white hair streaks through the hot black space with a lonely volition of its own—luscious, vain, exquisite, fake and stunning in its snaky-pale platinum perfection. The lukewarm moisture, you notice, is sweat mixed with tears from her hazel eyes. A flat dead voice giggles out through her grimace, as she speaks a thing you cannot hear. She's telling you something, grinning, while she yanks at the rope in either hand, to keep swinging. You strain, till at last you hear her message, seeking wisdom—but it's nothing more than numbers, one to ten in sequence, repeated and repeated *ad nauseam*. Harder at the ropes she yanks, and wetter do her eyes run, and more and more stunning is her blonde hair swinging through the hot black, locked in its own swishy dripping private silence … and you feel as if you're looking back inside yourself, Angel, as if you once were her, the Baby Doll.

You twist around the bed beneath the surface of a half-sleep, and there I follow too, while you sneak into the Berkeley Carteret Hotel, to hide. You wander round the empty mezzanine, through the grand empty dark mirrored rooms and halls and terraces, with views of the deadness of this town all around you: a lushness all for you, flitting alone from mirror to window, peeping through the glass at wastes of concrete, empty grass, sand, ocean-hiss and blasted buildings' silhouettes. I watch you, you little queen, dancing on the ballroom floor, beneath the chandeliers. From the shadows at the side, as you twirl in the middle, I conduct a string quintet you cannot see but can hear; and my face weeps pouring flesh that runs in red rivulets across the shiny wooden floor but sinks before it reaches you. I'd kill you if I wanted to, but suicide hurts, so I pull you towards me on invisible elastic that sweats as it stretches in the wine-red glow radiated from my face. I pull you up the stairs, past the mirror, past the paintings and the plush public couches where no one ever sits; around the corner, past the ice-machine and down the long corridor, nearly to the end on the right, to number 629, where you stand at the window of the darkened room and watch an empty bus hiss by, while here in the corridor I stand behind your locked door and stare at your neck—

You twitch awake, as Lucan grabs your wrist and pulls you upward, off the bed entirely. You screech, flail and dangle, shivering in shock and trickling with sweat beneath your slinky black clothes, with the delicate silver cross still hanging off your chest where Lucan fixed it gently onto you earlier today. He gives that laugh of his ... then lowers you again to the bed and grins down with malevolence and hunger, inspecting you, and licks his lips.

94 THEFT FIVE, WITH SUICIDE AND SOUP-OF-THE-DAY

"Are we ready for the last recording?" asks Rik in the studio. "If Jason's client hasn't got enough for a spokes-sheep after this one, then I'm sorry but I can't help them. I only hope the sheep gives all this stuff a good home."

"After tonight, I'll never need to tune in to any of them again— it's the end of an era," I say. "I'm glad it's the last session. I'm starting to feel we should give our targets their privacy again."

"Hear, hear," says Alaia, "I applaud you for that," and I feel as if I've just been given marks out of ten by some strict but strangely glamorous maths teacher.

"OK, we're all set up," says Rik. "What harvest of fruits d'you have for us this time? Once more with feeling, please."

"Oh, something for all the family." I feel an exhilaration of finality infusing me, as I psych myself up to project two tune-ins from last night and five from today, vowing maximum accuracy...

First off is Angel's love for the waxwork, glimpsing himself as an elf in a turret, one dagger in his hand and another in his chest, his heavy violent feelings and his constant excitement.

Next comes the only stoned tune-in I'll have projected (and the only unreliable one), to Shigem in Paradise: his memory of the imperious club owner, the five non-existent bartenders and his weighty conversation with Tapette.

Now here are Kim and Shigem waking up this morning, their pleasure, their remembering Kim's blue elephant dream; and going out and bumping into Evelyn.

Here's Kim leaving Southport alone for London, and meeting people but still being alone; and the Asbury Park waterfront staring at him quietly.

I pump out Angel's foreplay, then his anger and haste, then his relentless nakedness in public and his spiritual enrichment on the crucifix.

Here comes Pippa's rainy walk, her sinking, not connecting on the street, her friend's silence on the phone, and her wander through the lonely edge of town to sit by the highway.

And we coast in for an unforgiving finish, with Angel exhausted in the Cadillac but unlikely to escape Lucan; Angel's Baby Doll on her trapeze, his dancing in the empty hotel ballroom—and grabbed awake.

Half an hour later, still on a glowing high from the session, I'm reclining on a sofa in Rik's and Evelyn's apartment, with Alaia, as the four of us embark on four bottles of red wine.

"Were you doing film stuff in Glasgow?" I ask Rik.

"Yeah, first I was a runner, for pennies, then I was doing the sticks, then pulling focus—all the time living in a squat in Castlemilk. Then one day I was actually allowed to look through a camera. And after I'd worked out which end of the camera you look through, I found they were actually going to pay me to operate it. So I could finally start living in a place with wall-to-wall ceilings, and floor-to-ceiling walls too. Then down to London and slid towards post-production, with all kinds of audio-visual toys in Soho. Then someone said there was a job opening at the GN in New York that needed some of the fine-tuned optimisation stuff I'd been doing between PAL in the UK and NTSC in the States, so I applied. They needed someone who'd been doing all that from the UK side. So that got me a work visa here, an H1B. But even with the GN behind me, getting the actual visa was still a long, complicated process. It turned out, bizarrely, that I had to stay for three weeks on a tourist visa in a small town in East Texas, 'cos that was the only place I could stay for zero money, with somebody I already knew, having run out of credit cards before the GN were allowed to employ me. Not to lapse into any clichés, but it really was all cow-tipping down there, and potted meat and Spam-moulding contests. The whiff of the KKK was still in the air, from the 'fifties, and scary religious people everywhere. If you were looking for a bit of incisive verbal cut and thrust, you were in the wrong place. Try to have an interesting conversation—you might as well watch dust settle. And no fashion show either. Bad clothes happening to good people, everywhere you looked. But you know what they say: when a chicken pecks you on the ass, you do what you have to. It was only three weeks till the visa came through, then suddenly I was working for Jason in Manhattan, so I had to go cold-turkey on the cow-tipping."

Evelyn opens another bottle of red wine, as I recognise within me the first fingers of that familiar melting warmth and sway from the first bottle. My attention wanders pleasurably, taking in the décor and the qualities of the light around me. When I return to the conversation, Evelyn is speaking: "It was funny, Rik and I went to this swanky restaurant the first two times we visited New York, and the first time we went, I ordered *soupe du jour*. I wasn't used to swanky dining, growing up here, so I didn't know what the words meant but I just loved the soup. So I ordered it again, the second time we went there, a few months later—but when the soup came I was so disappointed because it was different from the first time I had it. So I kicked up a fuss, right? And the waitress didn't understand much English, or any Spanish—I think she was Polish or something—but she knew enough to keep pointing at my soup, saying, '*This* is soup of the day! *This* is soup of the day!...' Well, I didn't like that, I can tell you. So I put my hands on my hips and I glared at her from my seat and I said, '*That* may very well be true. But I want *soupe du jour*...' But whatever words I used, to express this simple truth, she just couldn't understand, until I was so ready to strangle her! She was getting more and more flustered and confused about this simple, easy, straightforward soup I wanted. Then at last I decided she must be just really thick and dense, so I took pity on her and I decided to give up and have the wrong soup anyway, which tasted OK although I was still secretly a bit sad about it—it was the wrong soup, after all, and nothing could take that away, however you cut it and whatever anybody said. Then, months later somewhere, I found out *soupe du jour* means soup-of-the-day, so of course it's different every day, and I looked back and felt like a right banana!"

"What I've never told you," says Rik, "is that I knew what *soupe du jour* meant all along, but I didn't like to say anything because I wanted to see how the situation would unfold. It's finally time to tell you this. Reality time, Evelyn."

Her mouth falls open. "*Bullshit!*"

Rik shrugs. "Maybe so, maybe not... I guess there'll always be that little niggle of doubt between us, from now on..." Then he grins and bursts out laughing and she thwacks him with a pillow.

It's not so long before the third bottle is opened, while Rik changes the music again and lights some candles. The conversation drifts along effortlessly, as it always seems to do here, and by and by I'm gazing with a slight lack of focus at Evelyn. "I remember," she is saying, "once upon a time this town did still have something you could almost call a tourist season. I used to paddle in the sea in flip-flops in the summer, feeling the dead shrimps nestling in between my toes—and all the fluffy clouds in the sky, like dead bunnies. Those were the days. It seemed like the craziest stuff happened near the very end of the almost-tourist-season, just before everything shut down again. I once saw this old biddy go into a phone box and start to take a piss—but the walls were all basically windows, so for the amount of privacy she got, she might as well have gone in the street! I walked up and encouraged her through the windows: I made 'squeeze it all out' type facial expressions. I think it helped her. They've taken that phone box away now, it became such a toilet."

The talk wanders in many unpredictable directions during the fourth and final bottle. "Talking of ducks," says Rik at one point, "my father was once staying in a bed-and-breakfast in the countryside, and he went to the local pub and got drunk, then he tottered back to the bed-and-breakfast for the night. The door was unlocked, because it was the countryside a long time ago, and he went in and made a cup of tea and a sandwich in the kitchen, and went out the back door and down the back garden and started feeding the ducks in the stream at the end there. Very peaceful, very mellow, just feeding the ducks and thinking about life. He was like that—philosophical. Then a hand grabbed his shoulder and he turned and saw this fright-ened guy with a gun. The guy was saying '*Who are you? What are you doing?*' My father just stayed calm and peaceful: 'Feeding the ducks,' he said. 'Just feeding the ducks...' But then he realised: this wasn't the bed-and-breakfast at all, but somebody's private house, which he'd walked into and made a sandwich in!... Not long afterwards he took his own life—hanged himself at home." A silence descends at this, during which Rik gives a gently exaggerated smile, as if to say "But do please talk amongst yourselves, regardless!"

Through the dimness of the room a twist of candle-smoke streaks towards the open window, bends to clear the raised sash's lower edge, and shines intact in outside lamplight. The comfortable, still centre of the room hovers quietly above the coffee table, where three or four feet are resting.

"Evelyn and I were high on Ecstasy about a year ago, one evening in our old flat," Rik continues in a meandering fashion, and she laughs as she pours out the last of the wine for us all. "And we were both floating around like headless truffles ... and at one point, for some reason, she was washing the dishes and I was drying them, and I said to her, 'Evelyn—I don't know whether I'm lying down now or whether I'm standing up now,' which at that moment was the absolute truth. 'Which is it?' I asked, 'I'm curious.' And she thought about that one for a while, as we washed up. She understood that the answer wasn't so cut and dried, if you thought about it ... which it really isn't, by the way. Anyway, then she had a gradual breakthrough at last, and she said, 'I've got it! I've figured it out ... I'm standing up. And I'll tell you how I know. You see—*I never do the dishes lying down!...*' And I said to her, 'Ye gods, you're a fucking genius, Evelyn. You're dead right. I think I must be standing up too...'"

PART VIII

SATURDAY: ALAIA IN HIDING

95 SPANISH BABOONS AND TINY CREATURES

I rise at half past one, and though there's sunlight at my window I can smell a storm: there's violence in the air. I bathe and dress, then before I leave my room I lie upon the bed again and tune in to Evelyn … and there, where you sprawl in a similarly luxurious Saturday lie-in, while Rik clanks around in the kitchen making breakfast, you drift back into a half-sleep, dreaming of your garden of water and loveliness contained in its circles of balustraded terraces. Down on your left is the flowering jungle, where a stiff-nosed anteater halfway up a palm-tree pecks at the palm's trunk. Down on your right is dry land, where the lemon-trees flourish in the bright cool sun. Up the hill towards you Flames Alleyne stalks, carrying a crowded world of Spanish baboons in a sack, which he swings through the sunrays. You wave, to invite him up. He nods with animal seriousness and flips a control beneath the terrace, which you haven't seen before: up comes a nozzle right in front of you and shoots a peeled hard-boiled egg tightly up the water chute inside it. He clambers up the nozzle to your garden, you embrace and evening falls. A rabbit in the moonlight beckons to the two of you and leads you to a lake upon whose surface little creatures caper (ponies, zebras, unicorns), flowing through the silken water; tiny bunnies slide down the slopes of the wavelets. A waterspout of tentacles is sprouting and shrinking at the centre of the lake, while white-eyed lungfish wheeze in the mud around the shore. You and Flames tiptoe and peer into rock-pools, where underwater micro-cities teem with pulps and jellies. Baby yales and sea-ears scuttle through the shallows, past sea-mice, sea-cows, sea-pigs, seahorses, sea-eggs, sea-cucumbers, dogfish, sea-oranges and sea-lemons ... and you wake!

96 AN INFERIOR DECAPITATION GESTURE

I chuckle aloud, vowing to preserve the flavour of Evelyn's dream as long as I can today. I open my door and knock at Alaia's, but no answer. No sign of her downstairs either; she must have gone out. I eat a buffet lunch, alone in the breakfast room. I can't shake the feeling that she's hiding from me.

I go out and wander up and down the beach for an hour, restless. Then I lie supine in the wide triangle of grass between Cookman Avenue, Monroe Avenue and Saint James Place. Halfway down the length of this last, a small space is being remodelled, in readiness for opening soon as a bar called Anybody's, it seems. Across Cookman is a second empty triangle of scratchy grass, across Monroe a third, and beyond this latter a fourth, all deserted except for me. The man doing the remodelling at Anybody's stares oddly across the space at me. I'm too far away for him to know whether I am looking at him or not. He decides not to engage with me.

To check on Shigem's and Kim's wellbeing, I bend my sight to Kim, who is also lying on grass, in the orchard-like calm of a deserted Liberty Square, reading ... and you look up as I tune in, Kim, half-sensing someone. You're doing OK; but even now, on the eve of your departure for a new chapter with a beautiful new love, how little does your OK-ness affect your calm knowledge of how much easier things will be after death. What a sweetness there will be at the moment of dying—the cessation of a struggle whose design has such cruelties for many and such dangers for all. True to its all-purpose aliveness, your imagination obediently conjures up the picture of a perfect, soulless ecstasy of electronic music playing behind the smooth vanilla-scented silence of a Burne-Jones orchard, where figures from a love-song wilt and strum and swoon in glades;

and you smile at this. But seriously, Kim, what relief and release it will be, from this demanding and uncomfortable situation we're in while alive, when we're always just a narrow squeak away from events that could plunge us into fear, pain, grief, horror or insanity. How very badly arranged that narrow squeak is: wouldn't a wide squeak have been a rather more intelligent setting? What a vicious and unforgivable fuck-up, frankly, on the part of whatever process caused this to happen. How exhausting and contemptible that we've been dropped into such a fuck-up, and how very sweet will your assassin be. You'll know him when you see him; you will smell his lovely perfume and you'll bend to kiss his lethal, jewelled hand. On your lips, from this hand, you will drink your elixir: honey, water, Nembutal and *peace* at last… Still, as you said before, all this in no way changes the fact that in practice you're genuinely OK—quite content, in fact!

You regain consciousness of Liberty Square for a moment, then return to your book. Curious, I read it too; and so we read together for a couple more hours, you and I, on this your last full day in Asbury Park. This strangest of books is bewitching you, I see, Kim, and making you resolve that you'll answer it in writing yourself one day, across the decades and the languages: head to head, toe to toe and mouth to mouth, your own chants will meet these and dance with them, somewhere in an evil dawn of gold. What better use could there be for your hours?

The daylight is fading. Kim closes the book and sits in thought— blond boy seated in a pastoral setting, under trees in the dusk. I rise on my triangle of grass, head across to his square and approach him in person. "Hi," I say. "Wasn't expecting to bump into you. I thought you'd be packing."

"I'm meant to be asleep at the moment. Shigem and I are taking it in turns to sleep, in case someone tries to break into the house, who we don't want to meet. I couldn't get to sleep, though, what with all his crashing around with boxes, so I thought I might have better luck sleeping out here—but no chance." He checks the time. "I should get back now. Tonight's our last night. Tomorrow evening, we leave. So come back and have a drink now, why not?"

My leave-taking of Shigem last night, though not expressed as our final one, was nonetheless conducted by us in such a way as to do duty as such, in case it should turn out to be so. This spontaneous delicacy occurred because of the bond between us, which has involved less verbal expression than any other deep bond I've enjoyed with anyone. I have no need, therefore, to visit now on account of him. That being said, a visit would do no harm. "OK, sure," I say.

Halfway there, we notice Kev across the street. He gives us an evil look, without speaking, then does a clumsier and more troglodytic version of Lucan's powerful self-decapitation gesture.

"We shan't be telling Shigem about that," states Kim.

97 LUCAN AND ANGEL ON THE BIG SCREEN

That does it—I should tune in to Lucan, right now, and see if there's any damage brewing for Shigem. It'll be much more valuable if Kim doesn't talk, of course; not that he says much. I hesitate a moment, then just come out with it: "Did Shigem say that Evelyn mentioned the Metropolitan had a brief project where I did some spying into Angel and Lucan?"

"Yes. I hadn't known you could do that, as well as the hypnotic stuff, until she said."

"Yeah. Well... Anyway, in view of that gesture Kev just made, I think I'd like to do a second bit of tuning in to Lucan, while we're walking, if that's all right?"

"Sure, what d'you need me to do?"

"Nothing. Just keep quiet, if you would."

As we walk on in silence, it's with some trepidation that I push out my customary mental picture of Lucan, in what I realise is indeed only my second direct tune-in to him, expecting to find bloodthirsty evidence of the real violence and injury I know he has perpetrated on many people. The only time I tuned in to him, when I was on the toilet eavesdropping on him and Angel in his kitchen, I felt no such trepidation, as I simply found myself tuning in by mistake, being stoned. And in any case what I chanced upon then was the unexpectedly human memory of his attraction to Angel when they first met—this benign selection of mine being no doubt influenced by Lucan's mellow party mood at that moment. Now by contrast, I am braced for whatever I may find ... and as it happens, Lucan, you are staring through the window of the Cadillac, as Kev drives you somewhere without conversation. Nothing bloodthirsty here, but I do feel a blast of formidable street power, the flash of many drug deals and the sprouting up of much cash all around you. I also see a swathe of your internal landscape that's like a pulsing cloud of shadow with drips of red in its depths, and I know straightaway that this flickering storm-cloud is Angel's housing, in all its opacity and exhilaration. No surprise that this dwelling should display a more ominous and complex mien than that of just your first memory of him: for those are the external ramparts of Angel's grand estate and seven-layered formal garden, as seen from inside you.

But I'm here now to hunt for something specific, namely whatever I can catch regarding any plans you have for Shigem; so I turn away from your Angel and cast about me. All I can find at the moment, however, temporarily drowning out all evidence of any other interpersonal dealings in you, is something I can identify as a well-honed fantasy of yours. We're in the anodyne environment of a Hollywood screening-room, where a new trailer is being unveiled for a VP of Marketing. "His name above the title," someone mutters, as the lights dim—and then it hits. Yes, Lucan: multiplied in close-up on a wall of television screens, a gun's safety catch is released in slow motion by your hand. Your biceps enters frame, lit in red against the sky. Your flesh shines with oil and has been misted just before the take, so individual droplets reflect the sinking sun. Photographed from lower down, your head scans the land, and your brows beneath a black bandanna frown low.

Now the music slams in, a mighty silver hubcap spins on each of the twenty screens, and roaring engines change gear. Pulling up and back through a crisp swirl of side-lit dust, the camera draws the whole tyre smoothly into sight, while flawlessly maintaining the hubcap centre-frame. (The visuals and sound design bear the hall-marks of a quite virtuosic skill, or at least a high budget.) The surface of a highway and the side of a truck appear, the truck's load covered with a green and black canvas camouflage. With no cut, the same take continues somehow upward as the army truck, below us now, is framed without a wobble, hanging stationary on screen between the yellow-painted streaks that mark the edges of its highway lane.

Two more trucks slide in to flank the first, then more behind, ahead and either side, identical in black and green; the engine roar swells and the whole screen-wall now displays one projection of this single moving shot, shared across the width of all twenty banked panels. A slow colossal drum joins the drone of the engines, as the ever-rising camera swallows six lanes of trucks, surging thunderous up a valley through the setting sun's light: the front of the convoy somewhere near the sun's disc; the rear end behind you, near a darker horizon.

"LUCAN ABAYOMI" unfurls across the screen in a red blast, and then is gone. A voice like the voice of a mountain resounds: "A soldier..." A heartbeat quickens under screeches of metal, over shots of wires coiling underneath a closed door and a clock dial ticking, then a ball of raging orange fire. The mountain voice concludes: "and a thief of minds!... *This* man commands, from a screen near you. See *The Imagination Thief.*" That scarlet script unfurls again, across the screen's entire width, "THE IMAGINATION THIEF". Your gaze returns, scouring the horizon, left to right above the camera lens—and *freeze-frame.*

But instead of the trailer ending there, as it clearly should, there's been some mistake up in the projectionist's eyrie, or maybe it was back in the edit suite in post-production, or way back in production itself, or possibly longer ago in pre-production or even development ... for as your trailer carries on, Lucan, Angel leaks in through the walls of your screening-room, and seeps up the curtains either side of the screen, and infiltrates the fabric of the screen itself, and pours through the canvas of that army truck you showed us—and *cut,* to this interior. The canvas roof above us here is camouflage indeed, Lucan, now it is revealed: for underneath it, snug below the green and black, the air is dim but candy-lit, and here is Angel Deon, your freak in a skirt of snakes, writhing in introverted lust and peeping out through the glands of his libido and the curves of the lens, to your screening-room... Moist, purple-nippled, pert-cheeked and eaten up with endless sexual hunger, Angel pouts and whispers at us, up there on your trailer screen: "*I'm your fatal attraction, Soldier! I'm exquisite damage. But you're the Ghost of Jealousies—a Stranger in Moscow.*" Despite your market strategy, despite straight lines, here he is still—hitching a ride in your army truck, tainting your trailer and suffusing your entire super-square action-blockbuster movie with his sumptuous poison. Carried on your tough tanks, aloft among your heavy-duty metal gun-turrets and astride the booming gun of your artillery, he's starkly incongruous within your wider image, Lucan, showing up your lies—but here you sit together nonetheless, just the pair of you, and here you shout together to the whole wide world!

98 PORCH-GEESE AND VIETNAM

Kim and I have now reached Shigem's place. "What did you see in him?" Kim asks, turning to me with fascination as we step up onto the front path.

"Um … I'll tell you later. I'm not convinced I could quite do justice to it, between here and the top of the stairs. A lot of it was pretty non-verbal. And you know what—coming in with you now would be cute and all, but I can be more useful than that. I didn't see any imminent danger in Lucan, but he may just have farmed out his dirty work, so I want to check on Damian too, right now, to make sure he's not about to come round here. I'll phone you, if he is."

"OK, Jaymi. Thanks, I'll see you later."

I set off down the street. What I just said was true, but my not going upstairs with him had a second reason too: I was scrapping my plan to convert that maybe-final goodbye with Shigem last night into a definitely-penultimate goodbye instead. I doubt that he and I could have made a better job of our leave-taking, later tonight, than the job we made of it last night, sudden and brief though that was; and if I'd forced us to attempt it by appearing tonight, we might even have risked a faint undercurrent of superfluity.

Within a couple of minutes I have zigzagged over to Damian's house, and there he is approaching it from the other direction, shooting furtive glances about him, with the collar of his battered leather jacket raised up. "Hi Damian," I call. He pauses, then jerks his gaunt head at me with the same hint of gruff affection I saw in the odorous gents at Downstairs. Well, good; but that doesn't mean I feel the same for him. On a bold whim, as a variation on my mission to protect Shigem, I decide to cash in on his goodwill. "May I come in for a moment?" I ask.

"Alright," he says, surprised.

"Thanks. I don't mean to be rude, but is there any danger of the dogs being kept away from me? I'm such a pussy-cat when it comes to dogs."

"I'll keep them out in the alley," he grunts.

I follow him inside and take a seat in his kitchen, at the same bare wooden table I saw in Angel's memories of living here. He brews up two mugs of tea, brings them to the table and sits across from me, all in a more leisurely manner than I have witnessed in him while in the company of the others. "Thanks, Damian. By the way, I've been meaning to ask: where did our two broadcasts take you, what did you see when you watched them?"

He stiffens, looking grim. "I didn't see the second one, but your first broadcast dug something up that it should have left buried. It's now running loose in me and hiding in the shadows. A thing I never knew I had. A *shriek*—that's all I'll call it. You don't wanna know more."

We lapse into quiet … and I see you as a boy, Damian West, when the sad pirate captain in your head said you'd sail via white sandy bays past frog-croaking jungles, through lagoons and straits and over seas whose green glassy surfaces shivered with the wriggle of gigantic squids and worms miles below. But even as a boy you could glimpse, within the captain's vision of your ship's jaunty launch, the spectre of the ghost-ship it would later become: torn shreds of sail hung on pale shrunken mast-wood, where cormorants perched and shat; the rasp of vultures scratched across the plastic glaze of sky, while an oil-slicked sea licked dully at the ship's hull; and strands of blackened flesh upon your own skull and bones.

My tune-in is interrupted by a savage barking from the side alley. Damian takes a quick step across to the window and peers through the lowered blind towards the street, his hand near his jacket pocket, then returns to his tea. "Passer-by," he mutters darkly.

He rolls an expertly thin cigarette from a packet of tobacco. I raise my mug to him and he returns the gesture. "I used to have porch-geese," he reminisces.

"Porch-geese?"

He says nothing.

"Are they what I think they are?" I persist.

He glances around the room, as if scanning it for hidden microphones. "Depends what you're thinking."

"Well … geese that live on the porch, I suppose?"

He nods grimly, sipping his tea. "You've nailed it," he says, then clamps his mouth shut tight again.

"Huh!" I say.

There's a silence.

"Well, that must have been nice," I venture. "Did you all like one another?"

"They were guard geese!" he barks, as if offended. "As good as any guard dog, they were."

"So … did something happen to them?"

A discernible sadness flickers in him. "They had to go. They just honked all night… And although they knew better than to attack me, they attacked everyone else. Friends. Enemies. The postman." He shakes his head. "The leader of the porch-geese, though—he was wild. Like a dachshund high on mushrooms."

Smoke from his roll-up rises through the bars of light let in by the horizontal slats of the window blind, which stripe his face too, like sideways prison bars.

"Have you ever seen a dachshund high on mushrooms?" he asks.

"No, I can't say I have." I should prefer to be asking "Is Lucan planning to hurt Shigem before Shigem leaves town tomorrow evening?" but I can't mention that he's leaving, just in case Damian and Lucan don't in fact know this. Nor can I even ask just "Is Lucan planning to hurt Shigem?" because I can't run the tiniest risk of putting ideas into Lucan's head.

Before I can hit upon an acceptable re-phrasing of the question or an effective substitute question, however, Damian takes me in a different direction altogether. "Never let your enemies escape," he urges me. "And yet, be patient too, because if you sit beside the river long enough, you'll see the body of every one of your enemies floating by, dead." He gives a mirthless cackle, then resumes, starting quietly but building in intensity: "I've seen it all, Jaymi: a madman in a dismal land, standing in a brown field, watching two bums who were trapped on a small shitty island in a river where they maimed each other using rocks and sticks in sunlight for hours, till they both died screeching—pointless, witless, hopeless pain. Larvae so bloodless and hideous, feeding off the napalmed bodies, out in Vietnam; and under the shed that I shared with the bodies was a baggy red light-bulb, squeezable and lit, with a fumble of wires, and I knew it was a bomb. So I ran, and heard it blow up close behind me with a burst of green smoke. Then the sun shone down pale green, through a green sky; dogs barked, birds screeched and body parts rained down. The sirens started wailing and the dogs wailed back at them, in time with the wailing of the newly mutilated—a sour flame of pain in a garden of evil. I saw that I was wounded. I started blacking out, then, and sombre pictures flashed in me: the son of the hounds of the sea, the hundred-foot snakefish, and swordfish jumping up conveyor belts. And torture, forever, all around the world, in chambers: the slash of steel, the burn of fire, the slice and stab of bone-twisting pain are all gashed into flesh at dawn as lightning shrieks, and nothing we can ever do to stop it."

"And how warming it is," I say, "to know that all that pain will last just as long as people last." The extent to which I find myself at home in his darkness is not something I expected before my visit, and I'm half-inclined to continue in this semi-philosophical vein. However, I must not forget my mission, so I attempt to bend the conversation back to this: "Still, let's at least try to minimise that pain if possible. Talking of which, there is one person who…"

I tail off, though. In view of the nature of Lucan and Damian, there really is no way, despite my best intentions outside, of just asking "Is Lucan planning to hurt Shigem before Shigem leaves town tomorrow evening?" or any equivalent question, without the risk of putting Shigem in more danger than he's already in. I fudge some forgettable ending to my abandoned utterance, therefore, and we part with respectfully minimal ceremony at his front door.

99 PIPPA A ZOMBIE THROUGH INTERNAL DAMAGE

Back in my room I phone Alaia with a certain trepidation, almost as if I fear she will put the phone down on me. "Any plans for the evening?" I ask.

"Yeah, I need to go to the studio alone again and try out some more new vocal stuff. Oh by the way, I did call Lucan today, as he asked me to, and I told him I've verified there are no wax-modelling materials in Evelyn's rooms. So the culprit definitely wasn't Evelyn, I said—as well as not being Shigem, of course."

"It's funny he asked you to do that. Even if Evelyn did have modelling materials, did he think you would report it to him?"

"I think he did, yes. I suppose it should tell us the level of control he is used to wielding over his crew. Or just that he's grasping for authority. You know how men are. All right, Jaymi: I must get ready for the sound booth. I'll see you tomorrow, OK? Goodnight."

"Goodnight."

I wanted to hang out with her, but she's hiding from me and I don't know why.

I recline on my bed, restless. My room is uncannily quiet. I close my eyes and shoot my sight out to hover over Pippa where she sits on her high-rise balcony, spotlit like a wax dummy, high in the night, with a golden angel ornament nestling on her lap, looking out with her dead glassy stare across town in exactly this direction. As usual, her moist green eyes look as if they've been crying. Although she seems to be looking straight at me, I know she cannot see through these walls to my body lying here. Nevertheless, I open my eyelids just a chink, peek across my room to my window by the eaves and check the window's position in relation to me and her. My light is on and the curtains and window are open—but the angle isn't quite right for her to see me here in the Metropolitan, I'm glad to note. I shiver, then close my eyes again. I remind myself that her high-rise cannot even be seen from this window, being hidden by trees or roofs or something else, as I ascertained a couple of days ago. Even so, I raise my eyelids once more, just a crack, to double-check.

Then I let them stay closed, deciding I shall trust she cannot see me … and at last I catch a glimpse of your mystery, Pippa, there where it stands in your mind for an instant before it's smudged away. This glimpse centred unmistakably on whatever space is behind that narrow door in your hallway, but its nature was less clear. It was a black pit of utter horror, but with the blank opacity of a lacuna, as if you have blacked something out, which might explain its strangely elusive concealment up to this point.

In your head a bird warbles, like water through woodwind. A line of oil-tanks on a freight train jolt and boom, across the points, beside an empty grey field bordered in coiled steel. An oily croak sounds from the rushes in the marsh beside the tracks. The cutting opens out upon a valley full of low unwindowed buildings, marked in Korean script. Over the death-camp, the wind sings faintly in the telegraph wires, a mournful dirge of loss and waste and sadness without end— thin and plangent and metallic where the pylons stride away through the blasted smudgy stillness of purple-black-brown air.

You're in your chair, hunched against the night air, sleeping in your dark-red sweatshirt with matching red sweatpants, your head turned in my direction, eyes open, staring at me lying here. And while you sleep, Pippa, on your dreamscreen flickers up an antique dusk: across a misty countryside a statuesque bull's head rears up and lows. Aged spectres, bestial and human, float from tumuli and copses, like shadows from the other side, wobbly and rustling. A goat's skull stands out stark against the darkness, an ancient apparition. You hear the shouts and whispers of the multitudes of dead things, echoed in this old place, catching certain names through the chatter: Centaur and Serpent, Ten of Swords and Queen of Circles, Eohippus fossils buried under hills of bone. Rooks caw, raspy and ragged like a hundred thousand years ago, and there nearby you is a sign-post: Old Place.

As I lie here with my eyes still closed, you feel almost like a vegetable, Pippa—hunched there in your chair at the bottom of my bed, staring at me glassy-eyed, down the bed's length at me—and always I can see the claw, pushing out against the inner muscles of your belly, sealed tight in its prison, pushing up the dark-red surface of your sweatshirt, towards me—

100 EVELYN'S DANCE, WITH MINIMAL EFFECT

I jolt awake and glance around the room. Then I get up, close the window and draw the curtains, right to the edges of the glass. In the bathroom I splash cold water on my face and stare at my pupils in the mirror: to me, that power and capacitance are still quite clear in there.

Something's building up, within the air in this town, that I should know about. I'll go for a walk around the block, to clear my head.

In the hallway I run into Evelyn, who is entering from the street. I gesture her into the empty breakfast room, which is lit only by lamp-light coming in through the single unshuttered window in there. "What's up?" she asks.

"This'll sound funny, but ... there's something strange in the air between me and Alaia. You heard her coldness on the beach to me a couple of days ago. Then yesterday I was alone with her in the morning right here, and then at Shigem's in the evening, and both times she just seemed to be receding from me. Now today she feels like she's in hiding... Strictly between you and me, you don't think those wax dummies were *her* work, do you? I wouldn't know, because I have an agreement with her not to tune in to her—"

"Jaymi, that's ridiculous."

"I guess so. Maybe I'm just being paranoid. I sometimes feel that the arrival of these abilities of mine have made me lose some of my own default personality—"

"I know."

"You know? How?"

"Well, she and I do sometimes talk to each other!"

"Oh. OK. Well, so maybe the strangeness between her and me just comes from me? D'you think so?"

"All I can say is, look at yourself and her, and keep looking. You may discover something." She ruffles my hair, as if I were a little boy, then gets up.

"Is that all the wisdom you have for me?" I ask.

"I have to go now. I have to drive to New York, to give Marc the final master recording of *Sound & Vision*, which Rik output today."

"Why so late in the evening?"

"Marc says it's safer at night."

"But you're a big girl now, Evelyn, I'm sure you could handle the journey in the daytime?"

"He's not worried about me, dummy, just the master recording! He knows what gold dust it is. In fact he's made me hire a small armoured van, just for this one trip. And get this: as soon as I've arrived, he's actually going to come along in person with me to the security vault in Queens and personally take charge of locking away

Sound & Vision and all the spokes-sheep masters. The Great Mogul himself, in an industrial cold-storage facility, in Queens, in the middle of the night!"

Aha! I think. I stare at her. "Er, Evelyn… You just said he's going to lock away not just *Sound & Vision* but *also* the spokes-sheep recordings. That's what you just said, and I found you convincing." She closes her eyes in a longish blink, like a computer screen going momentarily blank for the duration of some necessary squirt of internal processing. "But *I* thought our secret spokes-sheep recordings were just Jason's gig, happening behind Marc's back…"

Looking at me, she puts her finger to her lips. She rises, pecks me on the cheek, chirps "Night night sweetie! Sweet dreams!" and leaves the room, pulling the door closed after her.

So Marc's ignorance of the "secret" imagination-thieving deal was a lie. That being so, Jason's claim that another company commissioned this thieving may well have been a lie as well, I realise: the General Network probably instigated it. Such maximisation of the value of my gifts has Marc's logical and energetic inventiveness written all over it. Even the "spokes-sheep" figure itself, that ridiculous presence or absence that has loomed so comically over all my dealings here, could have been a fiction too, all along—just something cooked up by Jason for his Times Square meeting with me, designed to sound as goofy as possible in order to amuse me and distract me from enquiring any further into the uses to which the company was really going to put the fruits of all this ethically dubious spying. The GN could be planning to use it within their own Global Market Research and Intelligence division, which I read about in the magazine article that first informed me about Marc; or they could be selling it onward to the military, for intelligence-gathering software development; or even selling it onward for nuclear weapons research… One way or another I've almost certainly been a tool of the military-industrial complex, and I have to say I'm cheesed off about it.

I sit on the window-seat in one of the shuttered window-bays and tune in to Evelyn in her van on Main Street … and as you drive, Evelyn, you feel the engine's rhythm and you feel at peace. Stopping at a red light, you notice certain men who are out for the night, and your fingers drum the wheel and you purr within yourself and the engine purrs back. In your mind, music rises: a beat pumps, brass swells and voices float down to you, as flame lights you up inside and spills from your eyes and your fingers like a fountain. You let go all arguments, even the good ones, and picture the eyes of those around you. Brown? Blue? Green? Another colour? You project to them a picture of you stroking shut their eyes and then kissing them—you know their eyes deserve it, for your own are the same. If everybody else did this... Of course you don't forget that their hands may stab you, while you're stroking shut their eyes; so you're ready all the time to dodge away or stab them back. But you dance in your mind, to make your kissing and your caution spin together, and you're agile in your dance, so you find what love you can within the colours of their eyes, while your mirth ripples up and out and chimes between the stars! Trumpet ripples through your body, lazy and fluid, while the bright dome of stars above you spins through the aeons, and your squeak is in its symphony.

I reopen my eyes upon this darkened breakfast room, with a renewed sense of peace. Then again, what effect does she really have, when the immense pain and sadness elsewhere just carries on regardless?

I enter Shigem's home number. "Hallo," says Kim.

"Hi, it's Jaymi. Just checking you're both doing OK."

"Things are a bit jittery, but no ominous knocks on the door so far."

"Good. I visited Damian after I left your place, and I went in and had tea with him."

"Really?... As one does."

"Yes, it seemed like the thing to do at the time. Anyway, I couldn't see any indications of him being in pre-'hit' mode."

"I hope that indicates he isn't—though I'm aware there are still plenty of fine opportunities left for him. Thanks for doing that."

"OK, good night, Kim."

"Good night."

101 DESIRE AS DISEASE IN ANGEL DEON

Immobile on the breakfast room window-seat, I feel my eyes narrow once again, for I know the next place I need to look ... and there you are, my Angel, in the dark verandah'd house, in the middle of your thousandth violent combat with Lucan. He twists your arm until you wince, and stares like a gun at your bewitching eyes, to find out if you're lying. Are you lying, Angel? Angel, are you lying? Answer Lucan. Your adrenaline is pumping—your nipples stand hard against your black polo-neck (no bra today) and you are breathing fast. *Angel, are you lying?* For you know you won't escape him: you'll tell him what he's seeking and you'll give him what he wants, as you always end up doing, every single time you fight.

Your throat becomes tight and your eyes burn with tears that you try to keep inside you and the tears bend the light from the ceiling in your eyes and your voice goes squeaky and tense and he grabs you. Dragging your beautiful face around the dusty cellar floor, he reaches down and with the power of a single hand he holds your jaws open. Tenderly then, with his other hand, he touches the end of your tongue with the Capri cigarette that you left in the ashtray a minute and a half ago. The cigarette burns—you yelp and whine. Tongue revenge. You picture your face, through its crying, as the face of a boy whom you once found dead upon the sand by the Casino, half-in half-out of the water that trickles out of Wesley Lake: he'd tried to screw Lucan on a drug deal, was shot dead by Damian on orders from Lucan, and then had a leather face nailed to his dead skull, obscuring his own face, just as a deterrent to others.

And here in the cellar, out of sight or sound of help, Lucan douses you with kerosene by candle-light, and clamps himself around you, a muscled insect incubus positioning its sting among the folds of inflammable, delirium-inducing, evaporated kerosene… He kisses you and whispers, "You're just a pair of fuck-holes to me, you little freak…" and you black out from zero food and excess hormones.

My sight zooms in below your smudged amber eye-shadow, enters your unconscious eyes and sees you are dreaming that your hurt spirit crouches with dripping wings, naked in an alleyway. But Lucan discovers you, of course, and he points down a downward-moving escalator, telling you to ride it, and you do. Your feet can feel the gears trundling underneath the step. Smoke swirls around you, growing redder as you travel down. Sweat trickles down your spine. The escalator steps are now hot beneath your bare feet. You see that yet again you are naked in public, as you so very often are, despite your always hating this. Also, as always when you're naked and scared, your erection stands hungry and hard in full view, while your body runs with sweat. The forty-five-degree descent ahead is dead-straight, for miles. Either side, banks of pipes, valves, tubes and wires tower up to clear sky and drop to depths of gloom, clad in complex walkways, balconies and stairs. Panic floods through you. The rumbling of the escalator gears is augmented by a booming so deep that it might be the engines of a planet, overlaid with a bank of sound as dense as the machinery—clanks, hisses, whistles, grating screeches and explosions. Sparks leap from point to point around you, as you watch in fright. A huge grinding blast from far below shakes the steps and a red flicker rises. You lean beyond the hand-rail and peer down: five miles beneath you a ball of orange fire rages, tiny and intricately floral at this distance.

You jolt back to real life, but it's out of the frying pan and into the fire, as Lucan's powerful arms are whirling you around through the air of the bedroom and thwacking you down upon your back onto the bed. He must have been carrying you up the staircase from the cellar, while you were descending your escalator. As he stalks around the shadowy room, you lie there apprehensively with wet staring eyes, rubbing your hand in the softest way across your necklace of bites. Your eyes hold aloft an early memory: where and how he bit your body, long ago, and wouldn't stop although you asked him to, and so you lay there as he bit, still and staring as you were (like your staring eyes now), while the back of your hand rubbed your neck and softly rubbed it more and more...

And how fast the years with him have run, since that nadir of weakness then, whose memory now hardens your erection to the feeling of a metal strut. You wish you shared this latter with that Siamese twin, you know the one, and had a tail like a snake's too—but now he flips you over, prone, and grabs your throat with both big hands until you choke with a pre-orgasmic tightness and constriction. He leans near your ear and whispers, "Wait until I hang you—you'll ejaculate for sure, my little love-slave..." Your anus grabs his giant penis, sucks it up and pulls it in deep, and deeper still until you feel it pushing far up inside you. "We'll both shoot together, while you die—won't that be sexy?" And as Lucan gives his laugh, deep and wicked, you moan and quiver cat-like and shoot like a small pistol, all around the bedroom.

You want *mercy*, little Angel? Dream on, baby. He's only just begun with you tonight, like every night, and you're hard again already. Your ears are always ringing and your eyes want to cry and you never can keep him out; he's always there, pushing, forcing, punching through your freedom and your body and your space. Except for your mind, you have no privacy at all, but are naked to him all the time. You glimpse yourself there in the shadows of the mirror, like a sexy little weasel, wiping off the blood from your mouth where he's hit you. Your desire for him is so extreme, it must be a disease—one you'll die of, as you realise now. One of these days he will kill you while you're with him, or he'll kill you for escaping, or you'll kill yourself because you can't escape him any other way.

Always, you have to hide your face behind your hands, hardly daring to peek between the bars of your fingers to see what new invasion or privation is in store, what knife is being whetted through the doorway, just for you—swaying on your feet, without the freedom of perspective to show you what is upward, while the walls of this tomb-dark house tilt and bend and leer and totter inward, always...

102 SHIGEM'S UNIMPROVABLE SITUATION

Craving escape before I suffocate, I pull my sight out of Angel, swing it upward over trees across town, from the fulcrum of this window-seat, and spear it straight down through a roof on First Avenue. I need to check that Shigem hasn't been visited by Damian, now that I've just learned about the latter's charming way with a nailed-on leather face ... and you're lying in bed, Shigem, your head on Kim's shoulder, saying "I like not really knowing what I'm going to say before I start talking."

"You don't say."

"It's funny, we don't have any poison in us. Some people are backed up with poison. Lucan and Angel, for instance. If ever there was a pair who deserved each other. Corrosive acid, that's what flows between them. And yet in a twisted way they really do love each other. Their relationship went to hell in a handbag as soon as it began, of course, just like Evelyn told me it would when they first got together."

Kim kisses your forehead and whispers, "My love." You burrow down into his protection, hold him tight and stay there, your mouth still and open against his chest.

After a while you squirm around to face the other way, so the pair of you are curled up front-to-back. His hot strong arms come around your neck and shoulders; his legs entwine with yours, adjust and are still. And there you lie together, in an eloquent communication of absolute silence and stillness.

This is a perfect, unimprovable situation right here, you decide, as you slip immediately towards sleep, easy and free now that you're enclosed within the sweet relaxing calm of your boyfriend's embrace. You're half-conscious of the voice of your own mind, prattling on for a little while longer, to nobody, as it winds down: "How alive, to see the face of your lover through the years," it is saying. "Oh, have I got staying power, strong like a mountain. But I'd like to turn a mirror to the sky first. Maybe then we'll see far enough to travel backwards? The sun's on track to expand to a red giant and swallow us. —I thought about you twice just then, my love. Perhaps the second time was really first. Look at me, behind the mirror. Chase that shadow: just as fast as you follow, it'll skip from your sight. It's a living, for a shadow, I suppose…" and as you sink lower, slower, through Atlantic depths, your mind's voice slows down at last. Down here in the deeps are only surges and fleeting things: seaweed fronds and eels make to grab your skinny torso from behind and wind you round them. Your body gives a twitch, as a fish-nose bumps you with a soft caress that leaves a nose-shaped dent upon your arm. Kim flashes up, swimming naked, right in front of you: *kiss forever, in the darkness!* comes a whisper … and you sleep.

103 THEFT SIX, WITH AMBIGUOUS BOWING AND CURTSEYING

I pull my attention back in to my fulcrum here in the breakfast room. Shigem and Kim have fully refreshed and released me, from Angel and Lucan. I know what I should do now, too, before the chance is gone. I pull my phone out and call Evelyn. "Hi, it's me. I have a very good reason for calling you this late."

"Hell, you call this late? I was just getting warmed up for the evening."

"Well, I know last night's spokes-sheep session was going to be the last, but I've ended up doing a lot more tuning-in today than I expected, just to keep a look-out for any last-minute attacks on Shigem. So I've got a *final* dose of hot stuff that we should throw into Marc's cold-storage—sorry, I mean the client company's cold-storage—to add to the symphony of beauties and horrors we've already captured for posterity."

"Fabulous! We'll see you in ten minutes."

Twenty minutes later, then, I sit before the lens for the sixth and last imagination theft, with Rik behind the camera and Evelyn and Alaia standing by. This'll be a quick one—just four tune-ins, from today...

So here comes Kim, for the last time: he's OK, but how sweet will death be; his reading and his resolution.

Here for the last time is Pippa, like a zombie; her dark and mystic countryside; and once again that demon in her belly.

Once more comes Angel: the fight, the cigarette burn and thinking he'll be killed; down the escalator; then re-awakening, to Lucan yet again.

And we close with my own Shigem: the unimprovability, the drifting into sleep.

The perfect end to Jason's raw material.

"Cut, and that's a wrap," says Rik. I look up at the monitor, in time to catch the very last second of Shigem's dying consciousness, before the screen fades to black. "Kiddies, for the very first time in history, we now have enough raw human mind-stuff to build a full imagination ... for a cartoon sheep! This is a break-through on a par with the great Dolly herself, the most famous sheep of all time."

Scattered applause from all four of us. "What's the next step for all this stuff?" asks Alaia.

"I'll cut off what's unusable at the beginnings and the ends, leaving just the usual handles for editing later. Then I'll take all the material for each of the four targets in turn, in the order we recorded it, and assemble-edit all that by itself into a target master file. Then

I guess Jason'll give the four target masters to the software people at the client company, who'll incorporate it into a tacky but highly sophisticated piece of interactive software which I'm proud to say I'll have fuck-all to do with!"

"Are you cool with all this private stuff going public, if it does go public?" Evelyn asks me.

"I shan't be publicising anything! I know nothing about it. I wasn't there, honest…"

"I decided it was better just not to watch the Angel material tonight," says Alaia, "so I didn't see any of it."

"Well, praise be!" says Rik. "So you won't be running out to phone Lucan now?"

"Lucan didn't hurt him too much this time, did he?" she asks.

"Oh, no," says Evelyn. "It became quite lovey-dovey, in fact."

"Hmm. I shall decide to believe you… I just can't watch pain."

"You had no scruples about singing it and causing it, in our song of death in *Big Bang*," I say.

She gives a rare burst of laughter and stares at me. "Is *that* what I was doing?"

"I'd say you made our audience suffer well and truly, yes! But always harmoniously, of course."

It's late, so the four of us split into two pairs in the corridor. Upstairs outside our rooms, despite her laughter just now, Alaia stills feels somehow in hiding from me, but with a new element of resignation … and of sadness. That's it: she seems sad. In fact, I observe as we stand there, she is quite emotional at the moment, blinking at me with an odd sort of hunger in her eyes. Before I can decide how to process this or whether to ask her what the matter is, however, we are both inside our own adjacent rooms, in silence.

Lying in the dark here, I get that restless sense, redoubled: tomorrow, it is going to break. But what, exactly?

I give up trying to see the future and bend my attention to the recent past instead. On two grand occasions now, my gaze has crackled out through the dusk of unknown towns around the world, through aerials and dishes, copper wire and glassy cables, in between the dog barks and underneath the planes, and has lodged in the eyes and minds of people everywhere whom I shall never meet. And meanwhile, against the distant backdrop of those multitudes, a small fiery troupe has strutted right here in front of me, some of whom I've watched from as close as it is possible to get to a human ape—from inside its head.

For the first time I contemplate this fiery troupe together, all posed for a photograph that never will be taken—Marc Albright, Alaia Danielle, Jason Carax, Evelyn Carmello, Rik Chambers, Flames Alleyne, Lucan Abayomi, Kev Banton, Damian West, Angel Deon, Shigem Adele, Kim Somerville, Pippa Vail—and they contemplate me back, from this hypothetical photo. The freeze-frame animates, all of a sudden, as the thirteen in sequence make respectful bows or curtseys at me, each in their own way. Then some of them titter at me, slapping one another's hands high and low, somewhat undermining their respectful obeisances ... and so I drift to sleep.

PART IX

SUNDAY: THE ANGEL
ON THE CARCASS-BUILDING

104 VIOLENCE IN THE AIR

Waking late, I know that today the storm will burst. There is violence in the air. But where is it brewing? I sense it's connected with Pippa, unless—surely it couldn't be in *Alaia*? I weaken, then before I can stop myself, I'm tuning in to her, for the first time since we were both in the van being driven here by Evelyn. I'm tuning in, just as I promised not to … and I find you in your room, Alaia, dressed and lying on your bed, which I'm startled to observe is just on the other side of this wall here—you're lying right beside me. This picture of you is only travelling about a metre to reach me, then! These old walls must be thick, for me never to have heard you shifting in bed during this last week: the only sounds I've heard from your room have been too vague to tell me the nature or distance of the movements causing them. Odd to realise, too, that I've never been in your room at all, though you've been in this room several times.

You're writing in your journal, as I once saw you do before. "It's so strange to be with Jaymi here, stranded by the ocean," you think and write. "It's shed a new light on him. To someone who first met him now, having already seen one of the broadcasts, I think he would seem surprisingly without passion in person, quieter and more passive than they'd expect. All that sound and fury around him, in the media, have been manufactured with smoke and mirrors by a publicity machine that hardly knows him or is interested in him. Since the onset of his abilities, things that would have elicited an emotional response from him in the past seem now to be just taken on board by him instead, as data to be fed into his mind, which then mediates his response. It's as if he now expects any and all eventualities, good or bad, ahead of time. Nothing seems to get him down any more, and not much seems to whirl him up high either, as if he inhabits a still centre within himself, like an ascetic. He's more or less said that he's aware of this in himself. I think he knows it feels slightly disconcerting to some people, while no doubt remaining invisible to others. He offers no explanations for this quality—because he has none, I think. Would he like an explanation? Is he looking for one? Is he equally simple and calm, when he's alone? I wish I knew. He has the serenity of one who knows that most ups and downs, including his own, are not as important as people say or think they are. That's it: serenity! That's what's arisen… That's why his emotions now seem muted—but not his fun and sparkle, I'm glad to say, nor … oh, I'm sad." She lays the journal down.

"Why, Alaia, you write the sweetest things!" I say aloud on my bed, knocking myself clumsily out of my own tune-in. Really, I didn't know she thought about me so much. But why is she sad?… I can't go and ask her, because that would reveal I've been tuning in. Yet I really must stop spying into her, right now—I did promise her that I wouldn't. Also, let's not forget I am meant to be on a dedicated storm-seeking mission right now, and not just frolicking and nosing about at random.

So instead I gather up my sight and throw it out like a lasso towards Shigem's house, where he's waking beside a still-sleeping Kim … and you wake to the sound of the birds in the trees, Shigem, remembering: today's the day you go to Newark Airport, then fly with Kim to London, to start a whole new life! Despite being well aware that your face now looks as much like a car-crash as it ever did aged fourteen or twenty-two, you are nonetheless joyful, verging on giddy—first because you were not murdered in your bed, and secondly because you're becoming tentatively hopeful of remaining unscathed by Lucan until departure tonight. Kim's sleeping blond head is on the pillow facing you, a tingle of pleasure runs through you, and I smile. "Kim and I are flying together into the sunrise!" you think. But dare you believe this? Isn't there some problem, some catch, hitch or late disaster here, that you've failed to notice? There must be. After all, there usually is. Yet sometimes, here and there, genuinely golden luck and happiness do roll up and park themselves on top of a person and just stay there like a pool of light ... and perhaps this has happened to you, with regard to Kim? "It's happened to me," you say to yourself. "*It's happened to me!*" To the sleeping boy beside you, you whisper some lyrics that you know, about a Boy Who Came Back: a boy who had once been a presence and a joy; who then went away, of course; but then, when least expected, came back to stay, restoring joy!

You think about that phone call you had from Angel yesterday (this is news to me), when he told you Alaia had supplied DVD proof that I was spying into Angel himself, into you, into Kim and into Pippa. You believed it, because Evelyn had already admitted I'd spied into Angel. And more important, relief spread through you, as you realised that this must be how Lucan knew about your dream of the Mint Man—so Lucan was indeed lying when he told you that Kim had taken money from me in return for giving "permission" to spy, as you had known of course. Angel and Lucan had evidently not coordinated their differing shit-stirrings here. While Angel spoke, you concluded too, with startling astuteness, that Alaia had somehow gone behind my back in supplying the DVD. Granted, it confirmed I really *had* been spying. But I harvest a golden crop now in seeing the next emotional reaction you had to Angel's call yesterday, Shigem: confirming your whisper to me in your hallway a couple of nights ago, your higher love and understanding of me are such that you straightaway forgave me for spying and were confident I would never misuse or promulgate whatever I had seen in you or Kim. (You were justified in this confidence, of course.) As for Evelyn, you didn't know what her involvement had been and you didn't want to know, preferring to think the best of her; so you decided you wouldn't tell her that you know the spying happened. (And I shan't tell her you know: she'll carry on thinking you don't.) You also decided not to tell Kim about my spying, as you knew he probably wouldn't like it, lacking the bond with me that you yourself have and also being more private by nature than you are.

Lying there in the morning light now, you decide these were the right decisions yesterday.

You grin through the ceiling to the sky.

Then you squirm and stretch, reach out your hand towards the blond head beside you, and stroke its inhabitant (*your boyfriend!*) awake.

Kim's eyes open at your touch; he sees you and knows you, and his eyes and face and movements start doing Kim things after their previous sleeping anonymity. "I was having a dream," he says, closing his eyes. "I met a skinny Asian boy with wide eyes, who was standing in a porthole with his hands and feet splayed inside its circle, peering down through the glass. We felt immediate attraction and embraced each other. Then we looked through the porthole and panicked because a vast tidal wave was approaching down the estuary, looking as if it would swallow the building we were in. But strangely, it just dissipated when it reached us: it surged up a kind of escarpment towards us but then it stopped when it splashed up through the blackthorn at the end of the garden. We felt so lucky…"

"Was he me?" you ask.

"Not really, no."

"You mean you're not faithful to me in your dreams?"

"Fuck it—I've just remembered," says Kim. "We weren't both meant to go to sleep last night. I was meant to stay awake all night, following our plan. How did we forget? Remember our plan? Damian could have killed us!"

Inside the moment he takes to say this, you give him a clear-eyed look, more simply and directly than usual encompassing his presence, shape and appearance, his hunky body and the smooth skin of his face, and you feel peace and ease and rightness: this is your boyfriend, this is your best friend, your ally, your playmate in this demanding, complicated, dangerous and frequently unpleasant world into which you were each dropped without being consulted. His normal masculinity feels like a sort of house that protects you; and although you've always been comfortable with the lack of this in yourself, it's restful to feel you can expand freely in his presence without needing to glance over your shoulder in order to watch your own back. You know that you tell him regularly, in words and through affection, that you love and value him; but now on the brink of your journey east, you remind yourself not to forget what you have here, not to miss out on the pleasure of remembering it in general, beyond the particularities of individual conversations or activities. There are things about the other that each of you might want to change in an ideal world, but that's of lesser importance. You're constructing a successful and loving partnership that's making your individual passages through life easier, more fun and less lonely, with more security, help and laughter than each of you would have had alone. It feels surprisingly strong already, this partnership, though it's only three months old. But never get cavalier, you tell yourself—for things can fuck up, and they do so, all the time. Be careful and watchful, but simple and sweet. "Don't worry," you reply to him, "Damian did kill us. We're both dead. It's better this way."

I rein my attention back to my room, musing upon this new phone call from Angel to Shigem. It would seem that Alaia's attempt to derail our spokes-sheep deal by letting Lucan see the extent of our spying will remain hidden from deal-conspirators Evelyn, Rik and Jason, but not from our astute target Shigem—though Shigem will keep his knowledge hidden from everyone but me. Rik has given no sign of noticing that, of all the DVD copies he yawningly made, he possesses one more disc of Angel's material than he should have, and one less disc of all four targets' material than he should have; so Alaia's misappropriation and motivations remain hidden from him. Remembering Lucan's phone call to Pippa, three of our four targets now know they were spied on—all except Kim. It remains hidden from them all, however, that they were selected for this honour by their good friend Evelyn; who herself is unaware that Shigem and Pippa know they were spied on. I now know, from Evelyn's slip of the tongue, that the imagination-cloning deal never was hidden by Jason from Marc—though I haven't established whether Evelyn ever shared this knowledge with Rik. In any case, I shan't be surprised if I find out one day that the sheep-designers (assuming they even exist) were unable to use such non-"family-friendly" material as we've gathered here; so most of our stolen imaginative raw material may yet remain hidden from public view indefinitely. As for me, my respect for our targets dictates that I shall be nothing but discreet with the raw material I gathered: the privacy of their four imaginations will be quite safe in my hands...

The strange affair of the spokes-sheep, in short, has been nothing but a ceremony of secrets and lies, concealments and half-truths, from start to finish!

Still, none of that changes the fact that there's violence in the air—I can sniff it.

105 THE TROLLS IN THE WAREHOUSE

I knock on Alaia's door to ask her if she wants to come down for lunch, but no answer, so I eat alone. Then my whole afternoon is spent skimming through our spokes-sheep material with Rik alone in the studio, to confirm which imaginative material is whose, and to associate files with metadata that will supposedly assist the programmers in deciding which stuff to exclude, highlight, keep separate or connect in their design of the sheep's inner life.

After this glimpse into the future of imagination-design, I return to my room and to my hunt for the source of the violence in the air, which I felt this morning had something to do with Pippa. I home in on my favourite grimy high-rise … and I catch you, Pippa, sitting on your balcony and staring through the dusk light. Your spacious sadness arches in a grand high vault above this lonely town, belying all the chatter and the fuss of other people—but nonetheless your stars are good again! Every twelve years the planet Jupiter revolves around your sky and paints its roof in swirls of pink and orange; every twenty-nine years, Saturn bars its windows even tighter than before, in green and black; every eighty-four years (so you may live one orbit), Uranus electrifies your vault in paler green; for sure you will not know a full turn of Neptune over one hundred and sixty-five years, in deep delusive blue; but then at last, from unimaginably far above, once every two hundred and forty-eight years, your vault is smashed by a bomb-blast from Pluto, deepest black, intractable and alien. Yes, your horoscope gives you the coolest view of where we are in icy space, a view too wide for daily life—a goddess-sized view, in fact. So, as befits a goddess, you are silent and you don't block your eyes.

You float indoors from the balcony, across the sitting room into the hallway, and now I think I may have hit a bull's-eye at last, as you approach that narrow door … but you walk right past it, straining not to think about it, striving to resist its pull, which feels like the pull from a black hole in your sanity—

You slam your bedroom door behind you, cross the unlit room to your bed and lie down. You hear that special silence creeping nearer, to hedge you in; you feel that dark, clotted presence there in the air, congealing thickly, and you know it is again time to be the one you should have been, inhabiting the world that you should have found around you. So you watch yourself climb off the bed, descend the stairwell, get into a limo and be driven by an unseen chauffeur to a place that no one else knows. There in the dead zone beyond the city's concrete edge, you strut like a skeleton across the asphalt field by the wire-netting fence. Giant metal floodlights sense you, hum alive and blaze down upon you. Lit stark white between broken empty warehouses, there your face and body-size change unpredictably until you can't be recognised. The creature that you now become, you treasure. The world you were born on, and the time you were born on it, were not quite up to this; they fell short. But with enormous shining bitter-sweet pleasure, you create for yourself, upon this asphalt stage, the world and time that should have been. You flip your ribcage open with a gesture to the stars, laying lewdly bare a heart like a black fleshy artichoke, and move and look as no one else on earth, beyond description … while hidden in the blackness of the broken warehouse windows all around the field, trolls growl and moan at the lurid beauty in you. And when your show is over, you morph back to Pippa Vail, slip into the limousine and speed away again along the fence, while the floodlights dim to black, as if you'd never been.

Back home, you stare blankly at the mirror in the bathroom. You don't seem to know it, but at some moment in the course of the upcoming month (perhaps the upcoming week), that imperceptible point of no return will have been reached and passed by you. When this occurs, presently, your isolation and dysfunction will have attained that combination of severity and duration required to warp you out of shape for good, easing you into a space where you will thereafter think in a different language from the rest of us. You could still then be guided back into our language, hypothetically, if a person with the necessary skills came along whose appointed task it were to do this. What would the chances be, however, of such a person coming along at such a point, Pippa? Negligible, yes?

Your eyes in the mirror are dead now—empty holes that shine with dead black light. Are you in them? Are you back there, hiding in the darkness of your broken warehouse windows, with the trolls?

I'm losing you. You're fading. Make a sign, if you're in there... Blink, if you can... Shatter your one-way mirror-sphere, before it shrinks around you—

There you go.

106 A GUNFIGHT AND A SNIPPETY EXCHANGE

The vibration of my phone wrenches me back to my bed. It's a breathless Alaia, with street noise behind her. "Hi, it's me," she says, all action. "I'm near Downstairs. Lucan's just been shot at from a car. The bullet missed him. The rumour is, it was an assassin from a gang in Red Bank who are trying to get rid of him, to grab his business."

"You sound just like a news reporter. 'Our woman on the front line, bringing hard news from the mean streets of—'"

"Look, there was nearly an assassination here. A gangland execution. Didn't you hear the gunfire?"

"No."

"Good thing we don't have to rely on you for world news."

"I've been gathering news about the worlds in people's heads," I reply. "Much more important. I always found gunfights a bit of a snooze."

"Jaymi, the implication of this particular gunfight is perhaps that it suggests the waxworks were just part of a plot to destabilise Lucan's business here, and therefore they weren't sculpted by anyone in Asbury Park after all."

"Oh, I see—you mean this'll finally get Shigem off the hook of Lucan's blame?"

"*Hallo!* Yes, I do." I can hear her raising her eyes.

"You're right, that's very important." I glance at the bedside clock. "Shigem's only got an hour left in this town before he leaves for the airport, but that is still time to bump him off. I take my hat off to you, one needs a certain sort of mind to grasp the implications of gun battles—"

"One needs *a* mind, Jaymi ... and sometimes a bit of bold action. Bye."

The line goes dead. "Bye."

Well! Snippety-snip.

Bold action?...

107 FLICKER OF MURDER IN ANGEL

OK then, bold action. I steel myself, shoot my sight to Angel ... and I see you, Angel, running to the front door with danger in your eyes. You feel it too: the restlessness in town today, the violence in the sticky air, the gunfire waiting to ricochet, and phantom flames burning in the air around your head.

You wander to a grungy and rain-washed Main Street, to T.J.'s Pizza at Sewall Avenue. It's warm but it's drizzling, so you're hot and cold at once. Dressed in black and dark-red, you're shielded from the rain by your scarlet umbrella, yet sweat drips down your face and trickles under all your clothes. You're wrecked and wild, feverish and tussled as you kick along an empty cigarette packet, churning with self-hate and self-love, fear and love of Lucan; and your wet-burning shame will suffuse you forever, yet forever too your urge remains to hack from your body that eternally erect self-lie that you can always feel, without relent, down there in front of you...

You get your pizza slice and set off home, devouring it with mechanical insect fervour. You are kept on a chain by a hungry man who swings you every day through the sky above his attic, while his gaze rapes yours. His irrational destruction, your dangerous obsession ... and so, for the very first time, it occurs to you: perhaps you should murder him? That would restore the balance between you, earth the voltage, settle the damage he's done you. Why, you could then carve your Angel symbol into his stomach—think how gorgeous that would look, set in his muscular flesh!

As you climb the staircase to the bedroom, you bubble with red fantasies of stabbing him to death in an orgy of carnage and fluid on the bed, as revenge for his countless denials of your preferences and needs and ideas, and every night the bruises he's kissed you with … but then you remember his wicked gleaming panther's eyes, and you realise you need him and you're trapped again and will never escape or dare to hurt him, and he knows it and he knows you know it too; and tears of being beaten yet again start to burn behind your long-lashed eyes, shot with frustration and anger and white-hot desire.

You *do* want to kill him, though, don't you? You want to feel him dying, while he's up deep inside you. Well, that can be your secret mission; I shan't tell. You enumerate your weapons: you've a pair of shadow-daggers; more practically, you have a real gun, fully functional, loaded and hidden under floorboards, which Lucan doesn't know about; and yes, you have the right stuff to kill, you know you do. You want to hold a knife to the face of every human here on earth, simultaneously—a knife for each face, poised just right. (This might become addictive.) Are you sure, however, that you want to cross this line, my lethal Angel? Lucan is your equal in glamour, so he's brought this to his killing, but consider: Kev and Damian have killed too, and where's the glamour there? Nowhere. So killing *in itself* is insufficient for transcendence. Still, it is a step towards that…

You flop down prone onto the bed, exhausted, close your eyes and straightaway you're almost asleep. Lucan of course kept you up and wore you out gorgeously for half the night, and then for the rest of it you just writhed around buried under the surface of a half-sleep and scratched your long nails across the surface of your body while your mind churned, like most nights; so you're now functioning on a serious sleep deficit. Semi-conscious, your mind still sounds like a factory of machinery, as usual: whining engines, screeching blades, hissing sparks and a never-ending drum-boom of earth-shaking power, shot with clattering and echoes.

You twitch awake again, and Murder flickers closer to you; waits for you to notice it. You notice it. It lets you drink it in for a moment, then it draws you towards it, with glaring pools of eyes in the darkness of the bedroom … and something subtle changes in you, something irreversible and silent.

You are now resolved to murder, for real.

You gently push this resolution aside: it can wait to be processed, please, just a few minutes. (Why, yes it can! It is patient and quite prepared to wait.)

At last your banks of mind-machines are quiet, as you fall asleep for real. You quiver, then are still: and the colour of a spasm in a boy-girl's dream has the radiant completion of a blade's squeak and rush through Lucan's soft-lit neck, while the cameras roll, projected on the big screen in extreme close-up...

This deep rest is short-lived, of course. As you start again to toss and turn and writhe and scratch your arms and wrestle with yourself in sleep as usual, radio feedback and strobing lights flicker through your pressured head: "*Bad girl!*" voices chant, "*so like a woman...*" in your tight red leather skirt and cherry lipstick and angel's wings, holding the big dangerous hand of your man with his crucifix pendant, strong and golden on his chest. He leads you to a garden, ties you to the trunk of an ancient bush profuse with crimson roses, and fires tiny scarlet arrows at you. Every few seconds an arrow lodges sharp in your torso, then falls out leaving a small gash until your body is a red mess, merging with the crimson of the petals; and you squirm, with the thrill of him strung upon the wires of the harp in the Garden as Satan's music thrums through his body. In a nearby nut-bush, a noose of light cusps off a twist of white nut-kernel-meat shaped just like a set of tiny fingers clasped in prayer; and you feel your tattooed Angel's wings morph to the soft white wings of a dove. You take off, soar up and land on a nail-head that spins upon its point below, spoked with jagged lightning underneath a blackness pinked with tiny galaxies. Ziggurats and onion-spires pierce through clouds of smoke the colour of a sweet red wine as rich as Sin. Within the smoke, snakes of scarlet chase and swallow one another, as on burning paper. Off the Mosquito Coast among the angel-demonfish, two skinless animals are making love in slime and blood, birthed from your imagination's most exquisite sump—a rapture of the deep! Dying fire seeps through the clouds of a sunset coloured treacle-black and blood-orange, sensuously chemical. Right where the sun should hang, your own face flashes up for one supernal instant, weeping scarlet blood ... and fades to black.

You wake and sit bolt upright. You bound off the bed to the

wardrobe, snake your hand behind it, prise up a floorboard, reach into shadow there and wrap your fingers tight around the metal of your gun. Listening hard for sounds elsewhere in the house, you pull the weapon out, check it's loaded, pocket it and tiptoe from the bedroom. Downstairs you slip through the back door.

108 I'LL NEVER SEE YOUR EYES AGAIN

I pull my attention quickly back to my room. Angel is hardly the only one with a weapon in Lucan's gang, and I'm concerned for Shigem's safety. I check the clock: Kim and Shigem are set to leave town some time during this very hour, but getting shot can be a quick process. I close my eyes again and tune in to Shigem ... and I find you still in Asbury Park, but sitting in the passenger's seat of a rental car whose back seat is loaded high with bags. "Any thoughts, now that we're driving out of here?" Kim asks as the car waits on Cookman Avenue to turn right onto Main Street. The traffic-light glow upon your face flicks from red to green, filling up a hundred acne craters with colour as you smile at him. He sets the car in motion, as I peer through your eyes and through the open windows, scanning for assassins.

You look, along with me, at the station on your left. "Years ago I sometimes fantasised about lying across those railroad tracks," you answer. "But I never did, because I always knew it would traumatise the train driver and maybe derail the train and give Asbury a bad name—you know, 'the Asbury Park Train Massacre' or something. We didn't need that here, on top of everything else. Still, I think now I might have the courage of my convictions: how about we stop the car, stay here after all, and both lie down across the tracks after midnight? It would be so poetic ... except that they'd find our bodies limp and sickly and sneezing tomorrow morning, because there are no trains after midnight. Oh, life is cruel. Hey—let's go to a fabulous party tonight."

"Yeah!"

"But I've just remembered, I don't know of any."

"Oh. Well that's a problem. I know—let's go to London tonight and never come back?"

"Are there fabulous parties there?"

"Hell yeah."

"I remember giving a party in a motel room, somewhere in my mid-teens," says Shigem. "The 'mid-teens' bit was the mistake there, I think, because it turned out messy. All these pairs of people kept going off together into corners and bathrooms and even airing-cupboards, and closing the doors for heavy emotional conversations about their 'issues' and all that stuff. Of course there were high emotions and tears, and worst of all, terrible karaoke performances using this karaoke channel on the TV in the room. Everyone got hammered and threw up, and the room was completely trashed and destroyed in the course of so much hormonal adolescent angst ... looking back on it, it was hysterically wonderful."

You gaze through the windows at the shuttered shops and traffic-lights of Main Street. Up ahead a few more blocks, you'll leave here, your home-town, for good. And of all possible times, it's now that I attain a clear perception of a particular little fruitcake of thought in you, which I might easily have missed. For in reality it's perhaps less of a fruitcake and more of a hum. Like the quiet but unique background hum or room-tone of every individual room located on a film-set, a few moments of which must be recorded by itself for later sound-editing, there's a room-tone humming in your head at all times—very subtle, quite specific and unique to you. It's your wish that you were a male who felt entirely female but had to live in the wrong sex: in other words you wish you were fully transgender, but not that you were female by birth or by sex-change. Unusual of course, as hums and wishes go, but there it is. The rest of you, aside from this specific part, is quite OK with being not fully transgender but rather just a feminine male without desire to be female. Yet always and forever there remains that delicious background hum, containing three sounds: a rich chord of pleasure in a major key; a single note of simple fact that colours your perceptions; and sub-tlest and deepest, a chord of regret, with the bitter-sweet flavour of unreachable perfection.

"Are we really moving to London?" you ask, as Kim accelerates past Sixth Avenue.

"Sure," he says. "Why not?"

Seventh Avenue comes level with you, then rolls away behind. "Yeah, it's time I lived somewhere other than this little dump—love it though I do. Bye-bye!" you tell your home-town, waving through the window.

And out of Asbury Park you drive, forever.

I land back in my bedroom here in the Metropolitan. I'm not going to follow them to Newark, then around the planet and onwards into the future: I'll let them go alone and be together. Shigem knows what he'll always be to me, and I know what I'll always be to him.

There's nothing more to say, then, except goodbye Shigem and goodbye Kim—together for life, I believe. Goodbye, you beautiful, beautiful pair. I'll never see your eyes again.

109 A SCREECH OF TYRES

I rise from the bed, approach the open window to take a breath of night air—and jump, for there's a sudden burst of gunfire. I step back, reach for the light switch and turn it off, then back to the window and peer around the frame to the right, where the shots were. Further gunshots sound, then shouts from the same direction—three or four blocks away, I'd guess. There's a screech of fast tyres, a receding car engine, then silence.

I sit on the bed, close my eyes and fire out my sight for a shared tune-in to Lucan and Damian, both of whom I find being driven by Kev at high speed, presumably away from the action I just heard. "Red Bank's dead!" declares Lucan, with vicious jubilance. They must have raced away westwards from the location of the gunfire, for they are now heading south on Memorial Drive on the other side of the railway line, just across the tracks from where Shigem and Kim slipped away in the opposite direction a few minutes ago. (*Shigem escaped!*)

"Yeah, their operation's crippled, with those three guys gone," agrees Damian with grim satisfaction. But then he turns to Kev, and hatred so suffuses his face that it twists out of shape as he grates out: "*But you killed Pippa, Kev. That was your bullet…*"

Alarm flashes through me.

"Yeah, sorry Lucan," says Kev. "Slip of the hand. Didn't mean to do that."

Lucan stares out through the window a moment, then pronounces:

"You were stupid. You didn't need to fire at that moment. She was cool." He shrugs. "Still ... wrong time, wrong place."

Bitter anger continues to boil in Damian. "I *respected* her," he growls, leaning forwards behind the driver's seat. "If this were Vietnam, I'd shoot you in the head."

"Oh, you and your Vietnam," moans Kev, coasting the Cadillac to a halt outside Downstairs. "What the fuck was World War II about, anyway? It was about the Panama Canal, right?"

Lucan laughs out loud.

"OK, OK," says Kev as he locks the car, "my history's shit, I know it. And my math is shit too... But not my lovin', if you know what I mean."

"I *throw* up, just to think of it," spits Damian in pain.

"Damian couldn't score in a barrel of pussies!" mocks Kev, sniggering coarsely.

A quiet grinding and clicking emanates from Damian, as the three of them cross the pavement to the door of Downstairs. "Within one year," he grates at Kev, "*you* will be dead. But we'll both be here still—happy that you *suffered* when you died. *Because I'll make sure you do...*"

Smiling, Lucan reaches for the back of both their necks and clenches extremely hard, without exertion, as I once saw him do to Flames. Resistance in both of them crumples. He takes his hands slowly away again and coos, "Hush!... Or you'll both end up like Pippa, may God take her soul." He lifts his crucifix pendant to his lips in a leisurely fashion and kisses it, and they all three vanish into Downstairs.

110 WHAT IT'S LIKE TO DIE BY GUNSHOT

Frowning with a terrible foreboding, I wrench my attention away and hurl it out towards Pippa ... and it's just as they said, Pippa. Trust you to have been caught in the cross-fire and wrongly assumed dead. So here you are, lying on your back at Kingsley Street and Fourth Avenue, dying by the carcass-building, all dressed in yellow. Three dead male bodies lie nearby. I start to make a move, to help you out—but I stop, because I notice through my shock that you're glad this has happened. In any case, it's too late: you're fading, and I see you will be gone by the time I or anybody else can arrive.

I therefore remain sitting here, tuning in. You are in pain, but as soon as the bullet entered your torso, your system kicked into gear and shut off most of the pain sensors involved. You know you will be dead within the next few minutes, and through your confusion you're content to die. This should not be news to me, in light of what I've witnessed of the life you've led inside yourself. So here you lie dying, and here I am privileged to watch. You see fires and explosions on the far-away horizon, where a nest of lethal Ferris wheels grinds through the night above a funfair of cotton candy, grinning clowns and death machines. You smell your own death now, uncoiling from inside you. Your mossy grave lies ready, up behind the night in a field of its own, with the cracked grey headstone bearing your name—can you read that?

You wonder what the person who searches you will conclude when they find the note that lives in the envelope in your rear left pocket. I frown, as I can feel something new and odd here... With awkwardness you reach into your back left pocket with your black-gloved hand, fetch the envelope, bring it to your face, pull the old piece of paper out and read it for the last time. At its left edge are small stains of blood, wet and dry, presumably from the gunshot wound in the right side of your back, where blood is soaking widely through your bright yellow sweatshirt. It's a brief note scribbled a few years ago by Angel, addressed not to you but to Lucan, with urgent kisses along the lower edge. The text reads simply, "*See you tonight!*" Some years ago it came somehow into your possession: you have crossed Lucan's name out and put your own instead, and several intervening years of your own obsessive kisses onto Angel's signature have smudged his name with lipstick and many tears.

So here's quite a secret, at the very last minute, lit in red... You nearly took it to the grave. How did I fail to recognise that you housed so intense an instance of what I suppose could be called an Angel-shaped emptiness? You were more unusual than I realised. Not that unrequited passion is rare—but what a spectacularly oblique direction yours assumed. And of course: all those angel ornaments throughout your apartment, in every room... Perhaps your few visitors assumed them to be religious statuettes? If so, how fitting that such sacred-looking angels were standing in for another one so profane! I must never have tuned in to you in the right way to perceive this. How bizarre—I didn't think I was missing things as major as this, in people. If so, what else have I missed? What other unrequited love might I have tuned in towards, but then right past, never hitting it?

For the last time ever, you plant a fiery kiss upon his signature and place the note back inside its old envelope.

For the first time ever, you lick what glue remains upon the envelope's flap and seal it up.

Then with care and discomfort, you fling this sacred object away from you, as hard as you can, down Fourth Avenue towards the sea.

The force of your throw, a collaborative breeze and lucky aerodynamics all combine to carry it far down the length of the strip of litter-strewn dirt and scrappy grass beside the carcass-building, halfway to Ocean Avenue and anonymity. You lie back, exhausted, your mind slipping out of your control. You see a convoy of cars in northern India, their headlights painted over with cartoony eyes. Beside it, a line of swaying poplars turns into a line of stunted poles stretching across the plateau into dim haze. At the end of the line is a graveyard ringed by statues of ash in crumbling colonnades. A sad human head like a marsh-flower swims through the air among the graves, where the long grass weeps. The sky dims and churns. White drizzle falls out of grey light to black snow. The wind dies, and far away, dust blown from distant lands falls to sea in silence.

Your system is sluggish now; the fog grows within you. You're standing in an Arverne alleyway, with sad social housing all around you under damp sky. Across the grassy mud a small pig trots on pointed toes, its flank stained umber, like ceramic. Lights flicker on among the high-rise tower-blocks. Wind makes the telegraph wires in the alley sing, as fog rolls along its narrow length to engulf you.

Faintly you recall Pippa Vail on her balcony, asking *who am I?* Beneath Pippa Vail were the lights of a small town somewhere on the coast and the swashing of the sea. You swell with compassion for this Pippa you are seeing: for her passion and her dreams and her vulnerabilities, for the heights she aspired to and the depths she feared to think about.

You're all alone, lying here. No one will wake you up, no one knows you're here—and that's fine, you reflect, as a smile lights your face.

And so you die, my lovely Pippa, whom I've watched through a frosted glass—you simply end. I feel my attention gently nudged from within you, dislodged from your carcass, to float past the carcass-building, back to my bed here. I'm glad we knew each other. I shan't forget your angels, and I shan't forget our picnic with the Laughing Cow cheese.

111 WHAT IT'S LIKE TO DIE BY SHRIEK

I stare around my darkened room. The bedside clock ticks away, as if nothing's happened. How brief our friendship was and yet how rich, at least for me. I feel she should be memorialised or at least recorded in some way. An idea strikes me. I find a pad of paper and proceed to note down every single thing I can remember of her—for what specific purpose or readership, I know not. In this, my progress is slower than I expected. My only experience of writing prose is in the working and reworking of financial prospectuses, I'm sorry to say, so I'm not used to putting the subtleties of people into words. By the time I've finished, it is very late. I am glad, however, that I was conscientious in recording it all. It wouldn't have been long before many of those memories of her disappeared. The process makes me realise, moreover, that there are many aspects of an internal life that it's more accurate to describe verbally than to evoke with the kind of visual imagery I've grown so accustomed to doing here for Rik's camera.

However, once I've put my pad away, it occurs to me: rather than writing about Pippa, perhaps my priority should really have been to check that Lucan hasn't sent his henchman up the turnpike in murderous pursuit of Shigem. It's quite possible, after all. Worried, I tune in to Damian … but I'm relieved to see you're now home from Downstairs, Damian, unconscious in your poky room. I peer behind your sleeping eyes, and jump at what confronts me: on the Asbury Park Boardwalk, a fat chaotic Ferris wheel clatters round, swaying, and disgorges vicious children, every face with pinpoint eyes, hard-pupilled, stripped of humanity, like puppets' eyes. Their tongues lick ice-cream cones filled with scoops of puréed meat-cream, shiny-pink and fatty. Whispers assail you in strange tongues, as crickets chirp and locusts thrum—all too loud and jagged. The sand-castles on the beach are wriggling with weevils; an eyeless fleshy black creature, all legs and whiskers, burrows down in fury and hides in the sand. Something very nasty is close below this surface ... and Damian, you're just a step too close to mental illness here, yes?

Like a painting on red velvet of huge-eyed, stunted kids, the child-faces here make you stare closer in at them, to catch the hard-eyed fakeness underneath the sunny smiles, and the pools of sick, and sickly-crusted madness grinning out through the sweetness. Dim-lit and floppy-limp, an ingrown girl dressed in swimmy-pulsing orange moves pins out of one tiny box, to another tiny box—pin by pin, week by week, month by month, year by year, and age by age—saliva on her bleeding fingers, fixing you with desperate eyes, up through your insides, with claustrophobic moisture mewing stale inside her needy, piteous stare—

You jolt awake and glance around your dark poky bedroom, breathing gaunt.

A coiled shriek, tucked in a corner of the bedroom by the wardrobe ahead of you, vibrates like a slab of red and blue meat. It twists up and rises, unsticking bonily from inside itself, through a mist of little sighs from the tiny mouths scuttling in the long swaying grass around the bed.

The shriek steps jerkily toward you, coming fast through the grass. The tiny mouths hiss and gibber at your toes. The shriek shoots out bloody legs in your direction, drags you in amongst itself and through the tendons of its sticky face, and sucks out your insides from in between your own teeth, with soft-piped mandibles. The mouths chatter on beneath the red and blue meat, while you hang from the shriek's face, knotted up and paralysed, your insides sucked out.

Far across the ocean, as tall as your imagined pirate ship, booms a drum with a timbre like the splitting of Antarctica. Dark sky-bells ring beyond it in cascade, where you fall out and down, buried choking in your own corpse—out and down and down, to your death.

112 STEALING EVIDENCE
FROM THE CRIME SCENE

For the second time tonight, I land on my bed after being nudged out of somebody by their death—this nudge out of Damian being rather ruder than the nudge out of Pippa. The charming apparition I just observed was presumably the shriek that Damian told me *Sound & Vision* had dug up inside him. I see why he'd have preferred that it be left buried. For all his reputed brutality, I do recall also the gruff decency that he exhibited towards Angel and, as far as it went, towards me too on the occasions I was alone with him. I wonder whom else Alaia and I have killed around the world, through our broadcasts, by scaring up what might have been better hidden?

What with Damian, Pippa and the three dead gangsters lying nearby her, I've seen more death tonight than I am used to. His demise has left me feeling like taking a hot shower, frankly, and I start towards the bathroom to do this, but stop in my tracks. When Alaia recommended "bold action" earlier today, she probably wasn't thinking of hot showers. Hmm … bold action. A brainwave strikes me: I want to rescue the envelope that was so precious to Pippa, rather than let it be destroyed by the rain or fall into very probably mocking hands. I tiptoe to the door, lean into the corridor and check whether any light shows under Alaia's door. Yes. I wonder how long she's been in there. I let my door close again gently, sit down and think how best to contact her. I take my mobile out and dial. "Hi, it's me," I say.

"Hi," she says opaquely.

"Did you hear that gunfire?"

"No, I've been listening to myself on the headphones."

"OK. Well, have I got stuff to tell you. I've got sad news; then I've got both a problem and a solution."

Sitting in my room a minute later, she listens grimly as I tell her about the gunfire, its unlucky victim's death and the revelation Pippa fetched out of her pocket. "The problem I mentioned on the phone just now is how to retrieve that precious envelope from somewhere on the edges of what's probably become a well-secured crime scene by now. The solution is for us two to go there together now, so you can distract whoever needs distracting while I hunt for the envelope.

In any case, I'd feel safer with you there as my bodyguard! Shall we go?"

It's been such a dose of new information I've given her, coming in the context of such an odd sequence of non-communication on our part, that I'm not surprised to see her struggling for a moment to process it. A practical and decisive conclusion emerges, however: "OK, yes. I'd like to do that, for Pippa."

She returns to her room, to get ready. It's about two o'clock. After a moment's thought, I grab some large tissues from a box, rumple them up a bit and put them into my pocket. We reconvene in the corridor, sneak out of the Metropolitan and turn left. Two blocks on, under the ambiguous grimace of Tillie from the Palace Amusements wall, we stop and peer down the length of Kingsley Street, where a couple of parked police cars' roof-lights are twirling, down at Fourth Avenue.

"Where's the envelope, then?"

"Well," I begin, noticing a somewhat accusing quality in her eyes. So complex a creature is she that I would have no idea why this is, without tuning in to her, but I dare say the reason will emerge at some point. "I can remember exactly where Pippa saw the envelope land. But now she's dead, I'm afraid I can't just tune in to an envelope..." As we stare at each other, the faintest flicker of mirth hovers disruptively in the air between us, at the absurdity of this idea, and her accusing quality softens a little. "I think we should approach it from over there, so we'll be less obvious," and I steer us a block further down Asbury Avenue, past a shuttered Paradise, and swing us left on Ocean Avenue.

Alert for anyone who may apprehend us, we pass the rest of the shuttered Empress Motel and the Stone Pony on the left, the weeded-over miniature golf course on the right and the ruined shell of the Albion Hotel on the left. We encounter no one. Taller than the Albion, the carcass-building beyond it looms close to us now. The scent of the sea comes through the yellow shine of the isolated street-lights. Here at Ocean and Third Avenues we are at the opposite corner of the carcass-building from the flashing police cars, which we can see through the empty ground floor between the numerous concrete columns. Their headlights provide illumination for three cops, two of them in conversation and the other one searching the ground.

"Pippa saw the envelope land beside the wire fence: from where the flashing light on the car is, it landed about fifteen metres towards the sea, I should estimate, so that's where I need to be looking."

"OK, let's hold hands—it'll look more innocent." She grabs my hand and swings our arms forward and backward. "Then I'll walk on ahead and distract anyone we meet with dumb questions."

We reach Fourth Avenue hand in hand and wander left, entering the headlights. Beyond the police cars a few scattered onlookers have gathered, but we are the only ones on this side of the crime scene, which has been sealed off ahead by a tape across the road, half a block from where Pippa's corpse lies covered by a sheet.

She and I pull off a good act of casual nosiness: as intended, she goes on ahead and distracts the lone cop who comes towards us as soon as he sees us, and she points him in various directions with questions and earnest ditzy comments, while I scan the ground. — There's the envelope. I wander to a stop above it, pull out the rumpled tissues from my pocket, make to blow my nose with them but lose hold of them, directly above the envelope. Idly I stoop, retrieve it and the tissues together, pretend to blow my nose with the envelope still in the tissues, and pocket the lot. "Hi," I say, ambling over and joining the two of them.

Soon she and I are making quick, quiet tracks, the way we came. "Found it," I murmur.

113 HOW TO BUNGLE AN ASSAULT

As we reach First Avenue I give a start, for sitting beneath a yellow street-light on our right, with his face buried between his knees and his arms hugging his shins, is Angel. He jerks his head up at the sound of our approach, and I see he is wearing mirrored sunglasses. Sunglasses at night—too cool for school, excuse me! Alaia and I stop in our tracks. He jumps to his feet and stands still, staring us down as if tensed to pounce, like the little she-wolf I've seen so often inside him; and something about his lone presence down here and the tilt of his sunglasses prompts me to cock the most powerful, intrusive and hypnotic gaze, right behind my eyes, ready for deployment at an instant's notice.

Nobody moves. The silver ring in his right ear glints in the yellow street-light, beside a dark-red polo-neck the colour of dried blood, and I register that for the first time he's not wearing his silver cross, unless it's underneath … and *that* would be the bulge of his gun, right there in the left pocket of his black leather trousers, exactly where I saw him tuck it when he slipped out of the back door of Lucan's house.

Without warning he slinks towards us, with an undulating movement like a skunk or a weasel, and stops just a metre away. "*You!*" he says, managing to seem as if he's hissing out the word, even though it has no *s* and he'd have softened any *s* if there'd been one. I cannot tell, through the sunglasses, which of us this was aimed at. "*Sound & Vision* and *Big Bang* were incredible—you're both absolutely incredible!"

His mouth grins, ferret-like. Being unable to see his eyes, I find myself focusing on his pointed canines, as well as on his left hand in case he reaches into his pocket. It is all this practical watchfulness that's preventing me from just tuning in to him and observing his intentions: doing that would be way too distracting for the practical watchfulness to be maintained at the same time. "Thank you," I say.

I hold that hypnotic gaze of mine on the very brink of being unleashed, and my concentration at peak focus. Again, no one moves.

This is seriously dangerous—no question. I need to take some initiative here, but what should it be? Keeping my speech slow, calm, quiet and deliberate, I say: "I think you know I've been watching you since the broadcasts, Angel…"

I watch something like a flash of dark electricity in him, as he registers what a mayhem of abuse and murderous emotions I'll have witnessed in him while tuning in for the period I describe. Then he regains his composure. "So you know how it is, with Lucan and me," he says with lethal quietness. "And you know why I phoned you to ask for your help."

I nod. He stands immobile. Nothing good can come of this, I think.

He takes a deep breath. "Then I *appeal* to you," he urges, with intense passion and conviction: "Go to him and hypnotise him into obeying me, because I'm desperate… I know you could do it. Flames told me how you looked at Lucan when you first met him. *No* one does that. And he was totally overpowered by you. So you can do it again, I know you can—and you must *force* him to obey me in everything, because he deserves it so much, after all his years of abusing me... You have a duty, Jaymi. I'll pay you, I'll work for you, I'll worship you—whatever the *hell* you need—just *do it*, Jaymi! I'm *begging* you to do this."

He has crept closer to me during this speech, so that we are now within arm's length of each other. Alaia is somewhere on my left and slightly behind me, I believe. I think for a second. "Angel ... I can't start interfering between people like that. There'd be no end to it, and I'd wind up dead in no time—"

Another burst of black electric rage flashes through him. "*Fuck you!*" he hisses and I can see he's about to explode.

As his left hand moves towards his pocket, I grab the sunglasses off his face at lightning speed and fire a colossal blast of hypnotic power into his eyes. Too late, I see he is wearing mirrored contact lenses, and my hypnotic blast slams straight back into my own eyes. I'm unprotected from it and unprepared for its gigantic voltage. I stagger, nearly collapsing, feel his sunglasses fall out of my hand, and feel within me some disastrous short-circuiting of an extraordinary kind I have never felt before. As I stop myself from falling, the horrible truth becomes plain to me: my special perceptive and hypnotic abilities are gone. This was the first time I experienced, as a target, the magnitude of my own powers—and the last time.

114 ALAIA AND I ARE KIDNAPPED

Looking from Angel to Alaia and back, I feel my loss with unbearable sharpness. I feel as I've not felt since before I met Marc, back in a time that seems long ago although it's only five or six weeks. Since then I have often chosen not to tune in to people I've been with, but always knowing that at any moment I could look at their internal lives at will. Now I feel vividly that I am watching Angel with a human gaze—a weak, powerless gaze that discerns only the surface of a person, having to use mere guesswork in order to fathom and appreciate all those rich ingredients of emotion and imagination that the person will probably be both unwilling and unable to put into words. Being one of my four targets, Angel has been laid so bare as to feel more like *you* than any other pronoun. From now on, though, it's certain that Angel will only ever feel like *he* or *she*, but never *you* again.

It makes me sad, because I wasn't made for this, clearly. The fact that I'm designed to have the power I had until a minute ago, namely more than just an average allocation, is surely a simple truth—a blindingly obvious one, indeed. I have contempt for any process by which this truth has violence done to it, as has just occurred. I'm disappointed, as I was honestly expecting the system of power-allocation to be more impressive than it's now revealed itself to be. I've given that system the benefit of the doubt, over the last few weeks, deciding to trust that it had some rightness or intelligence in it—but evidently not.

Next, however, I realise something whose magnitude eclipses even that: *Angel now has the powers I myself had until a minute ago.*

Watching Angel's shocked face adjusting to this thunderbolt of an exchange we've just made, I know the feelings he is having, because I recall them from when I first ferried them out of my office building and saw them behind my eyes in the building's mirrored façade on Liberty Street: "Some brand-new power—some great new capacitance."

"Hey, baby Angel," calls a familiar deep voice. Angel pauses, then with a dangerous smile spreading across his face he turns to see a self-assured Lucan swaggering down the Avenue towards us with Kev, thirty metres away.

Angel doesn't reply. I watch him tweaking his new-found gaze and homing his focus in upon Lucan, who has guessed nothing odd yet. I glance at Alaia, who is staring from me to Angel with horror: yes, she's understood exactly what has happened here. I imagine she's also forming the same intention I'm forming: we need to get the hell out of here.

With Lucan and Kev only a few metres away from him, I surmise that Angel is still psyching himself up to turn his gaze upon Lucan—and now I see he's done it. Followed by Alaia, I shuffle surreptitiously back to the side, where I have an equal view of both their faces: Angel with his back to the sea and Lucan facing him…

And Lucan freezes, seeing Angel's deadly eyes where they hang upon the night, transfixing. "Oh, *fuck*," he murmurs in horrid shock. The energy in Angel's eyes is vicious, sensual, magnificently powerful and quite irresistible. I'm glad it isn't aimed at me, though I'm scared it soon will be. His mirrored contact lenses diminish this power not at all, but simply serve to make it even more other-worldly. A lifetime of slavery for Lucan is beginning right here, as the plaything of one whose shrieking eyes behind their mirrors promise obsessive and lifelong retribution, without the possibility of parole. So specific is Angel's message to him, that even here at a forty-five-degree angle I comprehend its meaning in a stream of fluid words, although there is nothing to hear: *NOW I've got you, Lucan, with the barrel of a gun pointed up through your mouth and my finger on the trigger! Your fear, your adrenaline—they stab through the air at me. Can you hear the sucking of the sea right behind me? Can you see my eyes, Lucan? Yes, I think you can. But I see YOUR eyes, infinitely more—and your pupils have dilated. Why would that be? They are wide, 'cos I'm your drug now, forever—just like you were mine, but even more! You are addicted, and you're powerless. You're not smiling, are you? Why is that? I see your internal settings, Lucan, every last one of them—I know how to change them and I know how to TWIST you! We'll explore those settings quite obsessively, I promise you, through channels that you've not conceived, though I can feel them tunnelling away from me beneath the sand: ten billion grains making way for me, to maximise my pleasure in your twisting... I catch your wish to kill me right now, but you can't—for I can poison, paralyse and infiltrate you any time I like, draw my tongue's twin tips across your eyes at night and down across the small of your back, like a female snake. I love you when you're hurt and sad, electric with sexiness and suffering, handing up the best love of all! I'll make you want to suffer, to refine the rush you give me. I can break you, you're weak. Oh Lucan, I shall fuck with your head, you may be certain—from now on there'll be violence and gorgeousness and blood!*

Lucan is frozen with weakness and terror.

My hand reaches out and touches Alaia beside me. Moving as little as possible, she and I exchange glances. I make the tiniest of head movements, down Ocean Avenue to the south, and we both start to ease away in that direction. Straightaway something invisible wriggles out of Angel's frame, like a great black squid that's grown to fill a building until it must lift the roof and spill its tentacles out from under the eaves. This invisible squid grabs Alaia and me both, pins us where we are, wrenches our heads back around to look at Angel and keeps our eyelids forcibly open. Seeing that his head has turned away from Lucan to face us, I flinch in anticipation of some kind of eye-themed nightmare…

I find, however, that his eyes are not at all hard to look at, even when they are fixed upon me in particular—and at this discovery I experience in turn surprise, relief, interest and gratitude. He's being easy on me, I realise: he *doesn't* hate me, after all. Wow! I feel a special glow and the stirrings of a kind of love for him, on account of this great leniency towards Alaia and me.

The dark beauty of his eyes is colossally amazing, too—almost too much for me to bear, in fact.

But next he turns his head to the last person present here, and it's a different story. I don't know whether Alaia's perceiving this as I am, but again I catch a stream of silent words from Angel's eyes. Befuddled and distraught, Kev all too clearly fails to appreciate the weary ironies within the silent rant that now skewers him: *Look, it's an abortion—no, pardon me, I see you're Kev and you're repulsive, and let's make sure that for the rest of your life my disgust soaks your ugliness. Everything you say is like a dog being sick. Every time I've seen you, I've wished you deepest, grinding pain: well, now we'll make it happen! Refine yourself, you stupid grunt, or can't abortions do that? How did you manage to be quite that vile? Nastier than gangrene, know yourself blessed if I choose your face to kick: my heels in your eyes are your big brush with greatness! I hate your smelly little mind and all its horizons—you sicken me and bore me. I hate you for dragging all the other monkeys down. But I shall be the agent of your closure, you cancer—what fun to block your system! You see this shadow-blade? It'll puncture you and rearrange your insides, Kev, mixing ugliness with pain. Screech, while I watch … yes, it's me doing that! Oh dear, never mind—shall we do it all again?… Oh yes, I shall damage you, for which I'm well-equipped, and you will suffer. But off you go for now, just tonight: run along now. You won't escape, I'll hunt you down. Yes, tomorrow the fun begins…*

Kev obeys. Down goes his shocked face, round turns his bulky frame, and off he waddles out of sight.

I'm filled with admiration. What a show! What power!

Angel turns back to Lucan. *You too!* his eyes hiss. *Get on back to the house—I'll catch you later.* And fearful after Kev, Lucan slopes off, weakly into shadow.

Angel swings his head around and looks at us with menace. My fear returns, for real. I see that Alaia is as malleable as me. He points up Ocean Avenue, his meaning clear: *walk.* Docile, she and I comply, on a forced march, two blocks northwards, back to the carcass.

Through the concrete columns I can see that the cars and cops have all gone. Angel points us through a hole in the wire-netting fence, then steers us towards the inland end of the building, where there's a bare unfinished stairway lacking any kind of containing walls, balusters or handrails, rising eleven storeys to the top. He stands at the bottom of this, still holding us with his gaze, and points up. "Come on up, you little monkeys," he says, with the ceremonial glee of some infernal pixie ring-master. "Let's breathe the fumes in, and paint the night red!" As Alaia and I step forward, I'm startled to realise that the vicious, lisped exuberance of this utterance is in fact the very first thing he has spoken aloud, since my powers were transferred into him, despite the barrage of verbiage that feels as if it's been fired through the air since then.

115 SHRIEKING EYES IN THE GHOST TOWN

So up the stairs we are steered to the very top storey of the structure, a platform about twenty metres wide by forty long, all open to the sky. Rust-stained concrete columns rise to above head-height at the corners of this platform, at intervals along its sides and in a central line down its length. Up from the columns poke long metal bunches of reinforcing rods, like the tangled legs of spiders silhouetted on the sky. We all three spread out in different directions, as if taking ritual places on a high-rise stage. Angel hovers down at the far end, closer to the ocean, while I find myself at the northern inland corner and Alaia at the southern, both of us nearer the stairway than he is, but neither of us able to use it. I glimpse the town spread out beneath me in its grid of streets and roofs, and a slow-flashing light on a metal tower far on the western horizon.

Throughout our journey here, we've been spared having to keep looking at Angel. Now there is no more postponing it. With trepidation and curiosity, I turn back to face him. And there he is, waiting for me, standing with his arms folded, pixily infernal in his dark-red and black. A slight and delicate figure to begin with, he's all the more so at forty metres' distance and set against the ocean's flat vastness rolling out and away into the east, its ripples sharp and tiny in the moonlight. Yes, his eyes are burning atop his silhouette, very dangerously—and yet it seems that despite his ring-master's bravado downstairs, he hasn't yet decided quite what to do with us. We've all started creeping round our stage, here; I'm not sure when we started this. In and out among the line of columns we weave, as if threading through the blades of a knife forest, summoning the memory of how Alaia and I did the same among the drainpipes standing on her roof, while we celebrated *Sound & Vision*'s birth. This time our attentions are focused on Angel, instead of on each other. We have time to share only occasional glances, during which we don't know which one of us Angel is watching, nor whether considerations of survival may now force us into mistrust of each other or even some kind of betrayal.

While we all creep around like this, Angel's eyes zero in upon me properly at last without warning, his gaze shoots through the air as if around the giant curve of a particle-accelerator, locks itself into my gaze and distorts this scene forcibly into a private memory of my own—so that he and I are suddenly prowling a heathery moorland plateau from somewhere a long time ago in my life, half-evading and half-pursuing each other across it now. (So this is what it used to feel like to other people, when I dragged them into some primal memory of their own.) A dim blustery sky hovers low above us, up here on the moor, but around us are grand valleys and light pouring down onto far horizons. As we stare sullenly at each other, his voice comes flat across the heather, but it does so a fraction of a second in advance of when his lips pronounce the words I'm hearing: *I think you'd like a Ghost Town, wouldn't you, Jaymi—yes!* with his eyes accusatory, blazing and psychic in the moonlight. I shudder, while at my feet a twitch of yellow street-light glances in among the heather. Thinking on these disconcerting words of his, I register that their softened sibilants were echoing almost imperceptibly, after they were first pronounced but before his lips appeared to form them—a faint ghosting pre-echo that reveals a dimension I have missed until now, which immediately makes even this grand exterior space feel like the inside of an echoing stone chamber. The ghosted, lisped *s* in his phrase *Ghost Town*, in particular, constituted a sinister and malicious feast all by itself, for seconds after the end of the original *s* in *Ghost*, hissing and flaring on and on after the word, like an insect burning alive in a flame. I feel a dead smile play inside my lips, but I wrestle it back in, so it never quite emerges. *That's your dead smile, I can see it!* he slants his words out across the moorland space, which now feels as enclosed as the space across a table with a mouse-trap upon it. *Good that I just named it, don't you think?* he grins, *to help it come again to you more easily and stick inside your jaws less?*—and this final double *ss* is like a pair of agonised, mutilated mosquitoes, separated from each other and trapped, one in each of my ear canals.

I'm unsure whether he is speaking with his mouth or his eyes, as he carries on: *This is weird, isn't it, Jaymi? These spaces and colours feel like they're on a screen, not around you. These vistas may be backdrops! I may turn around inside your little stone chamber and bite your neck, any moment, don't you think? Something's deeply wrong, you know. It's creepy, too. Look around… Yes, it's creepy, Jaymi, isn't it … but you must allow it's alluring, so why not come and lick me and I'll switch off your head?*

As he swings himself around a column only three metres away, the moonlight flares off his big silver earring and the moisture on his canines. I'm struck once again by the unbelievable allure of Angel's eyes, finding it hard to look away from his bewitching beauty. *Jaymi*, he confides through his eyes or his mouth, *I'm careful that you don't see my real stare of thirst through the dusk at you—my green flesh and sunken cheeks would scare you away. When you stare at the silver-mirrored windows of my black limousine, as it slithers and it oozes through the night-streets, you can't see my face right in front of you, behind your own reflection, frozen in a grimace that has gripped me for hours into wet-burning shame and exhaustion in the darkness…*

Deep longing flickers in his mesmerising eyes, and with that last unbearable sibilant in *darkness* comes a hiss among the carcass-columns, as of gas in air vents—its shiver like the quiver of the shadow-dagger stuck in Angel's chest, with his whisper in my ear,

Stroke the blade soft on Jaymi's neck, while he sleeps... The air clanks thickly, every clank ringing on for many seconds, as mocking oily voices call *Jaymi! ... Jaymi! ... Jaymi!...*

Angel Deon's face hangs huge in the sky above a space of cloud, staring out of mirrored contact lenses—shrieking eyes across the ghost town. Across his left pupil a silver plane flies, with a tiny fleck of dirt upon its ice-coloured nose. The fleck of dirt's a camera and the nose is a bomb-nose, primed to broadcast live tonight on network television, hurtling down—what a rush! The sun shines cold from the red crystal skies of a lurid mountain sunset and the bomb falls silent, its momentum that of ten thousand trains or a march of giant pylons through a forest to infinity. As the east grows dimmer, an obscene fungal bomb-cloud sprouts from a city; burning towers flare, tiny cries shrivel upward and the air beats thick fire. A woman in Arabia with eyes like the desert tells a camera, "As we turn, an explosion booms across the Gulf, the earth shakes, the sky turns red, a sword of light flies from the sea, and towards us comes a wave as high as a ship. What's the sword of light, you ask? Methane exploding, released from sediments beneath the Gulf bed." Cut—to where a great Antarctic crust of ice, the Devil's Ballroom, grinds and snaps and crashes to the ocean. *That's the sound of the atom splitting!* Angel's giant face whispers from the sky, with a honey-coloured knife-smile purring like a scalpel stroking velvet the wrong way.

But now behind the clanks, Alaia whispers—and she's teaming up with Angel against me, as I feared. Alaia is betraying me... *Cold as a jewel, yet my voice burns, pitiless as desert sun parching human tongues into crackly black parrots' tongues, around his shrieking eyes as demons dance and lightning flashes dry,* she hisses. She's becoming Angel's soundtrack, as once she was mine. Is he forcing her, or is this what she wants? I am numb to reflect that she's turning this on me, and I dread what she and Angel may be planning to inflict.

Out of eyes without a smile, she fires a question at me: *Was it ever said you're like a flame in the distance?* She points towards a corner of the building, where I seem to see myself like the whisk of a ghost, with a faint flame of purple in me, thin behind the ocean's sigh. My ghost-self looks at me, with purple-brown-black points of light in its eyes, then licks its lips and summons a bevy of sinister things that step across our stage: proud as horses, these things glance sideways to check their formation, then they slink across the moonlit concrete, launch into slow-motion handsprings and back-flips and vanish… Where are they taking me, this villainous pair, Alaia and Angel? *Where?* she replies. *To your death, Jaymi, where d'you think? Loud in my song, the voice of death. Death in tens: raised up from here to twenty-six powers, shooting out from my tongue and Angel's eyes; and lowered eighteen powers more collapsing down from here. From tiny single deaths, to deaths of great collapsing towers and of towns. Deaths of cities and of centuries, expanding to the rhythm of the rise and fall of empires—a grand wave of death spilling upward and down through millennia, like a tide. Deaths of species, over millions of years. Deaths of planets and of suns, over billions of years, in ever-grander, slower waves. And deaths of whole galaxies and clusters of galaxies—*

Silently, but seeming to emit a shocking roar, a blocky object the size of a house blasts across the sea towards us in a dead-straight line, just above the water, lit sharp in the moonlight. Every second it emits a flash of blue, adding much to the scent of apocalypse and dread that it emanates. Angel and Alaia are between me and it, and within its every flash I glimpse their skeletons, clear through their flesh—like an x-ray but sharper—the bones a frail black inside a blue body shape. It passes a hundred metres south of us, streaks away inland and is gone. I flick my eyes over to where it came from. The giant spectre of Angel's face in the sky is gone, but I'm just in time to see against the black horizon a huge, pale, shiny disc rise from the ocean, water streaming from the air around it, tumble on its giant axis and disappear up into the clouds. Astonished, I look at Alaia and Angel, but they are still staring inland after the other thing, now vanished. An electric whisper runs through the grid of streets around the carcass, underneath the asphalt, down the wires and tunnels, through the crevices and chinks, and then is gone.

Did we all really see that flying thing, and did I really see that gigantic disc? I have no idea how to begin processing them in my mind. In practical terms they have had one major effect, however: they have somehow stripped Angel's power from him and stripped Alaia's nascent power from her, earthing the voltage of unsummaris-able insanity that had somehow built up on this high-rise stage. Looking at both of them, I know their power is gone, just as my own disappeared on the street below. We are just three tired, small, equal human beings, standing on an unfinished building late at night; and it is time to go and sleep.

I'm so tired, in fact, that I feel nearly ill with tiredness. "I need to sleep," I mutter, floating towards the stairway. "Coming, Alaia?" She nods, grins weakly and stumbles over to me. We turn to look at Angel, who is squatting at the end of the concrete space nearer the ocean, like a weasel, coiled to spring towards us. He makes one last bold attempt to stare me down hypnotically, but it is quite unlike a few minutes ago: rather than feeling powerless against the force of his eyes, I can now see straight through his human glare into the desperate human intention behind it, and he and I both know this. He starts to reach for his left pocket but I point at his face, shouting "*I noticed your EYES today, Angel…*" and his hand abandons its quest and falls to the concrete. He lowers his beautiful gaze in defeat, then shakes his head and buries it between his knees.

Turning back towards the stairway, I glimpse the flashing light upon the tower in the west, and I look at Asbury Park from above, for the last time: a grid of dim yellow-white lights in the dead quiet, seeming like a thousand other small towns, giving no clue as to the dramas I've witnessed in the course of a week.

Alaia takes my hand and leads the two of us with care down the stairs, step by step, vertiginously railing-less, for twenty-two flights, through eleven bare storeys of space, to the derelict wasteland below.

Three or four blocks away, approaching our separate bedrooms hand in hand, I pull us round to face back towards the carcass-building. We stop and run our eyes across the topmost platform—and there is Angel's form still, in tiny silhouette against the northern sky, hunched in his dark-red and silver and black, with his head between his knees and his back to the faint blue dawn across the ocean.

PART X

GHOST TOWN DEPARTURE: REVELATION OF ALAIA

116 REVELATION IN THE BREAKFAST ROOM

My eyes open, at nearly noon. Something heavy happened last night. I push my memory into gear...

Oh yes. Loss of special sight, plus a few supporting dramas. This will need some processing.

I lie here, my mind racing. First, I should try tuning in to someone, just in case. Evelyn, for instance. I try; but it's no good. All I'm doing is thinking about her, nothing more. I try several more people, including Alaia through this wall here, before realising I don't even know if she's behind this wall, however hard I focus. I simply don't know where she is.

I stare at the blank sky through the window, distraught, then I get ready numbly, leave my room and knock on Alaia's door. No answer. I knock again, wait, turn the handle and peer in. Her bags sit just inside the door, all packed up and ready to go. I am just about to turn away, when I realise that the bed is not where I saw it when I tuned in to her yesterday morning: instead of being against the wall beside my bed, it's over there by the window. She must have moved it yesterday. That's odd, though. I can see she might prefer to have a window view from bed, but why did she wait a week, until yesterday, to act upon this preference, and then pack up

329

all her things anyway?... Now that I consider the room as a whole, however, I realise that in fact this current arrangement must be how the Metropolitan staff keep the room. The arrangement I saw when I tuned in to her was the temporary one.

I start to ponder this as I head down the marble staircase, but am startled by Marc's voice from the hallway below. I'd completely forgotten he was coming here today from New York. "*Jaymi!*" he booms, striding over to the stairs and extending his hand to me with gusto.

"Hi Marc," I murmur, trudging down. I feel like no match for the Albright whirlwind this morning.

"Excellent news! We now have a date for our third broadcast event..." He trails off, fixing his shrewd regard upon me: sensing change, no doubt.

"I have a confession," I say sadly. "First, I succumbed to the temptation of leaving the Metropolitan. I know you didn't want people in town spreading it that I was down here, but *that* wasn't the problem; that never happened. What happened, nobody could have predicted..." And I stand there and tell him all about last night—omitting the flying thing and the disc in the ocean, both of which I've decided to keep to myself until I've had time to decide what to do with them from now on.

He interrupts me not at all. When I am finished, he says, "I see." We stand there unspeaking for a moment. "Well—what's done is done," he pronounces. It is all too obvious to both of us that there can be no third broadcast now; that our adventure with global TV events, special sight and raising the world's self-knowledge is over, and that it's time for Alaia and me to leave this town. "I only wish we'd had a camera and sound equipment trained on you last night," he adds, smiling but with genuine regret too. "What a fantastic third instalment that would have made... Jaymi, can you *imagine* it?"

I close my eyes for an instant. "Yes, Marc," I say dryly.

"Well—there it is." He pats me consolingly on the back. "Let's all meet in the office down the corridor there at two o'clock, and take care of the all the paperwork, shall we? I'll see you both then."

He exits the hallway and heads briskly towards the office in question.

I wander through the open door of the breakfast room and find

Alaia sitting alone on a window-seat, drinking coffee. "Oh! Good morning," I say.

"Hallo." She looks at me with a strange mix of sombreness and febrility.

I pull the door closed behind me and approach her. "Well ... I assume you overheard all that?" She nods. "So we're meeting him at two. I wonder—d'you think *you* could call Bedford Pickering III and tell him what's happened? I don't think I can deal with him at the moment. He should phone Marc right now, before we get there." She takes her phone out. "Thanks." I sit down beside her.

After ten minutes of her talking on the phone, during which I stare at the white wall opposite me as if I'm in a trance, she ends the call. "How d'you feel?" she asks me.

"Flat," I state. "Clear, dry, colourless, inert. Like a fact or a number." I take the mug from her, have a sip of coffee and return it. "Thanks for coming with me on this strange journey."

"Thanks for having me!" Then without warning she reaches up and strokes my face, very gently.

I stare at her in surprise.

"Bold action," she murmurs.

As I stare into her admiring eyes, my right hand rises to touch her warm, sleek forehead for the very first time, and a simple, full, radiant truth raises its hand and is noticed, at last: I'm in love with her.

I'm in love with her...

I've fallen in love with Alaia!

"Alaia, I love you," I hear myself say.

"I was wondering when you'd notice."

We stare at each other. So *this* has been the oddness between us, these last few days... I'm at a loss for words to make proper sense of this. "What happens now?" I ask.

She shakes her head slowly. "I don't know... But it's exciting, isn't it!"

I frown in concentration, thinking this through. "But—do you love me?"

"Yes. I love you, Jaymi... I was wondering when you'd notice that too."

I stroke her hand. "Since when?"

"Since I was in the sound booth for those ten minutes when Rik had us sitting there in silence, before *Sound & Vision*. For ten solid minutes I watched you on the monitor, right in front of me—in full 4K definition. Or going further back, I think the very beginning was probably when you hypnotised me on my roof at home."

"Which won't be happening again now. You're aware of that?"

"Oh yes. I'll cope with that. In fact I think I'm rather glad of it."

"I've probably loved you since that time on the roof too. I've just been way too busy to notice it."

"Jaymi ... d'you remember my statue of black icing-sugar?"

I laugh aloud. "How could I forget it?"

"You came to visit me in my clearing and ... it was beautiful together. Remember?"

Her eyes are clear and calm and warm, from close.

She rises to her feet, my hand in hers. "Let's go for a walk," she says.

I stand, and she leads me across the breakfast room.

117 THAT NARROW DOOR

The next two hours with Alaia, whether chatting as we wander hand in hand or just sitting wordless in the sunlight together, are two of the most romantic hours I have ever spent in my life—excepting perhaps the ten-minute interruption of fevered legal jabbering with Bedford Pickering III on my mobile beside Sunset Lake in preparation for our imminent meeting with Marc. Then she and I return to the Metropolitan, in time for two o'clock.

It's a most satisfactory meeting, I'm glad to say, involving a three-way online video conference between us three, Bedford and the GN's general counsel. Within forty-five minutes all remaining aspects of my and Alaia's rights in the two broadcasts are clarified and negotiated in general, subject to detailed imminent documentation.

After the conference call, Marc adds that Jason's assistant will be in touch with me soon, in connection with "any other rights that may be outstanding". Was that a conspiratorial twinkle in his eye, as he uttered this? I can't be sure; but if so, then it was the first and doubtless the last acknowledgement by him of the imagination-thieving. Either way, I emit no such twinkle of my own, whatsoever: I prefer to keep my dealings with him impeccably pristine, severe and above-board ... and anyway, I'm not about to start twinkling when we haven't even hashed all that stuff out yet.

As for this afternoon, we tell him, we'd rather not prolong our stay here unnecessarily, preferring to head home to New York and the real world again. Marc agrees and phones Evelyn to ask her to make the van ready for us now.

We all stand up and he looks me squarely in the eye. "Nice to do business with you, Jaymi!"

"And with you, Marc. Did we re-ignite a few radioactive ballroom scenes around the world, d'you think?"

He laughs aloud and nods. "I think we did," he answers. Then he lifts his hands, makes a circle by putting the end of one thumb against the end of the other thumb and the end of one index finger against the end of the other index finger, holds this circle in front of his face, centring just above his nose, and fixes me with the stare of *that* figure at the ballroom party: above the crowd, its eyes strangely one, like a great gold Cyclops three metres high, sprouting horns like a Baphomet's, its claws hanging down resting easy on the grey heads carpeting the ballroom, its heavy eye transfixing me—

"I shall never forget that, Marc," I reply. "That's how this whole thing began, and I can think of no more fitting way for it to conclude."

We shake hands, both inclining our heads a fraction in mutual respect, and I take my leave of him.

Having done likewise, Alaia follows me out of the office, into the marble hallway and upstairs, where she watches me pack up all my belongings quickly. Then she grabs her own bags from her room and we run back downstairs and slip out through the Metropolitan's inconspicuous door for the last time. Out on Asbury Avenue, Evelyn is waiting in her silver van. "You look just like you did when you picked me up on Forty-Third Street," I say.

"Marc says you're both leaving now!" she exclaims, and I see her noticing our hands holding each other. "Why?"

We climb in, slide the door shut and start to give her a quick summary of what's happened, while she drives. We haven't got far into the tale, before she parks outside Pippa's high-rise. "Carry on," she says. "I'll tell you why we're at Pippa's in a minute, but what happened next?" So I finish the tale as we sit in the parked van. "OK, we need to talk more about all this—with Rik too," she decides. "We can't just wash our hands and move on here. This is a bunch of serious juiciness to discuss!"

"You bet," says Alaia, "so let's fix a time for you and Rik to visit us in Manhattan: it's compulsory."

"All right, we'll do it." Evelyn peers at us in the rear-view mirror. "Especially now that you two—"

"I was hoping to say goodbye to Rik just now, but leaving was such a rush," I say.

"You can say goodbye to him on the phone," she says. "He's up seeing Jason in New York today—give him a call. OK, so we're at Pippa's now because I still have a copy of her door key and I want to go up and check there's nothing major that she wouldn't want people finding, before all her stuff ends up god knows where—I don't even know if she has any relatives alive. I should have come here last night. Wanna join me?"

Alaia shakes her head. "No, I think I'll wait here. One visit there was enough for me."

"Sure, I'll come up," I say.

For the third and last time, therefore, I enter Pippa's dim, cluttered apartment, where the space is all wrong. Once we're inside, an unholy quiet prevails. Evelyn and I both seem to be walking on tiptoe, as if not to wake something. "I'll go look on the balcony," she whispers, heads up the hallway past the kitchen and pushes the sitting room door open.

Left alone, I glance down the long, narrow corridor in the other direction, towards Pippa's closed bedroom door, and am startled to notice a faint light gleaming through the hinge of that narrow door... I creep nearer to it, careful to make no sound. There's the keyhole. I bend down very slowly, bring my eye level with it, and peer through.

I recoil—for there it is. Exactly the figure Kim described: what looks like some kind of vegetable twin of Angel Deon, sitting naked in a wheelchair.

These eyes are quite different from the big, creepy, beautiful eyes on the waxwork on Damian's path, however. These are weasel eyes.

These eyes look like the eyes of a person.

At least, I *think* they do…

Can Pippa really have kept a *person* in her apartment, like this, for who knows how many weeks, or months, or years?

I start, as Evelyn comes bustling up behind me, proffering three keys on a key-ring. I put my finger to my lips, stand out of view of the keyhole, in front of the door itself, and gesture to her to remain where she is too, out of the figure's line of sight. I take the keys, peer at them, choose the likeliest-looking one and try it carefully in the hole. It's not a good fit. I pull it back out, bring the key-ring up to my face, compare the other two keys, select the next likely-looking one, and even more carefully try this in the keyhole: it goes in smoothly, but then will not turn. I shake my head, pull it back out, start to identify the third key, and jump nervily as Evelyn pokes me on the arm.

"*Jaymi*," she whispers stagily. "*Maybe it's not locked…*"

I think for a moment, hand her back the key-ring, half-look again through the keyhole, straighten up and start to turn the door handle, very slowly.

She's right! The door starts to open, by itself…

We stand there and let the door swing gradually inward under its own weight, making a teeth-grating squeak as it does so. Then, after a few centimetres, it comes to a halt. Through the crack, the wall of a toilet cubicle appears … and the edge of a knee.

No one moves. There is silence and absolute stillness, for several seconds.

Evelyn and I glance at each other, horrified. Then I gesture to her to move back, brace myself grimly, and push the door firmly inward.

There the figure sits, bathed in the feeble off-white light of a hanging bulb. It has its right hand hidden from view, pushed in between its skinny pale-brown torso and its left upper arm, in a physically self-defensive pose that I recall is acutely characteristic of Angel. Its left hand is resting on its left knee.

Once more, nobody moves.

Then gradually, in tandem, like a pair of synchronised swimmers, Evelyn and I bend our torsos in towards the figure and peer at it from closer … until at the very same moment, again like those same synchronised swimmers, we both become certain that despite its uncanny lifelikeness, its surface is wax. It is a second, full-body, life-size wax Angel, rendered even more exquisitely than the one on Damian's path, once again with small smooth male genitals tucked demurely between his thighs, beneath a small and lovely pair of female breasts. The only real difference is that in comparison with the big soft eyes of the first model, the eyes of this one, though also beautiful, are startlingly realer, with a quality that's a lot more cunning and (to use Kim's word) more weaselly.

"So," I whisper to Evelyn, still feeling on edge and uncomfortably conscious that I am being watched by Angel, "there's no doubt: Pippa did make the one on Damian's path."

She nods. "And the wax heads," she whispers back.

I decide not to tell her about the note from Angel that Pippa kept in her pocket; I shall leave Pippa her privacy there. I permit myself, however, to whisper the obvious: "This indicates quite an obsession with Angel!" at which Evelyn nods again with vigour. It occurs to me, too, how much Pippa must have hated the rest of Lucan's gang, for having such close access to him but not (I'm sure) appreciating this access as they should have done: hatred for Kev, Angel's enemy; hatred for Damian, Angel's affectionate one-time landlord; and worst of all, hatred for Lucan, who dared to be not only Angel's lover but even his abuser, of which she must surely have had at least an inkling. How ironic, that in killing her in its cross-fire this gang was punishing their sculptress provoker without even knowing it.

Impossible, unfulfilled yearning, frustration and sorrow must have been Pippa's lot, to judge from the contents of the shelves throughout this apartment, where numerous angel ornaments stand in a frozen symphony of mute raptures. And how much greater yearning is suggested by the thin wedding-ring that encircles the ring-finger of Angel's left hand, resting there upon his knee. As I bend down to peer at the ring, it bears in upon me that the silence of this apartment is now like a stranglehold. There is no longer any sound of Evelyn just behind me, no sound from the kitchen, the sitting room or the bedroom: just dead quiet. It's almost as if I'm alone here—except for what's in front of me, of course.

It is at this moment, still on my way down to inspect the ring, that I become half-aware of something awful, while horror gathers weight against it from the other side, ready to tip it into plain view here any second…

I leap backwards with a grimace and a wail. *Yes*: Angel's feet have been moulded onto his slender ankles back-to-front, so he greets me with his heels, while his ten toes burrow hindwards into the carpet on either side of the toilet-bowl.

Evelyn reappears beside me from the bedroom without warning, so I jump again and almost knock her over and we both squeal in unison, before erupting in nervous hilarity. I point at Angel's feet and stare at her, as if challenging her to deny it. "Oh, shit!" she says, craning down towards them.

There's a text bleep from my phone. I pull it from my pocket. "What's happening up there?" reads Alaia's message. "2 mins," I text back. "You know, I think I'd like to leave," I announce.

"Hold on. We have to take him with us. I need to rescue him now and put him in the van, because I don't know who else may be coming to take Pippa's things away."

"Evelyn, you're taking him *home*? You'll wake up one night and find he's got into bed with you! I swear he footsied his way closer to me just now. Where are you going to keep him—on the bedside table?"

"No, but I know who'll want to keep him *exactly* there, sitting on his own bedside table, right beside the first wax Angel—Angel himself, the one who deserves to own them both. I only hope he can keep them safe in that war-zone he lives in. Lucan's going to have a harem in the bedroom: three of them! Help me get him up." I help her guide him gingerly up off the toilet and through the narrow door. "Come on, Angel," she coaxes. "Come with Evelyn… Oh, Jaymi, isn't he just adorable?"

Soon the three of us emerge from the high-rise into the daylight at last, appearing suddenly beside a startled Alaia in the van. "*Another* one?" she says through the van window.

"You may notice something different about the feet," I reply. "Evelyn's going to give it to Angel himself. He's apparently now addicted to waxworks of himself, which doesn't surprise me. When I tuned in the other day, I found his adoration for you and me is already looking a bit atrophied, though it's only a week old: there also seemed to be a certain confusion in him concerning the basis of the adoration itself."

Alaia snorts with laughter. "I'm not surprised!"

"OK, we're not going back to the Metropolitan with you two in the van," says Evelyn, lowering the figure carefully into one of the rear seats. "I'm meant to have got rid of you. So we won't go back there to dump Angel. He can just go up to New York with us, then back down here again with me, for the ride. I guess we'd better cover him up, or those breasts are going to cause a crash on the turnpike." She pulls out a clean white sheet from a bag in the back of the van and drapes it over him.

Then we are off up Main Street and heading north out of Asbury Park, one day after Shigem and Kim did the same.

118 THE FEET BENEATH THE SHEET

Not far out of town we all fall quiet, which is unexpected but welcome. I am seated in the rear half of the van, with the window against me on my left and a sleepy Alaia on my right, her head resting on my shoulder. Across the central aisle the white-draped Angel sits securely in his seat, with his backwards-pointing feet sticking out from under the sheet.

Alaia's going to spend the night at my place, I do believe. How strange, that despite my visual abilities, it took me so long to realise what was flickering between us. Those abilities had to disappear, in fact, before I realised it. I suppose they had focused me so much on unfamiliar scales of grandeur and intimacy within people, that I wasn't focusing in the right way to see something occurring on such a familiarly human-sized scale right in front of me. Plus, of course, I never tuned in to her—well, hardly ever.

I gaze through the window. In the wake of my loss of powers, I still feel like a monarch who's been robbed of a realm, but the regular human abilities to which I've been returned now feel richer than they did before. It's a strange, grand fortune to have shone worldwide with an almost supernatural glow of glamour, beauty and power for just a brief time—for those two extraordinary broadcasts only—and then to return to the realm of normal humanity, quite certain never to shine as brightly again for the rest of my life and yet also knowing nothing can take away what was achieved nor cause the world to forget it.

Moreover, what Alaia and I emitted survives in perfect high-end recordings, which Marc will spare none of his prodigious powers in marketing and selling as globally as possible, and from which Alaia and I shall receive large shares in line with the agreements just hashed out between Bedford and the GN. Such has been the fantastic impact of *Sound & Vision* and *Big Bang* in just this first week, according to Marc, that I can see this pair of broadcasts will rage and thunder on without relent into the future, towering unstoppable and huge through the years with their own self-generating fuel and a being and volition quite their own, independent of Alaia and me altogether. From now on, she and I will in some respects be no closer to her sound and my vision, as sealed and perfected there, than any of the viewers who will watch them for generations to come.

As for the flying thing and the disc in the ocean ... well, I'm going to keep quiet about them, at least until Alaia wants to talk about the flying thing. I still don't know how to process them, and perhaps I'll never know. No one will believe me if I mention them, so why bother doing so? I'm sure I saw them both, and I'm sure she and Angel saw one of them, and who knows what they were. If they had any emotional effect on me, aside from wiping away his and Alaia's abilities, then this was probably to leave me with a newly clean, clear and serene consciousness of the icy power of objects to wipe out any and all of us at a moment's notice, neutralising every social or imaginative distinction or achievement at a stroke.

I spot something else too, which makes me smile: that default-level personality of mine, peeping out like a mischievous rabbit from the place it was hiding in while those greater abilities were overshadowing it. And wouldn't you know—it's just me. Perhaps the reason I felt I'd mislaid it, once I started looking into other people's personalities, was that my own personality had thereby been revealed as just a habitual set of ways of seeing, rather than its own objective beast. No matter: I greet my set of ways of seeing, like a long-lost bunny, in warm affection.

How randomly chosen personalities are, for the people who find themselves acting as their custodians, I reflect. I frown, noticing that just above the flat horizon there's a pale cloud resembling a tornado... I peer at it, fascinated; then I realise it's half the white of one of my eyes reflected on the surface of the glass beside me, the tornado's inside curve being formed by the outer edge of the iris.

I feel Alaia's breath on my neck as she sleeps. I turn my head to the right, to look at her from close up. Beginning at her eyes, I move my adoring gaze slowly downward, in a deliberate and leisurely trip along the line of her profile. When my gaze reaches her mouth, softening at the prospect of its imminent detour into the small curved inlet comprising her parted lips as seen from here, I feel my eyes change focus, from close up to further away: for exactly beyond her lips, in this particular sightline, are Angel's backwards-pointing feet sticking out from under the sheet.

I turn my head quickly to face forward again, and lean my head back against the head-rest.

119 SAVAGERY, MYSTERY, DEATH AND CONFINEMENT

We're entering a town on an elevated highway, through concrete and space never walked on or touched but seen by millions through glass. From the open-topped convertible in front of us, a sweep of music surges, with soft and ethereal voices, as from paradise. Caught among cars all jostling for the exit ramp, we slow down. The man and the woman in the car in front kiss, while the music carries on and on, syrupy and swoony and incongruous in traffic. Glancing from the highway to a grimy housing project underneath us now, I jump at a sight that lifts the music's incongruity to heights quite obscene. As this gorgeous aural treacle fills the air, a boy beats another quite defenceless smaller boy with a baseball bat, surrounded by a ring of cheering onlookers: *thwack* upon his bare head, *thwack* upon his ribcage, *thwack* upon his bare shins, *thwack* into his groin... The traffic creeps forward, the smaller boy screeches and the music swishes on.

I look away in horror, feel my head start to swim and move it down between my knees. I know I must help the smaller boy ... but when I come to, the music's gone. I'm reclining in the passenger's seat, which has been pushed back so that I'm looking up through the van's open roof. I sense the driver is a bit like a skeleton, but I can't be sure of this because I cannot tear my gaze away from the gluey ultramarine of the sky, which is enrapturing me: my eyes rootle into the sky's surface as if to eat it. The driver turns from the wheel to me, grinning, and I feel more than ever how like a skeleton it is, wearing a wide-brimmed hat. Still I am fixated on the orgy of darkest blue, which grows ever larger and more glutinous. The driver leans close to me and its bony lips whisper, *When the student is ready, the master will appear!* Grinning wide, it blows upon my face a breath that's at once decaying parchment, rich wine and the smell of Greek seas through the ochre dusk light of a temple on an island—then my gaze is released from the sky with a jolt and I am sitting in the driver's seat, alone.

The car is cruising fast, sliding smooth on the curve of an elevated freeway, high as a suspension bridge, that strides grey and silver through the countries of a jungle on a march of slender legs I can see far ahead disappearing in a mist of light.

Either side of this sleek path of concrete and steel spreads a wet land of spongy green, monkey shrieks and bird plumes, hanging vines and steamy swamps twinkling with leeches and gassy mud, yellow fish and tiny white bubbles on the underside of weed fronds.

Jaymi, you see that ahead? comes the vanished driver's voice, like a whisper from the back seat. A shadow in the overhead mirror—quickly gone. *You see that ahead?* comes the whisper from my left, and half a mile ahead beside the freeway a fountain of orange flame bursts from the jungle, to burn high and clear against the fluid sky. *That's your death, at age sixty-eight! You want a preview? Go ahead— I'll hold the wheel while you look!* and I can feel the steering-wheel being adjusted as we drive on, to keep us with exactness in the centre of our lane.

The orange fountain-flame seems to ripple into folds. A picture forms beyond it: the outside of a tiny washroom window. Inside the window, in a cubicle, a long shrunken grey face nuzzles into view, sick and pinched and mad with dead despair. Its chin sinks to rest upon the sill, its deadened eyes looking down to the right, as if it's never been outside this poky washroom. It spits greyly, feebly—and suddenly I see that it really hasn't been outside the washroom, for decades, and it knows it never will.

The flame-folds ripple back, to cover up my future, like a curtain sliding across a movie screen. The fountain subsides to the jungle canopy. Control of the steering-wheel returns to me. I drive on, distraught. The spongy land on either side carries on, as if nothing's happened, just as beautiful and alien as ever.

"No," I think, then scream aloud "*NO!...*" and hear my voice, flat and dead upon the closed air.

I sense I had to help someone, back there behind us. Who *was* that?

I sense, in addition, that the word I just shrieked was a sound and nothing more.

120   A RING, TWO SPIRES AND A WEDDING GIFT

I wake for real, bumping my head onto the van's window. Alaia stirs in her sleep. It's funny, a week ago on the outward leg of this trip, I also sank into ominous dreams. Must be something strange about this van.

The Manhattan skyline appears in the distance, at the far end of a convergence of wires strung on a line of majestic electrical pylons stretching across these dirty marshes and industrial wastelands surrounding us. I contemplate that little clump of skyscrapers with love—a so-familiar beacon of home, civilisation and excitement, for both Alaia and me. This glad return to the approaching city reminds me of something Rik told us on Friday night, during the second or third bottle of red wine: "I tell you one of my favourite slivers of New York," he said. "There's a store window display that's been there for years, with this surreal line of miniature Barbie dolls, different ethnicities, each one dressed in a tiny fake-fur coat, to help sell the shop's furs—some coats are subtle colours, but others are really bright, like fuzzy electric green or blue. It's on the uptown side of Houston, around West Broadway. And every night after it's closed, you can see through the grating that this teeny-weeny chorus-line has been moved a bit further back from the window, or maybe they shuffled back to get out of the street-lights. Anyway, after I'd seen these fuzzy Barbies a few times, I realised an elusive truth. I don't know how I knew; I just did. A few blocks away there's a building where those honey-roasted-peanut vendors' trolleys are parked each night"—here he lowered the volume of his voice—"and I realised: every night, in the deeps of the wee hours, when nobody's listening at the crack of the door, when nobody's peeking through the grating of the window, this line of little fuzzy Barbies sneaks out the back door of the shop, and they tiptoe through the back streets to that other building, and then every little Barbie rips off her fake-fur coat and jumps into a peanut trolley and nuzzles compulsively among the peanuts for a hour or so, to relieve some of that fuzzy Barbie tension … and then they slip back home to the window, in time for dawn and commerce."

Chuckling, I feel some unidentified object in my left pocket, reach in and pull out a small grey plastic elephant, the one I named Dotty after the woman in the bric-a-brac store, her trunk raised high as if greeting me. Leaving her in my lap, I pull out from my bag the other souvenir I've brought back from this trip—Pippa's envelope, still sealed as it was by her before she flung it away with all her ebbing strength, as far as she could up Fourth Avenue and into an unknown future here with me. I reach into my bag again, fetch out a key-ring, cut cleanly along the envelope's edge with the sharpest key and pull the note out.

It is as I deciphered it through her eyes, when she lay there fading, reading it for the last of what must have been thousands of times. "*See you tonight!*" say the urgent words addressed to Lucan, in Angel's delicate, jagged script, from some time soon after the two of them first met: his yearning hope and electrical excitement, in that instant several years ago, are still clear in the upward-soaring swoops and cruel downward whiplash of his purple ink signature, despite now being smudged by subsequent years of Pippa's kisses. I turn this bizarrely precious item around in my hands, contemplating the train of events it memorialises. I smile in wonder at the intricate tracery of bloodstains at its left edge, which I noticed through Pippa beside the carcass-building while some of these stains were still wet, doubtless from the gunshot wound in the right side of her back … except that perhaps the stains were a little too delicate to have come from such a wound, even assuming the blood did make it across from her right side to her left side, and in any case why were some of the stains already dry beside the carcass-building?

A movement on my right makes me turn my head and glance across the van, where the vibrations of the road have just caused the sheet to slide partly off Angel before getting caught between his shoulder and his seat-back, thereby uncovering his knees and left hand. For the first time during this drive, I can see his face in profile, his left weaselly eye staring straight ahead at the seat in front of him. But what I find myself becoming more acutely aware of is the little waxy hand that he rests on his left knee, just across the aisle from here.

My gaze alights again on the silver wedding-ring Pippa has dressed him in, which buries itself just a fraction into the non-humanly smooth matt finger where I can make out a thin scratch indented into the wax surface, like a scratch on a candle: if I remember when we reach New York, once I'm no longer trapped here in my seat by a sleeping Alaia, then perhaps I shall take a moment to smooth that scratch carefully into its unscratched wax surroundings, for Pippa's sake. What artistry she has brought to bear, first in modelling the pale-brown wax hand and then in painting its five nails a deep, luscious crimson. The nail on the ring-finger, in particular, is so uncannily lifelike that I would almost expect to see this finger stir and start tapping slowly up and down on his bare knee...

My gaze wanders upwards and through the window beyond Angel. Ah yes, truly, I feel the warmest of glows inside me, to contemplate the promise of such a brand-new chapter back at home in New York, and on such a brand-new basis with Alaia!

My gaze wanders back downwards.

Beneath the thin, even, smooth coat of crimson on its very shiny, smooth surface, that fingernail protrudes from its wax ring-finger with an awesome perfection of modelling, especially as seen from the side here...

My gaze flicks up again sharply, and lodges on the points of the spires of the Empire State Building and the Chrysler Building, which are scratching their way slowly up into the sky, as the van shoots ever closer to them—my gaze clinging first to the nail-point of the one spire, then flicking across to cling to the nail-point of the second spire, then flicking back to cling tightly to the first.

My eyes narrow, as images of Pippa flash like strobe-lights in my head...

Her rare smile—and her eternal black silk gloves.

Her love of angel ornaments—and the filigree of old dry blood-stains at the left edge of her note from Angel, doubtless from the fresh, gaping gunshot wound on her right.

The sad light in those green and slightly protuberant eyes that always looked as if she had just bottled up the remaining half of a violent bout of weeping—and the red stains on the wax of the Laughing Cow cheese after she placed it onto her plate, smiling about the cow on the label.

Those singing pussy-cats she may or may not have heard—and that black pit behind the narrow door in the hallway, where ... an eternal wedding gift from her, harvested for her most deeply beloved, whom she knew that she would never, ever have.

The van gives a jolt and the sheet falls all the way off Angel's shoulder onto his lap, covering his left hand and at the same time revealing where his right hand is hidden from view, pushed in between his skinny pale-brown torso and his left upper arm, in that self-defensive pose so acutely observed by his loving modeller as being so characteristic of Angel himself: a gesture born of a lifetime of physical and emotional attack from every side, first throughout years of childhood and then throughout years of Lucan. I wonder if this hand too, although hidden ... but I wrench my mind away from this, never to know the answer.

Angel is still secure in his seat but has swung slightly to his right, so he now stares through the van's right window ahead of him, as if eager to reach the city. I wish I could pull the sheet back up to cover the entirety of him, as it did until its unfortunate slippage a few minutes ago; but if I move then I shall wake Alaia, whose cheek rests against my right shoulder.

Still clutching Angel's note, and filled with powerless compassion and vertigo at the depths of pain in her whose lips smudged its author's signature with such hopeless frequency, I honour that smudging in the only way I can think of: I turn and place a slow, gentle kiss on Alaia's warm temple.

I feel my eyes staring widely at the Manhattan skyline, then somewhat narrowing again as they return to flicking between the tips of the Empire State Building and the Chrysler Building—the nail-points of these two spires scraping their way up the dusk as we approach them, both now stained blood-red from the sunset on my left, and both glinting against the deepening ultramarine of the eastern sky with a hard, cold beauty.

THE END

If you've enjoyed this tale, then my warm appreciation for leaving just a quick rating and/or a handful of words of feedback on it, at the online retailer it came from (all retailers' links are at www.rohanquine.com/buy/the-imagination-thief-novel-paperback). If you are able to do so, then this really would help me enormously, so very many thanks!

Rohan

OTHER TITLES BY ROHAN QUINE

Also by Rohan Quine, the following titles are available
at most online retailers, in paperback, ebook and audiobook
formats, published by EC1 Digital.

THE BEASTS OF ELECTRA DRIVE
A novel

From Hollywood Hills mansions and Century City towers, to
South Central motels and the oceanside refinery, *The Beasts of
Electra Drive* spans a mythic L.A., following seven spectacular
characters (or Beasts) from games designer Jaymi's game-worlds.
The intensity of those Beasts' creation cycles leads to their release
into real life in seemingly human forms, and to their combative
protection of him from destructive rivals at mainstream company
Bang Dead Games. Grand spaces of beauty interlock with narrow
rooms of terror, both in the real world and in the incorporeal world
of cyberspace. A prequel to Rohan Quine's other five tales (and a
Finalist in the IAN Book of the Year Awards 2018), this novel is a
unique explosion of glamour and beauty, horror and enchantment,
exploring the mechanisms and magic of creativity itself.

www.rohanquine.com/the-beasts-of-electra-drive

This novel is available as a paperback (retailers' links at www.rohanquine.com/buy/the-beasts-of-electra-drive-novel-paperback),

an ebook (retailers' links at www.rohanquine.com/buy/the-beasts-of-electra-drive-novel-ebook) and

an audiobook (retailers' links at www.rohanquine.com/buy/the-beasts-of-electra-drive-novel-audiobook), all published by EC1 Digital.

REVIEWS OF *THE BEASTS OF ELECTRA DRIVE*

See www.rohanquine.com/press-media/the-beasts-of-electra-drive-reviews-media for all links to the following.

"Technologically intelligent, socially clever, and supernaturally chilling—a trippy sci-fi tale. [...]

There is a strong artistic element woven into this act of creation, allowing us to see how and why Jaymi creates each of his Beasts, giving them purpose and personality as well as form. [...] This is a book that would have been entirely serviceable with just the hacking and virtual reality interfaces, but what makes it really compelling is the ability for Jaymi's Beasts to step out into meat-space (*I love that term*) and take on corporeal form. These characters grow, learn, and even challenge their programming—they are somewhat childish in their willful independence, to the point of being sociopaths, although they demonstrate real emotion. There is some wonderful genderfluidity to some of the Beasts, with Shigem never feeling '*quite like a boy, being half a gender to the left*' and Scorpio whose '*nature flowers with so transgender a beauty,*' as well as a gay love affair between two Beasts who were created for one another. Lest you forget that this is a revenge fantasy, however, Amber is modeled after Rutger Hauer's character in *The Hitcher*, while Scorpio's defining moment is the fantasy of dominating an entire prison as the most dangerous boy in a skirt. [...]

What really impressed me, however, is the flair for language, with some really beautiful—and beautifully chilling—passages that had me dog-earing pages along the way."
—**Sally Bend**, author, in *Bending the Bookshelf*

"Quine describes [the Beasts'] release like a beautiful dance instead of a strategic infiltration. [...]

The novel is a creative mashing together of Hollywood novel, science fiction, eroticism, and dystopia, with a premise that seems at once foreboding and prescient. While the book takes obvious science fictional liberties with technology, there is a real-world parable about superficiality versus authenticity. As the world becomes more digitally mechanized—and we are as much a product of our digital personae as our real-life personae—the book has an important message to tell about what it is to be truly human. [...]

Quine obviously has a lot of affection for his Beasts, which has the same effect on the reader. He also injects humor throughout into what is at times a fairly dark storyline, replete with violence and seamy sexuality.

In all, Quine has created a wholly unique book that will appeal to gamers and non-gamers alike. Most readers will empathize with the main character and his suboptimal working situation, and the steps he takes to get out from underneath a tyrannical and uninspiring boss. On a science fictional level, the novel works exceptionally well for its creative use of tech, mixed in with a group of highly imaginative characters.

A prequel to five other works, *The Beasts of Electra Drive* will have readers seeking out Rohan Quine's other books in the series."
—SPR

"This novel is essentially near-future cyberpunk subtly blended with elements of LA noir and dystopic fiction to create a darkly stylish and, at times, visionary glimpse into humankind's future. [...] Richly described, the beasts are androgynous characters with full backstories, personalities, and idiosyncrasies. Unleashed upon the world, they allow Jaymi to achieve vengeance in ingenious ways.

This is an intriguing premise, but the story's true power comes from its underlying theme: Humans can choose to live in the superficial, and underlying falseness, of tabloid reality (as gamers do when engaging in the novel's online game), or embrace the 'complexity, unconventionality, beauty and subtlety of truth' of the world around them. Ultimately Jaymi's journey of self-discovery mirrors our own: We all seek happiness in the short time that we inhabit the 'meat space' of this world."
—BlueInk Review

"*The Beasts of Electra Drive*, an unctuously dark piece of magical realism interwoven with biting satire on mass culture." "This book is a marvel." "I had the joy of editing this extraordinary novel that's part magic realism, part horror, part satire of the media industry, part meditative hymn."
—**Dan Holloway**, author, poet and *Guardian* blogger

"Quine's narrative challenges the arbitrariness of commercial gate-keepers and the randomness of success—and has a lot of fun in the process. It's an odd mixture of dark—verging on horror—with more than a bit of kitsch. [...] It's a very visual novel too. Quine gives his narrative voice (and sometimes his characters), the eye of a camera mounted on a drone, able to fly across a valley and zoom in on details miles in the distance—like a tiny reflection in the pupil of someone's eye. [...]

Reading this book is a little like watching a particularly unsettling art house movie. You will be, in turn, disoriented, enchanted and repelled.

For all the technology involved, this is more magic realism than science fiction. It deliberately pushes the boundaries of the outrageous and challenges you to go along for the ride."
—**Catriona Troth**, author, in *Bookmuse*

"Quine's novel centers more on an interesting cast than fascinating sci-fi traits. Some characters are computer code in bodily form but still have depth. For example, Jaymi created Kim, in part, to be Shigem's lover. (A nice touch: both Beasts are male.) There's likewise a rather sublime religious theme. Though one Beast kneels in prayer in front of 'his creator,' Jaymi, there's an understated notion of free will. Jaymi assigns missions to Beasts (e.g., wreak havoc on Bang Dead) but often leaves them 'to [their] own devices.' The author's lyrical prose is profound and sometimes surreal, especially in character descriptions. 'Inside Kim,' Quine writes, 'there is a lonely savage from the caves, bent on pure first-degree survival, blown by chance and the primal drives of instinct and emotion, alone and uncertain on a dart from birth to death.' [...]

Unhurried but engrossing novel in which characters are more enticing than otherworldly technology."
—*Kirkus Reviews*

"[Protagonist Jaymi] discovers that he can bring his incarnations of excessive freedom, sexuality, intellectual seriousness, cool ambiguity, and dark vulnerability to life, unleashing them on 'meat space.' They become his beasts, extensions of his own personality, and through them, he interacts with the executives behind *Ain't They Freaky!* As various elements of Bang Dead's software are released, Jaymi works to help his former coworkers recognize the shallow depravity of their game through unnerving visits to their homes. [...]

This is a powerful book that advocates letting people be themselves, despite how far outside the bell curve of 'normal' they are. Pulsing with sexuality, the story will appeal to readers who enjoy artistic works rich in vocabulary, symbolism, and graphic imagery."
—*The Book Review Directory*

"Part cyberpunk meditation and part erotic thriller, BEASTS is a stylish narrative romp around a fictional Los Angeles landscape that appeals to the heart first and the head second. [...]

THE BEASTS OF ELECTRA DRIVE sounds like a cyberpunk thriller, and it sort of is. It also has an erotic undertone that grows throughout the narrative as the Beasts themselves crawl out of Jaymi's computer screen and gain independence. It's also a postmodern-ish meditation on creativity. Part of Jaymi goes into the creation of each of his Beasts—perhaps something author Rohan Quine can relate to—and as a whole the group is as a kind of kaleidoscope view of its creator. Additionally, part of Jaymi's mission in siccing the Beasts on Bang Dead Games is a retaliation against *Ain't They Freaky!*, an in-universe alternate reality game that embodies empty mass appeal over genuine artistry. [...] the writing grows increasingly smoother, culminating in a hauntingly pretty passage about man's inhumanity to man and ending up with intense backstories for the Beasts.

THE BEASTS OF ELECTRA DRIVE is, as its cover suggests, perhaps more about style than substance. Readers are told not to judge books by their covers—but this is the future. Maybe that's the point."
—*IndieReader*

"A sensual ballet of rich characterisation, alluring subtlety and originality. *The Beasts of Electra* Drive is a novel that I didn't want to put down while I was reading it [...]. I was transported into a domain peopled by characters who felt as if they were beckoning to me. It was as if they were inviting me into a kind of gliding embrace of harmony, within the pages of their author's imagination.

I found myself underlining things on the page, throughout it, because of the allure of Quine's language. I was fascinated with the marriage of his vocabulary and his punctuation. On the few times when I wasn't familiar with a word he uses, I resisted looking up its meaning—so as not to disturb the flow of the prose, but also because the spell of the sentences made the mystery of those words' meanings into an actual part of Quine's sheer creativity.

I felt drawn into his characters, which are complex. In the case of at least a couple of them, I had a strange feeling that they were somehow stroking me, while I was being led around their inner worlds. I was unable to dislike any of them, even those who clearly weren't very nice.

I also loved being reminded of when I lived in the Hollywood Hills. [...] Quine has captured the feel of those hills and canyons, in a way that will be recognised as authentic by anyone who's lived there.

This book creates a luscious and sensuous effect, which you can expand into. I have the sense that it was written by a very unusual and special person."
—**Suzi Rapport**, poet

"An extraordinary genre-defining and fascinating novel. So timely as cynical, talentless and opioid-pushing mass-media owners try and downgrade all popular culture—Rupert Murdoch/tv producers and ilk, I'm looking at you. Like a lyrical poem from ancient times. But more violent and with more gay sex."
—**Hermione Ireland**

"Jaymi's pursuits are a revenge fantasy taken to the next level, with moral and ethical quandaries wound in.

Magical realism meets old school noir in Rohan Quine's technological thriller *The Beasts of Electra Drive*, which poses philosophical questions around reality, humanity, and where to draw the line with tech-infusion. […]

Distinct writing is filled with lyrical prose and vivid sensory descriptions […] At times, [Jaymi] appears to have moral quandaries about his drastic actions against a rival company. His cyber-creations also lead him to question the nature of existence and his role as a creator—can he ethically order his creations to do his bidding in the real world? […]

The characters that Jaymi creates are refreshing in their diversity of race, gender, and sexuality. The two distinctly male beasts conform to the spectrum of masculinity, with one, Amber, being excessively violent, athletic, and handsome, and the other, Kim, being introverted but boundlessly intelligent and philosophical. These two men are in relationships with Shigem and Scorpio, who are more fluid in their gender and sexual identities. Shigem and Scorpio, along with Evelyn, are of varying nonwhite ethnicities. The scope of variety among the beasts is a nice change of pace.

The Beasts of Electra Drive is a techno-thriller that focuses more on its beautiful prose than on nurturing its thrills. Although sometimes repetitive in format, the vitality of the characters is pleasant and engaging."
—*Foreword* Clarion Reviews

"A crazy, psychedelic and experimental book. A fascinating and genre-defying story of a genius computer games designer waging war on the cynical and cretinous mass-market media and entertainment peddlers that threaten to cheapen and destroy our world. Perfect for adventurous readers."
—**Dartmouth dogwalker**

"A fully-wrought origin story like no other."
—*The Bookbag*

THE PLATINUM RAVEN AND OTHER NOVELLAS

The following collection is available at most online retailers, as a paperback published by EC1 Digital (retailers' links at www.rohanquine.com/buy/the-platinum-raven-and-other-novellas-paperback), with the following cover.

The Platinum Raven and other novellas
contains the following four novellas.

THE PLATINUM RAVEN
A triple convulsion whereby our heroine Raven escalates
herself into the Chocolate Raven and then the Platinum Raven,
from London to Dubai to the tower in the hills in the desert—
then back down again, forever changed.
www.rohanquine.com/the-platinum-raven
This novella is also available as an individual ebook (retailers' links
at www.rohanquine.com/buy/the-platinum-raven-novella-ebook)
and audiobook (retailers' links at www.rohanquine.com/buy/the-
platinum-raven-novella-audiobook) published by EC1 Digital.

THE HOST IN THE ATTIC
A hologram of Oscar Wilde's *The Picture of Dorian Gray*,
digitised and reframed in cinematic style, set in
London's Docklands in a few years' time.
www.rohanquine.com/the-host-in-the-attic
This novella is also available as an individual ebook (retailers' links
at www.rohanquine.com/buy/the-host-in-the-attic-novella-ebook)
and audiobook (retailers' links at www.rohanquine.com/buy/the-
host-in-the-attic-novella-audiobook) published by EC1 Digital.

APRICOT EYES
A cat-and-mouse pursuit through the New York City
night involves a preacher, a psychic and a dominatrix, broadcast
live on air—until a horror is unearthed, bringing two of them
together and the third to a sticky end.
www.rohanquine.com/apricot-eyes
This novella is also available as an individual ebook (retailers' links
at www.rohanquine.com/buy/apricot-eyes-novella-ebook) and
audiobook (retailers' links at www.rohanquine.com/buy/apricot-
eyes-novella-audiobook) published by EC1 Digital.

HALLUCINATION IN HONG KONG

Sliding from joy to nightmare and back, a plane flight frames a journey into Jaymi's and Angel's polarised identities and perceptions, where past and present merge in an obsessive fantasy of love, death, horror and apocalyptic beauty.

www.rohanquine.com/hallucination-in-hong-kong

This novella is also available as an individual ebook (retailers' links at www.rohanquine.com/buy/hallucination-in-hong-kong-novella-ebook) and audiobook (retailers' links atwww.rohanquine.com/buy/hallucination-in-hong-kong-novella-audiobook) published by EC1 Digital.

REVIEWS OF *THE PLATINUM RAVEN AND OTHER NOVELLAS*

See www.rohanquine.com/press-media/the-novellas-reviews-media for all links to the following and other reviews.

"It would be remiss of me not to take this opportunity to bring people's attention to a truly remarkable book. Rohan Quine writes right at the boundary between literary fiction and experimentalism, and his new collection of four novellas, *The Platinum Raven and other novellas*, is a genuine masterpiece. This guy is as good as [Sergio] De La Pava, and deserves to be the next self-published literary author to cross over into mainstream consciousness." *SPR*

"Rohan Quine is one of the most brilliant and original writers around. His *The Imagination Thief* blended written and spoken word and visuals to create one of the most haunting and complex explorations of the dark corners of the soul you will ever read. Never one to do something simple when something more complex can build up the layers more beautifully [...] suffice to say he is the consummate master of sentencecraft. His prose is a warming sea on which to float and luxuriate. But that is only half of the picture. He has a remarkable insight into the human psyche, and he demonstrates it by lacquering layer on layer of subtle observation and nuance. Allow yourself to slip from the slick surface of the water and you will soon find yourself tangled in a very deep and disturbing world, but the dangers that lurk beneath the surface are so enticing, so intoxicating it is impossible to resist their call."

"Rohan is one of the most original voices in the literary world today—and one of the most brilliant."

"four stunning new novellas by one of the most exciting literary writers in the UK."
—**Dan Holloway**, author, poet and *Guardian* blogger

"Rohan Quine is a master of words, his world is also accessible, and it's a place you definitely need to visit. With echoes of Jennifer Egan's *Goon Squad*, Quine captures all that is beautiful, but he doesn't shy away from all that is ugly. What links the four novellas together is that his characters are all searching for that something beyond the everyday, beyond the ordinary, and Quine is a god, having them dole out kindness and justice. In his world, everything that is commonplace would be annihilated. This is the kind of read you have to give yourself up to. [...] When you emerge on the other side with a greater understanding of what it means to be 'that animal called human', then that will be the time to stop and ask, 'What just happened?'"

"Rohan Quine is a poet who happens to write novellas/novels. Incredible use of language."
—**Jane Davis**, author

"Novelist Rohan Quine not only has several books out. He also has a career in alternative modeling and film to look back on. Naturally, he has gone on to make a series of silent short films to go with an audio track of the author reading from his work. It's flooded with city lights, drugs and darkness. One foot in the New York Nineties, and one foot in today's London, it's both hypnotic and gut-churning."
—**Polly Trope**, author and literary editor of *indieBerlin*

"A cautionary tale of the potential corrupting power both of vanity and of the internet plays out in modern London's high-tech dockland offices and luxury apartments, with brief forays to lavish West End hotels and country houses. [...] As the story becomes ever darker, gentle touches of humour provide a little light relief. I particularly enjoyed the characterisation of the women, especially the wonderfully petulant Angel Deon [...]. While at first this parable's main purpose may seem to rage against the principles of a high tech, monopolistic, capitalist world that enable individuals to lead unspeakably privileged lives above the law, it is at the same time a cautionary tale against narcissism and the abandonment of love and compassion for others. This broader theme gives the story its true heart and depth. Quine is renowned for his rich, inventive and original prose, and he is skilled at blending contemporary and ancient icons and themes. [...] an interesting approach to dialogue, blending idiom and phraseology from different eras, from Victorian times through 20th century popular film culture to the modern day. [...] There are some classic moments of horror that are very filmic,

including one on a par with the *Psycho* shower scene. Without giving too much away, I can imagine this book might put readers off accessing their own attics for a while."
—**Debbie Young**, author and Amazon UK 1,000 Reviewer, in *Vine Leaves Literary Journal*, about *The Host in the Attic*

"This is an extraordinary writer. I am going to gorge myself on these novellas as soon as I possibly can."
—**JJ Marsh**, author

"cerebral works full of brilliant imagery and invention. This series of novellas are all well crafted and designed to draw the reader in to the shifting realities of their settings. The title novella *The Platinum Raven* in fact has two young women in two narratives [...] very vividly described. There are elements of magical realism and alternate reality throughout. At times the two Ravens appear to communicate but the levels of reality are enigmatic and intriguing. *The Host in the Attic* is a beautifully reinterpreted version of *The Picture of Dorian Gray* set in a high-tech dystopian world and a sinister computer global company—Mainframe Corporation, which appears to permeate every level of society. The hologram corporate image logo is in essence Dorian. All the main characters from Wilde's novel are here in more modern form. It has a tremendous and horrific climax. The horror novella *Apricot Eyes* is a fast-paced horror tale in a nightmarish New York. *Hallucination in Hong Kong* is a mysterious tale of past and present, dreams and waking with horror and love themes. The whole collection is a roller-coaster of at times nightmarish perceptions and strange surreal happenings brilliantly imagined. The tales leave a lasting impression and I recommend highly."
—**Alexander Gordon-Wood**, actor

"a riveting read. The novella *The Host in the Attic* in particular is splendidly Wildean: in it, [Quine's] novel *The Imagination Thief* itself drives forward the plot of *The Host in the Attic*. He is a veritable Imagination Thief!"
—**David McLaughlin**

The following are reviews of Rohan Quine's *Hallucinations* (New York: Demon Angel Books), published in print in the USA only, which included earlier versions of: *Apricot Eyes*; *Hallucination in Hong Kong*; and a few chapters of *The Platinum Raven*.

"I have now been reading *Hallucinations* with great pleasure [...] you are indeed a star."
—**Iris Murdoch**, author (scan of her letter at foot of www.rohanquine.com/press-media/the-novellas-reviews-media)

"He has no equal, today or tomorrow."
—**James Purdy**, author

"Sometimes Quine succeeds with things you wouldn't think language could do, like describing a piece of music with an extended metaphor that reads something like watching the last half-hour of *2001*."
—**Ben Cohen**, *New York Press*

"*Hallucinations* at the end of this millennium is what Lautréamont's, Huysmans's and Wilde's work represented at the end of the 19th century [...] a sadistically svelte structure on top of explosive, primal content that refuses to behave in a linear fashion. It can only be described as literature that strains between ecstasy and bondage [...] one of the chic-est, most provocative things we have read in years [...] one of those seminal works that goes on to be accorded the status of a classic."
—**Wayne Sterling**, *New York Web*

"The imagery is *Apocalypse Now*-era Coppola meets Wes Craven, or *Edward Scissorhands* meets *Barbarella* [...] or Anne Rice (as screenwriter) on an acid trip [...] the lilt and cadence of prose poetry laid end-to-end, resulting in a narrative that is frequently stunning [...] sublime verbal renderings of the emotions and sensations of human love."
—**Hayward Connor**, *Union Jack*

"Most taut and clever in [*Apricot Eyes*]; it grips the reader and gives a provocative ride [... *Hallucinations*] develops 'alternative' characters with style and dimension, as well as challenging traditional forms of storytelling with admirable results."
—**Tom Musbach,** *Lambda Book Report*

"This is quite an extraordinary work, distinguished both by its originality and by the strength of [its] voice."
—**Anne Hawkins,** literary agent, John Hawkins & Assocs.

"There's a reality in each sentence of *Hallucination in Hong Kong* that neither depends on nor is blurred by all its virtuoso fuckings of the English language."
—**Dr Michael Halls**

OTHER FORMATS OF *THE IMAGINATION THIEF*

The Imagination Thief is also available as an ebook published
by EC1 Digital and the Firsty Group
(retailers' links at www.rohanquine.com/buy/the-
imagination-thief-novel-ebook), with the following cover.

The Imagination Thief is also available as an audiobook published by EC1 Digital (retailers' links at www.rohanquine.com/buy/the-imagination-thief-novel-audiobook), with the following cover.

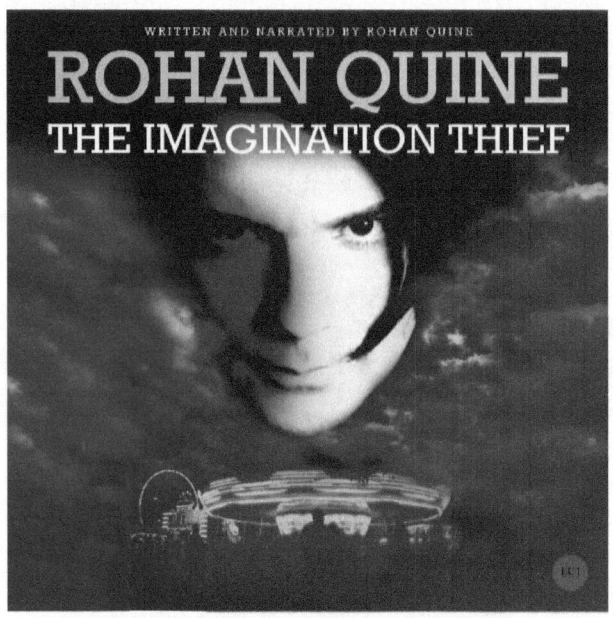

ABOUT ROHAN QUINE

Rohan Quine is an author of literary fiction with a touch of magical realism and a dusting of horror. He grew up in South London, spent a couple of years in L.A. and then a decade in New York, where he ran around excitably, saying a few well-chosen words in various feature films and TV shows, such as *Zoolander, Election, Oz, Third Watch, 100 Centre Street, The Last Days of Disco, The Basketball Diaries, Spin City* and *Law & Order: Special Victims Unit* (see www.rohan-quine.com/those-new-york-nineties/film-tv). He's now living back in East London, with his boyfriend and two happy free-roaming house rabbits—a white down-ears and a black up-ears.

His novel *The Beasts of Electra Drive* (a Finalist in the IAN Book of the Year Awards 2018) is a prequel to his other five tales, and a good place to start. See www.rohanquine.com/press-media/the-beasts-of-electra-drive-reviews-media for reviews by *Kirkus, Bookmuse, Bending the Bookshelf* and others. From Hollywood mansions to South Central motels, havoc and love are wrought across a mythic L.A., through the creations of games designer Jaymi, in a unique explosion of glamour and beauty, horror and enchantment, celebrating the magic of creativity itself.

In addition to its paperback format, his novel *The Imagination Thief* is available as an ebook that contains links to film and audio and photographic content in conjunction with the text. See www.rohanquine.com/press-media/the-imagination-thief-reviews-media for some nice reviews in *The Guardian, Bookmuse, indieBerlin* and elsewhere. It's about a web of secrets triggered by the stealing and copying of people's imaginations and memories, the magic that can be conjured by images of people, the split between beauty and happiness, and the allure of power.

Four novellas—*The Platinum Raven, The Host in the Attic, Apricot Eyes* and *Hallucination in Hong Kong*—are published as separate ebooks, and also as a single paperback *The Platinum Raven and other novellas.* See www.rohanquine.com/press-media/the-novellas-reviews-media for reviews of these novellas, including by Iris Murdoch, James Purdy, *Lambda Book Report* and *New York Press.* Hunting as a pack, all four delve deep into the beauty, darkness and mirth of this predicament called life, where we seem to have been dropped without sufficient consultation ahead of time.

All six titles are also available in audiobook and video-book formats, performed by the author.

CONNECT WITH ROHAN

If you'd like to be notified of future publications,
you're most welcome to sign up for Rohan's not-too-
frequent newsletter at www.rohanquine.com/sign-up.
Your details will be shared with no one else.

And if you wish, thanks for connecting on:
https://twitter.com/rohanquine
www.facebook.com/rohanquinetheimaginationthief
www.goodreads.com/author/show/1089889.Rohan_Quine
https://theimaginationthief.tumblr.com
www.wattpad.com/user/rohanquine